the PENALTY

the PENALTY

LYNN MONTAGANO

Book Cover Design by Lori Jackson
Interior design and formatting by

emtippettsbookdesigns.com
Proofreader: Emma Malito

ALSO BY
LYNN MONTAGANO

ROYALS AND LEGENDS
The Keeper

THE BREATHLESS SERIES
Catch My Breath
Unravel Me
Effortless

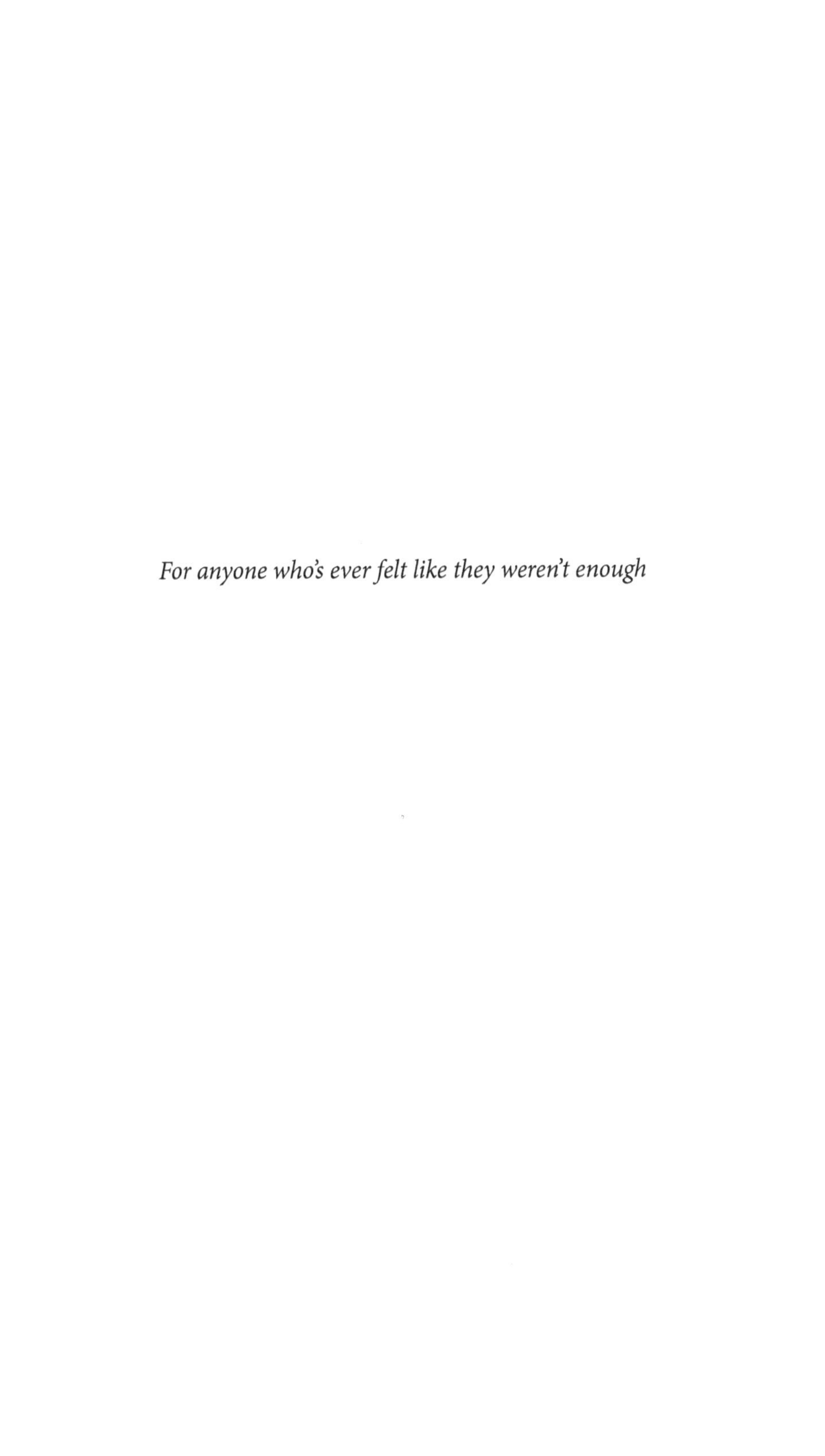

For anyone who's ever felt like they weren't enough

PLAYLIST

Unsteady - X Ambassadors
You're All I Have - Snow Patrol
Into You - Ariana Grande
Bad Things - Machine Gun Kelly ft. Camilla Cabello
Pillowtalk - Zayn
Clarity - Zedd ft. Foxes
Dynasty - MIIA
Beneath Your Beautiful - Labrinth ft. Emeli Sandé
Something Just Like This - Chainsmokers ft. Coldplay
Dark Side - Kelly Clarkson
Burn - Ellie Goulding
Centuries - Fall Out Boy

CONTENT WARNING

This book contains darker themes, including mentions of suicide and sexual assault, profanity, violence, explicit adult content, and past trauma.

CONTENTS

NOTE TO READERS:

This story has an over-lapping timeline with the preceding book, *The Keeper*.

Part One takes place through the end of *The Keeper*, picking up immediately after the revelations from Charlotte's final diary entry; Part Two brings us to the present.

It is recommended to read *The Keeper* first to follow what happens.

A scar I can't reverse
And the more it heals, the worse it hurts

- MIIA
"Dynasty"

PART ONE

Chapter

ONE

"It's cute that you thought this would go any other way."

Jordan's smug expression set off an explosion of rage within me. I squeezed the tumbler of whisky so tight I was surprised it didn't crack in my hand.

We were seated upstairs in the VIP section of his favorite gentleman's club, meaning we had our own private area with a scantily clad hostess tending to our every need. And I mean *every* need.

Pretty. Blonde. More Cade's type than mine since she was barely twenty.

"The night is young," I retorted, swallowing the drink.

"The Maddox arrogance. Like father, like son."

A sardonic grin curled my lips. "One of my better qualities."

Jordan leered at the young woman while she refilled my glass. Calling him a womanizer was too kind. He was a predator.

"Why'd you ask me out on a date, Xavier? We haven't spoken or seen one another in years. You've always seemed to be the love 'em and leave 'em type. Not sure I'm interested. I'm a sensitive girl."

I wanted to rip the smile off his face. He's the last person I want to see. Unfortunately for him, and me, this was how it had to be.

I didn't leave Victoria behind in New York to *not* deal with this piece of shit.

"There are a few things I need to make clear to you."

"Clear how? Like the night you overreacted when you found Millie with me? How is she doing these days?"

Anger streaked through my veins. He regarded me pleasantly enough but the distain simmering in his eyes was unmistakable.

"We both know my actions were justified. But I'm not here to rehash the past. At least not that night."

"Oh?" He cocked his head to the side. "Is there another blissful walk down memory lane you want to take? The time you stole my fiancée?" His eyes slid across my scar. "Bennet's party, perhaps?"

"I think you know that story well enough," I replied coldly. "I was thinking about the bonfire we all went to. Ring a bell?"

An oily smile tugged at his mouth. "I went to so many. You'll have to be more specific."

I finished the whisky and waited patiently for our hostess to refill my glass. She stood to my left, putting her directly in front of another languid stare. But she ignored Jordan's less than subtle intentions and looked at me with come-hither eyes.

I drank the whisky immediately and covered the empty glass with my hand, signaling I was finished.

"We're good for now," I told her. "If you wouldn't mind leaving us for a little while."

She offered an emotionless smile and left the area. Jordan scowled.

"I paid to have her all night."

"You'll live."

Part of me wanted to tear into Jordan about the night I was jumped at Bennet's party. Maybe I'll do it anyway. Might as well fire all my ammunition at once. See how indestructible he really is.

"While you try to figure out what you want to say, I noticed you're involved with someone again. An American?"

The muscle in my jaw twitched. He straightened his cufflinks.

"None of your business," I warned.

"So proper. When did you stop bragging—"

"I'd be very careful about what you say next."

Another arrogant smile. The muscle in my jaw ticked faster.

"Did you know we almost became neighbors? Lovely cottage down the street from you. The owners finally put it up for sa—"

Glass shattered on the floor the second I lunged across the table and grabbed his neck. I wanted to choke the life out of him and make him beg me to stop. Stunned, he stood up, giving me the perfect opportunity to pin him against the wall.

"Big mistake, Maddox," he rasped.

I didn't fucking care.

"How does it feel, Jordan? How does it feel to have someone stronger than you hold your pathetic life in the palm of their hand?" I squeezed his neck tighter, turning my knuckles white. "You want to talk about Bennet's party? Fine. Let's talk about how you put my girlfriend's twin sister in a chokehold after she saw your mates beat the shit out of me."

Some of the entitled bluster drained from his eyes.

"While we're at it, let's talk about the night you raped her at the bonfire."

I kneed him in the balls before he had a chance to counterstrike with his free hand. Air whooshed out of him.

"Fucking prick." His voice was barely above a whisper. "I've never raped—"

Another knee to the balls.

This was fun.

"She wanted it." Saliva dripped from his mouth with every word.

"She wanted none of it." My voice went dark and sinister. "You threatened her after she saw what you did and then a year later, you raped her. And now my girlfriend lives with the guilt from thinking it was all somehow *her* fault."

Jordan struggled in my grasp, much like a mouse trying to escape a cat that's toying with it. Then, he went limp. Not because I'd rendered him unconscious, although I really wanted to. Glaring at me, he lifted his chin in defiance.

"Those spoiled Americans? The Chase twins? That's what this is about." His tone dripped with vitriol. "Little tarts. What were their names? The fun one was Victoria—"

I slammed his head against the wall. "Say her name again and I'll end you."

"Thinking with your prick again, I see. She's quite an attractive woman. I can see why you'd—"

"Stay away from her."

A low, patronizing laugh vibrated through him. "Too late for that."

My grip tightened. "You have three seconds to explain before I snap your neck."

"I'd like to see you try."

"Don't tempt me."

Heavy anticipation filled the room. I could end him with one turn of my wrist. God, I fucking wanted to.

You'll lose her if you do.

The thing in my chest raged at the thought.

Jordan capitalized on my hesitation.

"She was very polite to me on the phone. Then again, I led her to believe I was a reporter who gave a shit about Royal City Athletic traveling to the States."

"Stay the fuck away from her."

"Not a chance. Don't you know anything about that family? The dad is some shady hedge fund guy. I invested—"

"Enough." I rammed his head into the wall again.

"You really haven't changed at all, have you. Still the same hot-headed prat. No wonder you need therapy."

"Fuck you."

His strangled laugh sent a chill through me. "Millie told me how you'd choke her like this. Squeeze until she almost passed out when you shagged her. She hated that."

A familiar wild energy coursed through my veins. For years I'd stopped it from swallowing me whole.

Not tonight.

I let go of his neck and punched him in the stomach, relishing his shocked grunt even though my hand flared in pain.

"You will *listen* to me now." I grabbed his neck again, shoving him back against the wall. "Stay away from Victoria. And admit what you did to Charlotte."

"You're delusional," he cackled. "I didn't do anything to her that you didn't do to Millie."

"This is where your lies will come back to haunt you. We both know I never did anything to Millie. But *you* did. Just like you did to Charlotte." I squeezed his neck harder. "You can't hide behind your family name and your money forever. I don't fucking care if it takes me fifty years. I will destroy you."

"Not before I destroy you first." Jordan's voice didn't sound as confident as before. "You're not squeaky clean either. Taking advantage of Millie. Manipulating her so you could act out all your fucked up fantasies."

"It wasn't like that and you know it."

"Oh no? What would you call it then? Coercion? Never did learn how to control your urges. Looks like Bennet wasn't able to teach you everything."

Another punch to the gut should shut him up. Pain burned through my hand the second it slammed into his stomach but I smiled when he gulped in a few breaths and couldn't speak.

"Watch yourself, Maddox," he wheezed. "You never know what can crawl out of the shadows and bring the past back to life."

"More empty threats? Looks like *you* haven't changed either."

"Not threats. Promises." A sinister grin pulled at his mouth. "You're nothing. Just some pretty boy footballer who thinks he's the anointed one."

You're nothing.

Never have two words filled me with more rage than those.

You're nothing.

I squeezed his neck harder. My lips curled in distaste. "You hurt the woman I love. You're the reason her twin isn't alive. I'm going to enjoy torturing you wherever and whenever the opportunity arises."

Terror flashed through Jordan's eyes before unbridled anger emerged.

There's no turning back now. I've ignited something dangerous.

"You have no idea what you've done," he said in a deceptively calm tone.

"Yes I do," I responded just as serene.

He tipped his head forward. "I know your weakness now. I'll find her. And it'll be more than a simple phone call next time."

"Touch her and it'll be my fucking pleasure to put an end to your shitty existence."

"Try and st—"

This time when I slammed his head into the wall, I knocked him out.

Chapter

TWO

"*That is nasty.*"

I turned to see Cade pointing at my bruised hand. "What the hell happened?"

The changing room was mostly empty after today's training session. A couple of the guys heard Cade's exclamation and looked over. I shot them both warning glances.

"It's nothing," I finally said.

"Whose face was on the other end?" Cade asked in a low voice.

"Nobody's." *Just that worthless shit's stomach.*

Cade's skeptical expression irked me. We've known one another since we were twelve. He could tell when I was being less than truthful.

"Whatever you say, mate."

Before I could respond, my fucking step-brother approached us.

"Xavier."

"Adam." I have to admit, he looked anxious about something. "What do you want?"

"We need to talk."

I forced a laugh. "Unless it's about Saturday's match, we don't."

His eyes narrowed when he folded his arms. "We do. Meet me in the car park when you're done here. And don't make me come back in to find you."

He left in a huff. Rolling my eyes, I tossed my training kit in with the rest of the dirty clothes and went to the recovery room for an ice pack. Cade followed close behind.

"Want me to come out with you in case things with Adam go, uh, not well?" he asked.

"Nah. I can't imagine this will last longer than ten seconds." I winced a bit when the ice touched my skin. I could feel Cade staring at it and looked up. "What?"

"Maybe you should talk to Victoria. It might help you," he paused, gauged my reaction and continued, "calm down a bit. You've been on edge since leaving her in New York."

My mind flashed to the night Victoria and I read through her twin's final journal entry. Victoria had been nearly inconsolable. I did my best to comfort her all the while imagining dozens of ways to make Jordan suffer.

The other night at the club was nothing. A mere warm-up for the main event.

"Xavier," Cade prompted. "Will you talk to her?"

Desire twisted around my heart. I wanted to talk to her. I wanted to hold her, kiss her, feel her skin on mine. Hear her laugh. See her smile.

"Not yet." I failed to avoid his steady gaze.

"Don't fuck this up." Cade looked solemn. "She's the best thing that's happened to you."

"I know," I admitted. "You still going to Bennet's?"

"Yeah. I'll be out in a bit."

I shook off the unease and sense of dread that's been eating away at me since Sunday. My impulsiveness ruled my life these days. Going after Jordan like that would probably end up biting me in the ass somehow.

Whatever.

Knocking him out felt bloody amazing.

Adam was waiting for me when I sauntered through the car park. If he looked agitated before, he was downright panicky now.

I won't lie. It made me uncomfortable.

Not that I'd let it show.

"What's this about?" I asked, stopping in front of him.

"Remember Philip?"

I stifled a smile. "The Duke of Edinburgh?"

Adam glared at me. "No, you asshole. Philip Edgewood from the Royal City under-eighteens. The one who busted his knee and couldn't play football anymore."

I shrugged. "Sort of. Why?"

"We've stayed in touch over the years. Still go out for a pint now and then. He told me he works for Jordan. Tech lead for all his security operations. Been there for a couple years."

My blood turned to ice. Jordan's family had as much, if not more, money and resources as Bennet's. His entitled ass decided to form a private security company fifteen years ago. It had more shady operations than legitimate ones. And since his sick and twisted mind got off on threatening and intimidating people, he made it a point not to be picky when choosing his targets.

I had to play this off like I didn't give a shit. "So? Why are you telling me?"

"You're not stirring up trouble with him again are you? You know what happened last time."

"Nope," I lied, keeping my expression as neutral as possible.

"Right." Adam shook his head. "I saw Philip last night. He said Jordan is livid and has it out for you."

For the first time in ages, I glimpsed a side to Adam I haven't seen since we were kids. The time when we *actually* looked out for one another, like brothers are supposed to.

I kept my gaze steady, waiting for him to continue.

"That's all." He shrugged. "Thought you should know."

I sunk my hands into my pockets, keeping a curious stare fixed on him. The last time Adam and I were even remotely civil to one another was the day he mistook Victoria for Charlotte. I still couldn't believe he'd dated her twin when we were teenagers.

"Thanks for the tip," I finally said, stepping to the side.

I was almost at my car when I heard him call after me. "Did she say anything else about me? In her diary?"

An unexpected jolt of anxiety shot through me. Adam and I only spoke about Charlotte and her diary that one time. I made it a point not to indulge in any further conversations about her with him.

Taking a deep breath, I turned to face him and answered with a curt, "No."

I watched him drive off, wondering how I was going to control the gathering storm I'd set off the other night. Finding out Jordan already contacted Victoria complicated everything. All I wanted to do was go back to New York, bring her somewhere secluded, and…and what?

Quit football?

Abandon everything I've worked so hard for?

You're nothing.

I shook myself out of this dangerous spiral.

Cade's voice echoed when he yelled out, "Maddox. Ready to go?"

"It's a little early, no?"

"Whatever." Cade waved his hand dismissively. "He won't mind."

I nodded, getting into my car.

The drive to Bennet's was pleasant enough. Cade often drove like he was trying out for the next Formula One race. I lost him pretty quick on the motorway. Fine by me. I wasn't in a rush to get there. Part of me considered calling to let him know I wasn't coming.

But then Bennet would moan and complain and tell me if he could take time out of his busy schedule, so could I.

Bennet's father dropped more responsibility on him for this season. Next year, Royal City Athletic would be fully under his control.

Not bad for the posh-looking teen who'd taken Cade and I under his wing when we were sixteen.

The day he'd come up to us on the pitch would forever be seared into my memory.

We'd just lost a match. Rare, since I've excelled at my position forever. But he extended an invitation for both of us to join the development league for the club. I signed on as their goalkeeper, Cade as their striker. Two years later, we had contracts.

Life-changing isn't a proper way to describe the opportunity. I'd felt it in my bones. It licked, sparked, and pinched my lust for being noticed, being seen, being watched.

All those eyes fixated on me. Waiting to see what I'd do next.

You're nothing.

I squeezed the steering wheel and turned down the long private road.

Logan Estate was massive. Not Buckingham Palace massive but close enough. The size and scope didn't intimidate me one bit. Quite the opposite. It comforted me. Let me know this was exactly where I belonged. Meant for something bigger, something bolder.

Cade leaned against his car when I pulled up. Without warning, a powerful sense of deja vu razored its way into my reality.

Footsteps.

My body twisted from a violent shove. I managed to regain my footing but...

Pain. Blunt and crushing against my jaw. I staggered and fell to my knees.

"That him?" an unfamiliar voice asked.

Silence.

The jangling of keys.

More pain. Bright and searing, above my left eye. A fist grabbed me by the hair, banging my head so hard against the car I saw stars. Something warm and sticky ran down my face.

Another sharp pull on my hair.

"If you try something like that again," the unfamiliar voice threatened, "I'll take your fucking eye out."

My head snapped back and hit the car again.

More footsteps. Two car doors slammed shut and an engine roared.

Rapid knocking on the window jolted me from the memory. I turned sharply to see Cade.

"We going in or what, mate?"

I nodded, getting out in a daze. I didn't let that particular memory consume me very often, if at all.

Gravel crunched beneath our feet as we walked to the door. A couple other cars were parked closer to the house. One belonged to Bennet's assistant. I didn't recognize the other.

Muffled voices wafted through the hall as we approached the library. One of the French doors was closed, which seemed odd. Bennet always kept these doors open.

Cade walked in first. I nearly crashed into him when he stopped short.

"Cade. Xavier. I wasn't expecting to see you for another hour," Bennet drawled from his usual spot at the fireplace. "I'm surprised you're early for something."

I was about to make a flippant remark when I noticed someone sitting on the couch. I could only see the back of their head but it looked—

"This *is* a lovely surprise, isn't it?" Jordan stood and turned to face us.

Another vivid, unpleasant memory from that fucking night came into sharp focus.

"*The bleeding finally stopped.*"

"*He should get stitches.*"

"*Do you really want to take him to hospital and deal with all the questions? I've already called my private physician. He'll be here any minute.*"

I opened my eyes, half expecting to see whatever medical drama was playing on the telly. But that's not where the voices came from. I blinked, getting a clearer picture of my surroundings.

Fireplace. Soft couch. Dark wood paneled walls. The smell of leather, smoke, and alcohol.

I blinked again, struggling to sit up. Pain lanced through my head, almost knocking me back down.

"*Careful.*" *Cade looked worried and angry.* "*You took a nasty hit to the head, mate.*"

"*What the fuck happened?*"

Nothing seemed to make much sense at the moment. All I remembered was being at a party and running out to get something from my car.

I reached up and touched above my left eye. It was hastily bandaged but holy shit the pain. I stared at the blood staining my fingertips when I pulled my hand back.

"*You got jumped in my own fucking driveway.*" *Bennet crouched down so he was eye level with me.* "*Do you know who it was?*"

"*No idea,*" *I mumbled.*

Bennet's stare overflowed with anger. "*My security team is going through the video. I'll find out. And there will be hell to pay.*"

I leaned back into the couch and must have closed my eyes because the next thing I knew a doctor hovered over me.

"*We need to stitch this up.*"

Fighting this wave of unconsciousness was tougher than I thought. When I opened my eyes again the doctor was gone and Cade was sitting in one of the big leather chairs with his elbows propped on his knees. I touched above my eye. Still bandaged but not hurting as much.

"You'll probably have a scar." Bennet's voice came from the same spot by the fireplace where he'd been standing when tonight's party started.

"Doctor said the cut was pretty deep," he continued. "Maybe keys. Possibly a knife."

My hands clenched into fists. "What the fuck are you doing here?" Vitriol and hate strangled each word as they came out of my mouth.

Cade's reassuring hand on my shoulder did nothing to slow the rage burning inside me. Neither did Bennet's warning glance.

"That's no way to greet an old friend, Maddox." The sound of Jordan's voice sliced through me. "Especially since our last date ended abruptly."

All I wanted to do was pound my fists into his face until those onyx pools that passed for his eyes closed from all the swelling. Permanently.

My hand twitched.

"Gallagher. Good seeing you, too. How long's it been?"

For his part, Cade remained silent, leveling an icy glare in Jordan's direction.

"I wish the two of you had called first," Bennet said smoothly.

"Nonsense," Jordan scoffed. "It's just like old times, right? A little chat. Some drink. Maybe a few ladies. Is your girlfriend visiting, Xavier?"

Blind rage consumed me. I covered the distance from the door to the couch within seconds and had Jordan in a chokehold. Cade tried to pull me off him but fuck that. I wasn't releasing this piece of shit's neck.

Fury spread from my chest to my limbs, ripping through me. I squeezed his neck tighter.

Bennet gripped my arm with inhuman force and yanked me back so hard I thought he dislocated my shoulder. His strength stunned me. I almost took a swing at him but the look in his eyes stopped me dead in my tracks.

"That's twice, Maddox. You should really work on your anger issues." Jordan rubbed his neck and aimed a dark stare at Bennet.

"We'll pick this up another time, yeah? You have your hands full."

Both Cade and Bennet restrained me while Jordan left the room.

Every breath I took drove a phantom spear through my lungs, making it impossible to retain enough oxygen. Maybe it was for the best.

Maybe I should just let it all rip me apart.

Maybe…

Maybe, maybe, maybe.

You're nothing.

All the muscles in my body tensed. The pressure building inside my chest exploded. A sharp yell ripped through the room.

It took a few seconds to realize it came from me.

"Let him go, Cade. I got it." Bennet kept an iron grip around my arm.

Blood pounded in my ears. "Sorry," I muttered.

"Sit" was all he said in return. I scrubbed my hands on my face and ran them through my hair before sitting on the couch. Heavy tension filled every corner of the library.

The cut was pretty deep. You'll probably have a scar. You got jumped in my own fucking driveway. That's no way to greet an old friend.

"Drink." Bennet held out a glass of scotch.

I extended a shaky hand and took it. The amber liquid coated my throat in smoky relief. Without saying a word, Bennet refilled my glass. The alcohol helped but it wasn't what I wanted.

What I really wanted was Victoria. If I could only pull her close, bury myself inside her, and lose myself in her warmth, her laugh, her embrace…I'd feel whole again.

Instead, I leaned my head back and listened to the silence.

"Why was he here?" Cade asked the question playing on the tip of my tongue. "And why didn't you tell us?"

"He was here because I invited him. And again, *you* weren't supposed to be here for another hour." Bennet's cold reply signaled there would be no further discussion.

"Whatever, mate." Cade sat next to me. "You feeling better?"

"I'll be fine," I lied, trying and failing to extinguish the persistent embers of wrath still coursing through me.

Bennet sat on the other side of me. The three of us must look ridiculous. Cade with his sour pout. Bennet with an exterior so icy it could freeze the sun. And me, a ball of rage and anxiety wound up tight enough to burst.

"You think I don't know what you did the other night?" Bennet scolded. "You think I don't have contacts at that club? What the fuck, Xavier?"

I lifted one shoulder in a nonchalant shrug. "I thought our chat was rather productive."

"You *assaulted* him for no reason."

"No reason?" I sat up straight. "Have you forgotten the hurt and guilt consuming Victoria? That prick—"

"It's over," he interrupted, standing up. "Almost twenty years have passed. It's not your place to—"

"Not my place?" I stood as well. Both hands balled into fists. I'd be more than happy to let one land on his face. I steadied myself, ready to swing at him.

But as angry as I was, I didn't move when Bennet clasped a reassuring hand on my shoulder and squeezed.

"I know this is hard for you. I know your instinct is always attack first and ask questions later. You don't want this trouble. Not over something that happened so long ago."

He's partly right. Getting jumped that night wasn't enough to set me off. At least not to this extent. But after learning what he did to Victoria's sister and the tragic aftermath and how she's lived with all that guilt for so long?

All the muscles in my body tensed again.

"Xavier, don't make the same mistakes. This isn't— You've worked too hard to get yourself right. Don't let Jordan get under your skin. He's not fucking worth it."

I felt Cade's presence when he rose to his feet. "Not really sure what you two are going on about. Does this have to do with Adam and the thing that happened at the Legends stadium?"

Bennet and I shared a knowing glance.

"That's part of it," I responded. "It's not my story to tell, Cade."

The star striker glanced from me to Bennet and back to me. "Is Victoria okay?"

Just hearing her name nearly shredded me. I swallowed hard, looking at my friend.

"I can check on her if you'd like," he offered. "Nothing dodgy or anything. Just a text here and there. Maybe—"

"Probably not a good idea, Cade," Bennet interrupted. "Let us handle this."

Cade shrugged and nodded. Bennet turned his attention back to me.

"Stay away from McKennie. I mean it. You're making things worse than they need to be. Leave him alone."

I clenched my jaw. Bennet could be a prick at times but he's right. I *am* complicating the situation. Reckon I still haven't learned my lesson from the last time.

Will I ever?

Cade and Bennet talked around me. I heard them, but I didn't. A million thoughts swarmed my brain. None of them made any sense.

That's not quite true.

Only one made sense.

If I continue along this path, I'm going to destroy everything I've achieved and lose the one person I can't live without.

Chapter

THREE

The next week passed in a cloud of monotony: Training. Won a match. More training. Therapy. No contact with Victoria.

Cutting off all communication with her destroyed me.

It had to be this way. At least for now. Jordan was hovering too close and I need to stay one step ahead of him.

Not even Dr. Frances could convince me otherwise.

"How does pushing her away keep her, as you put it, safe?" He looked up from where he'd been writing in his notepad.

I shoved back the insistent wave of emotion threatening to reveal everything.

"I'm not pushing her away."

"Okay. I'll ask it a different way. How does not being there for her after making this emotional discovery together keep her safe?"

Fucking hell. Why doesn't he just draw and quarter me? It would have the same damn effect. I could barely find a breath before I answered.

"It just does."

I always assumed therapists were supposed to be good at keeping their frustrations hidden when patients stonewall them. Not this guy. His eyebrows shot up.

"The anger living in here," he pointed to his chest, "will only worsen if you continue to suppress it."

Not after I bury my fists in that low life's face.

"It won't."

"It will." He looked at me over the rim of his glasses. "You carry around this anger like some badge of honor. Anger only lasts for so long. After that, it becomes something more dangerous. Rage. And rage will make you careless."

"Reckless," I said aloud without thinking.

"Yes," he responded. "Holding anger is like a poison. It destroys from within."

My shoulders slumped enough for him to notice he'd broken through a little.

More notes on the page.

More tapping of the pen.

More thoughtful stares.

"Have you ever really stopped to process what it is that makes you this angry?"

Lancing pain throbbed behind my eye, making it twitch.

You're nothing.

"No."

I braced for another long-winded response. All I got was a hard stare and a quick nod.

"Have you always been this protective with your girlfriends?"

I flinched. "I haven't had many girlfriends. Just casual hook ups."

"But you did date someone long-term while in your twenties. Six months? Is that correct?"

"Don't really see the point in bringing that up."

"You don't talk about it much," he challenged. "You've only alluded to making mistakes and letting your reckless decisions cause someone harm. Did she get hurt in some way?"

If this fucking guy keeps pushing me…

"I'm not talking about it."

"Holding it—"

"Fuck off," I shouted. The echo of my outburst lingered in the room.

Dr. Frances observed me for a few seconds. It was brief, but long enough for the quiet to suffocate me.

"Are you still doing what I suggested at the gym?"

"Yeah."

"Has it helped?"

"I guess."

"Xavier." His tone softened to a nurturing, parental octave. "Forgiveness is some—"

"There is no chance in hell I'm forgiving him."

"That's not what I was going to say. Consider forgiving yourself for whatever happened between you and him and your then-girlfriend. Try giving yourself some grace."

No matter how loud I turned the music up in the car on my drive to the gym, all I heard was the *thump-thump-thump* of my heart. I like this therapist but fuck all, he knows how to get under my skin. And if we're being honest here, it angered me even more.

I didn't need to forgive myself or give myself grace or whatever bullshit touchy-feely nonsense he spouted at me. I needed to protect the woman I love at all cost. And that meant doing whatever it takes to keep Jordan away from her.

Bennet was already inside the workout area when I arrived. I didn't say anything to him at first. I prowled around the room, stewing in my annoyance.

"I'm going to kill him."

The words came out of my mouth with such ease it shocked me.

"You'll do no such thing." Bennet didn't even bother to glance in my direction. He was too busy stacking weights on the barbell for another powerlifting round. "Go do what Frances suggested and hit the fucking bag."

"Not quite what I want to hit."

Bennet sighed, rubbing his temples. "We're not having this discussion again."

I secured the wraps around my hands. "This isn't about me or the shit that went down with—" I caught myself before continuing. "This is about Victoria. He's not getting away with it."

"And what do you plan to do?" He narrowed his eyes at me. "Avenge your girlfriend and her dead twin with an impulsive decision that will ruin your relationship and not only get you kicked off the team but thrown out of the league? Not to mention you'll lose your business, get arrested, and possibly hospitalized with a broken face."

"He called her," I yelled. "He found her and called her and…and I don't know what else he's going to do. I have to protect her."

Bennet's mouth flattened in a hard line. "Why didn't you tell me?"

"Because it's not really your fucking problem." Exasperated, I walked away. Anger and fear rolled through me. The anger was obvious. Fear? I'll never admit to it.

But my past is threatening to seep through cracks I thought I'd sealed. The fallout would be manageable, I suppose. Unless said fallout included losing Victoria.

The fucking *thing* in my chest went haywire at the mere thought of not having her in my life. She's my light. Without her, I'd be lost.

I can't lose her.

I **won't** *lose her.*

This unwanted concoction of emotions threatened to dismantle the control I needed to have over the situation. Otherwise, I'd lose my shit and take it out on the next person who looked at me sideways.

Instead, I took it out on the punching bag in front of me.

Over and over and over.

I hit it until my muscles burned, my hands ached, and sweat dripped down my brow into my eyes. This definitely wasn't part of my normal routine of strength training, running sprints, and working on my agility and quickness. Punching the ever-living shit out of an inanimate object didn't quite qualify as preparation for my next match.

But I figured I'd do what the good doctor said.

You don't want to be suspended again, do you?

I toweled the perspiration from my face and grabbed some water.

"Hope you got it all out of your system, mate," Bennet drawled from the far corner of the training studio. "Thought you were going to dismantle the bloody thing."

"Don't you have somewhere better to be?" My words came out sharp. He's been up my ass all week and I just wanted to get out of here without a litany of snarky comments or questions.

"Not this time," he replied. "You're too much of a loose cannon." He raised his hand to shush me. "And it'll be a cold day in hell before I let you anywhere near McKennie again. The mess I've had to clean up since—"

"Keep scolding me, Logan. You won't like what happens next."

"Xavier," he said calmly. "I understand why you went after him the other night." Concern tinged his voice. "But I'm worried you're conflating what happened with—" he caught himself "—you're conflating what happened when you were younger with what you've learned recently. You didn't know Victoria back then. It's not the same situation."

He's right but it didn't feel that way. I have to do something. He'll hurt her.

All the stress and anxiety from the last couple weeks caught up with me, suffocating me until everything sharpened into a singular, painful clarity.

I fucked up.

I never should have left her like that.

"I'm going to New York after the final match next week," I blurted without thinking. "I'm not doing anyone any good being far away."

My words hung in the air, heavy and determined.

If I stay here, I'll do something I'd regret. If I'm with her, I'm less likely to jeopardize my relationship and career.

Bennet's resigned sigh was all I needed to hear to ease some of this tension. Don't get me wrong. I was still ready to put him in his place if he so much as hinted at trying to stop me.

"Fine," he muttered. "But don't lose your head. And don't do anything stupid between now and then. I need you focused and ready."

"I'm always ready. You know that."

"Sure." His stony demeanor cracked a little. "We expect nothing short of perfection."

Right. I am, after all, Xavier Fucking Maddox.

England's number one.

As long as I'm in goal, there's no chance we'd lose.

Arrogant? Yes. I didn't work this hard or get this far to be modest.

A smug smile pulled at my lips. "If anyone scores on me I'll retire. How's that for perfection?"

Bennet's exaggerated eye roll punctuated his response. "The size of your ego is astounding."

"Go annoy someone else. I'm leaving."

"One more thing."

"What?"

"Remember how we discussed having Marcus keep an eye on Victoria?"

I tensed. Marcus is one of the Caldwell family's top security guards. He's assigned to Hannah's detail, along with one of Bennet's top men, Alex. It wouldn't be too difficult for him to also watch Victoria.

The problem?

"She'll lose her mind if I tell her she has a babysitter."

Bennet shrugged. He'd brought up Marcus several times but before I left Manhattan I promised her I wouldn't let it happen.

"Thought I'd give it another go."

I grinned, remembering how she'd put him in his place when he'd originally suggested it. "It *was* entertaining watching you get reprimanded that night."

The usual arrogant glow in Bennet's eyes softened to intrigue. "She's a handful."

I bristled a little at how he said that with a hint of intention. I know he'd never try anything but a reminder won't hurt. "For *my* hands only."

"Meeting Cade for dinner later?" he asked, ignoring me.

"Yeah. Figured we'd cause some trouble out in the city before the end of the season."

Bennet stared at me like he's done since we were teenagers. "Don't even think about it," he muttered, arching an eyebrow.

"Remember the day you first met us?"

"Vaguely."

"Do you still wear those ridiculous chinos?"

"Sod off, Maddox," he answered, giving me one of his *this topic is closed* stares. But I could tell he was amused. As much as he made my blood boil at times over the years, I appreciated his friendship more than I could ever express.

"Do me a favor." I walked toward the door. "Don't tell Hannah I'm going to Manhattan when you talk to her. She'll tell Victoria."

"As you wish, my liege."

I threw a towel at him and went home.

Since I still had a couple hours before meeting Cade, I decided to take my mind off everything and watch something on television. Something mindless.

I'd just sat down on the couch when my phone chimed. My heart jumped. Fuck, I wanted it to be her.

Adam: Dinner next week?

I scowled.

Nope. I tossed the phone on the cushion and leaned my head back. Unfortunately for me, he kept texting.

And texting.

And texting.

I swore under my breath, grabbing the phone.

Adam: Don't ignore me

Adam: Xavier

Adam: Answer me

Adam: Fuck you

Me: What's the urgency?

Me: And fuck you too

Adam: No urgency. Dinner next week after training. Don't blow me off

Adam: Asshole

Hard to believe we were close as kids. Well, not super close. We had a healthy, competitive relationship since we'd both started playing football so young. I can't pinpoint the exact moment our relationship turned hostile.

That's a fucking lie.

It was more like a muddled bunch of little moments that grew and festered, toying with my general feelings of inadequacy. The scales tipped shortly before I joined Royal City's development league and Adam befriended Jordan.

Screw this. I can't keep dredging up the past. It's done and gone. Aside from making sure Jordan gets what he deserves, the rest of it doesn't matter.

You can't bury your life away forever.

The words I spoke to Victoria not too long ago echoed through me. I'd said them to help her move past the guilt she carried over Charlotte's death. She'd been so open and vulnerable with me that day in the storage unit.

Trusting me with a part of herself that she'd kept locked away for years must have been difficult for her.

I'd tried to be just as vulnerable with her more than once. But I ended up shutting down each time. Didn't matter if we were talking or having sex, I couldn't let myself go with her.

And I wanted that more than anything.

To fully let myself go with the one woman who might understand how to handle me.

The following week proved to be less aggravating. My only obstacle was meeting Adam for dinner.

I arrived first at the small restaurant in downtown London. Since the weather was somewhat agreeable, I chose a table outside to minimize any chance of causing a scene if he pissed me off.

Dr. Frances and I spoke at length about finding ways to curb my anger. Aside from the punching bag, he suggested putting myself in situations where losing control would be detrimental to my public image.

It'll force you to stay present and be aware of how you react, he'd told me.

Why am I listening to this guy again?

Of course, sitting out here alone left me exposed to attention, which never bothered me in the slightest.

Several people recognized me and waved as they walked by. One guy gave me a dirty look. *Must be a West London United supporter.* I smiled at him anyway.

A couple of kids ran over asking for an autograph. They talked nonstop about their youth clubs until their parents managed to corral them. Both apologized profusely for interrupting my dinner.

I told them I really didn't mind at all.

A few minutes later, two young women stopped to ask for a photo. I obliged, taking some time to chat with them.

"We're really hoping to come watch you play in person someday," the brunette said. "It's so hard to get tickets."

"That's because you're so good," her friend fawned, looking at me with wide eyes. "You and your club, I mean. Yeah. Not…not just you." She blushed.

I smiled, aware that some fans get tongue-tied. My usual default was to make a bad joke at Gallagher's expense. "It's a good thing Cade isn't here. You know how he gets when he thinks he's not the favorite."

They both giggled.

The star striker did have a reputation for being pouty when the spotlight moved off him.

"We won't tell him."

The young women thanked me and went on their way.

"Some things never change. Center of attention as always, Maddox." Jordan stood next to the table with an arrogant grin blooming on his lips.

Metal scraped on concrete when I pushed to my feet. Guess we're about to test Frances' homework.

The more this asshole smiled at me, the more I wanted to shove his face into the ground.

As tempting as that sounded, I held back. A world-famous footballer speaking to a high-profile British aristocrat already caught the eye of more than a few people nearby.

"What brings you to this part of the city?" he asked, smoothing down his tie. "A date?"

"Not really your concern, is it?" I folded my arms, my cool voice at odds with the violent intentions swimming in my mind.

Jordan sized me up with contempt. "How's your lovely girlfriend these days?"

The tips of my fingers dug into my shirt. "Again, not your concern."

A ruthless smile appeared. "Am I safe to assume you won't be as open to sharing her as you've been with others in the past?"

In an effort to *not* kill him where he stood, I shoved my hands in my pockets and backed away.

"Touched a nerve, have I? Does she know what it's truly like to be one of your girls?"

My hands ached from fisting them tight.

Breathe.

Jordan kept baiting. "Still keeping yourself all chaste and proper these days? Well, *chaste* isn't right. It's more likely my own dick will fall off before you stop shagging any woman that crosses your path. Surprised you didn't grab those two for a quickie behind—"

I moved to swing at him, only to be blocked by Adam.

"Sorry I'm late," he said, standing in between us. "Traffic."

Neither Jordan nor I moved or said anything. Years of animosity and betrayal saturated our bitter stares. We remained locked in this silent battle until Jordan spoke.

"Socializing with the blended family? Not going to lie. This is out of character." Jordan donned casual surprise as easily as he did one of his expensive suits. "I'm sure you boys have quite a bit to catch up on."

He'd walked almost to the edge of the sidewalk before turning and saying, "Drove past that lovely cottage again this afternoon. Briarcliff Cottage, is it? Maybe I'll make another offer."

Ice ran through my veins.

A vicious smile tugged at his mouth. "Money can be so persuasive at times."

Chapter
FOUR

Dinner with Adam was not happening. I don't care how much he protested.

"Listen." My step-brother grabbed my arm. "He's planning something. I don't know what it is but you need to watch yourself."

"I'm not a child, Adam." I shook his hand off me. "I can handle him."

I walked down the street, ignoring whatever he shouted at my back. My only goal was to get home and try to relax.

Relax?

Who the fuck am I kidding?

I needed to get out of London.

After arriving at my flat, I grabbed my car keys and left the city.

The drive to Briarcliff Village passed in the blink of an eye. I parked in front of Victoria's cottage and admired the gray and white stone exterior. She'd given me a spare set of keys but I haven't been inside since we were there together.

I want my last memory of this house to be of you here with me.

Her words punched an even bigger hole in my chest. *Fuck.* I squeezed the steering wheel and exhaled slow.

Go inside. I need to go inside.

The scent of flowers filled the air as I approached the house. Gardeners still hadn't tended to the rose bushes. They bloomed among the wild brush and thorny vines.

My hands shook when I unlocked the door. Maybe I shouldn't be here but I just fucking need something to quiet this anger and fear and utter regret that's been plaguing me.

Heavy silence filled the dark foyer. The door clicked shut, echoing throughout the space. I'd only been in this house twice but I felt closer to her in here.

I didn't even mind sitting on this repugnant gold couch.

Color choices aside, it was a lovely old home. It just needed to be restored from the inside out.

"Beautiful but broken," I whispered.

My heart wrenched. That applied to so much more than this cottage.

I looked at the shadows on the walls, letting my gaze trail over to the staircase. *If I'd never run up there...*

Standing up, I walked through the double doors to the sitting room. Running my hand along the sturdy lines of the wood paneling gave me an idea. I renovate homes in much worse shape each year. This house didn't need a major rebuild but it definitely needed some sprucing up.

I could easily sand the floors, and some of the paneling. Maybe strip the wallpaper and give the walls a fresh coat of paint. Victoria *is* my neighbor after all. What good is it living down the street from her if I don't give her a proper welcome to the area?

A laugh rumbled in my chest. Yeah, she knows this area well enough. But still. I want to do this for her. She did ask me for some contacts to help with fixing up the place.

I texted one the contractors I've worked with for years to let him know I'd be starting a new project this summer. Then, I texted my home security guy. If Jordan insisted on circling this house like a vulture, I wanted it protected with the most state-of-the-art system money could buy.

Satisfied, I returned to the foyer and sat on the stairs. I should probably leave but I wanted to feel close to her for just a little bit longer.

It took an enormous amount of restraint not to text her. Instead, I scrolled through her social media.

Not my best plan.

I kept going back to the photos she'd posted from the Met Gala and some league event. Desire twisted and pulled on my heart the longer I stared at the pictures. Victoria's smile always affected me. Its radiance made a mark on my soul the first time I saw her.

And fuck me, this dress.

Her sexy body poured into gray satin and lace that hugged her curves with innocence and enough seduction to heat my blood.

Green eyes. Sun-kissed ivory skin. Red hair swept over her shoulder in loose waves. Glossy lips. All smiles and beauty and effortless grace.

The muscles in my jaw snapped into a rigid line.

How does pushing her away keep her, as you put it, safe?

Dr. Frances' question burned through me, exposing not only this colossal fuck up but every shitty mistake I've made.

I hung my head and sighed. I just need to get through the rest of this week.

"I can't do it that day," I said, folding my hands on the desk. "I'll be out of town."

Three sets of eyes locked onto me. None of them looked particularly pleased. This ad campaign for a new designer watch was scheduled to launch for the holidays. I'm actually quite excited about it so I'm not sure why they're annoyed since it's barely June.

"We'll just plan for when you come back then?" the account manager asked.

I stared blankly at him.

Julian. That's his name.

"I'm not planning on coming back until July. Will that throw off the launch schedule?"

Julian's eyes narrowed. "If you don't mind my asking, where will you be?"

"Manhattan."

"Perfect." Something that looked like a smile teased his mouth for a second. "We have offices in Times Square. I'll have Chloe set up the photoshoot there. We'll circle back in a few days with dates."

"Brilliant." I stood up, escorting them to the door. While I enjoyed running my own brand management company and securing my own partnerships and endorsements, I could do without the corporate speak. If one more person tells me they'll *circle back,* my head will explode.

It's my own fault for insisting I could take this meeting without my business partner. But I suppose his honeymoon is a reasonable excuse to be on holiday.

I flinched.

Marriage.

Christ.

I sat down heavily at my desk.

Not something I've spent a lot of time thinking about nor is it something I've ever considered. I never even liked it when a one night stand wanted to spend the night. I'd always ask them to leave. Politely, of course.

Well, except for the night I invited Victoria to stay...

My stepmother's name popped up when my phone started ringing.

I greeted her with as much cheer as I could muster these days.

"Are you busy tonight, Xavier? I can never keep track of what you're up to these days."

"I'm not busy."

"I made cottage pie for dinner. Your favorite. Feel like stopping by?"

Not really played on the tip of my tongue. Rebecca would be the sole reason I'd consider going. She's the only mother I've ever known and always treated me as her son.

With the way I've been feeling the past couple weeks, maybe seeing her wouldn't suck.

"You said the magic words. Set a place for me. I'll see you later."

Scars are weird things. They come in many sizes, shapes, and colors. But those are only the visible ones. The ones people stare at and ask *how'd you get that?* And if the scar is really big and really ugly, it's generally expected that a fantastical story will follow about how it came to be.

I knew mine would be a conversation starter. Part of me loved that aspect of it.

The other thing with scars is not all of them are as clear as the jagged line above my eye.

Some can't be seen. Some are so deep, so ugly, so painful, that they hide in the depths of a person.

They never heal. They scab over until the inevitable moment it rips open.

Sitting at the dinner table with my father and stepmother was one of those moments.

Not because my mum wasn't alive. I'd dealt with that growing up. Therapy started young with me. Funny thing about it? I reconciled any guilt I had about my mother's death faster than I've been able to deal with the anger that's been festering inside me.

Tonight's overwhelming burden wasn't anger. It was the persistent cloud of feeling inadequate.

"Big match this weekend," Rebecca gushed. "Think you'll win it all again?"

"That's the plan."

I didn't have to ask if they were coming to watch. They were. Surprising, since my dad showed minimal interest in my career. But Adam was playing too, so, you know, have to support the family and all that.

I glanced at him. Strong silent type, this one.

"You and Adam should come over Sunday. We'll celebrate."

I smiled at Rebecca. "I won't be here but thank you."

"Where are you off to now?" my dad finally spoke.

"New York."

He looked at me with wistful sadness. It's always brief but I never miss it. "What's in the States? More endorsement opportunities?"

Rebecca cleared her throat, shooting him a smug look. "No, James. It's a girl."

Oh for fuck's sake.

"The one I showed you from his social media," she continued. "The pretty American."

"Oh right," his voice went up an octave. "Didn't know it was this serious."

The way they both looked at me made me slightly uncomfortable. Like I'd done something sneaky. I'm a grown man. Why do I feel like a teenager who's been caught watching porn with his dick in his hand? And since when did my father *ever* take an interest in anything about my life?

"Nice to know I'm being stalked online by my parents," I quipped, running a finger over my eyelid. "I should block you."

"You will not." Rebecca sounded offended. "You haven't said anything about her. Not that you ever say *anything* about the girls you've dated. Did you meet her when you played in New York last month?"

"No."

"How did you meet?"

My eye twitched. *By chance.* "The usual way."

"On one of those dating apps where you swipe them, what is it, right? Left?"

"Don't really think it's smart for me to be on any of those." I softened a bit when she smiled at me. "I met her at Black Rose. She was here on holiday."

Mostly true.

"What's her name?"

"Victoria," I answered quietly.

"Lovely," my stepmom grinned. "We'd like to meet her the next time she visits. You never bring any girlfriends around anymore."

"It's not like I've had very many. Just a date or two here and there."

Rebecca eyed me with that knowing gaze only mothers have. Even if she didn't give birth to me, she could still sniff out when I was being vague. My reputation didn't shield itself from my family. They heard the rumors, saw the articles online. At one point in my career, I'd been linked with a different celebrity or model every week.

Speculation was one thing. I'd always respond to the rumors with a cheeky one-liner. Little did the media know what a cruel irony it was to be surrounded by adoration and desire only to feel completely alone. But that was how I'd wanted it.

"Well, you're rather public about her with the photos. It's refreshing to see you post something that isn't football."

Three pictures. I'd posted three pictures of Victoria while we were together in New York and my stepmom was acting like it's a royal decree of marriage.

I blanched.

There's that word again.

Focus.

"In any case," Rebecca kept talking. "It's only fair we get to spend time with her." She placed her hand on my dad's arm. "We'll have them both over for a relaxing dinner. Sound good, James?"

I braced for my father's standard answer.

"Maybe."

Chapter

FIVE

Friday's training proved to be more challenging than I anticipated. I thought I covered it well but Cade noticed. He pestered me until I agreed to grab a leisurely dinner with him before retiring to our hotel rooms.

"Mate, in four days I'll be laying on the sand in Dubai enjoying the scenery." Cade waggled his eyebrows at me. "Are you sure you don't want to join me?"

"Quite sure, thanks."

"You're going to stay here? In this cloudy, drizzly city? You've not been yourself since…well, you know. Give yourself a break. It's the off-season. Live a little."

I pushed the food around on my plate. "I'm going to see Victoria."

Cade's eyes practically bugged out of his sockets. "That's great," he exclaimed. "You finally pulled your head out of your ass."

I fought an urge to throw my napkin at him.

"Is Victoria happy you're going? She must be buzzing."

"She doesn't know."

"Why not?" He sounded incredulous. "You've been wallowing in misery for days." He knocked on the table for emphasis. "Weeks. Reckon you'd have called her for a naughty video chat to celebrate."

This time I did throw my napkin at him. He just laughed in his unaffected way.

"C'mon Maddox. This nonsense with McKennie really got you down. I've never seen you like this." Cade's voice lowered. "I know you hate when I say this shit, but I've been worried about you."

I rubbed my eyes. "I know. Thanks, mate."

"Wow. An actual acknowledgment." Cade sat back in the chair. "I'll have to mark this down." He made a sweeping gesture with his arm. "Xavier Maddox, Somewhat Moody Goalkeeper, Appreciates Cade Gallagher, Best Striker in the World."

"*Best* is a lofty title for a striker who hit the post *twice* at our last match."

"Arse," he snickered. "I did land that beauty of a free kick though."

"That's because Liverpool's keeper didn't react fast enough."

"For fuck's sake," he laughed. "Give me a little credit."

I laughed with him. Cade is always good for bringing some levity to any situation.

"Seriously though." His solemn tone gave me pause. "I remember what happened the last time Jordan interfered in your relationship." My muscles tensed. "You got blinded by revenge and—"

"Drop it, Cade."

"No. I realize you hear it from Logan almost daily but you've worked too fucking hard to get yourself right. Victoria is an amazing woman. Create a future with her. Don't burn down the past just because you think you can."

For a guy who walks through life like it's one giant red carpet, Cade does have his moments of deep reflection. He's not wrong. I should focus on creating a future with Victoria, not going scorched earth on Jordan.

Watching him burn is tempting though.

Our conversation soon shifted to more light-hearted topics. Cade mostly rambled on and on about what he planned to do in Dubai, Spain, and Greece.

"Vegas will be my final stop," he told me. "If you're still in Manhattan, let me know. I'll come crash your romantic escapades. Or maybe catch up with those American football players. We all got on really well after our match at that bar."

Catching up with Noah fucking Tate or Tre fucking Gideon was not going to happen.

"I'd rather peel grapes."

"Lighten up, Maddox."

Cade continued talking as we settled the check and walked back to the hotel. Being around him tonight helped get my mind back where it belonged.

We did have a trophy to win after all.

He walked backwards out of the elevator, spreading his arms wide. "Tomorrow at this time we'll be champions."

"Yes we will," I grinned. "See you on the pitch."

My hotel room was down the hall from Bennet's. I wasn't too surprised when I heard his voice through the door when I walked by.

He's probably on the phone with either his dad or Hannah. I paused to listen and thought I heard something that sounded like a muffled *are you close.*

I know he likes to play with Hannah when they're on a call. I stepped away and went to my room.

After showering and settling on the bed, I grabbed my phone.

Time to put my plan in motion.

Me: Need a huge favor. Please

I leaned my head back, wondering if I'd get a reply. After a few minutes passed, I turned on the TV hoping to occupy my mind. Reruns of an old American sitcom played back to back. I stared at it, not paying even the slightest amount of attention. Now I get why Victoria paces around in circles when she's stressed.

My phone vibrated, sending a wave of anxiety through me.

Killian: Why do you think I'll help

Me: I'm coming to Manhattan

Max: About time

Killian: What do you want

This is going to be rough.

Me: I'd like to see her. Do you know if she has plans tomorrow night?

Max: We might be going to a fundraiser

Killian: If you think I'm going to let you see her, you're high

My heart sank. Maybe this wasn't the smartest way to go about it.

Me: Sorry to bother you

I tossed the phone on the bed and scrubbed my hands over my face. Not sure why I expected them to jump at the chance to help. Killian is her best friend and fiercest protector. He probably dislikes me more than she does at this point. Max seemed to play the role of mediator but would most likely side with his partner.

I shut off the TV and tried to get some sleep. After staring into the darkness for what felt like hours, my phone vibrated again.

Max: If you really want to see her, I'll work on Killian

Me: I do

Max: Give me some time. Don't expect miracles

A little piece of hope was all I needed.

The final match of the season went exactly as planned on Saturday. We won (obviously) giving the club another league championship. Back-to-back, for anyone out there keeping score.

I recorded my twentieth clean sheet of the season and was named Goalkeeper of the Year.

Winning never gets old. Neither does the cheering or the accolades or the adoration. I fucking love it and will never get enough.

Victoria texted me after the match ended. She sent a photo of her TV screen with the message *I'm so proud of you.*

She must be just as desperate as I am for the smallest bit of connection.

I'd heard from Killian and Max at halftime. Fingers crossed all the texts would lead to the outcome I wanted. It took a mountain of convincing on my part, but I think I managed to get them in my corner for now.

The plan was for me to meet them at the fundraiser at nine. I made those two swear to secrecy and had to trust they'd do this one little thing for me.

After I completed all my post-match interviews, I showered, tossed all my clothes in my travel bag and went to the airport. My nerves didn't settle until we were about an hour into the flight.

"Hey." Bennet's serious tone gave me pause.

I looked over at him.

Oh shit.

His grim expression didn't help.

"Before I say this, I'd like to remind you we're on an airplane over the Atlantic. Don't do anything crazy like try to open a door."

Panic set in. I clutched the armrest and said as evenly as I could, "What happened?"

"Jordan confronted Victoria in Manhattan last night." His eyes widened at whatever expression burned itself on my face. "He pretended to be some guy from Missouri. She's fine. He only talked to her. Hannah was able to get rid of him when she found her."

Way too many fucking thoughts ran rampant through my mind. "Where? Why was she alone? How did Hannah manage to find her?"

Bennet ignored my concerns. "When you see her tonight, don't be surprised if she asks you some tough questions."

My heart nearly stopped. "Tough how?"

"According to Hannah, Jordan said a lot of shitty things about you."

"What *things*?"

"I don't know. Victoria didn't get into specifics with her."

Unbridled rage turned my vision to static. If I'd only *pictured* killing him before, now I'd make sure Jordan took his last breath the next time I saw him.

"Did you find out about this during the match?"

Bennet didn't answer straight away, which riled me up even more.

"I'm waiting, Logan."

"Last night," he finally admitted. "I talked to Victoria after it happened."

He stiffened against the seat when I stood up.

"What did you say to her?" Venom razored my every word.

"Sit down, mate," he said as tactful as a diplomat negotiating a treaty. Fear, anger, and impatience pounded behind my eyes. But I sat, because honestly what the fuck else could I do trapped in this flying tin can?

"She wanted to talk to you." Bennet's expression softened. "I told her I needed you focused for today. I wasn't wrong about that. You would have buggered off and flown to her the second you knew."

"Of course I would have," I shouted, almost pulling the armrest off this chair. "Fuck the match. Don't you *ever* stand in the way of her and I again."

Bennet wisely kept his mouth shut.

The flight to Manhattan dragged on. When we finally landed and arrived at the hotel, I changed into my tuxedo and hightailed it to the event.

Killian and Max were waiting for me in the lobby.

They looked annoyed.

Great.

I could tell Killian wanted to give me a piece of his mind. I'd let him at some point, but right now I needed to see Victoria.

"She's out on the terrace," he told me.

I turned to walk away.

"Not so fast. First I'm going to give you some unsolicited advice."

Fuck.

Exhaling slow, I clasped my hands behind my back and nodded.

"She'll see right through your bullshit. Be honest with her and don't rush anything." Killian narrowed his eyes. "I love her like family. If I ever see her go through what you put her through these last few weeks again, I'll rip your fucking heart out."

Not many people could talk to me this way and walk away unscathed. But Killian loved her as much as I did. Maybe even more.

"You have my word," I vowed.

Maxim cleared his throat. "We like you, Xavier. We want this to work for you guys. But much like Killian said, if you hurt her again—"

"You'll rip my heart out?" I interrupted, flashing a smile that accentuated the trademark Maddox dimple. If now isn't the perfect time to charm my way out of a situation, when is?

"No," he scowled. "I'll take a sledgehammer to your hands. Can't be a world-famous goalkeeper if your hands are broken."

Jesus Christ.

"Point taken." I swallowed, ready to bolt for the exit. "She's on the terrace, yeah?"

Killian nodded. "Silver silk dress. Probably nursing a martini."

We stood in awkward silence for a few seconds.

I didn't know if I should thank them or just leave, so I left. Maybe this reunion won't go as well as I'd hoped.

The closer my strides took me to the terrace, the more nervous I became. That's weird for me since I never get nervous around women. But Victoria isn't just any woman.

She challenges me, sees me, loves me at my worst. That last bit is debatable since I haven't been the greatest of boyfriends lately. I let rage blind my actions and it ended up hurting her even more. I'd be lucky if she didn't break up with me on the spot.

We'll just talk. No sex. Maybe a hug if she'll let me. I won't do anything an *actual* gentleman wouldn't do. She'll like that, right?

Yes.

Well, no.

I choose to play rough. I choose to be spanked, bitten, grabbed, tied up, used in public, used in private. I choose all of it because I choose you. All of you.

Her words from our last night together had imprinted onto the deepest, darkest parts of me. I wanted to do things with her, and to her, I've suppressed for years.

Not tonight.

Tonight I only wanted her forgiveness. Ironic, since I'd dismissed the whole forgive myself thing Dr. Frances suggested.

Great. Now I'm thinking about my therapist as I'm trying to find my girlfriend.

I shoved my hands in my pockets and followed a handful of other guests outside. They walked toward a section overflowing with trees and seasonal plants. I doubt she'd be there. It was such a pleasant night, I bet she found a spot to admire the city.

Another couple strolled toward a hightop table nestled to my left. I kept moving forward until I noticed a small table almost hidden from view. It was flanked by decorative trees and an ivy-covered wall.

When I slowed down and paused behind the redhead in a silver silk gown, my heart felt at peace for the first time in weeks. Her shoulders slumped a little when she tugged an olive off the skewer into her mouth.

She was indeed nursing a martini.

I lowered my gaze, savoring the slit climbing her left leg, exposing her smooth thigh. Lust pulsed through me.

Mine. If she'll still have me.

I relaxed my stance and said, "So, Victoria is it?"

Chapter

SIX

Of all the ways I'd pictured my Sunday afternoon going, driving along the coast with Xavier Maddox was *not* one of them.

But here we are.

All things being equal, I'm still sort of shocked he showed up at the fundraiser last night. There's so much more explaining he has to do. With the way we operate though, I'm not surprised.

We have a habit of fucking first and talking later. True, last night is on me. I let him off the hook. I wanted to indulge in my fantasy of having sex in public. It was more mind-blowing than I expected and I have zero regrets. Besides, he has a full three weeks' worth of apologizing to complete.

"You should let me drive." Xavier's silky voice filled the car. "I'll get us wherever we're going much faster."

My response was to press down on the accelerator. The engine rumbled as the car picked up speed.

"This fast enough for you?"

"Maybe." He squeezed my thigh. "Where are we going?"

"Just a little spot on the beach. It's a private area for residents only."

The warmth of his hand trailed under the hem of my sundress. His touch was casual but possessive, sending a pleasurable shiver down my spine.

"You have a house here?"

"No. I sold it years ago but the couple who bought it still let me use their private entrance to the beach." I glanced at him for a second. "My dad helped with their investments. They've been family friends forever. I always thought they let me use it out of pity but…" I shrugged, turning down the street toward another house I haven't seen in a long time.

Fortunately, I could park away from the house on a small section of the long driveway. A nearby path led to the water. I grabbed a blanket from the backseat and guided Xavier, listening as the sound of the waves crashing against the shore became louder and louder. When we finally reached the clearing I paused and took in the Atlantic.

Dark, powerful, majestic.

"You're not going to toss me in there, are you?"

"Maybe. Why? Can't swim?"

"I can swim just fine, city princess. Which way?"

I led him toward one of my favorite spots, laid out the blanket and sat near some grass covered dunes. The sun wasn't at its full summer strength yet. Even though it beat down on us, it wasn't unbearable.

Xavier stretched out on his back, lacing his hands behind his head. As hot as he looked in his tux at the event, he looked just as delicious in jeans and a t-shirt. I swear, the man could wear plastic bags and I'd drool.

Great. I've become *that* girl.

"What's on your mind, love? We're all by ourselves on this beautiful beach. You can tell me." His sapphire eyes locked onto mine.

I replayed all the things I've *wanted* to say to him over the last three weeks in my head. All the confusion and annoyance. But I also didn't want to create too much tension between us, especially after what we shared last night.

Balance. I needed to figure out the balance.

"Come here," he said, gently pulling me down so I could nestle into him. I rested my head on his chest, listening to his steady heartbeat and inhaling his clean scent. Somehow it was even more intoxicating mixed with the salty ocean air.

"How long are you staying?"

"As long as it takes."

"Don't you have training and international matches to—"

"I said as long as it takes. If I have to fly back and forth every week, I will." His answer came out low and rough, almost pained.

I propped myself up on an elbow, searching his face. It was neutral but his eyes always betrayed him. At least they did around me. Behind the tortured glow I saw his deep love and devotion.

And his fear.

Xavier's expression flickered from indifferent to covetous. He sat up, pulling me onto his lap.

"Is this where the picture of you and your sister is from? The one on your birthday?"

"Sort of. We took it in the yard." I motioned to my left. "The house is back that way." I glanced at Xavier. "You don't want to see it, do you?"

He smiled at whatever expression planted itself on my face. "No. Your aversion to your family's houses has been duly noted."

Relief flooded through me. I would have shown him if he'd asked but I'd rather not walk down memory lane if given the choice. Sitting on the beach in his lap seemed like a much better option. Part of me feared this was all an elaborate dream and I'd wake up alone and miserable.

"I stopped by your cottage the other day."

My lips parted in surprise. "Really? Why?"

The warmth of his hands bled through my clothes when he slid them around my waist, leaving a trail of fire in their wake. "I wanted to feel close to you."

My heart rate kicked up a notch. I'm not one to blush but I'll be damned if my cheeks didn't burn an obvious pink.

And the pièce du résistance? About a million butterflies (give or take) invaded my stomach.

Collecting myself on a breath I quipped, "I'm surprised it wasn't to toss the gold couch in the garbage."

"That's still a possibility," he drawled. "I actually sat on it, if you can believe that."

"Wow." I laughed. "Who are you and what have you done with the insufferably snobbish guy I met on the side of the road?"

My words hung in the air for a second before he laughed. The sound slid over me, rich and textured and sexy.

"Yeah, he's…he's been having a go of it lately." Melancholy replaced the remnants of amusement filling the corners of his mouth. "I really did go there to feel closer to you."

"Did it help?"

"More than you'll ever know."

That house caused me so much anxiety and stress. But it comforted him. The paradox floored me.

"I'm glad one of us likes being there."

Several strands of hair blew in my face on a strong breeze. Xavier gently tucked them behind my ear. "You like being there, too. Otherwise you wouldn't have fought so hard to keep it."

Somehow, he always seemed to know, and see, the inherent truth behind my deflections.

"Don't tell anyone." I traced a finger along his mouth.

"You'll have to kiss me to keep me quiet."

My whole body erupted in goosebumps when his hands slid along my thighs. If not for the rhythmic pounding of the waves, it felt like we were isolated in our own private world.

I leaned closer. "If you insist."

"I do."

Xavier's groan vibrated through me when his lips pressed to mine. He kissed me slow and lazy, our tongues swirling and exploring. I could kiss him like this all day.

"Talk to me," he requested when he pulled away. "You must have more questions." He rubbed his thumb along my jaw. Softly, just barely touching my skin, but it was enough to cloud my thoughts. He's good at knowing how to break down my defenses.

"Haven't lost your charm, Maddox."

The crooked, dimpled smile I adore spread across his face. Of course, it was also tinged with the arrogance that makes it impossible for me not to be sucked into his intoxicating aura.

His thumb made another slow sweep over my jaw.

No sense in delaying this any longer.

"What happened while you were in England?"

"Nothing you need to worry about." His answer chilled the warm, ocean breeze.

"*Something* must have happened. You were gone for—"

"I know, I know," he cut in, tightening his grip on me. "Shit. I— Okay. Just...don't hate me."

"Drama never did suit you." I reached for his hand and placed it over my heart. "The whole honesty thing is still in effect."

He exhaled, toying with the silver chain around my neck. The ring he'd given me before going back to London dangled from it.

"I had a few run-ins with Jordan."

"I'm not surprised." I responded with ease while my pulse raced.

An eyebrow arched. "You're not?"

"Well...I mean...a little but..." I struggled to find the right words. "The night we read the diary I thought you were going to commandeer an army and charge into battle. I've never seen a person get so angry. What happened?"

A scowl marred his sexy mouth. "We got into a bit of a fight. I knocked him out."

My shoulders slumped. "You what?"

Xavier's expression soured. "I fucking knocked him out. If you'd been there, you'd understand why."

"Please don't do that," I said quietly. "I don't think I can handle it if someone else I love gets hurt because of him." I glanced at the jagged scar above his left eye. "Did he hurt you?"

Regret passed over Xavier's face so fast I almost missed it.

"No." He leaned forward to rest his forehead on mine and continued his gentle strokes along my jaw. A slight restlessness moved through him. "But it's probably why he came to Manhattan. I didn't mean to put you directly in harm's way."

"You didn't. He would have found me anyway."

His entire body stiffened in my embrace. The sweet caresses stopped, replaced by firm pressure sinking into my skin. When his eyes met mine I struggled to find my next breath. Everything around us buzzed and crackled with an undercurrent of danger.

Nerves got the best of me and I kept talking.

"I can handle myself. It's not like he cornered me in a dark alley. He was just being an asshole."

"Just being an asshole." Xavier's lazy repetition of my words sent a shiver through me.

Something about his demeanor gave me pause. Like I'd approached a vault of secrets that was fortified with a lock no master thief could ever crack.

"What aren't you saying?" The question tumbled out against my better judgement, intensifying the crackling hum in the air.

The whisper-light touch of his hands on my skin did nothing to calm the erratic beating of my heart. But the way he looked at me…

Xavier's eyes darkened until the pupils swallowed all but the slimmest edge of sapphire.

"The thought of you being hurt or upset angers me in ways I didn't know existed. All that matters to me is *you*. All I think about, all I see, all I feel, is *you*." The velvet softness of his touch belied the cruel edge to his tone. "I will risk everything, Victoria. I will fucking destroy him if he comes near you again. I've never felt like this before, and I've never been more terrified of what I could lose."

Every word spiked my adrenaline until my heart beat so fast I feared it would burst. I might not know exactly what happened while he's been away but it pierced him to the core.

As though he could read my thoughts, Xavier's expression softened. Delicate, sensual strokes continued on my arms.

He apologized so softly I thought I imagined it.

"Is that all that happened?" I asked gently.

His fingers pressed into my arms. "I went after him again at Bennet's."

"Bennet's?" My jaw dropped. "Why was he there?"

"I don't know." A pained expression washed over his handsome features. I'm not used to this level of vulnerability coming from him.

…never been more terrified of what I could lose…

Discomfort seized hold of me. My sister lost her life when she put herself between me and Jordan. I didn't want to think about what Xavier could lose.

Silence stretched between us for several agonizing minutes. If not for the warmth of his touch on my skin, I'd have mistaken him for a statue.

"Still feeling okay about what we did last night?"

His question surprised me.

I caught his eye before answering. "Of course. Why? Do you have regrets?"

Both his eyebrows arched. "I'm going to pretend you didn't ask me that. Especially since I can still taste you on my tongue."

A rush of desire sped down my spine. Visions of our encounter on the terrace flashed through my memory. The roughness of his voice, the way his touch seared through my dress, the feel of his mouth.

There will never be a moment when I'm not affected by him. It's like I'm seeing him for the first time all over again. Beneath his tattooed, bad-boyish, arrogant exterior lies a heart so warm and giving I often catch myself wondering what I did to deserve his affection.

Liquid warmth pooled in my stomach. Every inch of my body became a hypersensitive nerve-ending.

Those hypnotic blue eyes flared. The tip of his tongue slid along his lower lip, savoring the secret that thrilled him to no end. He knew exactly what he did to me, and he relished in it.

"You're not angry with me anymore," he stated with a little too much confidence. "No more apologizing for me then."

Looks like Xavier the Charmer has entered the chat.

"Irritated," I corrected. "I'm irritated. One night hasn't erased that. Your apology tour won't end until I say it does."

"How many nights will it take?"

"Until you bring me to every balcony in Manhattan."

For someone as skilled as I am in media relations, I have the worst track record with failing to keep my inside thoughts on the actual inside around him.

His bemused expression morphed into something more wicked.

"Is that what you want?" Each word came out slow and deliberate. "My so-called apology tour to be me fucking you on every open air terrace in the city?"

The intended effect was immediate. Nothing else existed in this space except for unspoken promises, electricity, and anticipation.

When my eyelids fluttered, the rest of the world fell away except for him. The alleged balance I attempted to achieve flung itself out the window. How can I maintain *any* balance around this guy?

"Are you taking suggestions?" *What am I saying?*

"I'm listening."

I felt myself flush with anticipation. The sly grin on his face grew wider and more crooked when he saw it. Good to see our game of cause and effect was alive and well.

Okay, fine. I *did* have suggestions. While he slept like royalty in my bed last night, I laid there wide awake letting my fantasies run wild. *The darker ones.*

But now wasn't the time to indulge in fantasies.

"Tori." His eyes glinted with the soft glow of danger. "Tell me."

This stare could have melted the polar ice caps.

Okay, let's play.

"The first one is pretty tame. I want us to go away for a few days. Somewhere that has weak cell phone service. I really want us to disconnect from the outside world."

"Sounds doable. What else?"

I shook my head. "Maybe this isn't the right—"

"Tell. Me." The forbidden, dark edge to his tone sizzled through my veins.

I missed this tone. Judging by the look on his face, he did too.

The rarely used practical side of me emerged and waved a tiny caution flag. *Slow down. Keep your head on straight.*

"I want you to lose yourself with me," I blurted.

Nice one, Chase. Very practical.

Confusion clouded his features.

"More than you already do," I amended, trailing my fingers down his chest. "I want to see you really come undone. Lose control. Be rougher with me. Don't stop yourself when—"

His hand clamped around my throat. I gasped in surprise, panicking for only a second.

"Rougher. Like this?" His soft, rumbled warning vibrated through my body.

Words failed me. All I could do was stare at him and feel his possessive grip.

"Yes?" His fingers tightened slightly. "Or no?"

My reply fought its way out. "Yes."

A veil I didn't know existed slid from his face. An unfamiliar darkness filled his eyes.

"Yes, *what*?"

Every last bit of oxygen disappeared from my lungs.

The animalistic stare he pinned on me while flexing his hand around my neck didn't frighten me at all. It had the opposite effect. My arousal heightened, my pulse raced, and it all went to the heat throbbing between my legs.

"Yes, *what*?" he repeated, his tone razor sharp.

"*Please.*" I barely got the word out. "Yes, please. I want you raw and untamed. Always."

I loved how dangerous and feral he looked. The way his mouth parted in ecstasy. The absolute focus on me and nothing else.

"You should be careful what you wish for, love."

A violent shiver streaked through him when I put my hand around his and squeezed.

"You are what I wish for."

In an instant, the mysterious veil snapped back into place. The warmth and strength of his hand disappeared from my neck, leaving me flustered and a tad bit annoyed.

"What else?" His low growl and cold stare made me shudder.

Words, yet again, failed me. I swallowed, relishing the slight discomfort in my throat. "Maybe that's enough for—"

"Tell me."

Our eyes locked. I wanted to tell him. I really did. But there are too many other fucking issues we need to resolve right now. Pushing our boundaries and limits can wait.

"I will. I just—" I exhaled in frustration. "You know how we are. We can't control ourselves when we're together. It's hard for me to stay focused around you. We have some real shit to work through and talk about and I can't when you're sitting here with that…and the…and you're so…well, *look* at you."

His answering smile was all lazy charm and amusement.

Not helping.

Neither was the slow, deliberate slide of his hands along my thighs, up the curve of my hips to my waist.

"Are you objectifying me, Chase?"

"Maybe."

"You know how I feel about maybes."

"Oh yeah. Totally. Big, bad Xavier Maddox and his lifelong beef with the word *maybe*."

Warmth crept back into his eyes, replacing the strained distance that dominated them moments ago. His laugh wound through me like warm caramel.

"You still like wearing this?" He traced the silver chain around my neck, stopping at the ring.

"I love wearing it."

Something about the way he smiled when the sun hit his face and hair made him appear almost angelic, which was hilarious because Xavier was as devilish as they come.

Devilish. Sexy. Arrogant. Possessive.

Mine.

All of him. Just as all of me was his.

A content sigh rolled through his body. I rested my forehead to his, gently running my nails up and down his back. We slowly molded our bodies together in a sweet embrace and sat without saying a word for quite a while. Only the seagulls and the ocean provided a serene ambient soundtrack.

"You should stay with me while you're here."

Oh my God. The lack of control I have over my own mouth is astonishing.

"Yeah?" He leaned back to look at me. "That's awfully forward of you."

I shrugged. "Or you can waste your money staying alone at a hotel. Up to you."

The subtle etched lines fanning from his eyes when he laughed reignited the flurry of butterflies in my stomach. Yes, he was devilish and all of those other things but he was also beautiful and gentle and made me feel emotions I thought I'd locked away permanently.

"I would love nothing more than to spend every possible moment with you. Fall asleep next to you. Wake up with you in my arms. For as long as you'll have me."

I melted. For as long as I'll have him?

That's easy.

Forever, please.

Chapter
SEVEN

I love New York.

More specifically, I love the woman scurrying through her New York flat, flushed and breathless from being thoroughly shagged after stepping out of the shower.

We're supposed to be at some ring ceremony for her team but when I saw her standing in the bedroom wrapped in a towel and staring into the closet, it didn't take much convincing on my part that we could be late.

I'll steal every possible moment with her I can. The last week has already flown by in a hazy, lovesick blur. Tonight's event will be our first actual date since I arrived.

"Almost ready, love?"

Victoria shot me an incredulous look while slipping into her heels.

Even annoyed, she's gorgeous.

Wavy red hair. Emerald eyes glowing. And the short, fitted dress she wore? I won't last the whole party without ravaging her in a corner or wherever I damn well please.

"I would have been ready an hour ago but *someone* couldn't control themselves."

She's fucking adorable.

"I didn't hear any complaints. In fact, I distinctly heard several cries for more."

The pink blush crawling across her cheeks was so damn sexy. I wanted to trace the color with my tongue.

"Just because you're self aware about how irresistible you are doesn't make us any less late for this party."

"I told you I was everyone's type."

She huffed, walking past me in a musky vanilla scented swirl. "And I told you I'm not everyone. Let's go, Maddox."

Since this was an official New York Legends event and Victoria was one of the top executives, we were treated to our own driver and car for the evening. And of course, me being *me*, I made sure Victoria knew exactly what I wanted to do *to* her and *with* her on the ride over.

"I'll be surrounded by my coworkers," she scolded in a low voice once we arrived and walked toward the Caldwell estate. "Behave."

The rosy glow on her cheeks betrayed the futile effort she made to keep this night chaste and professional.

"Whatever you say, dirty princess," I told her, my mouth tipping up in a smile.

The massive estate reminded me a little of Bennet's place. It's not as big or grandiose but it's just as pretentious. No wonder he's drawn to Hannah.

A few members of the press were gathered to take photos and grab interviews with the players. There was even a red carpet and one of those backdrops with sponsor names splashed across it.

My good mood soured a little when I saw Noah Tate chatting with reporters. Victoria has told me countless times I have nothing to be jealous about but still. It's there and I'm feeling it.

I couldn't stop my scowl watching him charm members of the media.

Tall, clean cut, all-American.

We weren't too dissimilar physically with the tall part. I know Victoria gravitated more towards men with an edge. I filled that need for her. And I do clean up nice when the occasion calls for it.

"There she is," the quarterback exclaimed when he saw us approaching. "Our media relations director. Victoria, come get these vultures off my back."

Good natured laughter filled the space as reporters fawned over him. I know this game well. My media training started when I was only sixteen.

Smile. Be polite and charming. Bite your tongue. Stay on message. Don't take the bait.

Easier said than done at that age. Now? I had reporters eating out of the palm of my hand. And from the looks of things, so did Noah.

Victoria squeezed my hand and mouthed *be right back.*

I stepped off to the side and watched her. One of the reporters shot a curious glance in my direction but quickly turned their attention back to Noah.

As well known as I am in England and throughout Europe, it's a little different here in the States.

Football —the *proper* kind— isn't as popular here. Yes, I still have my admirers but it doesn't get to the frenzied level it sometimes reaches at home. Not that I'd shy away from it anyway.

Watching Victoria shine and charm the reporters filled me with pride.

She flashed me one of her demure smiles before turning her attention away.

Every fucking muscle in my body tensed when Noah rested his hand on her lower back. The casual movement looked completely normal to anyone else. Then he said something to her and she laughed. Jealousy clawed at me, shredding any trace of common sense or logic.

"Xavier, right?" a soft feminine voice said.

I tore my eyes away from them to see a pretty brunette woman standing next to me.

"I'm Tracey. We met in April after your game against the Knights. At the bar?" Her dark brown eyes watched me.

The bar. Tracey.

Oh.

"Yes, sorry, hello." I turned on the charm. "Noah's girlfriend."

Her smile tightened when she nodded. "And you're Victoria's boyfriend."

Fuck. I see what she did there.

"Wow. I'm a complete asshole," I said, showing off the Maddox dimple. "Let's start over, yeah? Pleasure to see you again Tracey… Watson, right? Enjoying the evening?"

"That English accent gets you out of trouble more often than you realize."

"So I've been told."

"I'm surprised they relegated you to the sidelines. This is usually where the girlfriends and wives wait while," she nodded her head towards Noah, "the boys get their minute in the spotlight."

Tracey wasn't wrong. I'm usually the one in the spotlight. Waiting in the wings felt weird but I didn't mind.

Fortunately we didn't have to wait much longer. Noah sauntered over and shook my hand.

"Good seeing you, man. We'll catch up in there for sure. I want to hear all about the big win. If you'll excuse us, I'm starving and want to get some appetizers before the offensive linemen eat it all."

He kissed Tracey, took her hand in his, and went inside. Victoria stood in front of me, looking effortlessly beautiful and regal. Sizing me up with a shrewd smile, she moved closer and placed a hand on my chest.

"Behave." Liquid green eyes gazed up at me through long, dark lashes.

Not a chance.

"Is that a challenge or an order?" I asked in a deceptively soft tone.

"A request." She placed her finger on my mouth. "Can you be a good boy for me?"

My cock stirred at the seductive rasp in her voice. The graceful sway to her hips stoked the low flames licking at my spine when she walked toward the front door. I fell into step behind her, close enough to feel the heat radiating from her body.

Be a good boy? Not tonight.

Hannah greeted us the moment we walked inside.

"I'm glad you're both here. Bennet's already waiting for us in the grand room."

I caught Victoria's eye and mouthed *grand room* as we followed Hannah through the hall. My redheaded beauty laughed and hooked her arm in mine. My heart swelled. This is what being on a proper date with the most perfect woman in the world is like.

My initial assumption about this palatial home wasn't wrong. It's not as grandiose but I'll be damned if it didn't rival the Logan Estate for pretentiousness. My step-mother would love all the detailed interior design. The grand room was filled with expensive pieces in polished black with gold accents. Elegant and exquisite.

There might not be royalty in the States but generational wealth is a close second. I can almost picture Hannah running through these gilded halls as a small girl.

Of course Bennet blended in perfectly with his tailored suit, noble bloodline, and smooth conversational skills. He swirled his drink in his glass and laughed at whatever Ethan Caldwell said.

"They'll let anybody in, won't they?" Bennet tipped his head in my direction and winked.

I rolled my eyes.

Mr. Caldwell greeted us pleasantly and then ushered everyone to the solarium.

A fucking *huge* solarium draped in soft lights, glass chandeliers, and flowing curtains. Dozens of tables filled one half of the room. It even had a stage and a dance floor.

As much as I appreciated design and architecture, this felt overdone.

One look at Victoria made me reconsider. She simply glowed like no one else could under all the lights. A room like this was made for her.

If I could freeze this moment, I would.

"What is it?" she asked, smiling in her captivating way.

"You're beautiful."

My compliment had the desired effect. Her cheeks turned pink. Victoria didn't blush often. I loved it when she did.

We sat with Bennet and Hannah at a table not too far from the stage. Caldwell addressed the room with some brief remarks before dinner was served. Once dessert was plated, the ceremony began. Well, *ceremony* probably wasn't the right word. This was a lavish party from top to bottom for a group of professional athletes who won a championship.

Hosts and hostesses dressed in formal attire carried trays of ring boxes to each table. Hannah looked over at Victoria and grinned when boxes emblazoned with the Legends logo were placed in front of them.

"Cheers to number six," Hannah gushed.

Victoria held the box in her hands. "Crazy, right?"

A commotion a few tables over caught all of our attention. Noah stood on his chair waving a microphone in the air.

"*Legends,*" he shouted into the mic. "They said we couldn't do it. They said we were too slow, too complacent, too spoiled. But guess what?"

An answering chorus of whoops and hollers filled the room.

I glanced over at Bennet and arched an eyebrow. A ghost of a smile crossed his lips.

"*We fucking showed all of them.*" The veins in Noah's neck popped with every word.

Mr. All-American has some fire in him. I can respect that.

I have no idea what else he shouted once people started yelling and his words became a garbled audio nightmare through the speakers.

Leaning close to Victoria, I slid my hand over her leg and asked, "Are you going to show me?"

A beautiful crimson flush crawled up her neck. "Show you what?"

"The ring."

I was treated to a fiery stare. "I thought you said they were gaudy."

"They are. I want to see. Show me."

She lifted my hand off her leg and placed it on the table. Slowly, and rather seductively, she removed the rings I already wore. "Let's see if we can make you look like a real football player," she teased, opening the box and revealing the biggest, sparkliest ring I've ever seen.

A sword encrusted in rubies was mounted in six championship trophies.

"Is this supposed to be like the sword in the stone or something?" I asked.

"Something like that." She pointed at different parts of the ring. "Everything is symbolic. The number of rubies and diamonds, the colors, what's engraved." Victoria slid the ring onto my finger.

"Does it have to be this bloody heavy?" I laughed, holding up my hand.

"Never felt the weight of more than two-hundred-fifty diamonds before?"

"It's a bit much."

"But it looks good on you."

"Looking minted, mate," Bennet commented, glancing up from his phone. "Mind if I steal you away from the lovely Victoria for a few minutes?"

I did mind. "Why?"

His even tone and expression gave him away. "Sponsorship opportunity. Don't want to bore the ladies with all that."

"Come on, Bennet," Victoria chastised. "If you want to go make out with him in a private corner, you have my permission. You don't have to speak in code. He's one hell of a kisser."

Bennet's eyes flared with amusement. "Meet us in the hall in five minutes to join the fun."

Hannah remained expressionless. Victoria's face turned scarlet.

Even with their playful banter, I didn't have a good feeling about this impending conversation. Bennet rarely interrupted a social event with business matters. This could only be about one thing.

I removed the gaudy beast of a ring, put mine back on, and stroked Victoria's flushed cheek. "Five minutes." She swallowed hard when my hand closed around her throat. "And then maybe I'll let Hannah and Bennet watch me fuck you in the hallway."

I didn't have to look at her when I stood up to know how much that affected her.

I *want you raw and untamed. Always.*

Her words burned themselves into my skin that day on the beach. I'll spend the rest of my life fulfilling all her fantasies.

Fucking Noah Tate passed by and grinned at me while I walked toward the hall. I turned in time to see him start up a conversation with my girlfriend. My hand clenched.

He's not a threat. Let it go.

When we left the solarium and paused in the main hallway, Bennet vocalized what I already sensed.

"McKennie's here."

And now my night is ruined.

"Are you sure?"

Bennet showed me the text.

Alex: In Manhattan. Tell Maddox

"How long?" I asked.

"A few days. Alex says he's been spending time at an office building in the financial district."

"What building? I'm putting an end to this. If he goes anywhere near her again—"

"No you're not." Bennet's broad-shouldered frame filled my view. "Let Alex handle it."

I thought back to what Adam told me. *He's planning something.*

"Any idea what he wants or why he's here?"

"Not yet."

Aggravation tunneled through my veins. I turned my attention back toward the solarium, scanning the crowd until Victoria came into view. She was still talking to Noah.

The sight of her calmed me. All the bullshit swirling around me fell away until we were the only two people who existed.

As long as I'm with her, nothing else mattered, not even knowing Jordan was in New York. In this moment, I no longer gave a shit. He wants to try and torture me with fabricated lies about what happened years ago? Let him. I'd love to see how far he gets. My only fucking priority was her.

"Xavier." Bennet's demanding tone irked me.

Reluctantly, I tore my eyes away from Victoria in time to see his expression cloud with displeasure.

I stared back, bored. "What."

"Don't do anything stupid."

"You sound like a broken record." I left without hesitation and returned to the only person I wanted to be with tonight.

Besides, she's spent enough time socializing with the Legends quarterback.

"…happy to help get things rolling. I love that idea," Tracey was saying as I wrapped an arm around Victoria's waist.

"Get things rolling for what?" I asked.

Victoria placed her hand on my stomach and looked up at me. "Remember when I mentioned starting a foundation in Charlotte's memory?"

I nodded.

"Tracey and Noah offered to brainstorm ideas. Tracey is a veterinarian and has quite a few contacts at shelters across the area who might benefit from donations for animal welfare."

"And my cousin's wife is a counselor at a mental health clinic for teens and young adults," Noah piped up. "I'm going to reach out to her to see what clinics need the most assistance."

Victoria's eyes outshined the brightest lights in this room. I know how important honoring her sister is. And that's why I refrained from snapping Noah's neck when she smiled.

"You're lucky to have such supportive friends." My words iced when I emphasized *friends*.

Not sure why I was behaving like such a prat. Tracey and Noah seemed like nice enough people. They obviously held Victoria in high regard, otherwise they wouldn't offer to assist her with such a personal project.

"I am," Victoria responded. "Thank you both."

They excused themselves to rejoin the party.

"You really have to work on your jealousy," she scolded, sinking her fingertips into my stomach.

"I know."

"Was that an actual admission?" she laughed, turning to stand in front of me.

"Don't push your luck."

"Or what?" she batted her lashes. "Maybe you should give me a stern talking to." Her hand trailed down my stomach to the waistband of my pants. "Or we could sneak off down the hall. Find a quiet place to—"

"Tori."

Her eyes flashed. "What's the matter, Maddox? Performance anxiety?"

I scanned the room, noticing a set of doors leading outside.

Without saying a word, I grabbed her hand and led her out to what I assumed was a patio.

It was actually a large stone terrace with wrought iron fencing and spiral topiaries. An arched entrance led deeper into a grassy area with even more shrubs and greeneries. For a second, I thought we'd walked out into the beginning of some type of maze.

Surprisingly, we were alone.

The solarium gleamed behind us, pulsing with music.

"I thought I was under orders to behave tonight," I said quietly, pulling her close.

"You don't want me to flirt with you?" she asked in a sweet, innocent tone.

"I like when you flirt with me. But if you tease me too much…" I let my voice trail off while I slid my hand up her thigh.

She failed at hiding a smile.

So this is the game she wants to play.

"I see." I bent my head, hovering my mouth at her ear. "I thought fucking you before we left to come here would hold us over. Guess I was wrong." My fingers dug into the soft flesh of her backside. "Take a few steps back."

This wasn't a suggestion. I released her, watching the subtle ways her body reacted to my order. The slight parting of her lips. The heavy-lidded stare pinned directly on me.

Fucking gorgeous.

I tucked my hands in my pockets.

"Dirty princess." My tone was deceptively soft. "You are *not* going to get what you want."

Defiance lit up her emerald eyes. Her chin lifted ever so slightly.

I observed and waited.

"What is it, exactly, that you think I want?" she asked with a small shake to her voice. Despite her attempt at playing coy, a deep pink bloomed on her cheeks.

Can't say I've seen her blush this much since we met.

I liked it.

I liked knowing I was the one who affected her this way. The *only* one.

Moving with calculated steps, I approached her until we were inches apart. Instead of touching her, I caressed her with my eyes. Bold and rough, dragging my gaze from her plush lips to her full breasts, down to the soft curves of her hips.

"What you want is far too easy for me to give."

"When has that ever stopped you?"

"This Ivy League mouth is just begging for trouble, isn't it?"

"Maybe."

The roughest part of me took over.

I fisted my hand in her hair, pulling hard. She moaned in surprise.

"You make such sexy little noises, Tori," I growled in her ear. "Maybe everyone should hear what you sound like tonight. Do you think Noah wants to hear the noises you make when I'm buried deep inside you? At least he'll finally get the hint that you belong to *me*. Should I remove all doubt that you're mine and let him hear you scream my name?"

The defiance glittering in her eyes deepened to arousal when she wet her lips.

"Naughty girl. You want them to hear you." I kept my hand in her hair but didn't touch her anywhere else. "How surprised would all those players be if they found out their proper, well-spoken media relations director got this turned on being my little toy? Mine to play with and use as I please, wherever I please."

Her body pressed into mine on a sigh.

This woman will be the death of me. I'd known it the moment I saw her pacing in circles on the side of the road. The death of my self-control, my self-imposed restrictions, my denial of who and what I am.

Let it die. All of it. None of it mattered. Not when her body felt this perfect against mine. Like she was tailor-made for me and no one else.

A burst of music filled the night air, pulling my attention away from Victoria. I loosened my grip on her hair.

"There you are," Noah exclaimed from the open door. *Fucking Noah.* "Come back inside."

Victoria smiled at my obvious annoyance and responded, "Be there in a few."

I didn't move or breathe until the door shut.

"His timing is impeccable," I grumbled.

"There's a reason he's been named league MVP four times," she deadpanned. "Do you want to finish what you were saying?"

She stared up at me with longing and something else shining in those beautiful eyes.

Whatever it was, it made my heart stutter. Part of me wanted to ravage her, tear off this dress, ruin her perfectly glossed lips, and mark her everywhere.

But I also wanted to savor her.

I slid my fingers through her hair, gentler this time. No more pulling for now. Then I trailed the pad of my thumb on her cheek, along her jaw, and over her mouth.

Victoria Chase deserves the world.

She deserves so much more than the reckless way I've behaved.

I refuse to repeat the mistakes of my past.

Chapter
EIGHT

I don't want to be at this party anymore.

I want to be at home with Xavier so I can drag out whatever he's *not* saying.

He isn't one to be this hot and cold. I mean, my God, I almost orgasmed from all the things he was telling me before Noah interrupted us.

Now he's stopped talking completely. True, the soft way he's touching me is quite lovely but…

Mine to play with and use as I please.

I held his hand and led him through the solarium to a long hallway. I've been to the Caldwell estate more than a few times over the years. I knew my way around.

After passing by a few doors, I went into one of the rooms I always loved to spend time in. Hannah called it the Empress Room. It lived up to the name with marble floors, plush couches, floor to ceiling windows, and my favorite part, the grand piano. It sat in the middle of the room, basking in the moonlight.

"What are we doing in here?" he asked.

I sat on the piano bench and crossed my legs. Xavier stared at me but didn't move. His guard was up.

"What's going on in that head of yours?"

A small smile. "Nothing. Remember? I'm a prepackaged snack with empty calories."

I appreciated his attempt at humor but couldn't hold back my eye roll if I tried.

"Maddox."

"Chase."

His smile grew wider. My patience thinned.

"Your apology tour hasn't ended yet, no matter how well it might be going." I crossed my arms. "I'm still in the dark about a lot of stuff."

"What stuff?"

"Really?" I cocked an eyebrow. "What did Bennet tell you earlier?"

Xavier tensed, anger rolling off him in waves. "Nothing."

"That's *two* nothings. I feel like I'm on a rollercoaster. Talk to me. Please."

Silence.

And to make it even more annoying, Xavier wouldn't look at me. Frustrated, I scanned the room, sneaking glances at him. Aside from the tortured expression, he really looked handsome tonight. Dark gray dress pants, white button down with the sleeves rolled up, all those tattoos, no tie, dark hair tousled to a fault.

One of the butterflies nudged my heart.

Stop it.

"Okay."

I was so surprised to hear his voice, I jumped. "Okay, what?"

An eyebrow arched as he walked closer. "I had no idea you were this forgetful." Oh good. The aristocratic tone has returned.

Xavier straddled the bench and faced me. "You wanted to talk. What's on your mind?"

"Can I tell you something?"

He dipped his head. "You can tell me anything, love."

"I wish you trusted me more."

He went still. So still, I thought maybe he didn't hear me. But then his eyes locked onto mine. They were filled with such aching and sadness it stole my breath.

"I do trust you," he said in an uncharacteristically timid voice. "I trust you with everything I am." He paused and looked down before continuing with, "It's me I don't trust."

Vulnerability wasn't a normal default for Xavier. He'd shown glimpses of it but this is the first time I've seen him deliberately strip off some of his armor.

"What don't you trust about yourself?"

A sullen expression washed over his face.

I brushed my finger over his scar. He flinched a little but didn't stop me. I held his face in my hands, leaned closer and kissed along the entire jagged length.

I'd done this more than a few times and I know it makes him uncomfortable, but I also know it's his way of letting me in, letting me see beyond the cracks and imperfections he guards with such fervor.

There was a long silence before he answered. "I hurt someone."

"When you were a teenager and got into fights?" I can't imagine he would have hurt someone to the point of hospitalization or serious injury. Maybe a black eye? Knocked out a few teeth?

The muscle in his jaw pulsed. "No."

I rested my hand on his thigh. My God, he was so tense. "You don't have to tell—"

"I want to," he cut in. "Pretending it never happened won't do me any good." He reached for my hand and held it to his chest. His heart raced beneath my touch. "I was reckless. Impulsive. I let my selfish needs dictate—"

The door swung open and slammed into the wall. A couple stumbled into the room, laughing and talking at the top of their lungs.

"Hey, it's Victory Victoria."

You have got to be fucking kidding me.

Jaxon Oliver, one of the tight ends, stood in the doorway with a girl draped on his left arm. "We're not interrupting are we? I was looking for a place to, uh…wow, this mansion is insane."

Any traces of Xavier's vulnerability or timid demeanor melted away. If looks could kill, his searing glance at Jax would have sent him plummeting through the floor.

"Yeah, it's a big house for sure." I placed my hand back on his thigh. "But I don't think Mr. Caldwell wants everyone roaming through it."

He did the finger point thing at me with both hands. "Special treatment for the media queen. I won't tell him I saw you in here with, uh, well, whoever that is."

The muscles in Xavier's thigh turned to stone.

Oh shit.

I squeezed it, gave him a look, and turned to Jax. "This is Xavier Maddox. His soccer team is hosting us in London this fall. Royal City Athletic. You were at their game in April against the Knights."

"Aw, dude, right. Sorry. Totally recognize you. The guys and I were just doing a shitload of shots and—" his date elbowed him in the side "—ow. Soccer. Good sport. Lots of kicking. You should come be the punter for us."

"That's enough, Jaxon," the young woman exclaimed, appearing mortified. She mouthed an apology, led him out, and closed the door.

Stunned silence spread around us for a minute. And then we spoke at once.

"I don't even know what to say."

"Who the fuck was that."

Caught between wanting to laugh and hoping the floor would swallow me whole, I rested my head on Xavier's chest.

"That was Jax. He's—"

"An absolute git." His tone dripped with indignation.

I looked up at him. "In his defense, he's taken quite a few hits to the head."

No reaction.

Cool.

My half-hearted attempt at lifting the mood fell flat.

"Is anyone else from your team going to interrupt us tonight?"

"Hopefully not."

"*Victory Victoria*? How many brain cells did he sacrifice for that gem?"

"Feel better now?" I laughed in spite of his dour expression. "Or is there—"

"Be the *punter*?" He sounded offended. "I'll have him know I could kick that egg shaped ball farther than—"

"You know what?" I clamped my hand over his mouth. "As fun as it would be to listen to sixteen-year-old Xavier whine about an encounter with a drunk football player, I'd like thirty-six-year-old Xavier to come back."

His sapphire eyes narrowed as he gazed at me. I held his stare, and kept my hand firmly planted over his mouth.

Just when I thought we'd sit like this for the rest of the night, he grabbed my waist, lifted me up, and put me on top of the piano. Much to my surprise, he hopped up next to me. We sat quietly, legs swinging, for several long minutes.

I stole a few quick glances at him. His whole demeanor was guarded. Not in a standoffish way. He just seemed…pensive? Maybe that was it.

I had a feeling we'd have to pick up our conversation another time.

Disappointing, since he really seemed to be opening up to me about something significant from his past. So many questions were poised and ready at the tip of my tongue.

But again, I had to find the balance.

"Where would you like to go?" he asked quietly.

"What do you mean?"

He laced his fingers with mine. "On our getaway. Do you have a specific place in mind?"

My default response was always *not really* when Killian and I would plan our little friend-cations. We'd usually end up somewhere on Nantucket at a cute hotel with great food and beautiful views.

But this wasn't a friend-cation with Killian. This was a weekend alone with Xavier. No interruptions. No distractions. No drunk tight ends barging in on delicate conversations.

"Honestly, just somewhere secluded and quiet and cozy and—" I paused. "What's that look for?"

One shoulder lifted in an elegant shrug. "You continue to surprise me, city princess. I'll handle all the plans. Just be ready to go when I give the word."

"Glad to see your little bossy side hasn't left the party."

He leaned in, hovering his mouth over mine. "You know you like it." His kiss was so soft and sweet it made my pulse race and heart jump. "We can finish our talk then, okay?" He brushed his lips on mine. "And bolt the door shut."

"Pretty good suggestion for a prepackaged snack with empty calories."

This time when he kissed me it was harder, more demanding. I tugged on his hair, my tongue tangling with his. Slowly, he started to relax in my arms. The tension in his muscles loosened with every firm, possessive movement of his mouth.

I breathed him in, cupping my hand behind his neck. A low moan vibrated through him when he broke our kiss. He stared at me, his eyes caressing every inch of me, memorizing every detail.

"I want to tell you everything," he whispered before fusing our mouths together again.

This kiss felt different. More desperate than possessive. Almost as though he needed to devour every last bit of me to survive.

When he pulled away, he asked "Would you like to get back to your celebration?" while brushing his fingers along my jaw.

"I'd rather hang out in here with you a little longer."

A wide smile pulled at his lips, softening his face. "Wow. Me? I've been a bit scattered tonight. Thought you might want an excuse to mingle with a better product."

The room echoed with my laughter.

"Impossible." I kissed the soft spot beneath his ear. His body shuddered. "I'm perfectly content sitting on this rock hard piano with you."

"It is a bit rough on the ass, isn't it?"

Granted, I've only known this man for a few months but I could sniff out a baited phrase like no other.

"Nice try."

"What?" He feigned innocence.

I leaned close, kissing beneath his ear again, gently biting and flicking my tongue on his skin.

"Is this helping you relax?"

"Yes." A hint of flirtatious arrogance crept back into his tone. "You can't resist me, can you. I don't think you'd stop if I told you to."

"You underestimate me." I scooted to the edge of the piano and got down. Without looking back at him, I walked toward the opposite end of the room.

I loved how it was decorated in here. The furnishings were ornate, opulent, and sensuous. But the attention to detail is what intrigued me. Subtle hints of gothic inspiration mixed with the overall renaissance vibe.

"How often do you come here?" Xavier's smooth voice broke the silence.

"It depends." I drank in every inch of him as he walked toward me. Something about the way he moved with sleek fluidity always sent a shiver skipping up and down my spine. "Hannah and I came here for meetings a few times. It's not like I hang out on the weekends or anything."

"Meetings? In this room?"

"No. Ethan's office. Hannah and I come in here to decompress. That's why I knew about it. Otherwise, you and I would have wandered through the house for hours and gotten lost."

"That sounds familiar. Took me a bit to get used to Bennet's place. Cade actually got lost in there a few times. He was rather vexed about us not coming to look for him."

"Vexed?"

"Angry."

"Be nice to Cade," I mock-scolded. "He's a sensitive soul."

Xavier's jaw dropped. He laughed so loud everyone could probably hear him in the solarium.

"How the fuck did you say that with a straight face?" His wide, genuine smile lit up the room.

I shrugged, staring up at him through my lashes. "Years of media training."

"You are something else." He wrapped me in a tight embrace, still laughing.

The longer I stayed secured in his arms, the more I felt the tension continue to melt from his body. Tonight hasn't really gone like I thought it would. It started off pretty on brand for us with the flirting and the dirty talk and Xavier's simmering jealousy.

It all seemed to change when Bennet pulled him away for that mysterious conversation.

As if reading my thoughts, he held me tighter. "Think anyone will care if we stay in here the rest of the night?"

"Well, I might care." I squeezed him. "I *would* like to celebrate with my coworkers and friends at some point."

His embrace loosened. "Pity."

I leaned my head back and caught his eye. His gaze was teasing and relaxed. *That's a relief.*

"I'll make a deal with you. Let's go back out to the party for a little while. Have a few drinks. Something to eat. Maybe do a little dancing and socializing."

"And where does the deal part come into play?"

"I'll let you hang out with me." I planted a lush kiss on his lips, grabbed his hand, and led him back to the solarium.

Bennet sat by himself at a table staring at his phone. I scanned the room and found Hannah. She was doing shots with Noah, Jax, and several other players.

From the looks of it, we'd arrived at the *anything* goes portion of the evening. And knowing these guys, the after-party would be even more insane.

Hannah waved me over. I waved back, tugging on Xavier's hand.

"C'mon," I coaxed. "Dance with me. Or do you want to be boring and lame like Bennet?"

He pulled me close, tipping my chin up. "I want to watch you dance. If I like what I see, I'll join you."

Tempting.

My intentions weren't quite the same. I wanted to ply him with alcohol and grind against him to every song the DJ played.

Between the things he'd said to me outside and the way he kissed me on the piano, my body needed release one way or another. For some reason, he didn't seem to be interested in playing in public. Maybe I was too convincing with my *be a good boy* routine.

"I know this look. Am I not supposed to behave anymore?" He glanced at the dance floor. "Hannah is waiting. You should really go to her."

"And what are you going to do?"

"Watch you." He dipped his head, as though he meant to kiss me. A level of desire swept through me so fierce and overwhelming, it nearly left me breathless. My eyes hooded at the slow, calculated slide of his hands over my hips.

"What will you think about while you watch me?" The catch in my voice sounded painfully obvious even with all the noise.

His mouth hovered at my ear. "The more appropriate question is, what will *you* be thinking about?"

A soft moan rose in my throat and burst into the thick, languid air enveloping us.

"Dance for me, love." Each word caressed my skin in sultry, warm strokes. The pulses of desire intensified. I was seconds away from unraveling.

Being with him at a sizable event surrounded by my coworkers and the media tested me on a level I didn't know existed. Sure, I've gone off with athletes or whomever at events similar to this in the past.

But those were meaningless (dare I say it) flings.

This was not a fling. This was real and raw and consuming and…

He slid his hand between my thighs. I parted my lips in an effort to breathe. I knew he could feel how turned on I was.

"Are you sure you want to do this?" he asked, teasing me with his fingers. The whisper-light strokes edged me closer to release.

"Yes."

The teasing stopped. I swallowed, looking into his eyes. A small tilt of his head reminded me of how I'm supposed to respond. One of these days we'll be able to bypass this part, right?

"Green."

A rough stroke across my clit nearly made me see stars.

"Dance for me, dirty princess. Don't make me say it again."

All I wanted to do was push him to the floor and, to put it bluntly, fuck his brains out. I could barely walk, let alone dance. But I peeled myself away from his body and went to Hannah.

"Is there a reason you're here with me instead of taking advantage of that delicious man?" she laughed, holding out a shot glass. "You should see your face. Drink this."

I didn't bother asking what it was. We clinked glasses and knocked them back.

Oh good.

Tequila.

This should get interesting fast.

More shots sat on a nearby table. Noah caught my eye and smiled. Normally, I'd go hug him or make some kind of friendly gesture but I could one hundred percent feel Xavier's stare burning through the back of my head.

I wanted him untamed, not annoyed.

We knocked back another shot. And another.

Hannah draped her arm over my shoulders. "I guess we're supposed to dance now." Her words slurred a little.

This was a rare treat. I haven't seen Drunk Hannah since the night we won the championship.

"What makes you say that?"

"No reason." She turned me to face where Bennet was sitting. He wasn't on his phone anymore. Instead, he ran a hand through his dirty blond hair and observed us with rapt interest.

Xavier stood off to the side, stroking his lip with his thumb. I fucking love when he does that. The corner of his mouth ticked up in a devilish grin when our eyes locked. And there goes my throbbing clit again.

"I can't speak for your guy but Bennet gave me very detailed instructions."

Her brown eyes sparkled through the blurry haze of alcohol.

"What kind of instructions?"

Normally I wouldn't ask my boss such personal questions about her love life but recent history has altered our friendship.

She twirled a strand of golden hair. "Do you really wanna know?"

YES. "Only if you feel comfortable telling me."

"Pfft. You're a terrible liar. You totally want to know." She pointed to the rows of shot glasses. "One more of these first."

Doing this many shots in rapid succession will most likely get her and I in trouble.

My body tingled.

Not a bad outcome, in all honesty.

We each grabbed two shots, clinked glasses, and downed the tequila.

Hannah appeared unsure about something when she banded her arms around my waist.

"I want to tell you," she murmured, wobbling a bit in her heels. "I feel like…I think you'd be the only one to understand."

Maybe the alcohol was affecting me quicker than normal. She didn't sound like herself. In all the years we've worked together and known one another, Hannah always portrayed herself as level-headed, composed, and regal.

Her usual poise seemed fractured.

I guess being an heiress wasn't as glamorous as it sounded.

"Understand what?"

The uncertainty evaporated when her forehead dropped to mine.

"Bennet likes to play this game where he picks someone out of a crowd for me to seduce."

I felt one of her hands slide to my lower back.

Uh oh.

I am the furthest thing from a prude. However, getting this cozy with not just my boss, but the director of the entire communications department, seemed like a bad idea.

I'm probably misreading this.

We weren't doing anything inappropriate. We were literally just standing here. Anyone would think I'm propping up an inebriated friend. I've probably stood this way with Killian hundreds of times and didn't even bat an eye.

"Who does he want you to seduce here?" I was genuinely curious.

"Dante's girlfriend." Her arm slid all the way around my waist, turning me so we both faced Dante Milano, another one of our tight ends. His girlfriend, Meghan, was talking to Tracey.

"Any particular reason?"

Hannah looked at me and grinned. "Do you want the real answer or the one he told me to tell you?"

My jaw dropped on an incredulous laugh. "The real fucking answer, please and thank you."

Uncertainty and regret washed across her features. "I shouldn't be telling you any of this. I'm sorry. It's unprofessional and—"

"Hey. You know you can tell me anything if you want to. I'm like a vault. Besides, I asked you to smuggle my underwear out of my desk drawer without anyone at work knowing."

Her eyes grew as wide as saucers. And then she threw her head back in laughter. "Oh my God, you're right." Our little scene caught the attention of a few players briefly. "That was a…that day was weird."

Weird is one way to describe it.

"Okay." She swayed a bit. I held her tighter. "I can trust you. Just don't tell Xavier. He'll get mad." Her words came out in a rush. "Unless Bennet tells him, which he probably will, then it won't really matter. Xavier can be mad at *him*."

Listening to her ramble in a stream of consciousness floored me. This is new even for Drunk Hannah. The absolute fascination I have with this whole situation is off the charts.

"Sure. My lips are sealed."

"The real answer." Hannah pushed a strand of my hair behind my ear. "Bennet thinks it would be hot if you and I hooked up. I do, too…"

I nearly lost my footing. Guess I wasn't misreading it.

"Not full on sex. A heavy make out session." Her voice had a rasp to it I've never heard before. I don't know what my face looked like but it made her giggle. "He'd want us to do that until he tells us to stop."

What world am I living in right now? Hannah Pruitt, the posh, savvy, heiress to the Caldwell family business and fortune has a dirty side that rivals my own. And here I thought the most surprising thing I've learned about her recently was that she's a submissive.

Might as well go for the main prize. "What was the answer he told you to tell me?"

She rested her head on my shoulder. "That I had to seduce Xavier."

Chapter
NINE

My entire body went rigid. "What?"

Hannah's head lifted sharply. Her brown eyes grew wide. She almost sobered up completely when she saw me fuming.

"Victoria, I would never. You know that, right?"

I mustered all the strength I had not to storm over to Bennet and give him a piece of my mind. I don't care if he's a Dominant or not, this was a shitty thing to do. I'm all for playing games and pushing limits but it had to be consensual once other people were pulled in.

He was all high and mighty while lecturing me on discussing my limits with Xavier and yet here he is, going rogue.

"I know you wouldn't," I finally said. And I meant it. Hannah is a good person. She's not conniving or manipulative or untrustworthy.

Neither is Bennet. He's just a colossal pain in the ass.

"Want to know what I think?" I asked.

She nodded, glancing over at Bennet. I looked over as well. His face was void of all expression. I shot him a dirty look.

"I think we should get you some water and some food and then go talk to the boys."

Before we could do any of that, Noah, Jax, and Dante surrounded us.

"We need a group photo," Jax proclaimed, loosening his tie. "All the core people from our draft class. You never know if something like this will ever happen again."

"What? You mean like last time?" Dante shook his head. "Weren't we doing this very thing exactly one year ago?"

"Dude, you know what I mean."

"What does any of this have to do with us?" I looked each one of them in the eye.

Hannah hiccuped and leaned into me. I started having flashbacks to frat parties.

"You," Noah rounded on us and draped an arm over my shoulders, "taught us everything we know about dealing with the New York media. You've been there for us. And let's face it, you put up with a lot of our bullshit."

"You left out the *on a daily basis* part," I said, trying to figure out a way to remove myself from his embrace.

"I'm an angel," Dante proclaimed. "The only bullshit she puts up with is yours, Tate."

"The fuck you are," Noah retorted.

While the two of them bickered back and forth, Jax fidgeted with his phone and complained about the dim lighting. Hannah sagged into me even more.

This is a circus and I'm failing at being the ringmaster.

The back of my head prickled with anticipation. And it wasn't the good kind.

"This must be where all the real fun is happening." Xavier's clipped tone sliced through me. *Oh shit.* "Hope I'm not interrupting."

"Xavier Fucking Maddox," Noah exclaimed, releasing me and turning around. "Where've you been all night? I want to hear about your back to back championships." He looked at me. "You don't brag enough about him." Noah elbowed Xavier in the side and winked. "Company policy. No bragging allowed."

Xavier's brows lifted in amusement. "Interesting. Victoria's been known to break policies when she feels like it."

"She does seem to be the type, doesn't she?" Noah joked. Xavier's expression iced.

"Keep it up, Tate," I warned. "I control the narrative for your career in this town."

"Okay, okay." He held up his hands. "You win."

Hannah's arm tightened around my waist. "I think I need to sit down," she whispered.

"If you boys will excuse us." I gave Xavier a look that said *behave for real* and gently led Hannah away.

Leaving him unsupervised with Noah could end in a number of ways.

An argument. A fist fight. A shouting match. World War Three.

None of the hypothetical outcomes gave me much hope.

Maybe he'll prove me wrong.

Oh right. He doesn't like maybes.

After I got Hannah a bottle of water and an assortment of heavy appetizers, I accompanied her to Bennet's table. She insisted on walking without help but I wasn't about to let her stumble her way through the room.

Besides, I had a few things to say to the god of thunder.

"Feeling alright, doll?" he asked, smiling at Hannah. She sat next to him, sipping on the water.

"I'm fine." She regained some of her poised stature.

"And how about you, Ms. Chase? Feeling okay?" His amber eyes glittered with self-satisfaction.

I started to say something and snapped my mouth shut.

Self edit.

I have to self edit or I'll say way too many things right now.

"Remember the night the three of us went out for drinks?" I asked.

"Of course. Lovely evening."

"Right." I rolled my eyes. "I would appreciate it if you took your own unsolicited advice about limits."

Bennet folded his hands, regarding me with interest. "Go on."

"If you want your little games to involve me or Xavier, maybe you should ask us if we want to be a part of them instead of imposing your will to get your fucking rocks off."

So much for self editing.

I half expected Bennet to launch into one of his lengthy speeches about how I'm not a true submissive and I wouldn't appreciate his definition of disobedience and blah, blah, blah.

Much to my surprise, he capitulated.

"You're right. Although, your boyfriend knows more than you think. But that's a conversation for the two of you to have at some point." His expression softened. "I apologize if any of what transpired made you uncomfortable. It wasn't my intention."

Sincerity coated every word. None of what he said felt rehearsed or forced.

Hannah snuggled into his side when he wrapped an arm around her. Just your average couple sharing a sweet moment.

"I'll give you a pass this time, Bennet. And for the record, I wasn't uncomfortable. Just…aggravated with you."

"Duly noted." He glanced down softly at Hannah. "If you'll excuse us, I'm going to bring this precious woman to a more suitable room so she can recover from all those shots."

As insufferable as Bennet can be at times, he really did care about Hannah. I watched him escort her out of the solarium.

One situation handled.

I braced myself and turned around.

Now, let's see what's going on with Xavier and—

What the...?

Xavier was holding court with Noah, Jax, and Dante, regaling them with a story. And he looked like he was *enjoying* himself. Obviously, he loved to be the center of attention. That part doesn't surprise me.

But the way his face lit up as he spoke? Mesmerizing.

Oh my God.

Is he *laughing and high-fiving with Noah*?

Never in my wildest dreams did I expect to see this.

Peaceful warmth spread through my chest.

Charlotte.

"Yeah, okay," I whispered, putting my hand on my heart. "I see what you're doing."

The familiar sting of sadness and guilt threatened to overtake me. Wrestling with what happened to her when we were teenagers always lingered deep in my soul. Some days were easier than others. Moments like this always brought me unexpected peace.

Inhaling slow, I walked toward my boyfriend and his brand new buddies.

"...bowling or duck-duck-goose," Jax was saying. "We like to keep the touchdown celebrations fun."

I caught Xavier's eye and smiled. He motioned for me to come closer.

"I preferred when you all did leap frog," I told Jax, leaning my back against Xavier's chest. His knuckles rasped across the front of my dress until the warmth of his hand rested on my stomach. I laced my fingers through his, relishing the soft rumble of satisfaction vibrating from him.

"We have a whole list of new ones for this season," Dante quipped.

"Is Hannah still around?" Noah asked me. "I really wanted to get this photo."

I shook my head. "She left. It'll have to be just the three of you."

"And *you*," Noah emphasized. "That was the plan." He took out his phone and looked at Xavier. "Would you mind taking it for us?"

I waited for the inevitable tensing of muscles or a deep sigh or something. Much to my surprise, Xavier pressed a kiss to my neck and responded, "I'd be happy to."

The second I stepped away from him, I studied his expression.

Friendly. Relaxed. Handsome as sin.

An eyebrow arched. "Do I have something on my face, love?"

"Um, uh, nope," I stammered a bit. "Just wanted to make sure it was actually you and not a clone."

"I see." A knowing smile played on his lips. "Your friends are waiting."

I walked over to the guys, opting to stand between Dante and Noah. Of course, they both put their arms around me. Xavier didn't bat an eye. He simply pointed the phone at us and took the picture. Then he took one of just the three of them.

"Would you mind if your guy joins us for a picture, Victoria? How cool is it to have the best quarterback, tight ends, *and* goalkeeper the world has ever seen all together."

"So cool." I answered Noah before looking Xavier dead in the eye. "All these egos crammed together in one photo is definitely unmatched."

His gaze swept over me in one heated motion filled with promises, sin, and filthy fantasies. I took the phone from him and grinned.

The four of them actually looked great together. And Noah's right. They *are* some of the best athletes in the world.

I took a few pictures and handed the phone to my quarterback. Jax and Dante thanked us and returned to their dates.

Noah lingered for a few minutes.

"How long are you in the States for?" he asked Xavier.

"At least another couple weeks. Training for our season starts next month plus I have an international friendly coming up in August that I have to get back to prepare for."

Noah gestured toward me. "He can use our gym while he's here, right? I don't think the Knights' training staff will mind having one of England's premiere players use the facility." He turned his attention to Xavier. "You'll be here for the Fourth of July then?"

My heart lodged itself in my throat. I flicked my eyes from Xavier to Noah, and back to Xavier.

He held my stare. "I plan to be. Why?"

"Tracey and I are renting a house on Lake George. We're having some of the guys over. Jax, Dante. Oh, yeah, and Tre Gideon. He's not here tonight but I think you met him after your game. Victoria and her friends always have an open invitation. You should come."

Xavier's pleasant smile punctuated the most unexpected conversation of the night. "I'll consider it. Thank you."

"I should get back to Tracey before she sends out a search party." Noah hugged me before extending his hand to Xavier. "Great talking to you, man."

Silence filled the space Noah previously occupied for several long moments before Xavier spoke.

"You seem surprised."

"You could honestly knock me down with a feather right now."

Navigating the ebbs and flows of his reactions and motivations tonight has been exhausting.

Flirtatious and filthy.

Pensive and stoic.

Charming and engaging.

"I think the internet experts call it *growth*."

"You're best friends now?"

"I wouldn't go that far," he drawled. "But he seems alright. Loves his teammates, loves the sport, loves competing." Xavier looked at me softly. "He respects and thinks highly of you. They all do. Do you know how proud I felt hearing that? Gaining the trust and respect of professional athletes isn't always easy. We can be selfish assholes."

"Not all of you." My words might have come out calm and even, but my heart pounded so hard I was afraid he'd hear it.

Proud.

He was proud to hear that about me.

Tears gathered in the corners of my eyes much too easily. *I shouldn't have had all the tequila.*

It took me years to finally learn that my own father was proud of me. My mother still hasn't acknowledged anything I've accomplished.

Since my twin died, I've walked through life convincing myself I didn't need anyone to validate me. I know what I've achieved. I know I'm great at what I do.

Didn't matter if it warred with the constant feelings of not deserving it.

Xavier held my chin and tilted it until my eyes met his.

"I know what you're thinking." He brushed his thumb over my cheek. "If you could see yourself the way others do, you wouldn't downplay or dismiss your accomplishments."

I'm always captivated by his eyes but right now they were magical. Golden shards reflected in the deep sapphire blue from all the soft lighting. *Like constellations in the night sky.*

"How do others see me?"

He held my stare. "Smart, confident, graceful, honest." Another soft stroke of his thumb brushed over my cheek. "One of a kind."

I swallowed. We both know that last part had nothing to do with other people. "And how do you see me?"

Xavier's breathing staggered for a split second before answering. "Like you are the most remarkable, beautiful, rare creature I've ever seen."

The words ignited every cell in my body.

"Never forget that, love."

"I won't."

"Good." His lips brushed mine in the softest of kisses, sending my heart galloping. "Come with me."

Chapter
TEN

Xavier led me outside to where we'd been earlier. The warm night air carried the sounds and smells of summer on it: insects calling, leaves rustling in a soft breeze, and the sweet, sharp scent of freshly cut grass.

"Ever been lost in there?" he motioned toward the hedge maze.

"No. I actually haven't been in there at all."

Wicked playfulness sparked in his eyes. "No time like the present."

"Wha— Xavier," I exclaimed as he pulled me onto the path.

"It'll be fine, city princess. Trust me."

We stayed silent through all the left and right turns, until arriving at a clearing with lights and columns. Large stone benches sat along the edges. They almost looked like sacrificial tables.

Did he just get us to the center of this thing?

"That was easy."

"How did—"

"Jax and Dante told me." His grin was so damn intoxicating.

"Apparently they've been out here many times and said there are two clearings. I asked how to find one of them."

"I guess Jax knows how to sacrifice *some* brain cells for the greater good."

I heard him laugh while I strolled around one of the square columns. The lights were dim, casting blurred shadows on the grass.

Stories about this maze spread like wildfire over the years. Some people got lost for hours trying to find their way. Others got lost on purpose to steal private moments in the darkness.

I stood in the middle, taking it all in. The quiet was gentle and comforting. A stark contrast to the frantic electricity skimming down my spine. Heat and anticipation crawled over every inch of my body. I could feel the intensity of Xavier's stare burning through the back of my dress.

Fidgeting with the ring hanging from my necklace, I turned to face him.

"If this soccer thing doesn't pan out for you, there's always a career in navigation." I gave him a playful wink, expecting a smart ass reply or a dark stare or maybe even a low, sexy laugh.

What I didn't expect was the utter chaos his sultry answering smile wrought on my heart.

"This soccer thing," he repeated, moving closer until I couldn't see anything else but him. "If that's the case, I guess I'd rather be the punter."

"You'd look good in a Legends jersey."

"Would you wear it?"

Without question. "Maybe."

"I'd love to see you with my name on your back." The soft, meaningful dip in his voice arrowed through me. "It would look perfect."

A seed of awareness blossomed at the underlying meaning. It grew when his hands circled my waist and rested at my lower back. It rooted deep in my soul when he kissed and nipped at my neck. I clutched onto his arms, afraid my knees would give out at any second.

"So, now that we're here," my words came out breathier than usual, "what do you have planned for us?"

His already amorous expression flipped to something darker, more dangerous. "I have a number of things planned for you, and every single one ends with you screaming my name in ecstasy."

He grabbed the back of my neck and crashed his lips to mine. I whimpered at the intensity of his kiss. Urgent. Possessive. Rough.

All my senses narrowed to focus solely on him. The feel of his toned body pressed against me, the taste of whisky and chocolate on my tongue, his fresh, clean scent, and the sounds of his low moans. The mere existence of this man consumed me.

"Tori," he grit out, collaring my neck and squeezing. "Kneel."

I didn't hesitate and dropped to my knees on the cool grass.

He grasped my chin, pressing his fingers into my skin. Desire pooled at my core immediately.

"You are so fucking gorgeous when you kneel for me," he growled, tipping my face up. "How should I take you first?" He shoved his thumb between my lips, sliding it in and out. "Do I fuck this Ivy League mouth to start? Maybe I'll play with your sweet little cunt." His tone went deeper and darker with every word. "Or…I'll do both at the same time."

I grazed my teeth against his thumb.

"Is that what you want, Tori? My cock in your mouth while I fuck your cunt with my tongue?" He knelt in front of me, reached around and squeezed my backside. "This is mine, too. Should I take your ass as well? Fill every part of you at once until you collapse in a used heap on the ground?"

Blood pounded in my ears so ferociously I thought I might explode. Seeing him on his knees always drove me wild. Not to mention the vulgar things he wants to do out here. My hand slid between my legs, desperate to provide relief to my throbbing clit.

We'd be exposed and vulnerable to anyone walking through this maze. Eyes watching. Hearts racing.

An unexplored, forbidden part of me unlocked and sprang to life.

I tucked my fingers under the edge of my panties, moaning when they brushed over my clit. My back arched as sparks of pleasure raced through my body.

Savoring it, I closed my eyes and imagined being watched like this.

"No." Xavier's gruff voice pulled me back to reality. "Look at me."

Staring into his eyes heightened everything. So did the absolute focus he pinned on me.

I shuddered.

"Show me," he commanded. "Show me how much you love this."

Small whimpers passed through my lips as I continued playing with myself. Different scenarios I've only fantasized about in the privacy of my bedroom unfolded in my mind.

Dark fantasies I've never shared with anyone.

Me, tied up and on display, while a faceless stranger had his way with me in front of a crowd. Hands wrapped around my neck, rough bites on my skin, sharp slaps on my ass, and being fucked so hard it ended with uninhibited screams and moans.

Xavier's lips parted as he watched me. His cheeks flushed with desire.

I rubbed my clit harder and faster. I wanted to please him. Show this side of myself only to *him*.

"*Xavier*. Oh my God. I want…"

"Come for me, love." His voice was pure gravel.

Pressure built between my thighs as the faceless stranger revealed himself to me.

Sapphire eyes. A jagged scar. Dirty words wrapped in an English accent. Tattoos and promises and…

The knot of pressure unraveled quickly.

I tumbled over the edge on a silent scream. Wave after wave of exquisite bliss washed through me. When my eyelids fluttered again, I couldn't stop them from closing.

I bowed my head and waited for my breathing to slow.

Xavier pulled my hand out from under my dress. I felt the damp heat of his mouth wrap around my fingers when he sucked them clean. The sensation nudged my waning orgasm.

"Stand up."

Opening my eyes proved to be more of a challenge than I thought. When Xavier's outstretched hand appeared I took it.

Next thing I knew, I was on my feet. Lust and possession gathered in his arctic eyes.

"Dirty princess." He backed me up against a column, yanked my dress up around my hips, ripped off my panties, and pushed my legs open with his knee. "That was quite the show you just gave me."

He remained fully clothed, only unzipping his pants enough to free his cock. Its warm, hard length pressed into my lower abdomen.

"What do you plan on doing about it?" I purred, grabbing a handful of his hair.

A sacrilegious grin appeared. "What do you think I should do?"

"Anything you want."

His deep laugh morphed into a groaned, "*Oh fuck*" when he slammed inside me.

I cried out even though I was so wet he slid in without much resistance. The sharp pleasure filled every part of me.

"I'm going to savor you," he whispered, pulling out almost all the way. "Then I'm going to fucking ruin you."

He rocked his hips forward, filling me to the hilt. Again. And again. Faster and harder.

Hot desire prickled over my skin. Energy and vibration ravaged me.

"Don't stop," I moaned. "I want more."

Xavier slowed, torturing me with exquisite control and precision.

Pulling out almost all the way, pushing in until he had nothing left to give. Edging me closer to the release I craved. It drove me crazy.

I clenched around him.

"*Fuck.* You're killing me," he rasped, dropping his forehead to mine.

A breeze caressed my heated skin as Xavier settled into a more brutal rhythm, making me take every inch, claiming me thoroughly.

"Harder," I pleaded. "*Please.* Let yourself go."

Ferocious eyes locked onto mine. The mysterious veil slipped away again. Seeing him stripped of any barriers stole my breath.

He stopped thrusting, wrapped my hair around his fist and held it close to the nape of my neck. Using his other hand, he unzipped my dress and pulled it down until it wrapped around me like a belt. His chest heaved when he raked his eyes all over my body. The sight of me standing exposed with his cock buried inside me affected him on a primal level.

"Demanding little thing, aren't you." He palmed my breast, hovering his mouth at my ear. "Do you want me to ruin you, love? I will. I'll discover just how much you can take before I tease, bite, lick, and fuck you until my name is the only thing you'll be able to say."

The more he spoke and touched me, the more I lost myself in his words. It's a powerful spell to wield and Xavier does it with such precision. Eyes that stop my breath. Hands that melt me with the faintest whisper of a touch. Taut face. Coiled muscles.

Pure, untamed masculinity. And I wanted every last piece of him.

"Answer me."

"*Yes.*" My voice cracked on a moan.

"Yes, what."

"I...*oh god*...ruin me. *Please.*"

With a grunt, he dipped his head, licking and sucking on my neck while he savagely drove in and out of me. Stretching me. Filling me. Breaking me into millions of pieces and putting me back together, over and over.

The sensations were too much. His mouth, his hands, his...

"*Xavier.*"

"Have you had enough already?"

I almost shattered when he looked at me. Unbridled, animalistic need reflected in his eyes.

"No…not enough. More."

"More?" He dragged his tongue up my neck, until he reached my ear. "Like this?"

He thrust into me so hard I hit my head on the stone column. I grabbed at his shirt for leverage. He was relentless, driving into me without mercy. Deep, possessive, and hard.

"*Fuck,* Tori. You feel too…fucking…good."

An orgasm ripped through me, ravaging my body in uncontrolled pulses and throbs and silent screams.

Xavier didn't stop. Another orgasm chased the first one. Then another until white-hot pleasure burned every cell in my body.

My knees buckled just as Xavier tumbled over the edge on a loud groan.

His hips continued pumping against me in small thrusts, stopping after he'd given every last bit of himself. We stood this way until our breathing slowed to a more natural tempo.

"Turn around and hold on," he ordered.

In a daze, I did as he instructed, gripping the sides of the stone column. Xavier pulled my hips back until I bent forward.

"Again," I panted.

"Yes, again. I'm not finished with you yet. I never will be."

A sharp slap stung my ass seconds before he pushed into me. I squealed in pleasure, arching my back to take him in deeper.

"It's so fucking hot how much you like this." He pulled my head back by the hair so hard I yelped. "Is it rough enough for you now, love?" Another slap. "Is this what you were thinking about when you fingered yourself? Me, taking you however I want, wherever I want?"

"M-maybe."

His hand clamped around my throat. "It's a yes or no question, Tori," he growled. "*Tell me.*"

"Yes." I shuddered when his fingers tightened.

"What was I doing to you?"

Jumbled images from my recurring fantasy played out. "I…I was tied up. Y-you tied me up and…*oh*." Another deep thrust. My thighs trembled.

"What else?" He reached down to play with my clit. "Tell me all of it."

Saying much of anything right now was nearly impossible. Warm breath caressed my ear before I heard, "I'm. Waiting. I want to hear you say it."

"I was on display. In front of strangers. You were" —thrust— "*oh my god*…y-you were choking me. Spanking me. Filling me with your cock. It was rough…and possessive."

A deep, guttural sound I'd never heard Xavier make before vibrated through him. He gripped my throat so hard I felt myself start to go limp.

"Maybe everyone at the party should see you like this." His voice was liquid heat. "Naked. Bent over. Getting your tight pussy wrecked."

"*Yes*. Let them watch."

"So. Fucking. Filthy." He released my neck and grabbed my hips, holding me still while he ravaged my body.

The sweet sounds and scents of summer mingled with sex and sweat, and panting and moaning.

Xavier buried himself so deep inside me I didn't think he'd ever get out.

Not that I wanted him to. This was all I wanted right now.

The beginnings of another orgasm knotted and twisted in my belly. "Oh, God, *Xavier*."

His vice-like grip on my hips tightened. "Every fucking inch of you was made for me." He withdrew almost all the way. "Scream for me, love. I want to feel you coming around my cock when you do."

One hand fisted my hair. The other reached down to rub my clit.

"I...*please* let me..."

My words dissolved into a hoarse scream when he pinched my clit and slammed into me in one brutal motion. This orgasm annihilated me on a level I've never experienced, tearing through me in waves. I felt him shudder and jerk inside me.

"*Tori*...so fucking *perfect*..."

I swore I blacked out for a second after his moan. Everything went still and silent.

When I came back to my senses, I felt Xavier's body against mine. His arms were wrapped around my waist, holding me up.

I trembled, slowly collecting myself with every breath.

"Are you okay?" He turned me to face him.

My foggy brain wasn't able to form any type of response. All I could do was breathe, and even that was challenging.

Xavier's soft kisses down my neck contrasted so sharply with how he just ravaged me.

Hard and soft. Dark and light. Two facets of the same man.

The gentle stroke of his thumb over my cheek preceded another question. "How do you feel? Alright?"

"I...I...wow."

That garnered a quiet laugh. "I'll take that as a yes."

He took his time redressing me and smoothing some of the hair out of my face. There was absolutely no way I looked presentable.

"Can you walk? I want to get you properly cleaned up."

"Y-yes. I..." My legs wobbled violently. I clutched onto his shoulders.

"We'll wait a bit."

Securing an arm around me, he led me to one of the stone benches. The second we sat down, I collapsed into a boneless heap, burying my head in his chest. He sifted his fingers through my hair, massaging my scalp.

The lust fueled fog slowly cleared. I luxuriated in his soothing caresses, intoxicated by comfort, by him, by…

"Feeling alright now?"

"Feeling alright," I answered on a yawn. "Mmhmm. Perfect. I don't want this night to end."

"It won't," he whispered, cupping my face.

I blinked up at him, still a little woozy from the after-effects of multiple orgasms. He bent his head to kiss me, the softest one of the night. I cherished it, trying to etch the taste and feel to my memory.

"Are you in any hurry to get me back inside?"

"No, love. I'm perfectly happy right where I am."

I held him tighter, never wanting to leave his side.

I only wanted to fill my soul with every piece of him.

Chapter
ELEVEN

"**S**end it back. It's undercooked."

The distain in Killian's tone made me laugh. I glanced at Victoria, who stared at her best friend.

"It's perfectly fine," she admonished. "Some of us like our steak a little juicy."

"Some of us don't want to see a horror movie on a plate. Could there be any more blood?"

"Since when did you become the beef police?"

"Since I stopped eating it."

"Children," Max chimed in.

Killian mimicked him silently while Victoria tried to enjoy her dinner.

It's been a while since I've seen the three of them in action together. Not much has changed. I was a little surprised when Victoria mentioned they wanted to have dinner with us, meaning her and I together.

This is the first time I've socialized with them since arriving in

New York. I've been here for almost a month now and could take a hint.

I assumed they still weren't huge fans of me. Maybe that's changed.

"What time's the big photo shoot tomorrow?" Killian asked me in a chilly, forced tone.

Guess not.

A satisfied smile pulled at his mouth when I lifted an eyebrow in surprise.

"She tells me everything. You should know this by now."

Victoria glared at him. "I do not."

"Right." He rolled his eyes and turned his attention to me. "Anyway. I hope it goes…ah-*MAZE*-ing."

Max choked on his drink. Victoria clenched a fist. Killian stabbed into his salad looking quite satisfied with himself.

I see what he did there. The maze. He knows.

And I get it.

He's the closest thing she has to family. *I* hurt her.

He's the protector. *I'm* the asshole.

But I could also play this game. And I can do it much, much better.

I cupped my hand behind Victoria's head and pulled her close. "It'll be more than amazing," I murmured, brushing my mouth along the column of her neck. Her pulse fluttered under my lips. "Especially since you'll be there with me." I kissed her before she could say anything. Not a chaste kiss either. A full-on fucking kiss. Deep and passionate. The kind that leads to dirty deeds in public places.

Victoria went limp when I pulled back. Her dazed expression intensified when I bit down on her lip.

"Tou-fucking-ché," Killian muttered.

Max dabbed his forehead with a napkin. "So, uh, when does your soccer season start, Xavier?"

"Mandatory training begins week after next. Then I have a couple of international matches. One in France, one at home."

"Paris?" Killian perked up.

"Yes."

My phone vibrated while the lads talked around me about shopping and cafés and French pastries.

Bennet: We have a problem

I tensed. This shit again. It's been a couple weeks since the party at the Caldwell Estate. The whole Jordan situation quieted down once he left Manhattan. Still not sure why he'd come here.

That's the problem. The not knowing. At least when I punched him and knocked him out I *knew* he retaliated by confronting Victoria.

Now?

I clenched my jaw. Maybe Bennet was right. Victoria needed someone to watch over her while I was away. I can't leave her exposed to whatever Jordan might have up his sleeve.

I started typing a reply.

"Are you going to Paris for the game, Victoria?" Maxim asked.

"I'm planning to. We have a preseason game that week so I'll fly out after that. It'll probably be a quick trip."

Me: Something that needs attention now or can it wait?

Bennet: Sooner rather than later

Me: Is he here?

Bennet: No. Alex has some information

Me: Will it hurt her?

Bennet: Can you talk?

"Xavier."

I looked up, unsure of who said my name. All three of them watched me.

"Texting your hot friends?" Killian sounded bored.

"Yeah," I muttered, sending another reply while fighting back my instinct to find McKennie and rip him apart.

Me: Not now. At dinner with Tori

Apprehension, anger, and the inability to control this situation burned through my blood. The warmth of Victoria's hand covered my thigh, soothing some of the unease. How she manages to relax me with a single touch is unreal.

"Everything alright?" she asked.

No. "Just an annoying situation."

"Stealing my lines, Maddox?" Her adorable little grin hit me right in the gut.

I will never get enough of her smiles. I'd seen Victoria naked, and in fancy dresses, using that mouth to do wondrous, filthy things to my body, but she was never more beautiful than when she was just being herself. Witty, charming, stripped of all her self doubts, and smiling.

I swear she gets more beautiful every day.

Fucking hell. I'm that guy now, aren't I? Completely under her spell.

For what it's worth, it's my favorite place to be.

I'll never let him hurt her.

Blushing a little, she squeezed my thigh. I took her hand in mine and held it in my lap. Killian's slightly arctic demeanor thawed.

"So I guess everything's been going well since we smuggled you into the fundraiser." His unwavering stare burned through me.

"Watch yourself, Killian," Victoria said quietly.

Max shifted in his chair. "We don't need to bring up—"

"It's okay," I interrupted. "Let him say what he has to say."

Whatever he needed to get off his chest couldn't be as rough as all the criticism and taunting I've been subjected to throughout my career. Some of it came from commentaries or sports writers who had nothing better to talk about. Most of it was just fans being fans, hiding behind their computer screens or mobile phones.

When I put on England's jersey, I was revered as a national hero. When I stood in goal for Royal City against another club, I was the villain.

Both roles fit me well enough.

My chest squeezed. This was different. I didn't want to be the villain now.

Strained silence clouded the table. Max grew more fidgety with every passing second. Victoria sat still next to me, the picture of poised elegance. Except for her eyes. They flared with warning.

"Fine." Killian cleared his throat. "Listen, it's no secret I haven't been your biggest fan lately. You did what you did. It was shitty and nothing can change it. But this one—" he waved a hand in Victoria's direction "—doesn't let just anyone in."

"We're back to calling me *this* one?" She tapped her nails on the table.

"Are you going to let me finish?"

"Are you going to be an adult?"

"Christ," he muttered. "Look, I'm not mad at you Xavier. We're all adults." He shot a petulant look at Victoria. "We all do stupid shit and mess up, even when the intention behind it comes from a good place." His tone softened for the first time tonight. "I've never seen Tori in love before. She…it's…it's hard to want to rip your fucking heart out when she looks at you the way she does."

"And how does she look at me?" I asked, turning to meet her big, green eyes. A small tremor rolled through her. Small enough so only I could see.

"The same way you look at her," Killian replied. "Like you never want to look away."

A few hours later, I surrendered to the truth behind Killian's words.

I never wanted to look away from Victoria.

Why would I? This fiery redhead with curves for miles, a smart mouth, and the most beautiful heart known to man was the only person who could bring me to my knees.

And I was perfectly happy to let her.

"I borrowed one of your shirts to wear as pajamas," she called out from the bedroom. "Hope you don't mind."

I hadn't even seen her in it yet and my cock jumped with interest. All things being equal, there wasn't much about Victoria that *didn't* interest my cock. Even after I'd spent the better part of the last hour fucking her.

"Fine by me," I answered, walking toward the kitchen. I grabbed two bottles of water from the refrigerator, turned, and immediately dropped them.

"That was smooth," she laughed. "Forget how to use your hands?"

Hands. What hands?

Intense lust paralyzed me. Victoria Chase was wearing my jersey. Not one that's sold in a store or online. *My* jersey. The one I wore during our final match. It's much too big on her but fuck me did she look sexy. My eyes flicked over every inch of her.

Hair pulled back.

No bra.

Nipples erect, poking the material.

No shorts or yoga pants.

Socks.

I exhaled a ragged breath and ordered, "Turn around."

Toying with the hem of the shirt, she turned slowly. "Like it?" She glanced at me over her shoulder. "The green is a little bright for my taste but—"

"I love it." Her body. My name. "You're only allowed to wear this from now on. Get rid of the rest of your clothes."

"Oh ha, ha. You're full of jokes." She waltzed up to me, bent down, and picked up the water bottles. Her eyes traced over my body. "But if that's the case, you're only allowed to walk around shirtless in these sweatpants. What's fair is fair."

"I'll consider it."

"By the way, next time you fly to see me right after a game, please wash your uniform. This," she pointed at my jersey, "was rancid. I had to wash it twice."

"Kit."

"What?"

"It's called a kit."

"Seriously? One of these days we're going to get through a soccer-related conversation without you correcting me."

"You know you like it when I do. And it's football."

She pressed a bottle into my bare chest. The cold felt good on my heated skin. "Uniform. Kit. Tie. Level. Soccer. Football. Nobody cares."

"Want me to bend you over that couch and prove you wrong?" I warned.

"Maybe." A sexy, teasing smile curved her full lips. It drugged me almost as much as the sight of her in my clothes. The primal, territorial part of me loved all the different ways I could stake my claim on her. Nobody else would ever see her this way.

"We should do something couple-y." She curled up on the couch.

"Haven't we been doing *couple-y* things since I've been here?"

"Things that don't involve brain-melting sex." Her lighthearted tone filled the room. "Let's watch a movie."

I laughed, sitting next to her. "Okay, city princess. What should we watch?"

"Nothing lame."

"That doesn't really narrow it down."

"Fine. No remakes. Those are the worst."

"Horror?"

"Maybe."

"Science fiction?"

Victoria rolled her eyes, grabbed the remote, and pulled up the menu. "Look at me."

I happily obliged because looking at her was all I really wanted to do anyway.

"Tell me when to stop scrolling. But you can't look at the screen. No cheating."

No problem. I could study the delicate lines of her profile all night. Soft, wavy hair pulled up in a loose bun. Long lashes framing gorgeous eyes. Lips made for hours of kissing.

More than a few seconds passed before I told her to stop.

"Finally," she giggled. "Oooh good choice."

I glanced at the television.

You've got to be fucking kidding me.

"*The Lion King*." Victoria's cheerful reaction did nothing to stop my muscles from locking up with tension. "A classic."

She lowered the lights, grabbed a blanket, and cozied up next to me.

I remained quiet while the sweeping opening scene played, sneaking glances at Victoria. She had the most captivating smile on her face and her eyes widened with joy. This was probably a childhood favorite for her.

"Charlotte and I used to watch this all the time," she said, confirming my thoughts. "*We sang Hakuna Matata* so much it drove my mother crazy."

Once Scar lost his lunch, she turned to face me, still smiling. "Don't tell me you've never seen it."

A better man wouldn't have tried to come up with fake answers. But it's *her* and the truth fell out of me before I could stop it. "My dad and I would watch it together on my birthday."

Victoria's expression softened. "Oh. We can watch something else."

I shook my head. "It's fine. Besides, I like seeing how happy it makes you."

"When is your birthday anyway?"

"October."

She stared at me with an expectant look in her eyes. When I didn't say anything further, she shook her head in frustration.

"The whole month? Or do you pick a random day each year?"

"Keep sassing me and your ass will be red before Simba reaches the water hole."

"Promises."

"So much trouble." I paused. "The twenty-fifth."

"Was that so hard?"

We fell into a comfortable silence as the movie played on. Victoria snuggled into my side and rested her head on my chest. I felt her tense up during the traumatic wildebeest scene. It always bugged me as well when I was younger. Good thing my fa—

No fucking way. I shook myself right out of that shit. I'm not going to let these bloody animated lions get the best of me.

"I wrote a thesis on *Hamlet* and *The Lion King* when I was in college," Victoria said out of nowhere.

A surprised laugh fell out of me. "Why?"

"It's fascinating. The movie is inspired by *Hamlet* and the themes are transcendent. Greed, power, revenge. And, at least in the movie, redemption." She lifted her head to look at me. "Obviously, there are differences. Hamlet didn't have a Timon or a Pumbaa to help him find happiness, so he spiraled into his own dark thoughts. And Simba thought he was doing the right thing when he followed Scar's order to run away because he believed he killed his own dad."

"Like I killed my mum," I said absently.

Victoria sat up straight. Concern seeped from her.

What the fuck did I just say?

No. No. NO.

FUCK.

"Xavier, you—"

"Drop it."

"I'm not going to drop it." She shut off the movie and fully faced me. "You didn't kill your mother. You were a baby. Nobody blames you."

"I never said anyone blamed me."

A deep ache pierced my heart from the gentle touch of her hand on my chest. Talking about my family wasn't a preferred topic. For some reason though, it didn't feel quite as daunting with Victoria.

I covered her hand with mine.

"I don't want you to think I haven't dealt with any of it. I have. I worked with a family therapist at a very young age. When I was old enough to understand some of the medical explanations, it helped ease the guilt I felt."

"It must have been really hard for you," she said quietly, placing her hands in her lap.

A shadow of sadness passed through her eyes. I knew she was thinking about her sister.

"It was. Fortunately my dad met Rebecca and she managed to make things a bit better."

Victoria picked at the blanket. I didn't plan on being open with her about any of this right now. Someday, yes. But not now.

"Do you see them often? Your dad and step-mother?"

"Occasionally." *Rarely.* "I had dinner with them a few days before coming here."

"You did?" Her warm smile thawed the chill crawling through my veins. "How was it?"

I shrugged. "The usual."

"I'm sorry." She climbed onto my lap and straddled me. "I don't want to make you uncomfortable and ask too many questions."

I'd never spoken this much about my childhood or family with anyone. Not even Bennet or Cade, and they knew some of the worst shit about me. Telling Victoria was…well, it was…comforting. Simple. Normal.

I wish you trusted me more.

Maybe this is also what she meant when she'd said that. Trusting her with all of it. All of me.

"I've told you before, love. You can always ask me anything."

Victoria appeared thoughtful. "I am curious about one thing."

"Tell me."

"What did your mom look like?"

Growing up, I had several old photos of my mother framed in my bedroom. Some showed her pregnant and joyful. Others were from her university days.

"Pretty. Brunette. When I was younger, my dad told me I had her eyes and her charming personality."

"Ohhh," Victoria laughed. "That's where it comes from."

A full grin bloomed on my lips. "Yeah."

She kept smiling at me. A beautiful, gentle, adoring smile. Emotion surged to the thing in my chest, nearly causing me to reveal my darkest mistakes. Not the ones related to disliking my step-brother or feeling inadequate in my father's eyes.

The dangerous ones. The ones where people got hurt because of my reckless decisions and impulsive behavior.

I wanted to fall apart in front of her. Piece by jagged piece, until she put me back together.

Beautiful but broken.

I pulled her closer. Not because I intended to shag her again. Although the feel of her pussy nestled against my cock put up a good argument. I just needed to have her close. Breathe her in.

She calmed me simply by existing.

"Thank you for telling me." The tenderness in her voice reached down and grabbed hold of my heart.

"There's nobody else I'd rather tell."

"Am I going to be the first you tell all your secrets to?"

"Do you want to be my first?" I dragged my hands along her thighs, picking up on the sensual note in her voice.

She ran her fingers through my hair. "First." She kissed my nose. "Last." Her lips pressed against my forehead. "Only." The softness of her mouth on my scar sent violent shivers through me.

I desperately wanted to hold onto this moment. Hold onto this happiness.

I had to.

My past keeps threatening to break free.

Dark thoughts. Spiral. Revenge. Redemption.

Chapter

TWELVE

Note to self: Attending photoshoots with Xavier Maddox can cause heart failure.

How ridiculously attractive can one person be? It's not natural.

This campaign will be huge for him. It's with Apex Jewelers for a fancy watch. Logic dictates that it requires him to be bare-chested in jeans sitting on a leather couch.

Sleek muscles. Tattoos. Tousled hair. Seductive smiles. Dark eyes.

Everything about him was a lethal, perfectly honed machine.

Perfect for telling time.

I bumped into the monitors. Hard. They rattled and shook so violently I feared they'd collapse.

Everyone turned to stare at the commotion.

"Sorry."

I internally scolded myself for being such a mess. This wasn't my first photoshoot and yet I'm acting like I've never seen anything like this in my life.

A tiny smirk tugged at the corners of Xavier's mouth. "You'll have to excuse Ms. Chase. It's our first time working together."

"Why don't you stand here." René, the photographer, pointed to an empty area behind him. "Not as many obstacles."

If you don't consider smoldering British soccer players to be an obstacle, then yeah.

While there wasn't anything for me to bump into or knock down, I was now directly in Xavier's line of sight.

I'll give him credit. He was the consummate professional, following the photographer's direction and shifting poses. Xavier didn't require much coaxing or encouragement. He embodied confidence and sex appeal. Every once in a while he'd glance in my direction, weakening my knees.

When they had him sprawl out on his back and stretch his arms over his head, I felt an ovary move. I must have touched and kissed every inch of that long, lean body more times than the legal limit. My eyes roamed over the strong column of his neck, the expanse of his chest, the tempting curve of his pelvic bone.

I wanted to unzip those jeans with my teeth and suck on his… *C'MON. Be professional.*

Sweat misted on my forehead.

But, you know, not as many obstacles standing over here.

"Doing alright Ms. Chase?" The seductive dip in Xavier's tone accentuated his come-hither stare.

"Perfect." The word scratched its way out of my dry throat.

The lighting assistant stepped in front of me, continuing with the shoot.

I managed to hold my shit together for the next hour.

"This one is great, isn't it?" The photographer scrolled through some shots and showed me the digital screen.

My heart skidded to a stop.

Stark desire etched across Xavier's face. His stare burned through the camera lens.

This pose.

I can't even call it a pose. I've seen him like this too many times. Mouth parted, thumb caressing his lower lip, the hint of a secret gleaming in his eyes.

"Really shows off the watch," a female voice commented nearby.

Yep. The fucking watch. Totally what I'm looking at.

"It's mesmerizing," I managed to vocalize a response.

"I'll show you more." René motioned for me to go to the monitors. I swallowed, remembering I was here in an official capacity, not as a woman in heat.

I took a step and nearly tripped over a cable. Xavier's deep chuckle carried across the studio.

I glared at him. He winked at me.

Menace.

Good thing I didn't have to pretend to like the photos. All of them were stunning. Even the ones where it's obvious Xavier wasn't ready or had his eyes closed.

"Everything looking alright, René?" Xavier asked, pulling a t-shirt over his head.

The photographer glanced over at him. "Looks great. Julian and the team will be pleased. Thanks for fitting this in while on vacation."

"My pleasure. Will you copy me on the email when you send the proofs?"

"I can."

They kept talking around me while my attention fully focused on one photo. I don't think it'll make the final cut but it spoke to me.

Xavier's attention was off-camera. A soft, adoring gaze replaced the lusty, beckoning stare from the other photos. It was subtle, but his lips curved in a gentle smile.

He appeared enamored with something.

One of the butterflies that took up residence in my stomach flailed.

He's looking at *me.*

"Best burgers and milkshakes in the city, huh?" Xavier's impish grin dragged me out of my thoughts.

Our server placed the food and drinks in front of us. We'd decided to grab lunch at a nearby diner before I had to get back to the stadium.

Needless to say, I've been less than attentive since leaving the photoshoot. I couldn't get over the way he looked at me in that picture.

"Yep. Says so on the menu."

"People toss around the word *best* to describe everything."

I gave him a look. "What? Like you're the *best* goalkeeper in the world?"

He reached across the table and squeezed my hand. "I am."

"The ego."

His pleasant laugh sent a shiver through me.

An array of condiments sat on the table. Xavier scrutinized them before choosing ketchup.

"I don't have to put ranch dressing on anything, do I?"

"No, Your Highness." I cut my burger in half.

"You sound like Cade." He grinned, tapping my foot under the table. "I bumped into Noah and Tre early this morning at the training facility."

I almost choked on the bite I'd just taken. Noah *and* Tre? Oh God.

"Don't look so panicked. We talked a bit. Good lads. Anyway, Noah really wants us to go to his cookout. I know it's your birthday, so I wanted to see if there was anything else you'd rather do before I text him."

Good lads? TEXT HIM?

I swallowed the mostly chewed piece of burger. I can see him maybe getting over the whole jealousy thing with Noah since he was never a threat. But Tre?

I can't imagine he would be totally fine socializing with a guy I had sex with months before we met. Granted, it was only a one night stand, but still.

Possessive Xavier was not something to be messed with. Neither was Jealous Xavier.

I washed down my food with the milkshake. My phone vibrated.

Unknown: Did you like the surprise?

I glanced at the number. *Who's texting me from a Chicago area code?*

"Work stuff?" Xavier asked before biting into his burger.

"Wrong number." I deleted the text. "Do *you* want to spend the Fourth of July with Noah and the guys?" I popped a french fry in my mouth.

"I want to be wherever you are. Besides, Bennet and Cade will be in town as well. Might as well make it an event."

"What's Cade been up to this summer? I miss his goofy personality."

"Fucking his way through Dubai, Spain, and Greece from what he's told me."

"There won't be an army of little Cades popping up in nine months, will there?" I joked, taking another bite of my burger.

"Hasn't happened yet," he answered, his tone dry. "He's in Vegas now. He should arrive in New York in a couple days."

I leaned back against the booth, considering my options. Well, there weren't too many options. My birthdays were either spent with Killian and Max on the beach watching fireworks, or with Killian and Max at a restaurant.

I'd never actually taken up Noah and Tracey on their invitations. Spending some time up at Lake George could be fun.

Text him?!?!

"You and Noah exchanged numbers?" I couldn't stop my disbelief from coloring the question.

"Yes."

"Noah. The guy you spanked me over for sitting in his lap."

His expression darkened. "Yes, and I'll do it again if I ever see you in his, or anyone else's lap." He leaned forward. "Besides, from what I remember, you liked it so much I ended up finger fucking you against the kitchen counter."

My body betrayed me like the weakling she is, and simmered with desire.

"Do you know what Bennet did the night of the ring ceremony?" *What am I saying?* I'd been wanting to bring this up, but now? Over burgers in a diner?

"Fuck," I mumbled.

Xavier studied me for a beat before responding. "I do know. I also know you put him in his place again, which I enjoy very much." A salacious grin curved his mouth. "I like how you handle him."

"He was so puffed up when he lectured me on limits. It annoyed me that he just went and did his own thing without asking if I was okay with it. Or you."

An uncomfortable thought filled my mind. Xavier's already admitted that he wasn't always alone at Bennet's parties. I wondered if this was something he's used to. *And gets off on.*

Both of us spoke at once.

"Do you like—"

"We should have this—"

Too many questions lingered on my tongue.

"How about we focus on one thing at a time," Xavier suggested. "Your birthday. What would you like to do?"

This birthday is going to be a little tougher than the others. I'm turning thirty-six, which means it's been twenty years since Charlotte was alive to celebrate a birthday with me. It also means the twentieth anniversary of her death will be here before I know it.

One thing at a time.

"Let's go to Lake George," I decided. "Besides, I'm still waiting on our weekend getaway. Your apology tour is seriously lacking."

All I got in response was a smile. Another message lit up my phone.

Unknown: you must not have seen it yet

A couple hours later, I heard the distinct *click-click-click* of football cleats on concrete approaching behind me.

"Hey, Victoria. Hold up a minute."

Dante Milano's voice echoed in the tunnel. I turned to see him and Jax jogging over.

"Good practice?" I asked.

"Practice is always good when we don't have to wear pads," Jax replied. "Gotta hit the showers. It's date night."

He patted Dante on the back and jogged to the locker room.

"What's up?"

"Uh, random question. And if it's not something you can do, don't worry about it."

"Ask away."

Dante scratched his head. "My sister's been working abroad. Spent the last, I don't know, four years in England doing sales or sponsorships or something with a soccer team." He grinned. "Not your boyfriend's. Don't worry. I already grilled her on all the info. They're not even in the same, what did she call it, tier for the league. Level two, she said. That's it. If they stay in the top spot this season they'll get promoted. She explained it all to me but I half listened after a while."

I folded my arms, widening my eyes. *Land the plane, Milano.*

"Anyway," he continued, "she's thinking about moving back to New York and she's interested in marketing or digital media or maybe what you do."

"Which is it?" I suppressed a laugh. "Marketing, digital media, or what I do?"

A heavy sigh wracked his massive body. The tight end listed at six-two on all his stat sheets but I'll bet my condo he's six-six.

"I don't know. Can she come in and talk to you? Maybe you could help point her in the right direction. Give her some contacts?"

"Yeah, sure. Have her send me an email. What's her name?"

"Chelsea. You have no idea how much I appreciate this. She's been having a rough time lately and…well, thanks." He started jogging toward the locker room. I noticed a piece of paper stuck to his shirt.

"Dante."

He stopped and turned.

"There's something on your back."

Confused, he reached around until he felt the paper. "Fuckin' Jax. He's been pranking us all afternoon. Taping shit to the ball. Tying water bottles together. Ass hat." He tossed the paper into a trash bin. "Thanks, Victoria. I'll tell my sister to email you tonight."

Dante's request aside, the rest of my day passed by without much variation from any other day. Although, I did notice the two large men stationed outside Hannah's office. I've seen her bodyguards before but never really thought anything of it. Her family has their own private security team. They mostly stay out of sight though, which makes this a little odd.

I'm assuming Hannah's in her office since these two guys are doing their best statue impersonations. Might as well go chat about the training camp schedule before I wrap up my day.

"Gentlemen," I greeted them as I walked to her door.

"Sorry ma'am. You can't go in there right now." The bigger guy on the right blocked the door with his arm.

"Oh." This is weird. "Is she okay?"

"Yes ma'am."

Neither one gave any inkling as to what was going on. Maybe something happened to her grandfather? A player was accused of harassment? That would be a nightmare.

Wild scenarios ran through my mind but none of them were serious enough to warrant two hulking bodyguards. Then again, the super rich do things different, I suppose.

"Okay, well, will you let her know I stopped by when she's finished? I'm Victoria. I'm right across the hall."

"I know, ma'am. We'll tell her."

Definitely weird.

I returned to my office and finished up the rest of my to-do list. Hannah never did come out. Even stranger than that? Nobody went in. I pulled out my phone as I walked to the parking lot and texted her.

Me: Hey. Stopped by to chat but your muscle men wouldn't let me in. Everything ok?

Me: Also, we're doing my bday at Lake George if you don't already have plans for the 4th. Talk later.

I slid the phone into my purse as I approached my car.

That's odd.

I stopped short.

A blue ribbon hung from the drivers' side door handle. It was tied in a neat bow. A tiny chill washed over me.

Before walking any closer, I checked out my surroundings. This lot wasn't open to the public. It was gated and loaded with security cameras. Only executives, coaches, and players had access. Nobody else was allowed.

I peeked through the windows. Everything was still locked. Nothing was missing or disturbed.

"Jax," I muttered, untying the ribbon.

Chapter
THIRTEEN

XAVIER

My final ten days in Manhattan flew by so fast it gave me whiplash. One minute, I was lounging in bed with Victoria, convincing her she didn't need to be on time for work. The next, packing a suitcase for my flight home to London.

The silver lining? We're finally having our weekend getaway.

"This is beautiful," she commented, stretching her arms over her head. "How did you manage to reserve it so close to the holiday?"

"Charm," I replied, admiring her supple curves and the fiery tattoo inked alongside her ribcage. We'd been outside lounging by the pool all evening. "And a sizable amount of money."

The description online referred to this place as a *cottage tucked away among spruce and cedar trees* when in reality it was a large, two-story home with a sprawling backyard, pool, and outdoor hot tub. Much too big for just the two of us but I liked how secluded it was.

As promised, all mobile phones were turned off and stuffed in a drawer.

I watched Victoria walk slowly to the edge of the pool. This fucking bikini she wore would live in my head rent free forever. There's no way in hell she's wearing it to the cookout. Birthday or not, nobody but me will ever see her in it.

"Impressive, Maddox."

"*This* is what finally impressed you?" I approached her from behind. "Thought it would never happen."

Her light, melodic laugh filled the night air.

"I'm always impressed by you." Victoria turned and wrapped her arms around my waist. "Try not to let it inflate your fragile ego."

"Too late."

She pressed a kiss to my chest before resting her head on it. I sifted my fingers through her damp, wavy hair, trying like hell to freeze time. Or at least memorize how soft she felt against me, the way her heart stuttered any time I caressed her, and the quiet moans of contentment that vibrated through her just from being close to me.

Leaving her while knowing there was still an unresolved threat looming wracked my body with unease.

Before we'd left to come here, Bennet texted me nonstop about convincing Victoria to let Marcus keep an eye on her. Something had gone down at the stadium last week, but he didn't elaborate. Victoria didn't mention anything out of the ordinary. Hopefully the disturbance was either contained or Bennet overreacted.

Regardless, knowing I'd be far away from her didn't sit well with me at all.

"Why are you so tense?"

"I'm not."

She stared up at me. "The weird thing about standing like this with you is I'm able to actually feel all your muscles bunch up. Sit on the lounger."

"Are you bossing me around?"

"Yes." She stood back and crossed her arms. "Sit."

I obliged out of curiosity more than anything. Victoria climbed on the lounger and knelt behind me.

"I'm giving you a massage so you can relax." She smoothed her palms over my neck and shoulders. Her touch immediately shot bolts of electricity through me, tightening my muscles further. "The *other* kind of relax, Xavier."

A quiet laugh rumbled in my chest. "Of course, city princess."

I purged all thoughts of Jordan and my lingering unease to focus on the firm, sure hands applying pressure to my shoulder blades. Her movements were controlled and methodical, shifting closer to my spine, moving out, down, and repeating.

By the time she reached my lower back, all the tension I didn't know I'd been holding melted away.

The air around us hummed with awareness when she scratched her nails up my neck and into my hair. Our breathing synced in soft, even breaths. I felt her breasts press into my back when she leaned into me and gently massaged my scalp.

This felt fucking good.

"Is it helping?" Victoria's warm breath tickled the back of my neck.

"Yes, love. Thank you."

"Anything for you."

Why did she sound melancholy?

When I felt her body pull away, I turned and saw her looking up at the sky. I tilted my head back. Can't say I've ever seen this many stars. Makes sense though. We're miles away from any big cities, so there's no light pollution. It's just us and the universe.

"Think they're fireflies or giant balls of burning gas?" I joked, catching her gaze.

A tiny smile touched her mouth before she looked up again.

At first I thought her eyes glistened from taking in all this beauty. But then I saw a single tear slide down her cheek. It nearly broke me.

"Thinking about your sister?"

Victoria nodded. Another tear left a damp trail. Her lip trembled slightly.

"I'm sorry. This weekend is supposed to be for us. Not me getting all emotional."

I cupped her face in my hand. "Don't ever apologize for this, Tori." More tears slipped down her cheek.

"It's been twenty years." Her voice cracked. "Twenty years since she was alive and we celebrated our birthday together. Do you know what that means?"

I did know but I stayed quiet, rubbing her tears away with my thumb.

"I've lived more years of my life without her, than when she was with me."

There were very few things in this world I couldn't withstand. Seeing Victoria cry was one of them. All I wanted to do was make this better for her.

I pulled her into a tight hug, holding her as close as I could. Somehow, I knew this was the first time she'd ever broken down this way in front of someone other than her best friend. The weight of this moment didn't escape me.

"It's not fair, Xavier," she choked back a sob. "Charlotte should be here. She should be thriving and happy and— I should have done more. I shouldn't have taken her that night. I shouldn't have left her alone. It's my fault."

I gripped her with such force I thought I might break her. "That's your mother talking, love. You were just a young girl yourself. What happened was completely out of your control."

Something caught fire in my chest. Something fiercely protective.

I'm going to fucking kill him.

There is no way in hell Jordan will get away with hurting her. I don't care about the consequences. I'll do whatever it takes to keep her safe and happy. Whatever it takes, for as long as it takes.

Victoria gently removed herself from my embrace, tilted her head back, and shouted, "*FUCK*," into the darkness. She covered her face and took several deep breaths.

Her pretty mouth twisted into a frown when she looked at me.

"I'm sorry. I don't ever break down like this in front of people not named Killian."

"I figured."

"I don't know what got into me. I was really enjoying giving you that massage. I'm sorry."

"No apology is necessary." I rubbed another tear away. "I'm glad you trusted me enough to break down like that."

She winced. "Sorry I said the thing about wishing you trusted me more."

"New rule." I wrapped an arm around her and pulled her so we both laid back on the lounger. "No more apologizing for things you shouldn't be apologizing for."

"Fair enough." She curled up closer to me, gently stroking my chest. Her fingers traced the tattoos I have near my collarbone. "*Cicatrix.* This means *scar*, right?"

"You do know more than just vulgar slang in Latin," I teased.

"Don't get cute." She propped herself up on an elbow. "What do the angel wings underneath it signify?"

I held her inquisitive stare. "What do *you* think it signifies?"

Empathy filled her eyes. "A tribute to your mother. That's why you have it close to your heart."

I nodded. "They were my first tattoos."

A wistful smile tugged at her mouth. "It's weird how similar our lives are in regards to loss. I just…it never entered the realm of possibility when I first saw you."

"I remember." I swept my thumb over her lips. "You couldn't stop undressing me with your eyes."

"Let's not ruin the memory with wild interpretations of what actually happened."

"Wild interpretations?" I laughed. "I fully admit I undressed you in my mind at least a dozen times on the side of that road. And again at Black Rose. Don't pretend you didn't do the same."

Victoria regained her confident, fiery composure, although a hint of vulnerability reflected in her eyes. "I plead the fifth."

"You can't plead the fifth when I know the truth."

Her soft laugh warmed me from the inside out.

"I've started some initial work on setting up the foundation in Charlotte's memory," she said after a few minutes. "Tracey's been a big help so far. Noah, too." I tensed slightly at the mention of Noah's name. Victoria noticed and placed her hand on my chest. "Would you be interested in throwing your celebrity status and support behind it when the time comes?"

"I'll throw whatever status and support you need right now. Just tell me what I can do to help."

My God, this smile. Good thing I was reclining on the lounger. It would have brought me to my knees.

"Consider yourself fully recruited." Playfulness sparked in the emerald depths of her eyes. "I was right about the product being more than just a pretty face."

We settled into a comfortable silence, staring at the sky for another hour. The more she relaxed next to me, the more I never wanted this night to end. I curled an arm around her. This was quickly becoming my favorite moment with Victoria.

"Xavier?"

"Yes, love."

"Do you ever think about fixing your relationship with your dad?"

"Sometimes," I admitted. "I guess I don't know where to start."

"I can definitely relate to that," she muttered.

"Your mum?"

She nodded. "My dad brought it up when we had dinner together. I wouldn't even know what to say to her. You saw what happened when she called that day. All of our conversations turn into shouting matches."

"At least there's *some* type of emotion," I said flatly.

"I bet your dad shows more emotion than you realize."

Aside from the fleeting wistful glances, I couldn't think of any. *Except for...*

"He seemed really proud of me when I signed with the Royal City development league." The words fell out of me too easily. "I thought that would be the thing to make me stand out in his eyes. Not my interest in architecture. It would be football. The thing we bonded over when I was six and he'd take me to the pitch. I thought maybe he'd look at me the way he did before Rebecca and Adam showed up. Maybe he'd *stop* looking at me with that fucking anguish when he thinks I can't see it."

I spoke so low I wasn't sure I'd actually said all of this out loud.

"I'm sorry, Xavier." Victoria's soothing voice filled some of the cracks I'd allowed to open. "I'm sure you *do* stand out in his eyes, even if he doesn't know how to show it."

My head fell back into the cushion. "No more talk about families tonight, okay love?"

"Okay." Her soft body pressed into mine. "Thank you for sharing this with me. It means a lot."

Neither one of us said anything further for a while. I liked being able to open up to her. I also liked that she didn't push when I'd reached my limit.

"Have you ever fallen asleep under the stars with someone?" she asked.

"No."

"Really? Not even to impress your legions of girlfriends?"

"Legions? I wouldn't go that far." I glanced down at Victoria. She looked peaceful. Eyes closed, long lashes fanning over her cheeks. "Have you?"

"No." She yawned, draping an arm across my stomach. "Never liked anyone enough to try all the romantic stuff."

Whatever the fuck my heart just did nearly killed me. Victoria's fingers brushed over my skin, settling me from…I don't even know what that was.

Another long stretch of relaxed silence fell around us.

Victoria's chest rose and fell with steady breaths. I watched her sleep for a bit, unable to tear my eyes away. She looked so content. Like she'd finally found the place she belonged.

My eyelids became heavy as I stroked her hair. I never really pegged myself as a romantic type of guy but falling asleep under the stars with Victoria might convince me otherwise.

Chapter

FOURTEEN

I've never seen so much cheese in my life.

Soft cheese, hard cheese, spreadable cheese, cheese with whisky, cheese with truffle.

Cheese with tea?

I have to admit, this shop was adorable. Rustic and cozy with some old-fashioned nostalgia thrown in for good measure.

"Try this one." Xavier sauntered over carrying cubes of cheese pierced by toothpicks. I grabbed one and popped it in my mouth.

"Not bad."

"Is that your default answer? Something has to be better than *not bad.*"

I laughed, bumping my shoulder against his arm when I walked away. We'd been roaming around one of the nearby towns all afternoon. Since it was peak tourist season, the small streets and shops were overflowing with visitors. Not a single one of them seemed to know or care who Xavier was. Although he did turn quite a few heads.

We stopped to have an early dinner at a small, family-owned Italian restaurant. The owner, a boisterous, round-faced older gentleman named Niccolò, greeted every guest when they walked in and treated us all like family.

"Focaccia drizzled with olive oil for the lovely couple." He placed the bread in front of us and turned to Xavier. "*La tua ragazza è bellissima. Sposala adesso.*"

I blamed my blush on being outside all day in the July heat.

Xavier's baffled expression deepened when he looked from me to the restaurant owner. "Sorry, I don't speak Italian."

"A charming Englishman," Niccolò said. "You are fortunate to have this woman by your side. She knows what I said." He winked at me. "May you be blessed with many children."

For his part, Xavier appeared unbothered. I whipped the menu up to hide my face.

"No menus." Niccolò took it away. "I will bring out a selection of our best dishes."

I only meant to take a sip of the water but downed all of it. This wasn't the first time someone threw out the word marriage in front of us. Cade made an off-the-cuff remark when we were all out to dinner in London. But he wasn't serious and at the time, Xavier was just a casual fling. *Or so I'd thought.* And then Killian couldn't stop saying it at the soccer game in April.

I smoothed down my sundress and placed the cloth napkin on my lap.

"Why do I get the feeling we have to send him Christmas cards for the rest of our lives?"

Xavier's flippant remark dissolved some of the awkward tension. I glanced over at him and failed to hold back my laughter. A wide smile split his handsome face. Spending uninterrupted time with him this weekend has been extraordinary.

Twenty minutes later, an army of servers arrived with several dishes for us to share. I learned all the food here was inspired by Niccolò's family in Tuscany. *Panzanella salad, tortelli di papate, pappardelle al cinghiale.* Each bite was more divine than the last.

"I'll be in a food coma for the next three days," I quipped after swallowing a mouthful of pasta. "You might have to carry me out of here."

"Have you ever been to Italy?"

"A few times. You?"

"More than a few times for football." He took a bite of tortelli. "We should go there on holiday together."

"Maybe," I winked.

Oh shit. Oh SHIT.

Xavier looked like he'd been whacked across the face with a brick.

"Hey." I reached across the table and held his hand. "I would love to go to Italy with you. You know I'm only teasing when I say *maybe.*"

"Yeah." He exhaled slow, not looking up from his plate. "Wasn't really expecting to hear it."

The pasta that had been so delicious a minute ago turned to sludge in my stomach. Clearly I still have more twists and turns to navigate when it comes to learning what makes him tick.

"When we do go," I said as brightly as I could, "promise you won't let me gorge myself on too much food. I'm sure the last thing you want is a sluggish American to drag around."

"I'll get some good practice dragging you around here." His dimple appeared. "We still have dessert to get through."

Xavier was right. No sooner did we finish the main dishes, the servers returned with dessert. Biscotti, small cakes, and gelato. I won't eat again for a week.

After we finished, Xavier and I strolled through the town. We bypassed the chocolatier and opted to browse the small shops. I bought a few souvenirs for Killian and Max. Several fliers posted outside the store mentioned fireworks over the lake this evening. We'd be able to see them from our rental and decided to take advantage of it.

A group of teenage boys pointed at Xavier and whispered amongst themselves.

"I think you've been recognized," I said, nudging him with my elbow.

Xavier glanced at the boys. One of them held up their phone and took a picture. "You would be correct," he grinned.

"Go say hello if you want. I'll hang back here."

"Yes ma'am." He kissed me. "Don't move."

Four sets of eyes widened in disbelief when Xavier sauntered over to them and introduced himself. My heart swelled with pride watching him. Then it almost stopped when he crooked a finger, signaling for me to join him.

"Gentlemen, this is my girlfriend. Victoria, say hello to the star players from Empire State FC."

They spoke at once, telling me all about their youth soccer league based in Buffalo. One of the boys was the goalkeeper, so he peppered Xavier with question after question about training, conditioning, and game preparation.

Before saying goodbye, I took a few pictures of the boys with Xavier.

"Still managed to be the center of attention all the way out here in the Adirondacks," I teased.

Xavier appeared thoughtful. "These are the moments I truly enjoy. Being recognized by the players who will shape the game for the future is exciting, especially here in the States where football continues to grow." He draped an arm over my shoulders. "Meeting my idols when I was their age definitely inspired me to keep going."

"Was there a time you wanted to quit?"

"Never. My desire to excel and be noticed outweighed any doubts."

"Do you still run into the players you admired when you were a kid?"

"Now? All the time." His eyes lit up. "One of them is the manager for England's national team. Playing for him is an absolute dream."

"You'll have to introduce me when I'm in Paris."

He grinned. "Maybe."

We walked around for another hour, stopping in a few shops here and there. By the time the sun started to sink into the horizon, I was ready to get back to the house.

"Excited for tomorrow?" Xavier asked, banding his arms around me while I stood at the kitchen counter and unpacked the shopping bags. One can never have too many touristy shot glasses.

"Depends. Did you get me a birthday present?"

He held me tighter. "Several."

"Do I get a hint?"

"One of them is something you specifically asked for."

Curiosity got the best of me. I turned to face him. "Is it you?" I stood on my toes and pressed a kiss to his grin.

"I'm not telling you."

My heart warmed seeing him relaxed. Last night, during my unexpected breakdown, he'd comforted me with such calm patience. Except for the few minutes when he'd appeared tense and determined about something. I thought I might have misread it, but I saw the same expression on his face this morning.

We still had another half hour before the fireworks started so I made the executive decision to cool off in the pool.

Xavier was writing in a notebook when I walked out onto the terrace after changing into my bikini. I'd seen him do this a handful of times over the last couple days when he thought I wasn't looking.

"What are you up to?"

"Getting some ideas down for a new renovation project I'm starting."

"Really? When do you start?" I paused in front of him.

"Probably next month." He didn't look up from his notebook. "It'll be a lot of work with football starting, too. Might take longer than usual."

"Is the house in bad shape?"

"Nah. Just want it to be perfect."

"Do you have pictures of it?"

He glanced up and lifted an eyebrow. "I do. But they're on my mobile phone which is turned off and locked away."

His gaze drifted down my bikini-clad body. I purposely brought this one to show off in front of him. It didn't leave much to the imagination.

"Are you coming in with me?" I pulled my hair free from the elastic, letting it fall in loose waves on my shoulders. He continued staring. "What's the matter? Cat got your tongue, Maddox?"

I added a little extra sway to my hips when I walked toward the pool. I even glanced over my shoulder when I waded in, biting down on my lip. Xavier's shoulders held a tension that hadn't been there before.

"You're missing out," I coaxed.

All flirtatious motivations aside, he actually *was* missing out. I luxuriated in the water, swimming a few laps while the sun completed its descent. When I finished, I slicked my hair back and blinked water out of my eyes. Xavier remained by one of the tables. His notebook sat closed beside him.

I held on to the edge of the pool.

"Were you watching me this whole time?"

"Does that bother you?"

"No."

Xavier rose to his feet, pulled off his shirt, and walked over. My lungs decided now would be a good time to malfunction. His lean, sculpted body sliced through the water, as silent and focused as a shark.

"Hi." He came up beside me, propping his arms on the pool's edge. A piece of dark hair fell over his eye. "Mind if I join you?"

"Took you long enough."

"Wow. Zero to feisty in less than three seconds. Must be a personal record for you." He motioned to the corner pool bench. "Come sit with me."

My intention was to sit beside him but once he positioned himself, he pulled me onto his lap.

"I like you here better."

"I bet you do," I smiled.

The fleeting colors of dusk reflected off the water before they faded, replaced by the vast darkness of night. I couldn't help but think of my sister again. The uncontrollable wave of emotion I'd felt last night didn't threaten now. Instead, a comforting peace settled over me.

I looked up.

A single star twinkled to life. Then another. And another, until they crowded the sky.

"They're fireflies," I said out of nowhere.

Xavier held my chin and tilted my head down.

"The stars. Last night you asked if I thought they were fireflies or giant balls of burning gas. Definitely fireflies."

A loud *pop* went off in the distance. Fireworks exploded above us in perfect bursts of chaos and predictability. Red, white, and blue blazed long trails against the dark sky. Shimmering pieces of color floated gracefully among the stars and burned out in the blink of an eye.

"Beautiful isn't...it..." My voice trailed the second I met Xavier's molten stare. Black swallowed blue, leaving nothing but promises and sin. Pinpricks of charged energy buzzed beneath my skin.

One of Xavier's hands moved to cup the back of my neck. His fingers gently scratched up into my hair.

"Most beautiful thing I've ever seen. Do you want one of your birthday presents now?"

Ravenous desire exploded through me.

"Yes." I pushed myself up on my knees, removed my bikini bottom, and pulled down his shorts. "I think you should give it to me right here."

He hissed out a breath when I lowered myself on his cock. "You're insatiable."

"You love it." I settled into a rhythm, rocking back and forth, using his hard length to rub against my clit.

"I do, dirty princess. I do."

Two hours, two rounds in the pool, one shower and countless orgasms later, we laid on the bed, talking and laughing and falling deeper into an abyss I never wanted to escape. As much as I was looking forward to seeing everyone tomorrow, I'd rather stay with him like this for one more day. Just us. Lost in our own world.

A lock of his hair fell across his forehead. I smoothed it back, sinking my fingers in the softness. Xavier glanced at the nightstand. His mouth tipped up in a smile.

"What?" I asked.

"It's midnight."

"And?"

He pulled me close, running his fingers up my thigh and over my hip, stopping beneath the curve of my bare breast. "Happy birthday, love."

His lips covered mine in a whisper of gentle warmth. He licked the seam of my mouth slowly, savoring me before pushing inside. The pad of his thumb teased along my nipple, coaxing it into a hard peak. On a moan, he deepened the kiss, inhaling me, pressing his body to mine. I kept my fingers in his hair, tugging gently.

The weight of his body pushed me into the mattress when he rolled on top, nudging my thighs apart with his knee.

"Again?" I asked against the dampness of his mouth.

"Not right now." He paused. "Tori…"

"Hmm?" I brushed my fingers along his jaw, still floating in the haze of his kiss.

"I…can I tell you something?" His raw whisper clawed at my heart.

"You can tell me anything."

Xavier exhaled a shuddering breath. He'd been more open with me on this trip than at any other time. I dipped my head, kissing the soft skin beneath his ear.

"Fuck. When you do that it feels…" The slight tremble in his voice nearly shattered me to pieces. "You bring light to my life, Tori. It's beautiful but it burns. It burns every part of me. And…I never want the light to end. I never want us to end. Please don't ever take your light away. "

Xavier and I didn't talk much on the drive to the airport. My thoughts still swirled around the days we'd spent together in blissful seclusion at the rental, the wonderful afternoon with friends, and the beautiful birthday present he'd given me.

If someone told me four months ago I'd not only fight to keep Briarcliff Cottage, but I'd have a boyfriend tell me he'd renovate it, I would have thought they'd been whacked in the head.

A boyfriend? Never.

Briarcliff Cottage? The last place my family vacationed together? Abso-fucking-lutely not.

But that was my reality and I wouldn't change it for anything.

"Want to walk me to the plane?" Xavier asked, squeezing my leg.

We'd arrived at the private executive airport. Bennet's jet sat on the tarmac, gleaming under the hangar lights. The last thing I wanted to do was say goodbye to Xavier and make the drive back to Manhattan alone.

"I'll walk you there but don't expect me to let you actually get on it."

His soft smile didn't help the situation.

Ground crew members performed their final checks on the plane as we approached. The engines idled, waiting for takeoff.

"Text me as soon as you land." I wrapped my arms around him.

"Don't forget to turn your phone back on."

True. It was still off.

"I'll see you in Paris?" I leaned back, holding his pretty stare.

"Yes, love." He cupped my face and kissed me. "I'm counting the minutes."

Watching him disappear into the sleek fuselage sucked. I went back to my car and sat there until the plane taxied down the runway and took off. I waited for the flashing lights to be swallowed by the night sky before starting the long drive home.

When I finally arrived, I greeted the night guard and went up to my condo.

My empty condo. The silence pressed down on me.

It's always been empty. I've lived alone forever. Always wanted it that way.

Now? I didn't want to be alone anymore. I wanted Xavier to waltz out of the kitchen and curl up on the couch with me. I wanted to feel his body next to mine, breathe him in, hold him forever.

I never want us to end. Please don't ever take your light away.

I dropped my bags and dug out my phone.

"Time to re-enter the real world," I muttered, turning it on.

Countless missed text messages lit up the notifications. Most were from Killian. Dawn and Ray texted to wish me a happy birthday. So did my dad. Nothing from my mother. I scowled.

The final message was from a local area code but I didn't recognize the number.

Unknown: Hope you enjoyed your vacation. Now the real fun begins.

PART TWO

Chapter
FIFTEEN

"**A**re you packing for three days or three weeks?" Killian asked, sprawling out on my bed. He rummaged through the pile of clothes I'd stacked neatly. His dog, Winston Furchill, rolled onto his back and panted.

"Stop touching my stuff."

He smirked, yanking out a green lace thong. "Will Xavier take this off you with his teeth? That would be so hot."

I stormed out of my closet and snatched the underwear from his hand. "You are worse than a toddler." I shoved it in the suitcase. Winston sat up, ready to play. I patted him on the head.

"A toddler? *Moi*?" He pursed his lips. "Someone has babies on their mind."

"Oh for the love of God, Killian. Zip it." I returned to the closet.

"That wasn't a denial," he shouted at my back.

I wasn't thinking about babies. I wasn't thinking about anything except packing. We had a preseason game on Friday in Miami. From there, I planned to fly directly to Paris for Xavier's international game.

Normally I wouldn't pack this far in advance but tomorrow, Tuesday, and Wednesday were stacked.

"When are we getting together again to talk about the foundation for Charlotte?"

I poked my head out the closet door. "Hopefully after Paris. Noah and Tracey can meet with you while I'm away if you want."

"Did you come up with a name yet?"

"Nope. Feel free to brainstorm."

"You have a text." Killian held up my phone.

"From?" A nervous chill washed over me.

Unknown texts have been popping up over the last few weeks. I'd dismissed them all as wrong numbers but the frequency was suspicious.

"Someone called Mildly Hot." Killian grinned. "Know anybody by that ridiculous name?"

I traipsed out of the closet. "What time is it?"

"Almost six. Why? Is it dirty talk time? Can I stay and watch?"

I glared at him and grabbed the phone.

Mildly Hot: Hey

Me: Video call?

Mildly Hot: Only if you're naked

Me: Guess not then :P

Mildly Hot: Is Killian still there?

Me: Yep. Give me a few minutes

Mildly Hot: Tell him I miss him

"Xavier misses you but he wants to know why you're still here."

"He's secretly in love with me," Killian gloated. "That's why I forgave him so quickly. When you finally dump him I will move in on that ass so fast."

"Be sure to tell Max all about it when you get home." I ushered him out of the bedroom. "Winston's hungry. Good night."

I heard Killian laughing all the way to the elevator.

My stomach growled. Might as well grab some food before I call Xavier. I pulled out a couple slices of cold pizza from the fridge, prepared a little bowl of ranch dressing, and poured myself some wine. I took a sip before running to grab my laptop. Once everything was all set up on the kitchen counter, I started the call.

"I'm having your favorite for dinner," I announced when he appeared on the screen. My heart screeched to a halt.

Damp hair, no shirt, lazy smile.

Oh, and he was laying on the bed. I silently cursed long-distance relationships.

"You're my favorite for dinner."

Deep breath. "Did you have training today?"

"No. Today I listened to Cade ramble about a girl he met last month. I think she was Italian. I don't know. I lost interest after about two minutes."

"What did I say about being nice to Cade?" I popped a ranch-covered pizza crust into my mouth. Xavier wrinkled his nose. "What's the matter, Maddox? See something that displeases you?"

"No, love. Every inch of you pleases me. And as soon as I see you again, I'll show you how much."

Even through the computer screen he could fucking make me blush. Maybe he can't see it. I finished chewing and stared at him. Yep. He can see it.

I cleared my throat. "Did you just get out of the shower?"

"A little while ago. Why? Did I miss a spot?"

"Not sure. I can only see you from the waist up."

"I can change the view if you'd like." He ran a hand through his hair.

"That will only lead to trouble." I dipped another piece of crust in the dressing and slowly sucked it into my mouth.

His demeanor changed in an instant. Relaxed and casual morphed into taut and carnal. We'd agreed to keep our video chats on the cleaner side. Needless to say, our track record was atrocious.

"Do you really want to go down this road, Tori?"

Yep.

I dragged the crust through more dressing, held it in front of my mouth, and licked it clean.

"Fucking hell," he muttered. "I shouldn't be this hard watching you lick ranch dressing off pizza."

I choked on the wine I'd just sipped. Spit it out everywhere. It landed on the screen, the keyboard, the counter, my food.

"Was not expecting that," I said once I'd composed myself and cleaned up. Xavier watched in silence, an amused expression on his face.

"It's what you get for breaking our policy. Then again, you're an expert in that department."

I shot him an incredulous look, scanning his shirtless, tattooed torso through the screen. If that body doesn't illustrate the saying *rules are made to be broken* then I don't know what does.

I grabbed some ice cream from the freezer.

"What flavor?"

"Mint chocolate chip. Does that meet your fussy standards?"

"So long as you don't drown it in ranch dressing."

I made a face. "Gross."

We filled each other in on our schedules for the week. He let me know he'll be training with the national team in London instead of using the facility near Birmingham as originally planned. We agreed to squeeze in one more video call before my flight to Miami.

"Everything else going alright?" The change in his tone gave me pause. He sounded uneasy.

"Yeah. Why? Something wrong on your end?" *You haven't knocked out Jordan again, have you?*

The longer he stayed quiet, the more my anxiety ramped up.

My phone vibrated.

Unknown: Almost time

Frustration overpowered me. "*Ugh.*" I deleted the text and slid the phone across the counter.

"What happened?" Xavier's sharp tone pushed through the speakers.

"Nothing. It's nothing." I balled my hands into fists.

"You seem awfully stressed about nothing."

I stabbed the spoon into the ice cream. "It was a wrong number. I must be on some spammer list. I keep getting random texts. It happened to one of the equipment guys too. So annoying."

"When did it start?"

"I don't know. June?"

Xavier didn't say anything. He just rubbed his thumb on his lip. Normally, the movement was sexy and deliberate. Not this time. He did it mindlessly, almost as though he was trying to figure something out.

"Would you consider letting me arrange for you to have a—"

"A babysitter?" I cut in. "Like Hannah? No."

"I think it would be a good idea." His tone hardened.

"No," I snapped at him, immediately regretting it. I looked down, taking a deep breath. "You and Bennet have tried before and I appreciate you both but I don't want a bodyguard or security detail or any of that."

A piercing blue stare was his only response. Not how I wanted this call to go at all.

"Xavier," I softened my tone. "Promise me."

"I promise, love."

Monday was a complete shit show.

One of the more tabloid-centric sports websites posted a rumor that Noah put his house on the market. Photos of his Manhasset home with a 'for sale' sign in front of it accompanied the story.

"It's fake." Noah paced around the media room. He was still dressed in his workout gear from this morning's practice. "I'm not moving. I don't even know where those pictures came from. Look." He pulled out his phone and showed me the screen. "This is my front yard right now from the security cameras. No signs. Nothing."

He was right. The yard was empty.

"Okay." I rubbed my temples. "Glen, see if you can connect with someone at the website. Maybe they're feeling generous and will let you know where they got their information."

"On it." Glen went back to his office.

"This is fucked up," Noah grumbled. "I'm going to be asked about it nonstop all week."

"You know the drill. I'll put together a statement for all the socials. Try to echo the sentiment as much as possible."

He rolled his eyes. "The usual shit? I'm the Legends quarterback… we're looking forward to another successful season…"

"Yeah."

"Don't hate me if I go off-script a bit."

"Depends on what you say. Be smart about it."

An aggravated grunt was his parting reply.

Tuesday coasted by without any major incidents. Noah handled the press with politeness, grace, and charm, like I knew he would. After some digging, and with the assistance of a few people in our tech department, the photos were deemed artificially generated.

Ethan called a meeting with Hannah and I. On top of all the other potential media-related problems we had to deal with, now we could add computer generated pictures to the list.

I passed along the directive to the social media team to be on alert for anything suspicious.

Wednesday announced itself without much fanfare. By lunchtime, I relaxed into the idea this would be just another boring day. The number of emails and phone calls I'd received about the Noah situation died down considerably.

News cycles were funny things. One minute, everyone's ravenous over a story. Then, they get distracted by the next big, shiny object. Nobody seemed to care much about the fake photos anymore. All the sports media outlets were now enamored with a baseball team accused in a sign-stealing scheme.

"Hey," Hannah poked her head into my office. "Feel like grabbing some dinner? Or do you have plans?"

"Plans?" I paused for dramatic effect. "Yeah. I'm having a forbidden affair with my couch."

"Oh please. That outfit and those heels need some attention. Let's go to Ghost. Their food is supposed to be outstanding."

Ghost was the trendy new place to see and be seen in lower Manhattan. All the influencers liked to post about it. Plus, several players enjoyed hanging out there. Jax and Dante were notorious for posing with the owner every time they showed up.

"Oh boy. A night out in the Financial District."

"Meet me at the car in twenty." Hannah went back to her office.

Alex, the oversized security guard, stood motionless by her door. He's been there every day for over a month. I finally walked up to him a few weeks ago and introduced myself.

He'd looked at me blankly and said, *I know who you are.*

I guess lacking a fun gene was a requirement to work in personal security.

Does he ever relax, I wondered.

An hour later I had my answer. Nope. He does not relax. In fact, he doesn't know the definition of the word. When we arrived, Alex made us wait so he could check out the surroundings before we went inside.

"Is he one of yours or is he courtesy of Bennet?" I asked, motioning toward him after we'd been seated and served our drinks.

"Bennet. Mine is only around during work hours." She fidgeted with her glass. "You know how Bennet is. Always pulling the strings from the shadows."

I sort of knew, I guess. Maybe? Intrigue bloomed. "Does it ever bother you how he likes to have his hands in everything you do?"

She didn't answer. I casually sipped on my martini, trying to appear nonchalant. Hannah's become an even bigger mystery to me since what happened at the ring ceremony.

Our conversation detoured from Bennet to Charlotte's foundation, and finally to our trip to Miami and Paris. We ordered some appetizers and another round of drinks. By the time the third round came out, we were both relaxed and giddy.

We even managed to convince Alex to stretch his legs for a few minutes. He scowled at us and muttered something about using the restroom.

"Good evening ladies," a deep voice greeted us.

I jumped, heart pounding. *He sounds like…*

My eyes fell on the well-dressed man who'd interrupted us. I relaxed a bit, realizing this wasn't a repeat of my encounter with Jordan. Although this guy could have emerged from the same business bro clone factory. Tailored suit, styled hair, gleaming cufflinks, arrogant smile.

Hannah glanced at him with disinterest.

He didn't seem to mind neither one of us greeted him with anything more than a cool stare.

"Sorry if I've interrupted you. My friend and I—" he gestured behind him "—would like to buy you both a drink."

I glanced to my left, noticing another three-piece suit sitting at a table. He lifted a glass and winked. I rolled my eyes.

"Thank you, but no," Hannah replied, sounding more like an annoyed princess than anything else.

The man smiled without any warmth. "You mean to tell me I'm being snubbed? And here I thought the esteemed executives with the vaunted New York Legends would jump at the chance to be pampered."

"Buying us a drink doesn't cut it." I paused to sip my martini. "But thanks for noticing."

Hang around posh venues in the city long enough, and running into this type of guy wasn't too much of a shock. Our photos were plastered all over the Legends website. Plus, Hannah's been part of the Manhattan social scene her entire life as the sole heiress to the Caldwell fortune.

Any person with half a brain who fancies themselves to be on the prowl would recognize her.

I get noticed occasionally but nobody cares about the media relations person for a football team. Unless they want an interview. Although these days my visibility on social media was more prevalent thanks to being linked with Xavier.

This guy had a different motive. I just couldn't figure it out yet.

"In that case," he continued, lowering his tone, "would you both care to join us at The Guild? It's an ultra exclusive…club. Invite only. We have a private room reserved for the night."

I've heard my share of bad pick up lines but this one takes the cake.

Hannah remained void of expression. I barreled ahead.

"It's an ultra exclusive *sex* club, right? You left that part out."

"I had a feeling you'd know about it," he told my chest. *Asshole.*

Hannah tapped my foot under the table. *Don't engage,* she mouthed. My vodka-fueled smile said otherwise. If this guy wanted an adventure, he's going to get one. Just not the kind he's expecting.

I angled myself to face him, draping one arm on the back of my chair. My other hand toyed with the martini glass. "What about me gave you that feeling?" My voice dripped with poisonous honey.

He didn't bother hiding his intentions anymore. "You look like the type. Big tits, expensive clothes, hot friend. I bet you two eat each other out and like getting railed by two guys at once. My friend and I are willing to take that bet."

I really had to fight back the nausea. This guy went from smarmy to revolting in an instant.

Hannah's whole body tensed but she maintained her poise. "If this place is as exclusive as you say, I'd hope they wouldn't allow people like you inside."

He ignored her. The longer he stared at my breasts, the harder it was for me not to kick him in the balls. But I did like the adrenaline of the situation.

Except for the part where he reached out and fondled me. I shoved him away. "What the fuck do you think you're doing?"

"Baby, you can't be this hot and this much of a cock tease without giving me a taste."

One cursory glance at his crotch told me all I needed to know. "Not much cock to tease, is there?"

He grabbed himself. "I would love to stuff this in your smart fucking mouth and prove you wrong." Then he groped me again.

"Step away from the table." A steel edge ran beneath Alex's calm tone when he gripped the guy's arm. I didn't even hear him approach.

Suit Guy paled.

"You should probably listen to him," I said coolly, ignoring the rapid beating of my heart. "He's already had to send his food back once because it wasn't cooked right."

"Entitled bitch."

"I think you're confusing that with *confident.* What's the matter? Don't know how to handle a strong woman?" Venom laced my tone. Alex appeared ready to strangle this guy. "And what does that make you? Asshole is too kind." His eyes latched on to my chest again. *Idiot.* "By the way, my face is up here, dipshit. Go back to the cave you crawled out from before I have my friend here throw you out."

A cunning smile appeared. "I got what I came for. Nothin' like copping a feel on some rich bitch who likes to run her mouth."

Alex yanked him toward the exit by the shirt collar. Hannah exhaled sharply. I knocked back the rest of my drink. *Copping a feel? Who the hell still says that?*

His table buddy strode toward the exit but not before pausing near us. He looked me over, smirked, and walked away.

"Let's go." Alex's clipped tone left no room for discussion when he returned.

As I was climbing into the car, I noticed the two douche bags talking to the valet. He handed them both an envelope. Panic surged through me.

I didn't say anything to Hannah about it on the drive back to the stadium. She'd been texting with someone the whole time. It couldn't be Bennet. It was after ten here, meaning it's the middle of the night in England.

My car was the only one still sitting in the lot. Alex pulled up and parked perpendicular to it.

"Thanks, Alex. See you tomorrow, Hannah."

"Drive safe," she called after me, not looking away from her phone. "Text me when you get home."

Something crunched beneath my feet when I approached my car. It was dark, but I could see objects glittering on the ground under the lights.

I looked closer.

Shards of glass.

Every muscle in my body screamed at me to run.

What remained of my driver's side window lay shattered on the asphalt.

Chapter
SIXTEEN

"Is she alright?"

My pulse spiked, eradicating any remnants of sleep. I couldn't get these fucking jeans on fast enough.

"She's upset." Bennet's reassuring tone didn't help. I grabbed my keys and a shirt, and ran down to my car. The alarm beeped when I unlocked it.

"Xavier, it's four in the morning. What are you—"

"Not now, mate." I ended the call and dialed Victoria's number.

"I'm fine," she answered.

"You don't sound fine." I clipped my phone to the holder, put her on speaker, and sped toward the motorway. Not quite sure where I'd end up yet.

That's a fucking lie. Jordan won't know what hit him.

"I'm not hurt or anything. Just shaken up a bit."

"Tell me everything."

An aggravated sigh preceded her description of events. "I was out with Hannah. We had dinner. She took me back to the stadium and that's when I found my car smashed up."

So much for the state of the art security systems at the New York Legends facility. How the fuck did they not see a random person roaming through the car park?

I get it. It's a stadium and there's a shop for fans to buy jerseys and other team shit but that doesn't mean anyone gets to walk over to where the executives park. Especially since that lot is gated.

"I want you to come directly here tomorrow. Fuck Miami."

"You're being ridiculous. And where are you going? I know you're driving."

"I have to take care of something." *I'm going to kill him.*

"In the middle of the night? That's crazy. Go home."

"No." I pressed down on the accelerator. The streets were empty. Nobody will care if I run a few red lights.

Reality narrowed into a razor thin focus. Someone threatened her. They won't get away with it. I refuse to let anyone hurt her.

The muscles in my arms ached from pushing against the steering wheel, willing the car to move faster. Lights and buildings flew by in a blur. I swerved around one car, pushing the accelerator down as far as it would go.

Squealing tires screeched just as a horn blew. I barely made it through the intersection without being hit.

"Xavier, please stop." Victoria's panicked plea arrowed straight into my heart.

Listen to her, my brain screamed.

Sucking in a breath brought clarity back to the world.

Too fast. I'm going too fast.

I yanked my foot off the accelerator and felt the car slow down. When I found a safe place to pull over and park, I cut the engine.

"Tori? Are you still there?" My heart thundered, slipping into an erratic rhythm. *Oxygen.* I needed more oxygen. "Answer me."

"I'm here," she responded in a dull tone. "Go home before you get hurt."

"I need to see you. I'll start a video call." I hung up, not waiting for her to say anything. My finger shook trying to touch the little fucking camera icon.

Victoria appeared. My anxiety level lowered immediately. She looked aggravated but okay.

"Where are you?"

"Parking lot." She reversed the camera so I could see Hannah and her bodyguard, Alex. *Bodyguard. That happens now whether she wants one or not.* Her face reappeared. "The night security guard said he'd wait for the tow truck. Hannah's giving me a ride home."

Night security. Where was this guy when it happened?

Her astute emerald eyes studied me through the screen. I swallowed hard, feeling the intensity of her stare. "Why are you out driving like a maniac?"

"I don't know," I admitted. "I felt—" *I can't lose you* "—I had to do something."

"There's nothing you can do from London." Exhaustion lined her eyes and mouth. "We don't even know who did—"

"It was *him*," I seethed. "He won't get away with it."

"Xavier." Her voice trembled. "You don't know that. Please stop making reckless decisions. I can't handle the thought of you getting hurt or—" a pained expression passed over her face "—please go home. I'll stay on the call with you. That way you'll know I'm home safe, too."

Fury darkened the edges of my vision hearing her this upset. But then it hit me like a fucking brick.

I made her this upset. *I* added to her stress by acting like a lunatic. Tearing through the streets of London to exact revenge on…on what? A gut feeling? An instinctual assumption based on past events? I had zero proof Jordan had a hand in this. Zero. Yet here I was, ready to burn down the world.

The hairs on the back of my neck stood up. *What the fuck is wrong with me?*

"I'm sorry, Tori." I barely managed to get the words out. "I didn't mean to upset you. I'm just…sometimes I can't control my impulses."

Her head rested against the window of Hannah's car. Even through the lights and shadows of the interior, I could see a small smile. "I've heard that about you."

My lips curved as I started the car. My pulse slowed back to its normal pattern.

"You shouldn't believe everything you hear. Especially if it's about me."

We stared at one another quietly for a few minutes. Six weeks was too long to be without her.

"Did you have a good night out? Aside from this?"

Victoria's eyes widened. "It was interesting." She pointed the camera at Hannah. "Wasn't it?"

Hannah's eyebrows winged up. "Yeah. Definitely."

"I'm about to drive. Is there something else you two want to tell me before I do?" I kept my tone light for the most part.

Victoria appeared. "Nope. I need you to get home safe. You have a soccer game to win in a few days."

"Football match," I muttered, grinning into the darkness.

"I heard that."

"Did you really? I could swear the word *soccer* keeps coming out of your mouth."

"You're insufferable."

"I've been called worse."

I heard Hannah laughing in the background.

"When do you have to be at the training facility tomorrow?"

"Early." I glanced at the time. "Doubt I'll be getting any more sleep when I get home."

"Try to nap."

Impossible. "I'll be fine. Getting you home in one piece is all I'm worried about right now."

"Mmhmm. Same."

Stopping at the traffic light gave me an excuse to focus on her. She must have propped the phone on something. Her eyes were closed and I could see her arms folded up to cradle her head against the window.

"Tired from all the drinks or all the excitement?" I asked.

"Both."

She must be exhausted. Not even an attempt at sarcasm.

"You should hang up if you want to rest," I said gently. "I'm almost home anyway."

"No. I like having you with me."

The mood shifted to something softer, almost achingly vulnerable.

"And I like being with you. I'm not going anywhere."

We fell into a comfortable silence for the remainder of our drive. The sky grew brighter as I walked into my flat. Definitely no more sleeping for me. I'll probably go for a quick run before leaving.

I sat by the fireplace, putting my feet up on the ottoman.

"I know that chair." Victoria watched me. "I like when you sit in it."

"Yeah? Haven't used it since you were here."

"We'll have to fix that next time I'm in London." A bright light illuminated the interior of the car. "Home sweet home." She blinked against the sudden light. "Thank you for staying on with me."

"Will Alex be picking you up in the morning?"

A brief silence followed. Victoria glanced over at Hannah. "Eight? Okay." Her eyes focused on me. "He'll come get me at eight."

"Good. Now go to bed."

"Just because you're sitting in the bossy chair doesn't mean I want to be bossed around." A tantalizing rasp edged her voice. "I'm about to get in the elevator. I might lose you."

"You'll never lose me, love."

"Tell that to all the steel in this building. Good night, country prince."

"Good night, city princess."

Training was awful.

Let me correct that.

I was awful.

Lack of focus. Lack of conviction. Lack of any desire or drive that made me…*me.*

"Get your head straight, Maddox," Ashton Clarke said, pulling me aside in the changing room. "Those should be routine saves for you."

The manager was right. All of this should be routine. Fucking up on the national team didn't sit well with me at all. The last thing I wanted to do was disappoint him or the rest of the guys.

Ashton had been the biggest football star in England when he was the midfielder for West London. Even though that club was now my biggest rival, I idolized him growing up.

"Having a shitty morning I suppose." I shrugged, unable to fully shake off what happened last night.

"Get some lunch. Regroup. Have a better afternoon, yeah?" He patted my shoulder and returned to his office.

After showering and changing, I met up with Cade and some other players in the dining hall. One of them was Zach Donovan. I'd sucker punched him a few months ago during a match, leading to my multi-game suspension. We've worked things out since, but he eyed my warily.

"Alright." Cade rubbed his hands together. "I've finalized the chateau rental for after the match. Who's in?"

"Another night of debauchery, Gallagher?" Liam Turner chided, sitting in the remaining empty chair.

"If that's what you want to call it."

"You're more likely to score at the party than on the pitch."

"Care to make it interesting, Turner?" Cade smirked.

I glanced around the table at my teammates. Well, at least for international matches. Liam excelled as a defender in Newcastle. Zach was a superstar at West London United. The other lads were called up from Liverpool, Chelsea, and Brighton.

We don't train together often but when we do, it sometimes turned into a good-natured battle of egos.

"How about you, Maddox?" Zach addressed me. "How many saves can you guarantee?"

I shot him a warning glance. I knew what he was up to and I didn't want to take the bait.

"What? Nothing to say? You couldn't stop mouthing off before our match against you lot. Guaranteed a clean sheet if I recall correctly. Too bad you didn't last the whole game."

A hush fell over the group. This was the last fucking thing I needed today.

"I guarantee I'll make more saves than you," I retorted, mentally kicking myself for even giving this guy the satisfaction of a lame answer.

"I'm a striker, asshole. I don't need to save anything."

Guess the amends we'd made were in name only. *Prick.*

"Tell that to your reputation," I snapped. "Driving your fancy Porsche through a store window isn't a good look."

Zach stood up, leaned forward and pressed his hands on the table. "You're one to talk about reputations."

A sharp whistle cut through the mounting tension. "That's enough, gents," Cade said, looking from Zach to me. "We're all here for the same reason. To get a win in Paris. Nothing else—" he looked pointedly at me "—matters."

I scowled at my friend. He responded with a knowing head tilt.

Seriously?

Fine. FINE. I'll be the bigger person.

"Sorry," I grit out.

Zach's satisfied smirk doused my annoyance with jet fuel. So much for regrouping and getting my head on straight at lunch. I rubbed a finger over my eyelid to stop it from twitching.

The remainder of our break passed without further incident, aside from Cade and Liam's spirited jabs at one another. I'd tried not to let my sour mood from last night spill into today's preparations. Guess I'm failing at that, too.

Once everyone stood up to get back to work, I approached Zach.

"Sorry. Again," I said, actually meaning it this time. "The Porsche remark was a low blow."

Zach stared at me with a glint of disbelief in his eyes. "Fair play. Apology accepted."

"Yeah, well, figure United won't win the league anytime soon so I'll let you have this one."

"Arrogant bastard. Just for that, I'm gunning for you this season. Mark my words. Back of the net every time."

We started walking toward the strength and conditioning room.

"Back of the net. You know how often I hear that? More times than anyone's actually scored on me."

"I've scored on you," he boasted. "Many times. You're good, Maddox. But you're not *that* good." He paused. "You do have a killer left hook though."

I laughed. "Been working on it since I was twelve."

"Listen." He stopped walking. "I shouldn't have baited you like that, with the whole guaranteeing saves." Zach studied me with caution. "We're both hot-tempered assholes."

Technically, he's not wrong. It'll be a cold day in hell before I say it to his face.

"Let's leave it all on the pitch, yeah? Show me that so-called talent everyone keeps talking about."

"I'll do you one better," he said with a smug smile. "I'll show you what a great striker can do if you show me one decent save."

We both laughed and went on our way.

The rest of the afternoon went much better than the morning. Even though most of us were rivals on the pitch, being around the guys and prepping for an international match together had a different energy.

After all the stress and anger and general unpleasantness from last night, this felt good. I felt more like myself. I loved this sport. Loved competing. Loved bonding with my teammates. Even the ones who got on my nerves.

This training facility was just as nice as our usual one near Birmingham. World-class, actually. The complex sat on nearly one hundred acres. It was lush and private and just what I needed to get focused. Ashton wanted us to stay closer to London for this trip. I wasn't complaining. Plus, we all had rooms in the hotel on the private campus tonight.

My improved mood carried me through dinner. Cade invited a bunch of us to his room to watch a movie before curfew. I went for a little while and excused myself early to hopefully get some time with Victoria. We haven't spoken since last night and I couldn't stop thinking about her all day.

I sent her a text before walking into my room.

Me: How's Miami?

I kicked off my trainers, grabbed some water and stood by the window.

Tori: Hot and humid. How's training?

Me: I've had better

Tori: Give me a sec. I'll call you

I sat on the couch, phone in hand.

"Hey," I answered after one ring. I heard muffled conversations in the background.

"Why have you had better?" This voice. It sounded even brighter and more soothing tonight. "Did someone score a little goal on you?"

"Maybe."

"Poor boy. How will you survive the embarrassment?" I could hear her moving around, as though she were walking to a more private place to talk.

"Where are you?"

"Some fancy restaurant downtown."

I heard heels clicking. She must be walking down a hallway. Then I heard a door shut. Was that a lock snapping into place?

"Did you just lock yourself in a vault?"

"Not quite. I'm in the bathroom. Actually the powder room area. It's more private."

Nothing sexy about that statement at all, yet my cock jumped with interest. "Why?"

"Because I miss you and I've had a few drinks and I'm really horny and feel like playing." Her tone was laced with want and hunger. "Are you alone?"

"Yes." I put her on speaker, unzipped my jeans and pushed them down. "Not like that would matter anyway."

A silvery laugh pealed through the phone. "No, it wouldn't. I can picture you sneaking off to another room. Would you put me on speaker so everyone could hear?"

This fucking woman. I fisted myself and slowly started stroking. "You know I would."

"Good boy," she purred. Somehow I could tell she was touching herself too. "Are you laying down? Sitting up?"

Her questions came out low and husky. It made me grip myself tighter. "Sitting up. Like I'm in my bossy chair."

"Perfect. Are you stroking yourself rough and hard? I liked watching you do that."

Fuck. "Yes. You were on your knees watching me. Are you kneeling now? Tell me what you're doing."

"I'll do better than that." A few seconds of silence followed. Then my phone vibrated. "You should really check your texts."

When I did, I nearly passed out. A picture of her seated on a velvet couch stared back at me. The couch faced a full-length mirror.

Her reflection.

Fucking hell.

One leg was up on the couch, a black high heel braced against the cushion. The other leg spread wide. She had her dress hiked up with her fingers buried in her cunt. I couldn't see her face because the goddam phone was in the way but her head was tilted back slightly.

Another text came through.

It was a selfie. *Holy shit.* She was licking her fingers.

"You are so fucking dirty," I growled. "I love it."

"How much do you love it, country prince?" She spoke in low, gentle tone. "Do you love it enough to make yourself come for me right now?"

I stroked myself harder.

"I can hear you. I can hear your hand moving over your cock. God…I wish I was there, kneeling in front of you. Sucking you—" her voice grew thicker with desire "—teasing you…swallowing you…I miss you…*Xavier.*"

My grip tightened hearing my name fall out of her mouth on a moan. An orgasm coiled at the base of my spine.

"I want you kneeling in front of me right now, taking every inch down your throat." I let out a harsh grunt. "Do you know how fucking good your mouth feels on me? How much I love it?"

Sweat beaded over my skin as I stared at the picture she'd sent.

"*Xavier…*"

The phantom scent of warm, musky vanilla invaded my senses.

I should be fucking her right now. Feeling her nails clawing at my back. Hearing her greedy demands for *more* and *harder.*

My breathing grew harsh, impatient.

I bit out a low curse. My cock was hard and swollen, begging for release. I edged myself closer.

"Say my name again, dirty princess," I ordered. "Say my name until I come."

A long pause and then…

"*Xavier Fucking Maddox*…do you have any idea what you do to me…" Breathy little gasps punctuated her words.

Oh my fucking God. My orgasm tightened, threatening to explode. I slowed my movements.

Not yet. I needed to savor this.

"*Tori.*" I thrust into my own fist.

"Come undone." Her sultry command washed over me. "*Xavier*…center of attention…everyone loves you…but you're mine…all of you…come undone for me…only me…*Xavier.*"

"*Fuck.*"

My climax burst in one blinding, deafening moment, drowning out any of Victoria's sounds. The force of it left me breathless and shaking. I rested my head back against the cushion, waiting for my heartbeat to slow and the fog to clear from my brain.

Mine. All of you.

After a few seconds I heard, "Are you still there?"

"Yes, love." *Barely.*

"I can't wait to see you on Saturday." The smile caressing her voice reached through the phone and punctured my soul.

Chapter
SEVENTEEN

VICTORIA

Having an entourage is *not* as glamorous as it sounds.

"How do you put up with this?" I grumbled, speed-walking with Hannah through Charles de Gaulle airport. We'd just arrived in Paris for Xavier's game tonight.

"You get used to it." Her flaxen hair bounced with every purposeful step.

"We'll see," I muttered. "I'm still not used to the freaking royal guard posted at work."

Alex has been hovering since Wednesday night. Not only did he drive me home, he also picked me up for work the next day.

And he drove me to the airport for the team flight to Miami.

Oh, and he was at the dinner for the marketing staff on Thursday night.

And the game on Friday.

And the flight here.

I tried not to let it bother me too much.

Since we'd taken the red-eye, our plan for the day was pretty flexible. We'll check in at the hotel, freshen up, then find a spot for brunch. I haven't been to Paris in a hot minute so I was actually looking forward to an authentic French roast coffee. And maybe a croissant or twelve.

"Ladies, the car is this way," Alex's gruff voice cut through the hustle and bustle of the airport.

Hannah stopped walking and looked at him funny. "No it's not. I hired a service to—"

She frowned, seeing the stern expression on Alex's face. Her subtle eye roll said everything.

"Busted," I laughed.

"I adore that man but sometimes I wish he wasn't so—"

"So what?" Bennet sauntered over from God-knows where. Even in the middle of an airport he commanded the space, exuding power and control.

"Hands on," Hannah finished.

Bennet whispered something in her ear that made her cheeks turn crimson before kissing her.

"Victoria." He greeted me with a smile.

"God of thunder."

"That never gets old for you, does it?"

"Nope. And it never will."

Bennet's amber eyes danced with amusement. "Alex will see to it that your belongings get to the hotel. You ladies are coming with me." His statement sounded pretty final but I wasn't about to be bossed around so soon after deplaning.

"I'd rather go to the room and shower, if that's okay with the lord of the manor." I stifled a smile, knowing this nickname ruffled his feathers.

Before Bennet could react, Hannah put her two cents in. "Same for me. There's nothing worse than sitting on an airplane all night and not freshening up. Especially after being in the Miami humidity before we left."

A ghost of a smile touched his lips. He's been on the receiving end of my defiance, or whatever his definition of it is, but probably not Hannah's. Then again, judging by the look on her face maybe my secretly kinky friend enjoyed pushing her Dom's buttons.

"Seems I'm outnumbered by the Americans." He turned to Alex. "I'll meet you all at the hotel."

"Sir." Alex nodded and motioned for us to follow him toward the exit.

Deciding to come to France, at least for me, was driven solely by my desire to see Xavier. Otherwise, I'd be laser focused on the upcoming football season. It starts in less than three weeks. We lost our preseason game in Miami last night. Plus, the rumors and speculation surrounding Noah's future with the team ramped up again.

Word leaked that no movement has been made yet to extend his contract. It expires at the end of next season, but negotiations have been on-going all summer. I half-wished the fake photos of his house regained traction.

I sank into the comfort of our car and enjoyed the views on the way to the hotel. Hannah took care of booking the room so I had no idea where we were staying. She sat quietly next to me, tapping on her phone.

"Um," she hesitated. "There's been a slight change."

"What do you mean?"

She frowned. "Bennet changed our reservations. We're each getting a penthouse suite at the Four Seasons."

"He did what?" My jaw dropped. "No. No way. Tell him that's not necessary."

Hannah's *have-you-met-Bennet-Logan* look said it all.

Over the course of my life and career I've been around all different types of alpha males. CEOs, politicians, international sports stars, celebrities. The list goes on. None of them, and I do mean none, hold a candle to the level of influence Bennet has over any situation. He is quite honestly the most controlling man I've ever met and I don't know how Hannah can spend more than five minutes in his presence without wanting to pull her hair out.

"Why do I get the feeling he's going to intrude on our brunch and eat all my croissants?" I pouted.

"He knows not to interfere in our plans. He just wanted to pamper us."

I didn't have the heart to tell her changing our hotel reservations *was* interfering in our plans but she looked so glowy and happy and smitten.

Shaking my head in amusement, I settled into the seat and relaxed. Once we arrived at the hotel, we were ushered inside like royalty.

Alex escorted us to our respective suites. Hannah's door was at the end of the hallway in one corner, mine on the opposite end. We were basically neighbors for the night.

First thing I did when I got inside was text Xavier.

Me: Bonjour

Mildly Hot: You're here?

Me: Yep. At the hotel.

Mildly Hot: Get some rest. I plan to keep you up all night

Me: Promise?

Mildly Hot: Is that a challenge?

Me: Maybe

Mildly Hot: Careful what you wish for

I hopped in the shower to wash off the remnants of Miami and the long flight.

Since we were going to a soccer game, I thought it would be fun to wear Xavier's jersey. He really enjoyed seeing me in his Royal City one. And I really enjoyed wearing it for him.

It was way too big though. I pulled out the England jersey I bought last week, running my hand over the name *Maddox*.

A smile played on my lips. *He's going to love this.*

Intense quiet filled every corner of the suite's luxurious bedroom. I wish he was here with me now, enjoying the beautiful panoramic view of Paris with the Eiffel Tower standing in all its iron elegance.

I'd just walked back into the living room area when a knock sounded at the door. A hotel employee stood holding a small, elegantly wrapped box.

"This arrived for you."

He handed me the box and left. I watched him disappear into the elevator. I also noticed there was no sign of Alex lurking in the hallway. That struck me as odd but then again maybe the poor guy was scarfing down some food in peace.

I eyed the pretty box with a healthy dose of curiosity. Xavier wouldn't send a present. He's not a surprise romantic gift type of guy.

Wait. He didn't know where I was staying.

A tiny wave of anxiety pushed through me. There wasn't a card or anything with it.

I did the only rational thing I could think of. I shook it. Silly? Yes.

"Might as well," I muttered, opening the box.

There was so much tissue paper I thought maybe it was empty. Then I noticed the slim, black flash drive wrapped in a small slip of paper.

I unfolded it.

THIS IS THE KEY: 08010401

What the hell?

My curiosity evaporated, replaced with an eerie crawling sensation up the back of my neck. I went to the door again and opened it. The hallway remained empty. The eerie sensation intensified.

"Get it together," I mumbled to myself, shutting the door.

It's the jet lag. The flash drive was probably meant for someone else. Bennet *did* just make these reservations, and knowing him, he probably had the original guest booted so fast they weren't able to tell anyone.

I relaxed a bit but wasn't able to shake the weird sensation. I put the flash drive back in the box and left it on the table. I'll talk to the concierge after brunch.

Half an hour later, Hannah and I sipped on mimosas at an adorable little café near the hotel. Of course, Alex hovered nearby.

I snapped some photos of the Eiffel Tower, our drinks, and us. Likes and comments flooded my notifications seconds after I posted them.

Enjoy Paris!

Lucky girl.

Queen.

Belle femme.

My following on social media had grown dramatically the last couple of months. I went from twelve hundred followers to fifty thousand. To say Xavier's fans were ravenous was an understatement.

"You're officially a WAG now," Hannah teased. "How does it feel?"

"I'm not that interesting. They'll get bored really fast."

"They're curious about you. Xavier was usually spotted with models or actresses or party girls. You're different."

"Is that your way of saying I'm a nobody?" I laughed.

"Stop it. You know what I mean. The way you two met was so… organic. People eat that shit up."

My phone chimed.

Killian: If you don't bring me something Parisian I'll cry

Me: Grab the tissues

Killian: Love you, mean it

"Was that Xavier?" Hannah giggled. "His ears must have been burning."

"It was Killian begging for a souvenir."

I finished my drink and excused myself to use the restroom. The café was bustling now. Tourists and regulars filled the sidewalk tables. I waited patiently for an elderly couple to pass by before squeezing through the door.

Someone bumped into me from behind, apologizing profusely. I whacked a pretty large, and from the looks of it, expensive camera lens when I turned around. Horrified, I told him in French how sorry I was and hoped I didn't damage the camera. He smiled and shook his head, waving off the notion. Then he told me to *have a lovely day* in English.

After I returned to Hannah, she leaned in and spoke low. "There's a reporter following you."

"How do you know?" I pulled out my phone and started scrolling.

"I saw him. Besides, the camera was a dead giveaway."

I stopped mid-scroll and glanced up. "Big lens?" I relayed my encounter with the stranger.

"This will probably happen more often now." Hannah straightened her posture. "Will it bother you?"

"I honestly don't know. I've had cameras shoved in my face by default when I'm escorting Noah or Jax around." I shrugged. "How different can this be?"

We spent the next hour or so shopping. I did grab something Parisian for Killian but it was more of gag gift than anything. He's afraid of mimes. When I saw a small ceramic mime holding a flower, I bought it immediately.

Before leaving the shop, I noticed a print of Baroque architecture, featuring Palais du Luxembourg and the Louvre.

The Louvre?

I read the information sheet near the print. Apparently the Baroque style was added in the seventeenth century during an expansion project.

Fascinating.

I bought it for Xavier on a whim, knowing how much he appreciates the inner workings of a structure.

Hannah and I returned to the hotel, agreeing to meet in the lobby around four to head over to the stadium. I put my stuff down, noticing the little box.

I should bring it down to the concierge so they can deliver it to its rightful owner.

My cell phone started ringing. Of course it was buried at the bottom of my bag. I rummaged through, feeling my way around.

Lip gloss, sunglasses, passport...

The ringing stopped when my hand brushed an envelope. Must be a piece of mail I shoved in there before leaving for Miami. I pulled it out.

Plain, white, no address.

Oh. It's probably the itinerary from Miami.

I tossed it in the trash and continued looking for my phone.

One missed call from an unknown number. The eerie sensation I'd had earlier returned. Never really thought Paris would bring out the creepy, horror movie vibes.

"I'm being fucking ridiculous," I grumbled, grabbing the box and heading to the lobby. I exchanged a pleasant smile with one of the room attendants on my way to the elevator.

The concierge was as polite as can be, apologizing for the mistake. She checked the computer several times, glancing at me nervously.

"*Mademoiselle, je suis désolé,* this is for you. Hannah Pruitt, *non?*"

Confused, I answered, "No. That's my friend, She's in the room down the hall from me."

"Apologies, *mademoiselle,* " she said, placing her hand on the box. "They must have misread the room number. I can have someone deliver it to her."

"That's not necessary." I reached for the small package. "I can give it to her. Do you have a record of who delivered it?"

"A local courier. They come and go all day."

"Thanks for your help. Sorry for the inconvenience."

"Not a problem. *Ça m'a fait plaisir.*"

Tapping my nails on the box, I waited by the elevator. Why would Hannah need a flash drive? More importantly, why would she be working on a girls' weekend? When I reached my floor, I continued down the hall and knocked on Hannah's door.

Alex answered because of course he would. Steely gray eyes skirted over my face before he greeted me with a monotone, "Can I help you with something?"

"Always a pleasure, Alex." I stifled an eye roll and held up the box. "This was delivered to my room by accident. It's for Hannah."

He plucked the box from my fingers. "I'll see that she gets it. Thank you."

The door closed in my face before I could say anything.

"Rude," I muttered, pulling my vibrating phone out of my pocket.

Unknown: Never know who's watching

A photo of Hannah and I having brunch accompanied the text.

Chapter

EIGHTEEN

XAVIER

Whoever said losing builds character never competed in an international football match.

Plus, they're an idiot.

The crowd chanted *allez les bleus* all around me while I sat in front of my goal. The ball still rested against the net after the referee blew his whistle to end the game. French flags waved everywhere in a sea of blue jerseys.

I slammed my hands down on the grass before standing up.

"We'll get 'em next time, mate."

Cade's reassuring words did nothing to soothe my bruised ego.

Four goals.

Four fucking goals.

Two of them grazed my fingertips. I should have been able to stop them.

"Whatever."

"This face is too pretty to pout." He squeezed my cheeks before we started walking around the pitch. "It's only a friendly. And it's not like we lost."

"A draw isn't a win, especially when I played like shit." I stopped short of saying the rest of the squad lacked any passion or commitment to actually want to win the fucking match.

"Not our best performance for sure." Cade remarked unfazed, waving to the England fans. His love of attention and adoration often drowned out the more practical matters of football. Admittedly, so did mine.

After shaking hands and acknowledging members of the opposing team, we went back toward the England fans. Some held signs and jerseys. Others waved flags or scarves. At one point, a group started chanting our names, making an *X* with their arms.

"Hear that? They bloody love us." Cade nudged me with his elbow. "Too bad you're not available anymore. Look at these girls. We could do some damage tonight."

I followed his hungry stare. It took me a second to latch on to whatever unsuspecting girl caught his eye. A trio of pretty young women leaned over the barrier, clamoring for our attention. Two of them turned so we could see the last name *Gallagher* on their jerseys.

The star striker noticed. "Excuse me. My audience awaits."

I shook my head, watching my friend run over to bask in their attention up close.

"Well played, Maddox." Liam clapped me on the back. "We'll tighten up and be more prepared for the Dutch next month."

"You better." I faced him while I walked backwards to where Cade stood. "I'm still waiting to see what all the fuss is about you."

"I'll show you when you come to Newcastle and we beat your ass in November."

Liam was a talented defender but excelled more at talking shit than actually performing well. His laugh faded slightly when something in the stands distracted him. Probably another overeager fan.

When I rejoined Cade, I fake-smiled my way through a stretch of vapid flirting. These girls were just like all the rest, batting their lashes, fawning over us, trying to act demure and mysterious.

Yeah, there was a time I enjoyed all of this. I took advantage of it on some occasions. There's a reason I have the reputation I do.

Not anymore.

But Cade ate it up.

"Would you ladies be interested in joining us and some of the other lads for a little post-match party?" He flashed the girls his trademark smile. "We rented a chateau for the night."

"Will both of you be there?" a petite brunette asked, staring directly at me.

"Of course," Cade answered, ruffling my hair. I almost pummeled him on the spot. "Xavier loves a good party."

"So does my girlfriend." My words came out in a glacial tone.

"She's welcome to join the fun if she wants," the brunette purred, wrapping an arm around her blonde friend.

Cade muttered something vulgar under his breath. He eyed the young women like he'd been served the most decadent food on earth. A few years ago, I'd be right in the mix with him. Most men would do anything for an opportunity like this. All *we* had to do was exist.

I turned away, scanning the crowd for Victoria or Bennet. Both had been suspiciously quiet. Victoria wasn't her normal flirty self when we exchanged texts before the match started. And Bennet only texted to say he'd be watching with some league executives.

I noticed Liam chatting with someone by the barricade near the stands. Mild curiosity got the best of me. I stepped back to see who held his attention with such rapt enthusiasm.

Intense jealousy paralyzed me.

Victoria smiled and laughed, leaning against the barricade with enough elegance to outshine any member of the royal family.

She was an absolute vision. Red hair swept up in a ponytail. Glossy lips. Curves accentuated by a jersey —*my* number— and jeans. I might be biased but I've never seen a sexier woman in my life.

Part of me wanted to gouge Liam's eyes out. They traced over her body with obvious lust and intention. It was evident from where I stood, which felt too fucking far away at the moment.

"See you inside," I said to Cade and started walking.

Someone blocked my path before I could get to her.

"Xavier."

I recognized the voice and lavender scent.

"Phoebe," I muttered, side-stepping her. "If you'll excuse me."

She moved with me, putting her hand on my chest to prevent me from escaping. "I haven't heard from you in a while. Did you forget how to answer texts?"

Her dark hair and eyes matched the blatant come-hither tone. The corners of her pouty lips curled up in a knowing smile. Not too long ago this would turn me on enough to get something out of it.

My history with Phoebe was long and mostly uncomplicated. She worked as a television presenter for one of the networks. She's also a model. Matches like this would sometimes end with her and I…well, they would end with her and I.

Not tonight though. *Or ever.*

"Been busy." I side-stepped her again. She mimicked my movements, keeping her hand on me.

"All the more reason to come to my hotel and take a break." Her words dripped with seduction. "You've never been too busy for a full body rubdown."

"That's where you're wrong." My smile lacked any warmth. "It's not happening Phoebe. Let's not make a scene."

Her tanned skin flushed with a red tint. "Don't tell me this little thing with the American is still going on."

"I'm not telling you anything."

"This isn't over."

Oh it was. And so was this conversation.

"Wrong again," I said icily, irritated by her advances and furious at how engaged Liam still was with my girlfriend.

My long strides ate up the distance in no time. I arrived in time to hear Victoria laugh after whatever the fuck he said to her. The tic in my jaw pulsed harder at the bright sound. Then he put his hand on her arm and my vision turned red. Teammate or not, I wanted to shove his face into the grass.

I thought I'd stamped out my jealousy.

Wrong yet again.

"Did I miss something funny?" I asked, disguising my annoyance with a bored expression.

Victoria's eyes swept over me. Their emerald glow intensified as she drank in every inch of me before resting on my gloved hands.

"Just telling your lovely lady a funny story." Liam's hand was safely back at his side, thank fuck. "At your expense, of course."

He shot me a look that said *you lucky bastard* before saying his goodbyes and heading to the tunnel. The overheated temperature of my blood cooled a little.

"You're still hot when you're jealous for no reason." Victoria's words tumbled out breathier than I expected, making my cock twitch. I grabbed her and pulled her to me. "Hi," she smiled.

I kissed her with such fierce possession it shocked both of us.

"Hi," I said on her lips. "I missed you."

"I missed you, too." She laced her fingers behind my neck, pulling me in for another kiss.

My skin prickled from the light touch of her finger tracing my jaw. Holding her in my arms felt damn good. I was so caught up in her I almost missed the cloud of unease pass through her gorgeous features. It was brief though. Maybe I imagined it.

"Did you wear this for me?" I slid my hands up her back.

"I did but don't get used to it. As much as I like lions, if you ever play against the U.S. I'm afraid I have to support the stars and stripes."

"A discussion for another time."

She laughed. "You better enjoy this while you can then. Do you like it?"

"Fuck yes, I like it."

I lowered my mouth to hers, kissing her slow and deep. Her taste and scent mingled together with perfection, filling my senses. Mint and vanilla. Spring and winter.

Soft, sweet moans vibrated through her, igniting my instinct to be rough and possessive.

"Turn around," I ordered in a low voice.

Her eyes met mine before she did as I instructed. Knowing how much she trusted me turned me on in ways I never thought possible.

I placed my hands on her hips. Seeing my name on her back did something to me. I dipped my head so my breath skated on her neck. Her intoxicating scent drugged me and turned the sound of my voice hoarse and sinful.

"My name looks so fucking good on you. That's where it belongs, love. On what's mine."

A shudder rolled through us at the exact same time. Our bodies were so synced. I didn't even have to look at her to know what she wanted.

But I did want to hear her say it.

When I turned her toward me, she stared up with eyes shimmering from the lights.

"Hey, Mad— *Victoria*." Cade's boisterous shouting yanked me back into the chaos of the post-match environment. He bounded over like a puppy approaching a new toy and engulfed Victoria in a hug. She squealed in delight when he lifted her and spun her around. My earlier bout with jealousy still swirled beneath the surface but Cade was harmless. Plus he knew I'd knock him into the next millennium if he ever touched her inappropriately.

"Careful, Gallagher. I need her in one piece."

"I'm not touching that one, mate," he laughed, putting Victoria down. She hugged him one more time before returning to my side. I wrapped my arm around her waist and kissed the top of her head.

"When did you get here?" he asked her. "I would've sent you *my* jersey to wear."

Victoria looked toward the trio of young ladies taking a group selfie. "I can't possibly compete with your fan club."

"Them? They're not full members." He winked. "At least not yet."

One of the girls blew a kiss and waved at him.

"Big night planned?" I asked, arching an eyebrow.

"I'll have my hands full for sure."

"Pace yourself, Cade," Victoria quipped. "You don't want to frighten them off with all that overeager manliness."

A sly grin ghosted across my friend's mouth. I tossed him a warning glance.

"You would know all about overeager manliness, wouldn't you?" he teased her and fake-punched me in the chest. "We should head in, lover boy. I'm sure there's a lecture or twenty waiting for us lads about this shit performance."

"Before you go," Victoria reached for his arm, "would you mind taking our picture, Cade?"

"Queen Victoria, I would do anything for you." He took her phone and bowed dramatically.

She grabbed my hand and pulled me onto the pitch toward the goal.

"How do you want me?" I asked once we reached the penalty box.

"A few ways. But for right now, like this." She positioned me so I faced Cade, then pressed her body into mine, angled her back toward the camera and looked over her shoulder. I wrapped my arm around her waist.

"So everyone can see I'm yours," she whispered, looking up at me through her lashes.

I kissed her, holding her tight. "And I'm yours, love."

"You two ready? Or do you need a quick shag before we do this?" Cade shouted.

"Ready," we answered together.

Cade snapped a few shots and let out a low whistle. "Fucking hell, you two are a hot couple. I mean, you're okay Maddox…but *Victoria*." He fanned himself. "Mate, you really hit the lottery."

"Give me the phone before I launch you into next month," I grumbled.

He handed the phone back to Victoria with a smile and patted the top of my head. "I'm not wrong and you know it."

With those words, Cade sauntered toward the tunnel, laughing.

"He's in rare form," Victoria said quietly.

"Always is," I replied, gazing down at her. Another uneasy expression shadowed her features. She seemed off. "I should get in there as well, but are you alright? You look a little tense."

Victoria's eyes dropped down. "Yeah, I'm fine. Go finish your post-game stuff and we'll talk later, okay?"

I didn't like this. I didn't like it at fucking all.

We'd just made it to the sideline when I heard, "Maddox." Bennet's frigid tone announced his presence. "A word."

Victoria stiffened in my embrace before pulling away. She pressed a chaste kiss to my cheek and glared at Bennet when she stormed past him toward Hannah.

"What the fuck is *that* about?" I snapped.

"Marcus is assigned to her now," he answered smoothly.

I almost, *almost* lost my shit in front of all these people. I studied Bennet's placid expression. He assessed me with cool eyes.

"Why? We talked about this."

"I had no choice." He sounded bored. "Circumstances dictated—"

"Get to the point, Logan." I said between clenched teeth.

"A tabloid reporter was sniffing around the hotel. Hannah

mentioned she saw someone follow Victoria into the cafe where they had brunch. Looks like people are digging for information on you two."

Mild panic shot through me. As one of the most watched athletes in the world, I'm no stranger to the seedier side of being a celebrity. Stalkers, paparazzi, the quote-unquote gotcha moments at clubs or parties. My impulsive nature didn't help. In fact, it provided the perfect cocktail for rumors, gossip, and viral clickbait.

Fortunately, I'd managed to dodge potential scandals and kept my misadventures mostly discreet over the years. *Mostly.*

"Does she know?" I zeroed in on where Victoria stood.

Bennet's regal stature filled my line of vision, obscuring my view. "Yes. She also mentioned something about the night she and Hannah were out for dinner. The night her car was vandalized."

Anger flared through me. "You have three seconds to stop fucking around and tell me." I've known Bennet long enough to sense when he's being selective about what he reveals.

True to form, Bennet hardened his exterior and leveled one of his pompous, icy glares in my direction. "Go to the changing room, Maddox. Talk to your girlfriend later."

He walked off, leaving me to simmer in my own annoyance while fans screamed my name and reporters hovered with microphones at the ready.

Chapter

NINETEEN

Victoria nudged me with her elbow and gestured toward Cade as we walked through one of the chateau lounges. "He looks cozy."

I followed her gaze and noticed my friend in his element, basking in female attention. He sat on the couch with two of the three young women who'd been fawning over him at the stadium.

I guess the other one didn't make it.

Oh wait. There's the third.

She walked over and positioned herself comfortably on his lap. The expression on his face when he caught us looking said it all. *The more, the merrier.*

I grinned at Cade and gently pulled Victoria through the crowd toward another room. The post-match party was in full swing. Most of my teammates were milling about, along with a good mix of celebrities, models, and influencers. I knew quite a few of them. Some more than others.

In fact, two women eyed me with interest. One was a random hook up I'd had last summer.

The other was Phoebe. *Shit.* Her demeanor soured when she spotted Victoria.

I steered us clear of encountering a potentially awkward situation.

The last thing Victoria needed was to have her nose rubbed in my previous flings.

We ended up in the butler's kitchen, which was empty. Victoria hopped up on the counter and pulled me closer. I wedged myself between her legs, wrapping my arms around her waist.

"Do all soccer players rent castles in France to impress select female fans?" she asked, running her fingers through my hair.

"Maybe. But to be fair, those fans did travel to come see us play. It's the least we can do to thank them."

My smart ass remark was rewarded with a sharp poke in my side.

"Ow. Not into castles, city princess?"

"I love castles. How many of these parties would you go to after a game?"

"A few."

"Lies. You went to all of them." She leaned close and kissed my forehead. "Would you be here right now if I hadn't flown out to see you?"

"Probably. But I would have found an empty room to call you so I could hear your voice while I stroked myself. I like this better." I grabbed her hips. "I can fuck you for real."

Her cheeks flushed but a half-hearted smile tugged at her mouth. Honestly, seeing her like this upset me more than I expected.

"What's wrong, love?"

She didn't answer straight away. Her silence hung over us for several long, uncomfortable seconds. All I could think about was her car getting trashed and me not being there to protect her. *And probably being the reason why all this happened in the first place.*

Her beautiful, delicate features twisted into a frown. Annoyance flashed through her eyes when she finally looked at me.

"Weird stuff has been…" Her lips pressed together. "Maybe I'm paranoid but I think someone might be stalking me."

Rage.

Atomic levels of rage.

I used every public relations skill I've learned to sound calm and even. "Why do you think that?"

Victoria shrugged and pulled me into a tight hug. I held her in a vice-like grip. She's not one to show so much vulnerability.

I know your weakness now. I'll find her.

Panic flooded my body. *What have I done?*

"Stalking is too dramatic. But I have been getting random texts. And today, one of them had a photo attached of me and Hannah at brunch. I don't know how they got my number."

This was not fucking okay. "Was there a message?"

"Yeah." She loosened our embrace, sounding nervous. "*Never know who's watching.* It reminded me of—"

Her mouth clamped shut.

"Reminded you of what?" I tried like hell to remain calm and comforting.

"Nothing." A small head shake. "It's nothing."

"Victoria." I curled my fingers under her chin. "Tell me."

She fidgeted with her necklace, appearing distracted. Several beats passed before she spoke.

"There's just been a lot of annoying shit happening this summer. Text messages, my car got vandalized, some guy groped me at dinner and—"

"You were *groped*? *What guy?*" Fury crackled through my veins. Taking a breath, I softened the edge of my voice from a command to a request. "What guy?"

"Some asshole propositioned Hannah and I at dinner the other night. He wanted to buy us drinks. We said no thanks. Then he invited us to a sex club."

My hand clenched.

Stay calm.

"He told me he had a feeling I'd know about it because of the way I looked."

The muscle in my jaw ticked.

I will flay this bastard alive.

"Then he grabbed me. I shoved him and said he had a small dick. He called me an entitled bitch. I told him to go back to the cave he crawled out from. The end."

The last part cleared some of the turbulent thoughts running wild in my mind. I was actually impressed by her audaciousness.

"That's my girl." I ran a thumb over the elegant line of her jaw. "Do you think he's behind the texts?"

"No, but I did see the valet hand him an envelope when we left. I assumed there was money in it." Her tone sharpened. "We were at a trendy restaurant in Manhattan. Certain groups of people know who we are. The players hang out there. It's not out of the realm of possibility that someone wants to harass either Hannah or myself."

Victoria closed her eyes and exhaled in frustration before leaning back against the cabinets. A chill set in at the loss of her warmth. When she looked at me, my heart sank. Her expression hardened.

"And if you could fucking tell Bennet fucking Logan to stay the fuck out of my fucking business, I'd appreciate it."

I waited a beat before responding. "That's a lot of fucks to give, love."

Silence.

She glared at me in disbelief, opening her mouth to say something. I was the picture of perfect neutrality. Her lips pressed together, twisting into a reluctant smile. Small, and not what I'd call *happy*, but better than a scowl.

"That's the most I've heard you swear at one time since we met. Your Ivy League mouth is quite unladylike."

"Sorry."

"What did I say about apologizing for things you don't have to apologize for?" I spread my arms. "Come here."

She melted into my embrace. I stroked her back, inhaling her warm, sensual scent. "What did he do?"

Her fingers slid into my hair, tugging gently. The sensation tightened my groin.

"A package was delivered to my hotel suite after I arrived. It was a mistake since that fu— since *Bennet* changed our reservations without asking."

I nuzzled into her neck, kissing the soft skin. "He changed your reservations? I take it that's offense number one."

"The package was meant for Hannah. But that's not what annoyed me."

"What else happened?"

"He overheard Hannah and I talking about the guy from the restaurant. I hadn't told her about what I saw with the valet."

Typical.

I caressed down her arm. "Is there more?"

"I just…one thing I always prided myself on was the ability to take care of my own shit. I don't ask for help unless I've reached the end of my rope." Victoria's eyes met mine. "It's always been a struggle for me to let anyone in. Meeting you changed some of that but…I'm not willing to surrender my independence."

"Marcus." *Fucking Bennet.* "Offense number two?"

"I really don't want someone shadowing me."

I started to respond and paused.

Gently. I had to approach this topic gently.

"Maybe you and I can figure something out regarding Marcus." Another soft sweep of my fingers grazed her arm. "After what's happened with your car and that—" I scowled "—*guy* touching you, I'd feel better knowing someone had your back when I'm not there."

Discerning eyes flicked over my placid expression. "You and I can work on this. *Not* your friend. I know you guys are like brothers but I don't want him sticking his nose in our business."

"For what it's worth, Bennet doesn't always tell me what he has going on. And if he suspected any of this has to do with Jordan, he *wouldn't* tell me because he knows I'll lose my shit and do something stupid."

Fuck. Meant to keep that last part on the inside.

"If he *is* behind this," she bit out, "I'll join you in doing something stupid. That asshole still has to pay for what he did to my sister."

Despite her fiery energy, a note of nervousness ran beneath her declaration. The fierce need to protect her consumed me.

"He will. I promise you that."

Although my tone remained comforting, I was a ticking time bomb.

Targeted texts and a bottom-feeder who put his hands on her.

The thought of that fucking guy touching Victoria, let alone breathing in her presence, turned my blood to acid.

This whole scenario reeked of Jordan's influence but I couldn't prove it.

At least not yet.

"I wanted tonight to be about us." She frowned. "I wish we could go back to Lake George."

The air thickened with an electric charge so powerful it dissolved some of the tension between us.

"Me too, love."

Our eyes locked, filled with memories of our secluded weekend together. The welcome change in atmosphere dragged us away from our unpleasant situation.

No smashed car.

No frantic speeding through London.

No strange guys who can't keep their fucking hands to themselves.

Just us.

Victoria's lips parted on a soft exhale. I cupped the back of her neck, massaging it with my thumb in long, languid strokes. The reality of her was so addicting and raw and consuming. A living, breathing drug.

Before her, football was my drug of choice. I constantly chased the high of adoration and winning. I still wanted all that. But now?

Now I desperately craved beautiful smiles and bright laughter. Warmth, grace, and light, all packaged in the most stunning creature I've ever seen.

Victoria's hand slid under my shirt. Her touch was hot and real and felt so bloody good.

"I have a confession."

"Tell me." I continued my lazy strokes along the back of her neck.

The warmth of her hand traveled over my stomach. "I bought you a present."

Not sure if I shivered from her touch or the idea of a surprise gift. I don't even like surprises. "Really? What did I do to deserve one?"

I dipped my head. Our mouths hovered close. She buried her other hand in my hair again.

"Nothing. I just saw it and thought of you," she replied, pressing her lips to mine.

Elation surged through me when she teased my mouth with her tongue, deepening our kiss. So did a healthy dose of lust and my usual urge to take her any way I pleased.

She hooked her legs around my waist, making it easier for her to feel how much I wanted her. My cock has been a rod of steel since I saw her at the stadium. I kissed her harder, more possessive.

Pulling on her hair, I roughly positioned her head so I could plunder the softness of her mouth.

The silkiness of her tongue caressed mine, savoring me.

"You are going to be the death of me," I rasped on her lips. "I will never be able to get enough of you."

The sound of her laugh filled every broken part of me. "Looks like you have your work cut out, Maddox."

"I do." A full smile curved my mouth. "I like seeing you this way."

"What way? Sitting on a counter in the servant's quarters of an old French castle?"

"No." I squeezed her waist, eliciting a squeal. "Looking hot as fuck in my jersey. And kissing me, of course."

"Oh, right. Kissing you." She bit down on my lip, drawing a low moan out of me. "Your admirers out there might not agree with the kissing part."

"Do you think I care?"

Her fingers hooked into the waistband of my jeans. "No. Just wanted to put it out there that I noticed."

The casual tone didn't mask the visible tension lining Victoria's shoulders. She's seen how other women interacted with me in public, specifically fans and former one night stands. They always tend to touch me and lay it on pretty thick with the flirting.

A smile played on my lips.

"Are you jealous?" A deceptive softness wrapped around my low, mocking tone.

Victoria's eyes narrowed as she placed her hands in her lap. "Should I be?"

"That's not an answer."

"Your former sexual conquests aren't my concern." Indifference colored her words but the emotions swirling in the depths of her eyes told me otherwise.

She's jealous.

"Maybe, but I want you to ask me anyway."

Her lashes dipped before sweeping up, revealing a heated stare. "Which one?"

Victoria played this game well. She already knew the answer. She just wanted to hear me say it.

"The brunette."

An eyebrow arched. "The one who had her hands all over you on the sideline."

Well-played, city princess.

"Oh, you saw that," I confirmed in a cool tone. "I thought you were too busy laughing at Liam's stories."

Victoria's aggravated grunt vibrated in her chest. Pride lit a defiant fuse in her eyes. "Seems we both still have a lot of work to do when it comes to jealousy." A hard swallow disrupted the delicate lines of her throat. "But like I said, your former sexual conquests aren't my concern."

Astuteness stretched her features taut. Victoria's intelligence and power of observation always impressed me. She could play off being aloof or nonchalant but I know she has questions. A few have already tumbled out of her in the months since we met.

I always planned to have these conversations with her as we deepened our relationship and explored our limits together. My biggest desire was for her to find ways to approach me with her curiosities.

I'd seen flashes of it in some of our encounters. Our tryst in the maze comes to mind. Victoria was not shy about what she liked or what she wanted. I loved that about her.

"Ask me what you really want to know, Tori."

Subtle changes cycled through her features as she worked through and figured out what she wanted to say. Dilating pupils, faint traces of pink staining her cheeks, a nervous swallow.

"Was she ever with you at Bennet's parties?"

The vulnerability beneath her question pulled a dark smile out of me.

"Yes." I brushed a stray piece of hair out of her eyes. "That's not all you want to ask, is it?"

"I can figure out the rest."

"Can you?" My hands rested on her thighs. "Tell me what you think you know."

Our bodies were so close I could feel the heat radiating off her. When I stroked along her wrist, I felt the rapid beating of her pulse. I lifted her hand, kissing the frantic rhythm.

She watched me, drinking in my deliberate movements.

Another kiss on the wrist.

Another stroke along her jaw.

"Tell me."

A long stretch of silence followed. I simply studied her, memorizing every detail; the controlled rise and fall of her chest with each breath, and the flecks of jade sparking and burning in her emerald eyes.

"She's seen you in ways I haven't." Her voice trembled slightly. "Ways I want to see you."

"Is that what you think?" I wrapped one hand around her neck. "Nobody has seen me the way you do. Nobody ever will."

"You took her to—"

"She went to Bennet's parties. I didn't take her as a guest. She did more networking there than anything else."

"But you did fuck her." Icicles pierced each word.

I held her wrist. Circling my fingers around it, I slowly rubbed my thumb until I felt her pulse and pressed the metal ring I wore into her silky skin.

"Ask me what you really want to know, Victoria." My repeated request came out slower, more dangerous.

Pouty, full lips formed a tense line as an internal battle waged. Staring at me with severity, she fisted my shirt. "Have you done things with her I only fantasize about doing with you?"

There it was. There's the fire I've been waiting to see.

"No."

"Prove it." Her teeth dug into her lush lower lip, and the desire to take her overpowered me.

Chapter

TWENTY

I t didn't take me long to find an empty room down the hall from the main party area. Looked like a study or something. Didn't really matter.

Prove it.

I walked toward a desk, faced her, and leaned against it. "Take off everything except the jersey."

Victoria stood in the middle of the room, staring doe-eyed at me. Her cheeks flushed when she kicked off her trainers and wriggled out of her jeans.

Part of me wanted to bury myself inside her right now. A bigger part wanted to toy with her like a predator who'd just captured the one creature that eluded him for too long.

"*Everything* except the jersey," I ordered. "Don't make me say it again."

She did that really sexy thing where she unhooked her bra and removed it while keeping her shirt on. Then she removed her lace panties.

Possessiveness gripped at me.

The most gorgeous woman on the planet stood in front of me, wearing nothing but my jersey. She stared back, her eyes filled with trust and anticipation.

I approached slowly, circling her, intoxicated by the scent of her arousal. Natural and clean. Tangy with a hint of sweet. When I stopped behind her and pressed my body to hers, I heard a soft moan.

"Feel that?" I asked, rubbing my clothed erection against the soft curve of her ass. "This is what you fucking do to me. *You.* No one else." I reached around and wrapped my hand around her neck, enjoying the erratic flutter of her pulse. "How do you want me to prove it to you?"

The column of her throat expanded and contracted in my grip when she swallowed.

"Take me in a way you've only fantasized about." The unexpected sharpness in her tone hardened my already aching cock.

"Fuck," I groaned, giving in to my instincts.

Reckless taking.

It's gotten me into trouble before but I didn't care anymore. I was tired of denying who I was and suppressing what I wanted. Victoria showed me I could do as I pleased with her. I always asked, and she always consented.

What she didn't know was once I was through with her, she'd be ruined. Filthy. Depraved.

"Remember when I said you haven't seen me untamed yet?" I brushed my thumb over her lips. "You still haven't." I trailed my fingers down and squeezed her breast, pinching the nipple through her shirt. She arched her back. "Do you know what it will mean when I come undone?" I slid my hand down further, parting her thighs.

"Yes."

"No you don't, love." I dipped my fingers inside her. "This is mine. Every inch of you is mine. Mine to love. Mine to kiss. Mine to touch. Mine to fuck however I want." My fingers plunged in and out of her.

"If another man tries to touch or take what is mine, do you know what will happen? He'll wish he was never born. The first person on that list is the asshole who groped you." My other hand closed around her throat again. "And you. What will happen to you?"

I applied pressure to both sides of her neck. Not enough to restrict blood flow, but enough to make her squirm when I teased her clit.

"You'll be tied to my bed or wherever I want to restrain you. And then I'll fuck you so long and so hard you won't remember your own name. Only mine."

She clenched around my fingers. I loved how much she loves this.

"Do you understand, Tori?"

"Yes."

"Who do you belong to?" I shoved my fingers deeper inside her, curled them, and pulled out slow. When they hit the spot that drives her mad, her knees buckled.

"You," she whimpered. "I belong to you."

"Yes you fucking do, dirty princess." I let go of her neck and pulled my fingers out. When I stood in front of her to suck my fingers clean, she smiled.

"Do you want to continue?"

"Green."

I walked back over to the desk, turned to face her, and leaned against it.

"Kneel here." I pointed at my feet.

She hadn't taken a full step when I lifted a hand to stop her, lowered my voice, and commanded, "Crawl to me."

Her lips parted on a sharp exhale. A subtle pink stained her cheeks. Her hands shook ever so slightly. All the different ways her body reacted to me went straight to my groin, making my cock exceedingly happy.

The wanton stare she leveled at me as she sank to her knees was almost enough for me to abandon this little game and take her where she was. I could tell from the impassioned glow in her eyes she was having a hard time not saying something smart.

Despite a brief, shallow sigh, she started crawling. Slowly. Deliberately. Eyes locked on mine.

The dark fire burning between us intensified.

"I love watching you, my gorgeous girl. You are so sexy."

I memorized how her back dipped and the supple curve of her ass as she moved. The way pieces of her hair fell and framed her face.

Then she bit her lip and grinned.

Thank fuck I'd trained my body for years not to react until the precise moment. Not moving proved to be a challenge.

Her smile remained when she knelt in front of me. I grabbed her chin, tipping her head up.

I made short work of unzipping my jeans and releasing my cock. "Open."

With a flirtatious gleam in her eyes, she parted her lips. I slipped inside the warmth of her mouth, pushing until I was buried down her throat.

"Fuck...*Victoria*." No matter how many times we've done this, the sensation of her mouth on me always sent a shudder rippling through my body. When she swallowed against me and her throat squeezed around my length, I almost lost it.

"That's my filthy princess. So eager to please," I growled.

Her eyes watered when she looked up at me. My legs shook from the effort it took not to lose control and come down her throat.

Loud, raucous laughter echoed in the hallway. I couldn't remember if I'd locked the door or not. At this point, I did not give one flying shit.

Victoria didn't even flinch at the sound. In fact, she took me in deeper. Part of me wished someone would walk in and marvel at the perfect woman kneeling at my feet, wearing my name on her back, worshipping my cock.

"So good, love," I rasped. "This feels so fucking good." My head fell back. I closed my eyes, getting lost in the silky heat of her mouth, thrusting until I felt the back of her throat.

We settled into a rhythm, slow at first, then faster and harder.

I grabbed the back of her head. "Do you want them to open the door and watch? Do you want to show them all who I belong to?"

She looked up at me, gasping for air, tears spilling from her eyes. Christ, she was a beautiful disaster. Mascara running, her cheeks stained pink, and my cock stuffed in her mouth.

The vibration from her moan, combined with the sensation of her tongue and teeth on my shaft, destroyed me. Violent tremors shook my thighs. My orgasm seared through me, wild and ruthless. I clutched onto the desk and surrendered on a deep moan.

Victoria swallowed every bit, slowly pulled her mouth off me, and glanced up. With a sultry grin, she licked the corner of her mouth where a pearl of cum remained.

Holy. Fuck. That might be the sexiest thing I've ever seen.

The laughter died down out in the hall but I could see shadowed feet from under the door.

"Get up," I ordered, my voice thick with lust. "Go to the door."

Watching her pert ass walk away drove me to the edge. She'd barely made it there before I pressed my body into hers, shoving her against the ornate wood. The low hum of hushed voices saturated the air.

"We have company. Should I continue?"

Her hands pushed hard against the door when she arched her back. "Don't you dare fucking stop."

My hand drifted down to her ass. I slapped it hard. "Is that how you're supposed to answer me?"

Her breaths came out harsh and raspy. "You talk too much, Maddox."

I clamped my other hand around her neck and squeezed. "Is that so?" Another sharp slap on her ass. "Should I continue?"

"Green...*fucking green.*"

A loud, euphoric groan passed her lips when I slammed into her. I fucked her so hard I thought I'd break her. Or the door. It rattled with every brutal thrust, rhythmically announcing what we were doing to whoever stood on the other side of it. And they sure as hell still stood there.

Sex with Victoria always felt like heaven. But this? I've been so *starved* for her. Getting myself off on video chats or phone calls only helped so much. I craved her body, her scent, her moans. Everything.

When I slowed my frantic thrusts she whipped her head around.

"*Xavier*," she panted. "I'm so close…don't stop."

I pulled out, spun her to face me and lifted her. She hooked her legs around my waist just as I slid back inside.

"Do you like getting your pretty cunt pounded with others listening?"

"*Yes.* I…*fuck*…coming."

"You'll finish when I tell you."

Victoria uttered a small warning growl in response. My lips curved in a mixture of amusement and satisfaction.

I pulled almost all the way out, edging her with slow, measured thrusts. Her little moans of protest were all for show. I know she loves when I play like this.

"Beg me, dirty princess." I reached down between us and stroked her clit. "Tell me how much you need me to make you come."

"You feel so…just let me."

I pressed into her, savoring how our bodies molded together with perfection. "Beg me, Tori. I want to hear how much you need me."

Her head thudded against the door in surprise. Edging her was one thing. Making her beg was new.

I held her hips, preventing her from moving. A low growl rumbled in my chest when she clenched around me.

"Are you going to do as I say?"

"Maybe."

"That word will not get you what you want."

The fiery gleam in her eyes lit me up inside. So did the sight of her on the verge of breaking apart. Tousled hair, raspy breaths, skin shining with sweat. An absolute gorgeous fucking mess.

Holding back tortured me just as much but my darker side loved this push and pull.

"Beg." I thrust my hips enough to tease her. She clutched onto my shoulders, writhing from the denial.

"*Oh my God.* Let me, please."

"Let you what?"

"Come. Please, let me come."

I shook my head, grinding against her. "You can do so much better than that."

Her legs tightened around my thighs. She grabbed a handful of my hair and pulled to the point of delicious pain. "I need...*please.*"

I stroked my tongue along her lower lip, slowly thrusting my cock in and out. "You need what?"

She groaned in frustration. "You...I need you...*Xavier,*" she nearly sobbed. "Please let me come."

"That's my girl." I plunged deep inside her. She wanted rough, she's going to get fucking rough.

In and out. Harder and faster each time I staked my claim. Victoria's moans turned into squeals of ecstasy. I fucked her like a man possessed. A man who'd been deprived of how it feels to be inside a woman. When the pressure started building at the base of my spine, I groaned.

I slowed a little, just to prolong what was about to happen.

Victoria's nails dug into my ass, sending shockwaves through me. I reached between us to rub her clit, giving her the release she so clearly deserved.

"Come for me, love."

"*Xavier.*" She bit down on my lower lip. Shit, that hurt in the best way. "Harder. *Please.*"

The sound of her husky demand fueled me.

My mind went blank. I rubbed her clit faster, driving into her not for pleasure alone, but for survival. For my own selfish needs.

Watching her fall apart in front of me was sexy as hell. Her uninhibited screams, her body trembling, her eyelids fluttering shut. The way she held onto me so tight, like she'd never let go.

"*Fuck*," I yelled, surrendering to the electricity coursing through my body. I came so hard I had to press myself against her to remain standing.

My vision blurred. My hips jerked and thrusted. My cock throbbed, viciously pumping cum in a never-ending stream.

This had to be the most intense orgasm I've ever experienced.

Everything went hazy and quiet.

The first thing I became aware of was how gently Victoria ran her fingers through my hair. I didn't remember burying my face in her neck but since I was there, I kissed her glistening skin, breathing hard as my muscles started to loosen and relax. All the tension I'd shoved down the last few months dissipated. Something inside me rebalanced itself.

"Hey," she whispered, still stroking my hair. "You alright?"

I looked at her. "Never better. You?"

"Yeah, I'm…wow." She had a small, dream-like smile.

So beautiful.

An aftershock from my powerful release nearly knocked me to the floor. That never fucking happens. Never.

"Are you sure you're okay? You're a bit unsteady."

"Must be your imagination." I kissed her, wanting to claim her again so completely, so unapologetically, that we'd never be able to survive without each other.

Victoria trembled in my arms, framing my face with her hands. "You've never kissed me like that before."

"Like what?"

Her shy smile pierced the few remaining barriers I kept up. *This woman.* She had no idea the things I would do for her. The lengths I would go. The risks I would take.

"I can't explain it…it felt like…forever." The light touch of her fingers on my scar shook me to the core. "I'm not making any sense."

Forever.

"Makes perfect sense to me."

A silent promise passed between us as our breathing slowed and bodies relaxed.

"Are you okay to stand?" I asked, carrying her away from the door.

"Are you?" she sassed.

"I'm still semi-hard inside you. I don't think you're asking the right question."

"I do enjoy an encore."

"You'll get one. Several, in fact." I smirked, pulling out and holding her close when she slid her legs to the floor. "I'll be fucking you all night in this jersey when I take you to the hotel."

"You're obsessed with the jersey. Athletes and their god complexes."

"You love it." I zipped myself up, noticing a box of tissues on the desk. Not the best option but it'll do until I get her in the shower.

"Care to test that theory?"

"I think I just did." I went to grab the tissues and walked back.

"Ah-ha. The ego strikes first."

I knelt to clean her. When I looked up and met her soft gaze, I smiled.

"What?"

"I…I just really like you on your knees."

"Yeah?" I stood up. "I'll keep that in mind."

She shot me one of her trademark smart ass looks as she grabbed her clothes.

I leaned against the door, watching her redress and fix her makeup.

She pulled her hair out of the elastic, bent forward to comb through it with her hands, and gathered it up again. When she popped back upright, her radiant smile lit my soul on fire. We need to get to the hotel immediately.

"Let's go before I devour the rest of you on that desk."

"Please do," she purred, kissing my cheek.

When I opened the door, we were greeted by Cade. The flustered grin on his face actually made me laugh.

"Can I help you with something, mate?" I asked, wrapping an arm around Victoria's waist.

He shoved his hands in his pockets and looked down. "Uh, I was just walking by."

"Right. And I'm the crown prince of Norway."

"Cade." Victoria's melodic voice sent a shiver down my spine. "Are you blushing?"

The utter look of horror crossing his face amused me beyond reason. Cade and I were quite similar when it came to our confidence around women and the sexual activities we enjoyed. He wasn't embarrassed about what he'd heard. Not in the least.

"Gallagher isn't sure if he should tell us how much he enjoyed himself."

A small laugh escaped Victoria. "Don't be shy. I obviously had a good time."

Cade regained his bravado and announced, "I had three women making the same sounds tonight. Three." His eyes ping-ponged from Victoria to me. "Hearing you lot was alright."

"You have a little something on you." Victoria pointed to the corner of her own mouth.

He did. Lipstick. Bright red, from the looks of it.

"Proof of a good time had by all. You should see where else I have several badges of honor."

"*Cade.*" My low, threatening tone didn't faze him one bit.

"I'll take your word for it," she replied, sliding a hand under my shirt. "Are they full-fledged members of your fan club now?"

"Don't encourage him."

Cade's grin widened. "I'm glad one of you appreciates my recruiting process."

"I wouldn't go that far." I lobbed a good-natured punch to his shoulder before walking away.

By the time we made it back to the hotel, I was more than ready to go another round. And I did. Since I'd been a little too selfish with her at the party, I made sure to give Victoria every ounce of my attention.

I feasted on her until she couldn't breathe, alternating between gentle licks and long, hard pulls on her clit. It was so swollen and tender. When I grazed my teeth against it, her delicate moan arrowed straight to my cock.

Victoria fisted her hand in my hair as I deliberately kept my rhythm slow and soft at first. Her thighs trembled when I started to suck harder. I pushed two fingers inside her, pumping them in and out until my hand was soaked.

Drunk from her scent and greedy for more, I used my tongue. Nothing tasted as good as Victoria. Nothing.

"Xavier." She uttered my name on a whimpered moan.

When I lifted my head to look at her, my blood surged. The most beautiful shade of rose dusted her cheeks. Her lust-drunk eyes glittered in the dim glow from the lights.

"I'm not done yet, love." I dipped my tongue back inside her briefly. "I won't ever be done with you."

Victoria responded with a raspy sigh.

I returned to my slice of heaven, sucking and licking until she shook around me. When her breaths turned sharp and shallow, I hooked my hands around her thighs to keep her from moving. Slowly, and carefully, I nibbled on her clit while stroking my tongue on it. Then I pinched it hard between my teeth for a brief moment. Not even a second later, her entire body surrendered to violent tremors.

"You taste so good," I moaned when the slickness from her orgasm coated my tongue.

Fuck. Forget actual food. I could live off Victoria forever.

Her body relaxed briefly while I gently licked her clit in slow circles, soothing her and coaxing another orgasm.

Hearing her sultry moans and sighs when I laid next to her made the damn *thing* in my chest break into a million pieces.

"I love you," I whispered, pulling her close.

Cupping my face, she pressed a kiss to my mouth. "I love you, too."

Victoria will never fully know or understand what hearing those words come out of her means to me. How affected I am. Knowing she could possibly love the worst parts of me simultaneously terrified and calmed me.

"Xavier?"

"Mmhmm."

"We should take care of this." Her hand grazed over my hard length.

"We will." I moved her hand when she started stroking me. "Give yourself a few minutes to recover then we'll shower."

"Minutes," she scoffed. "I won't be able to walk right for the next few days after what you just did."

"Is that an official complaint?"

"Not even close."

She draped herself on my chest, her hair spilling over my skin in red satin waves. A thoughtful smile curved her lips while she drew lazy circles on my tattoos.

"What is it?" I asked.

"You let yourself go with me tonight. More than you have before."

I closed my eyes, caressing her arm. She's right. I did. And I hadn't even fought against it. I let instinct take over. I've not felt this free or whole since before…

Memories I'd rather not relive flooded my mind. I'll have to deal with them at some point. Not now. I shoved that shit right the fuck down and wrapped Victoria in my arms.

Chapter
TWENTY-ONE

VICTORIA

If Paris was a dream, London was my perfect reality.

Granted, I'd spent less than twenty-four hours in Paris, so essentially it felt like a dream. Xavier and I flew into London early this morning. Not together though. He traveled back with his team; I joined Hannah on her private jet.

Xavier and I met up at his townhouse to regroup before spending the afternoon in the city. My body remained delightfully sore from last night. I could only imagine what he had planned for today.

"Here," I said, handing him the print. "Your present."

The most adorable smile brightened his face and accentuated his dimple. "This is what made you think of me?"

"It was either this or a pillow with a dog wearing a beret."

An eyebrow arched but the smile remained. "Good call. Next time we're in Paris, I'll take you to the Louvre and explain in detail about how it started as a fortress and then became a palace."

"Sounds enchanting."

"Yeah? I can tell you all about who designed the Colonnade and why it's celebrated as a masterpiece of French architecture."

"Have I mentioned how sexy you are when you geek out about this stuff?"

"I'm not geeking out."

"You are one hundred percent geeking out." I kissed him. "I've told you before, it's not a bad trait to have. Embrace it."

"Maybe." An unreadable expression briefly washed over his features. "We should get going. Unless you want to spend all day in here."

"Tempting. But you promised there'd be shopping."

"You'd rather shop than have access to this—" he gestured at his body "—all day?"

"Having access to that—" I mimicked his hand motions "—isn't limited to this townhouse."

"No?"

"Remind me which one of us propositioned the other with public sex the first night we met?"

He smirked. "Regretting your decision to blow me off?"

"I didn't blow you off. I was suffocating under the weight of your ego."

"Wow." His tone dipped into the darker one I loved. "I'm going to save that remark for a rainy day."

"Good thing it rains in England every five minutes."

We decided to go to Leicester Square and Covent Garden. I only had today with him before heading back to Manhattan. My flight was scheduled for seven this evening and I planned to make the most of every second.

"Would you like to go see some of the work I've done on your cottage?" he asked while we strolled through the outdoor market. Several people stopped and whispered when they spotted us. It didn't faze Xavier one bit. Me either, to an extent.

Escorting professional athletes to press conferences or events was part of my job. However, it was much different holding hands with one of them on a crowded street. Especially if said athlete was a global soccer star and had millions of fans. I noticed more than a few onlookers pause to snap photos of us.

"I would but I don't want to waste all day in a car driving back and forth. Next time?"

"Next time." He draped an arm over my shoulders. "I haven't done any work upstairs. Would you prefer if I stay away from your sister's room for now?"

Wisps of guilt and remorse squeezed my chest. Being in Charlotte's room for the first time in nearly twenty years had such an effect on me. It was more than finding her diary or feeling her spirit in every corner.

It felt like I'd lost her all over again, even though everything in her room remained frozen in time.

"I would, yes," I responded quietly. "I'd like to take my time packing her belongings and…yeah, just stay downstairs for now."

He kissed the top of my head.

"How's everything going with the foundation?"

"Good. I think I figured out what the name should be."

We stopped walking to browse items on a vendor's table.

"Are you going to tell me or do I have to guess?" he asked.

"I'll tell you when I'm ready," I teased. "But I will give you a hint. It sort of ties into the meaning behind my tattoo."

Xavier's expression softened. "Still rising from the ashes?"

A lump formed in my throat. "Always."

Two teenage girls ran over and breathlessly asked Xavier for a picture. They giggled and blushed when he agreed.

"We'd like one with you as well," one of them said to me. "If you don't mind."

I smiled, taking the phone from her while they flanked Xavier. "I don't mind."

They were cute. Excited and shy about meeting their favorite soccer player.

Charm came so naturally to Xavier. The genuine smile. The eye contact. The friendly banter. He had an innate way of making people feel at ease, all while luxuriating in their attention.

When it was my turn, I passed the phone off to him and posed with the young girls. They thanked us over and over, looking at the photos and chatting with starstruck grins.

We continued our stroll, bypassing the numerous clothing shops and jewelry stores. I did take a detour into one shop to get a bottle of my favorite perfume.

"Is this what you use?" Xavier asked, spraying it onto a sample card.

"Every day."

His dimple appeared when he waved the card in front of his face. "I'm putting these all over my bedroom so it'll always smell like you."

"That almost sounds not creepy."

I heard him laughing when he walked outside to wait for me while I made my purchase.

"Where to next?" I rummaged through my bag as I approached him on the sidewalk. "Hungry? More shopping? Back to your place for a quickie?"

I found my lip gloss and reapplied some, observing the people around us. My sister would've loved this. All the stories we dreamed up while we people-watched as kids flooded my memory.

"That guy just had his heart broken," Charlotte said, motioning toward the man across from us.

"How can you tell?"

"Easy." She leaned closer to me. "Look at how he's staring into nothing."

"So? I stare into nothing all the time. My heart is in one piece." Honestly, my sister comes up with the weirdest stuff sometimes.

"Tori, you're not paying attention as usual," she scolded. "He's holding a box. I bet it's the engagement ring she turned down. Or something sentimental he gave her that she doesn't want."

I shot her a skeptical look. "You can tell all this from over here?"

"You're insufferable. That's my story for him. What's yours?"

I scrutinized the guy. Average looking. Medium height. Could use some help in the style department. "I bet he's a serial killer and he stuffed some of his victim's underwear in that box as a souvenir."

Charlotte looked at me, horrified. I couldn't hold back my laughter and broke character. "I'm kidding, Charlie. He looks like a high school science teacher about to meet a blind date. He'll bore her with anecdotes about plant cells versus animal cells. But she'll have sex with him because he's not ugly."

"I don't know how we're related," she muttered.

I shook my head and smiled. Poor Charlotte. I don't know how she put up with me.

"Xavier?" I glanced at him, surprised he hadn't responded to my quickie suggestion and found him staring into nothing. Well, not quite nothing. I followed his gaze to where a young boy stood with his father.

There wasn't anything unusual about it. They were talking and laughing. But then I noticed another little boy, standing quietly a couple feet behind them. The dad turned and asked him something. The little boy shrugged and nodded.

His eyes met Xavier's, who stared back with empathy.

That's my story for him. What's yours?

Sadness poured into my heart, dulling some of today's enjoyment. "Xavier? Are you okay?" I gently put my hand on his arm.

"I'm fine, love." He didn't sound fine.

"Let's go find a café and relax for a bit."

We walked until I spotted a small restaurant tucked away on a side street. Only a couple of tables were occupied in the outdoor dining area. Xavier and I were seated in the corner, away from everyone else.

After the server set our drinks on the table, I spoke.

"When Charlotte and I were younger, we'd make up random stories about people if we were out shopping or having lunch or whatever." I kept my tone light. "People watching was one of our favorite things to do."

Xavier rubbed his fingers on his lips, studying me.

I sipped my water and asked with as much sensitivity as I could, "What affected you so much seeing those boys with their dad?"

Even though he's naturally guarded when it comes to talking about his family, Xavier's been allowing himself to show more vulnerability around me. We're both navigating a delicate dance around events that affected us deeply in our youth. It hasn't been easy, but so far, it's been worth it.

Although, I wasn't sure if he'd entertain this question.

Much to my surprise, he did.

"Believe it or not, there was a time when Adam and I actually got along. I wouldn't describe us as *close*, like you were with Charlotte, but..."

I waited, not wanting to push him or ask anything.

"I got it in my head that my father had an easier time showing affection or attention to Adam because he wasn't directly responsible for my mother's death."

A deep, painful ache expanded in my chest.

"I know this look, Tori," he said quietly. "It's not about blame or guilt. I've seen enough therapists in my life, trust me. Disliking Adam was my coping mechanism. I channeled all the unresolved pain and directed it at him. Adam and I fought constantly. My dad didn't know what to do or how to deal with me, so we stopped communicating. We're both stubborn, so once that happened our relationship was pretty much done. After I was accepted into Royal City's development league, I threw myself into football and left everything else behind."

I blinked back tears. Xavier gave me a hard smile.

"Not what you expected?" His acerbic laugh scorched my lungs. "At sixteen, I alienated the only parent I had left, and he didn't give a shit. Pride and arrogance. The best of the Maddox family traits and I inherited both of them from my father."

I reached for his hand and held it. Tension lined every muscle in his face. Haunted sadness ghosted through his eyes before dissipating. So much of what he'd told me resonated with my own shattered past. My relationship with my mother remained fractured beyond repair.

"You once told me everyone responds to grief differently." I spoke low and gentle. "I am so sorry you carry this with you."

In situations like this, any words or platitudes felt hollow. I didn't know what else to say. All I wanted to do was ease this for him in some way. But how can one broken person possibly offer anything to heal another?

"I've never told anyone that before. About what happened with my dad. I..." Xavier's expression blanked as he stood up. "Let's go. I'm sure you don't want to listen to me tell sad stories all afternoon."

The ache returned to my chest. I did want to hear his stories. I wanted to know everything. Our time together was too short.

We paid and left the café. As we approached the main street, Xavier paused. "Tori."

"Yes?"

"I'm glad you're here."

I caught his eye in time to notice another mysterious veil dissolve. Only this one wasn't covering any hidden dark desires. This one revealed a deep affection I haven't seen before.

"There's no place else I'd rather be." I laced my fingers through his and squeezed.

His gaze held mine for one brief, burning moment before he looked away, jaw flexing.

"I'm changing your flight. There's somewhere I want to take you."

VICTORIA

A soccer field.

Not sure what I'd expected but an empty soccer field wasn't anywhere on my list.

The scent of fresh cut grass saturated the air as he guided me toward one of the goals. From the size of it, it was meant for children.

My heart stuttered.

Was this…?

"We aren't too far from where I grew up," he said, seemingly able to read my thoughts. "Which means we also aren't far from Briarcliff Village. I know you said you didn't want to spend the day in a car but now that your flight is much later, we have time."

"I'll remember to thank you for this when I'm half asleep at work tomorrow," I teased.

"As you may have guessed, this is the pitch I used when I was a kid."

"When you dreamed of being a striker?"

"You remembered. Impressive, Chase."

"I pay attention to everything you say, Maddox."

His throaty laugh slid across the humid, August air. I soaked in every part of him. He stood casually in the goal with his arms up, hands grasping the crossbar. Pieces of the detached, frayed net swayed in the soft breeze.

No designer clothes for him today. Just jeans, a t-shirt, and sneakers. Tousled hair and bright eyes.

"You look cute. I'm going to put you all over social media."

"Cute?" An eyebrow went up.

I pointed my phone at him. "Hot. Sexy. Insufferably snobbish. Is that better?" I snapped a few photos when he laughed.

"Did you get what you wanted?"

"Yeah." *He's perfect.* "I did."

The world saw him as an arrogant, talented athlete. The charmer. The unattainable object of so many desires. And he absolutely was all of those things.

But I got to see him like this.

Unguarded, relaxed, not craving the attention of millions.

Here, he was just Xavier. I could almost see the little boy who wanted to be a striker, and longed to impress his dad.

The air shifted when I looked at him. Playful flirting morphed into something more insistent.

"Come over here, city princess. I have to tell you something."

"Bossing me around?" I approached him, resting my hand on his chest. "What do you have to tell me that's so important I needed to be right here."

"I just like having you close to me."

"Sneaky flirt."

"You know you like it." He studied me for a few seconds. "Enjoying your day so far?"

"I am. Although I'm not entirely sure why you brought me to a soccer field."

"Football pitch." Xavier's devilish smile unfurled a forbidden puff of smoke in my stomach. "Stand against the post and see if you can reach the crossbar, like I'm doing."

My pulse fluttered. *He wouldn't.* "We both know I can't reach that. What is it? Almost seven feet high?"

"Probably." He backed me up against it anyway. "Arms up. Hold on where you can."

I reached over my head, gripping the post. The way he looked at me stole my breath.

"What do you have in mind?"

Xavier leaned close, rasping his fingers down the front of my strapless maxi dress. "I want to tie you to this post. And then I want to see how far I can push your limits." He watched me carefully, his dark eyes reflecting the sunlight. "Do you want that?"

I nodded without hesitation while trying to control the insistent throbbing between my thighs.

"I can't hear you."

"How much longer do I have to keep saying this?"

"Until I say otherwise." His heated gaze tore through me. "Do you want me to push your limits?"

"Green."

"Good," he whispered, kissing me softly. "Don't move."

A few thoughts ran through my mind while he went off to do whatever it was he was doing. The most obvious being someone could show up at any time. Not sure how it would play out in the media if England's number one was caught fucking a girl tied to a soccer goal.

I mean, it turned *me* on but...

Crawl to me.

What we'd done last night at the chateau sizzled through my veins. His visceral reaction to seeing me crawl across the room burned itself onto the deepest, darkest parts of my soul. I'd do it again in a heartbeat if he wanted.

"I told you not to move." Xavier's warning tone made me jump.

"I...oh." Dammit. My arms were down. "Sorry."

"You will be." He lifted a torn piece of netting. "Arms up."

I did as he ordered, keeping my eyes locked on his. The intensity of his stare complimented the silky darkness in his tone.

"Put your hands through here and then hold onto the post again."

I tucked my hands into the mesh squares and clenched my thighs together when I felt the first bite of material wrap tight around my wrists. Then I reached up and grabbed the post. Xavier grinned, binding my wrists together with the netting and securing them to the goal.

"Beautiful." He caressed my cheek. "Are you comfortable? Does anything hurt too much?"

He'd tied me up pretty tight but I liked how the mesh dug into my skin.

"I'm comfortable."

"You say that now." Dipping his head, he pressed his mouth to the base of my throat. My normal reflex is to sink my hands in his hair. I gasped from the inability to move and the sharp sting of the netting. His kisses branded a path from my neck to my mouth. "Still comfortable?"

Our lips hovered close. Dangerously close.

"Yes."

"I love seeing you like this." His eyes hooded. "Only you. And here's how I'll prove it."

My muscles pulled taut when his fingers skimmed along my arms, down my sides to my hips, and back up. He did it again. And again. The feather-light touches scattered goosebumps on my skin. Getting tickled wasn't one of my favorite things but every graze of his hands went straight to my clit.

"I've fantasized about doing this since you described your university experience." Xavier's warm breath caressed my lips. "I thought tying you to the goal would be more fun than kneeling on a floor."

Another long, slow caress traced the length of my body from the swell of my breasts to the top of my thigh. A sound between a gasp and a yelp clawed its way out of my throat when he pulled down my dress and brushed his thumbs over my nipples, teasing them into hard peaks.

"You are so soft," he whispered, cupping my breasts and tracing their curves. "Tell me, dirty princess, am I making you wet?"

Not breaking eye contact, I nodded.

The damp warmth of his breath tickled my ear when he said, "I know you are, love. Your scent is intoxicating."

Desire pulsed through my veins. The urge to touch him overpowered me. He stood so close, yet I was powerless to reach for him.

Slanting his head, he licked his lips and smiled. "Do you want something?" The teasing and seductive edge to his voice slid over my skin, along with his hands. *Those hands that don't miss.*

Velvet caresses outlined my jaw, neck, collarbone, and stomach. When I thought he was finished, he started again, stimulating different areas of my body.

"*Xavier*. You feel...*oh my god.*"

My breathing turned ragged and my heart raced. His hands...his hands were everywhere. Touching. Exploring. Taking.

"Xavier, *please.*"

The heat from his body disappeared when he pulled away, leaving me shaky and craving more. I squirmed against the restraint.

"Looks like we still have a lot of work to do on your patience, Victoria." Xavier yanked my dress all the way down, tapping my legs so I could step out of it. He slung it over the crossbar, then removed my panties and stuffed them in his pocket. A smile that screamed filthy fantasies curled his mouth when he stroked his jaw.

"You're so gorgeous tied up." He approached, clamping a hand around my neck. "What should I do with you now?" His other hand slid between my legs as his tone darkened. "I know. I'll make you come as hard and as often as I want."

A needy whimper escaped me.

"Oh, Victoria." His voice poured out like molten lava. "I'll make you beg for it first, love. You like that don't you?" My mouth dropped open on a silent moan when his finger slipped inside me. "The idea of begging me while you're helpless and bound turns you on, doesn't it?" Another finger entered me. "My fiery, independent city princess. So willing to trust me with your pleasure." A rough stroke on my clit nearly shredded me. "So willing to surrender everything to me." Another rough stroke. And another. "So. Fucking. Willing."

"*Please*," I begged as hot desire prickled over my skin. It wasn't simply the feel of him or the tight bindings or how he sounded that drove me closer to the edge. It was the feral play, the filthy ways he wanted me, and how he teased and tortured every inch of my body.

He withdrew his fingers and painted my lips with my own desire for him. Then he licked across them before kissing me hard and deep. I tugged against the mesh netting so ferociously I thought I might actually break free.

"You're not getting out yet." The damp heat of his lips brushed mine when he spoke. "I have something to give you first."

Without breaking eye contact, he lowered himself to his knees. I was already a soaking wet mess but now? Seeing Xavier Maddox fall to his knees for me? The intensity snatched the breath right from my lungs.

"You have the prettiest cunt I've ever seen." He leaned forward, tasting me with a lazy lick. "Fuck," he moaned. "Spread your legs wider, love. I'm going to savor you."

I trembled, doing as he requested.

Xavier took his time, using his tongue to seek out my clit. The steady licks buckled my knees. So did the long pulls and hard sucking.

Two fingers dipped inside me, plunging in and out. All my muscles pulled taut again when I felt his slick fingers slide back toward my ass.

"Wha-what are you…?" I've done quite a bit of experimenting but this wasn't something I ever tried.

He gazed up at me with sinful eyes and stroked the opening, rubbing it and applying gentle pressure. I nearly saw stars. He felt and looked like temptation and darkness. Then his tongue circled my clit.

"That…that feels…oh my god."

I fucking lost it. An orgasm exploded behind my eyes and shook me so violently I thought I'd pull the whole goal down.

All I felt was him.

His hands, his mouth, his tongue. All coaxing more.

I surrendered to the dark flames that burned between us, consumed by it.

This orgasm went on forever, sending electric shocks through me over and over. When it finally subsided, my senses rushed back in a deafening wave.

Xavier remained on his knees with his arms wrapped around my legs and his head pressed against my stomach. I don't know how long we stayed like this. I was so dazed I didn't even feel him stand up.

"Tori," he said silkily, unzipping his jeans but not fully undressing. The tip of his cock slid along my swollen pussy.

"I…I need you, Xavier." I almost didn't recognize the throaty dip in my voice. "I need all of you. I *want* all of you. Every piece you hide, I want to see them all. Let yourself go with me."

He let out a low groan. "I will. We'll be broken and beautiful together." Eyes wild with hunger flicked over me as he hooked my legs around him. "You're so perfect for me…so perfect."

His gentle praise ignited feelings I didn't know existed. And then he slammed into me and fucked me the way I wanted. The way we both wanted.

Brutal. Untamed.

Not only did he fill me to the hilt, he also rubbed my clit without mercy. He was relentless. His fingers, his thrusts, his sharp panting.

My world narrowed and devolved into a carnal haze of rough sex, deep moans and grunts, and the delicious pain from being strung up.

I craved release but I never wanted this to stop.

Xavier's grip on me tightened as he lifted my thighs higher. The angle let him slide in deeper.

"So fucking beautiful." He pushed into me harder and faster. "You're *mine*, Tori. Forever."

The dark possessiveness in his voice ignited the ache in my core. It built to an excruciating level.

He stopped his frantic thrusts, staying buried inside me.

"Show me who I belong to."

Reaching down between us, he pinched my clit.

"*Xavier….I…Oh…*" My screams echoed through the sultry summer air. I climaxed so hard tears streamed down my face.

His measured thrusts drew out my release while he rode through it, finally coming on a loud groan.

I collapsed, as much as I could, into a heap of liquid bones. Closing my eyes, I tried to catch my breath. Soft kisses covered my cheeks as even softer caresses wiped away my tears.

The haze of post-orgasmic sex settled over us in a thick cloud. If not for Xavier's gentle rubbing on my wrists, I never would have realized he untied me.

"I'll put something on these when I take you back to my flat," he said, sounding a little concerned.

I looked at the red marks on my wrists.

"Does it hurt?" he asked.

"No."

Xavier cupped my face with both hands, searching me with uneasy eyes. "You would tell me if it did?"

"Of course I would. It doesn't hurt. I promise."

"Okay." He reached for my clothes and helped me redress.

When we sat on the grass in the goal, the optics made me smile.

"What is it?"

"I think I just scored on you."

His breathless laugh charmed me. So did his flushed skin, lust-drunk eyes, and wide, dimpled smile. Somehow, he looked even more gorgeous than ever.

"Don't tell anyone."

I reclined against him, resting a hand on his thigh. Closing my eyes, I imagined Xavier as a teenager, honing his skills on this field. I know he met Cade when they were kids, and then Bennet entered the picture a few years later.

It still floored me to know I'd vacation here every summer with my family and never once did I run into him. My heart fluttered. But Charlotte did.

After a few minutes I asked, "Did you ever go to the bonfires when you were a teenager?"

Birds chirped in the distance to fill the prolonged silence.

"I went to all of them," he finally answered.

"Isn't it wild how we never crossed paths?" I looked up at him. "You probably wouldn't have noticed me anyway. Not with your harem always surrounding you."

His quiet laugh swathed my heart in warmth. "You make it sound like they covered the ground in rose petals everywhere I walked."

"I bet they would have if you'd asked."

"Probably." He pulled me onto his lap and swept a thumb over my cheek. "The only reason I know we never crossed paths back then is because if I *had* seen you, I would have made you mine from the start."

My pulse sped up. "You're too charming for your own good. I realize I'm not a wallflower but I'd still be just another faceless girl clamoring for your attention."

"You're wrong, love." He banded both arms around me. "You could no sooner blend into a crowd than a star could hide from the darkest night."

The weight of his words rooted deep in my soul.

"When I, um," I cleared my throat. "When I first started reading Charlotte's diary and learned she was dating your stepbrother, I had this…thought."

"Do I want to know?"

I smiled, pressing a hand to his cheek. "It's nothing bad. I just…I'm not a big believer in fate but it almost felt like she'd tethered us with an invisible ribbon. It's like she knew we'd eventually meet or—"

"The strength of your light would have led me to you." The warmth of his hands burned through my dress when he slid them around my waist. "I felt it the moment I saw you."

"Felt what?"

Eyes bluer than the summer sky latched onto mine. "That there's nobody else for me. That it's only…" He paused, inhaling a shaky breath. "Only you, Tori. For as long as I breathe, only you."

The slow sweep of his thumb over my lips sent shivers rushing in waves along my skin. Never in my wildest, most uninhibited dreams did I imagine someone would say that to me.

"Xavier, I—"

His firm, passionate kiss finished what I was about to say. If the world ended right now, I wouldn't have one regret because I was with the only man I could ever, and would ever, love.

"We should head out." Xavier's somber tone brought reality rushing back when he broke our kiss. "Unless you want to stay here with me."

"Forever?"

His grin took on a wicked slant. "Careful what you wish for, love."

"I told you already. *You* are what I wish for."

"And you have me." He squeezed my waist. "Up you go."

He helped me stand, and then hooked his hands on the crossbar again.

The longer I stared at him, the more my heart ached for a reason I couldn't name.

"Am I really not going to see you again until we come here for the game in October?"

A gentle smile pulled at his lips. "Miss me already?"

"Your arrogance is showing."

"You love it."

"Maybe."

"Almost as much as you love me."

"Wow. I'd almost forgotten about how highly you think of yourself."

"Glad I could be here to remind you." His smile grew wider. "To answer your question, I'm hoping to fly over to see you during my international break next month."

"Next *month*? How will I survive?"

"You'll manage."

I rested my hand on his chest, standing on my toes to kiss him. "Thank you for Paris. And for today." I pressed another light kiss to his lips. "Thank you for opening up the way you did about your dad. I know it wasn't easy."

Xavier released the crossbar and wrapped his arms around me.

"Everything is easier with you." The rawness in his voice twisted around my heart like a vine. Butterflies flitted through my stomach when he cupped his hand behind my neck, massaging it with his fingers. "The luckiest day of my life was seeing you on the side of that road. I feel like," he swallowed hard. "I feel like I could tell you everything and you'd still love me. You'd let me stay in your light and stop me from spiraling."

I hurt someone.

Tears burned my eyes recalling what he'd started to tell me all those weeks ago at the ring ceremony. "Everyone deals with trauma in their own time. When you're ready to confront it, I'll be here to listen."

His heartbeat thundered beneath my hand. A tumultuous storm swirled in the depths of his sapphire eyes. Confessing the hurt over what happened with his dad was only a small piece of a much more textured past. I sensed it from the way he held me.

He confirmed it when he kissed me like he was drowning, and I was the only thing keeping him alive.

I melted into him, letting myself get swept away. The love we shared was so powerful it nearly extinguished the nagging, persistent voice in my mind always whispering *you don't deserve any of this.*

Chapter
TWENTY-THREE

Reality slapped me in the face.

Hard.

Two weeks ago I'd been blissfully holed up with Xavier in Paris and London.

Now? Life in Manhattan imploded.

Tre Gideon bruised his knee in practice. Dante Milano failed a PED test and was promptly suspended four games. Oh, and Noah Tate thought it would be hilarious to go skateboarding for a stupid social media post and sprained his finger.

The silver lining was the finger happened to be on Noah's non-throwing hand. Little victories.

All of this happened as the final preseason game inched closer.

"Is your season ruined now?" Killian propped his feet up on the coffee table.

We were lounging in his living room after returning from Sunday brunch. We'd met up with Noah and Tracey to finalize some of the marketing and financial plans for Charlotte's foundation. Most of the discussion revolved around the inaugural event, which Killian nearly hijacked and turned into a masquerade ball.

Thank goodness Max stepped in as the voice of reason.

"I don't know." I rubbed my temples, trying to ignore the muted pain throbbing behind my eyes.

Aside from the player injuries, preparing for the home opener has been insane. The Legends were kicking off the regular season with a primetime game. My days were filled with media requests, pre-interviews, player and coach availabilities, digging myself out of a never-ending string of emails, and putting the final touches on the media plan for the entire season.

I haven't even had a chance to see the boys until today. And Xavier? Let's just say our communication has been minimal at best now that his new season was in full swing.

"I'm the best sports-baller fill in if you need one." Killian clasped his hands together. "Or you could ask Hotty McBodyguard to be the new quarterback. What's the deal with him anyway?"

I flopped back against the couch with an audible sigh. "His name is Marcus Hanson and he works for the Caldwells. That's all I know."

Xavier and I did manage to work out the whole babysitter situation. I really didn't like how frantic he'd become the night my car was vandalized. If having someone shadow me meant peace of mind for him, I'd be willing to bend. I agreed to have Marcus be my security detail only if he didn't interfere with every little thing in my life.

So far, so good.

"Baby girl, I don't need names. I need vital stats. Single?"

Maxim cleared his throat loudly. "I. Am. Right. Here."

I flung a pillow at my best friend. "Stop."

A boisterous laugh echoed through the room. "When did the two of you become such prudes? Max knows I'd never do anything. And you—" he threw the pillow at my head "—haven't said one word about what happened with that photo. You're a minor celebrity in England."

Right. The photo of Xavier and I from after the game in Paris.

It went viral and got picked up by several tabloids in the U.K. Apparently dating England's number one can't be kept a secret forever. Not that we were hiding it.

My social media following shot through the roof. Captioning it *Mon amour* probably sped up the whole process. So did posting the picture of him from our late afternoon tryst at his childhood soccer field. I'd captioned that one *He's a keeper* with a blue heart emoji. People ate it up.

"It was bound to happen." I shrugged.

Killian propped his head on his hand. "You're so blasé about it. I'd be terrified of a stalker or something."

"That's what Marcus is for," I responded, trying to sound unbothered. Not sure if I succeeded.

My best friend eyed me with interest. "Does he still drive you everywhere?"

"Yep."

"But your car is fixed."

"I know."

"Then tell him to go take a long walk off a short pier. You're a big girl. You can drive yourself to work."

"Babe." Max's tone was stern. "Leave her alone."

"I almost forgot," I said, ignoring them. "I bought you something Parisian."

Killian's face lit up. A small part of me felt bad when I handed him the gift bag.

He dug out the present, tossing tissue paper to the floor. His exuberant expression fell.

"Why?" He glowered, holding up the little mime statue.

"It's whimsical."

"You're a heathen." The way Killian tossed it over to Max reminded me of when we played hot potato as kids.

"It's a *mime* not a spider." I took it from Max and put it on the table. "See? It's just like you. Expressive, almost to a ridiculous degree."

Winston galloped over and jumped on the couch next to me. I scratched him behind the ears. "Mind if I take him outside?"

Winston tilted his head and stared at me. I haven't met a dog yet who doesn't get excited by *outside.*

"Please. And take your time." Killian grabbed the leash for me. "Make sure he doesn't get into anything gross."

"Yes, your grace. The little prince shall have his paws wiped after every step."

"The sarcasm isn't necessary."

"But it *is* fun." I blew a kiss and headed to the elevator.

On cue, Marcus appeared at the front door when I walked outside. Clad in a designer suit with his hands clasped behind his back, he looked like a rogue Secret Service agent. Or an assassin. Either way, totally intimidating.

As much as I don't want to admit it, I've gotten used to the quiet, statuesque man following me around.

Seriously. Marcus embodied the strong but silent type.

We walked toward the dog park without saying a word. The silence didn't bother me much when he drove me to and from work but it did now. I slowed my stride a little.

"Everything okay, Ms. Chase?" His deep voice sounded behind me.

"Yep. I just figured since you're walking with me we could, you know, chat. If that's okay with you."

"Yes, ma'am." He fell into step next to me.

"First thing, please don't call me *ma'am*. Ms. Chase is alright, I suppose. But it's not against the law to call me Victoria."

A beat passed before he responded. "Yes, ma'am."

Christ on a stick.

"So what's your story, Marcus?" I asked, opening the gate. Not many people were in the park. "Did you dream of working for a private security firm when you were a kid?"

Winston stopped to sniff around. I took the opportunity to study my brooding, tall escort. No smile, no hint of amusement, nothing.

"I'll take your lack of response as a yes." I peeked at Winston. He rolled around in the dirt. *Killian will love that.*

"I'm a former Navy SEAL, ma'am."

My eye twitched. "How'd you make the leap from special ops to personal security?"

Was that a shrug?

"Training athletes has always been a bit of a side hobby. Most of my clients after I left the SEALs were football players. When this detail opened up years ago with the Caldwell family, I jumped at it."

Interesting.

"Have you ever considered working on the strength and conditioning staff? I know a few teams in the league are hiring."

"Thought about it."

"The idea of shadowing a media relations director seemed more exciting?" I joked.

Another bout of stern silence.

"I do what the Caldwell family asks."

Winston tugged at his leash when a squirrel ran by. I double wrapped it around my wrist. He might be little but he's feisty.

I wasn't going to pull any additional information out of Marcus. I could tell by the way he stared at the tree.

Fine.

Winston happily followed me when I sat down on a nearby bench to text Xavier.

XAVIER

"Thanks for agreeing to see me." Adam strolled through my flat, pausing at the display case filled with awards and medals. "At least nobody will ever mistake you for being humble."

"This is how you're starting? You're welcome to leave."

"Relax, Xavier. I'm only teasing you." He waved a hand at the shelves. "It's impressive." Adam's drawl reminded me of my father's; smooth and casual. He'd picked up a few of the Maddox family traits over the years. Hard not to.

A debonair charmer, Adam always made everyone feel at ease.

People often mistook us for brothers by birth. Physically, I could sort of see why. We're both tall with dark hair and light eyes.

But he lacked the one trait that made me an actual Maddox, and him just Adam Bourne.

Arrogance.

He oozed charisma without the sharp edge I inherited.

Spending Sunday evening hanging out with my stepbrother wasn't high on my list of things to do. But he'd insisted.

"What do you want?" I asked, pulling my phone out of my pocket when it vibrated.

Tori: Tell me your day is way more interesting than mine

I smiled, typing a reply.

"I think I know what Jordan is up to," he told me just as I sent *it's terribly boring* to Victoria.

Not so boring anymore. "Explain."

Adam tapped his fingers on the arm of the couch before sitting. "Remember Philip?"

I groaned in frustration. "Yes. We had this conversation already. What's—"

"He's working on a new project for one of their clients. It's a start-up tech company that specializes in creating computer generated content. Images, videos, that sort of thing."

"I thought he was just the security guy."

I was subjected to one of Adam's dramatic eye rolls. "For fuck's sake, Xavier, you never listen to me. Tech lead. He's the tech lead for the security team."

"Meaning?"

A blank stare preceded his answer. "Meaning he detects and responds to cyberthreats, and he makes sure the clients' networks are safe. It also means he could *cause* those cyberthreats. Should I simplify or did you grasp all that?"

Tori: Want me to make it not boring?

I squeezed the phone, wishing Adam would go away. "Why are you telling me this?"

A tense silence vibrated between us.

"The new client is based in Manhattan," he finally said.

I dropped my phone. Adam flicked his eyes down and back up.

"Philip is working out of that office until the end of the year."

The muscles in my jaw twitched. "What does any of this have to do with Jordan?"

"I don't know. But Philip told me Jordan also has an office in the same building. It's not related to the tech company stuff but…it's weird. Jordan mainly focuses his attention on London, Paris, and Frankfurt, vying for business on the political and financial stages in Europe, not in the States." Adam held my laser stare. "I told you he has it out for you. What happened?"

That's a fucking loaded question.

"It's a long story," I admitted, sitting on the arm of the chair. "You know how he can be."

"Yeah." Adam examined me with empathy. Not something I've seen from him in a long time. "I've been thinking a lot about back then. I was friends with that prick. I saw what he did to people and I stayed friends with him." He hung his head, shoulders slumping. "I was so blinded by trying to be like you that I couldn't see what was really going on."

Wait one fucking second. "Repeat that last part."

Regret flooded my stepbrother's demeanor when he stood up and walked to the door. "You heard what I said, asshole. We'll get into all that another time. I just thought you needed to know about Jordan."

"How do you know all this?"

"I told you. Philip and I have remained in touch over the years." He spoke so low I almost didn't catch it. "Do you remember what happened at the bonfire that one summer? When you and Jordan got into a fight?"

I snickered. "Narrow it down for me. All we did was fight."

Adam looked thoughtful. "True. He was quite miffed about not making the Royal City development team. He sucked as a striker though. Come to think of it, he sucked as a winger, too. He shouldn't have been surprised they didn't want him."

The way Adam looked at me transported me back to the first day I met him. We were eight. My father and Rebecca thought it would be easier if they introduced us in a casual setting. We'd been on the pitch, kicking the ball around.

I remembered not thinking much about him except it would be fun to have a younger brother, even though we're only five months apart. But he'd looked at me like he already idolized me in some way. Like I was the older brother he'd always wanted.

A grin tugged at my lips. "He did suck."

For a split second, all the animosity between us dissipated.

"Anyway." Adam shoved his hands in his pockets. "Thought you'd want to know since Victoria lives there. Hope everything's going alright with you two now that you're splashed all over the gossip sites."

"One thing about Victoria is she knows how to handle the media. We're fine. Thanks though."

Without saying another word, he left. The door closed quietly behind him.

What the fuck is going on?

Chapter
TWENTY-FOUR

The following week flew by faster than I thought it would. We had a match on Wednesday, and another one set for Sunday. I still wasn't able to talk to Victoria much since her schedule this week was just as hectic.

Cade pestered me nonstop Friday at training for a night out in London. Begrudgingly, I agreed.

"Should we show up unannounced at the estate after this?" Cade asked, pulling at the sleeves of his shirt. "We haven't been there in nearly a month."

We'd just arrived at Constellations, one of the more exclusive lounges in the city for dinner. The clientele generally consisted of business professionals, athletes, politicians, and celebrities.

Contrary to my reputation, being here wasn't quite what I wanted to do tonight. Going to Bennet's? Not even an option. I had a small window of opportunity to speak with Victoria later, and wanted to be home.

"It's your funeral, mate."

"Oh, come on. It's fucking Bennet, not some psycho."

"You've obviously never been golfing with him."

"Neither have you," he laughed. "Besides, golfing isn't my thing."

"You need a hobby."

"I have one." Cade stopped walking. His lips stretched into a smug smile. "In fact, I have three. They're all coming over tomorrow night."

"Are they of legal age?"

I barely managed to avoid his poor attempt at punching my arm.

"Come over and find out."

Cade's general demeanor on any given day fluctuated between smart ass, charmer, and asshole. We're quite similar in that regard and it's probably one of the reasons we get on so well.

We sat at a table near the bar where I spent way too much time half-listening to him talk about his three 'hobbies.'

"Everything good with Victoria?" His question surprised me.

"Yeah. We haven't really spoken much lately."

He cocked his head to the side. "Care to elaborate?"

"Nothing to elaborate on. She's busy. I'm busy."

"Lot of bullshit falling out of your mouth," he scolded. "How can you be too busy for her?"

I arched an eyebrow. "We text every day. And we're going to speak later. Not that it's any of your bloody business."

Cade leaned back in his chair, casually sipping his beer and smirking at me. "You're going to marry her, aren't you?"

A weird ache in my chest briefly prevented me from breathing.

That's not normal.

I dismissed it as acid reflux from all the scotch.

"People keep throwing that word around." I downed the rest of my drink, adding to the discomfort.

Cade laughed. "Mate, you should see your face right now. You shouldn't be afraid of marriage."

"Says the guy with three hobbies on stand by."

He waved his hand dismissively. "I will say I'm surprised it's you diving into the whole long-term relationship thing. Always thought Bennet would settle down first."

The more Cade examined me with amusement, the more I wanted to go home. Larger-than-life personality aside, he was observant as fuck and as soon as he'd catch a whiff of vulnerability from me, he'd pounce.

My silence only confirmed whatever he was thinking.

"I'm happy for you." He knocked his glass against mine. "But if I'm not the best man, there will be hell to pay."

I shook my head and laughed. Cade glanced over my shoulder with intrigue.

"Interested duo moving in behind you."

"Of course," I muttered. Normally I didn't mind getting noticed. Wasn't really feeling it tonight, though.

"Gentlemen." A statuesque blonde paused next to me, resting her hand on my shoulder. "Hope we're not bothering you. My friend here—" she gestured at the petite brunette standing next to Cade "—tells me you're both footballers. I don't really follow the sport. I said you both worked in advertising. Do I owe her a drink or what?"

Cade didn't waste any time indulging them. "You do. But I insist on paying if you'd both like to join us."

They did.

The blonde sat next to me, the brunette next to Cade. It didn't take long for us to learn their names, occupations, and favorite drinks.

Stacia (the blonde) worked in real estate and loved red wine. Pippa (the brunette) was a candy heiress who only drank beer.

A candy heiress? Scotch, and annoyance at my friend, burned through my blood. I did my best at fake smiling while they flirted around me.

The usual shit.

A wanton smile. A soft laugh.

A hand on an arm or a leg.

In my case, Stacia not only grabbed my thigh but made sure to curl her hand around it.

"My flat isn't too far from here." Her low voice pushed through the hum of conversation and into my ear. "You should take me home. Teach me everything you know about—" her hand slid further up my thigh "—football."

How many times have I been in this situation and decided to take someone up on their offer without batting an eye? Fuck. Too many times.

"Sorry. Not interested." My answer came out gruffer than I'd meant. I don't like being rude unless the moment calls for it.

Her skin flushed a faint red. "I don't see any wedding ring. It's impossible for a man as attractive as you to be single."

For some reason, I don't think it would matter to her if I was, in fact, married.

"I have a serious girlfriend. I'm not looking to ruin my relationship." I stood up. "If you'll excuse me."

Stacia's stunned expression told me everything I needed to know about her. Apparently she wasn't used to rejection.

Cade didn't seem to mind that I'd abandoned him. Suppose now he could add these two to his growing list of hobbies.

I stopped at the bar and ordered another scotch.

While I waited, I scanned the room. It was fairly crowded here tonight. I recognized some of the lads from United at a table in the corner. I didn't see Zach, though.

We'd been on better terms since the friendly in Paris. We even exchanged a few texts and made plans to meet for dinner before the London derby. Pretty sure Royal City would come out on top for this one.

Just as I turned to collect my drink I heard, "Out charming the socialites, Maddox?"

Jesus Christ.

Jordan stood next to me and leaned against the bar without a fucking care in the world.

I glared at him in silence. Figures he'd show up here. It'd been weeks since we've crossed paths. In fact, the last time we did, I nearly throttled him.

My hand clenched into a fist. All I could think about was him cornering Victoria in Manhattan.

A knowing smile spread across his face.

"They do like to buzz around you, don't they? Must be tempting with so many women always wanting a piece of you."

I had a couple of options. I could ignore this piss poor excuse for a human and go back to my friend.

Or…

"Surprised to see you here. Thought you'd be moonlighting in New York again."

Some of the bluster faded from his eyes. If there's one thing Jordan couldn't stand, it's when someone was one step ahead of him. I kept my expression neutral and pressed him further.

"I hear you're branching out in business. Taking an interest in American tech start-ups. Or are you offering your unique brand of security protection to the upper echelon of New York? Money and European politics aren't exciting enough for you anymore?"

I casually sipped my drink, relishing the absolute look of shock seizing hold of his face. Maybe having Adam's information could work in my favor after all.

A slight twitch of his lips preceded a rather chilly response. "The thing about footballers is they're not very smart off the pitch. Stick with what you know."

"What's the matter? Did I break some aristocratic code?" I smirked. "Is your useless title tarnished now?"

"Good to see the Maddox arrogance is on full display as usual." He regained his composure. "I do like New York. So much...*opportunity* there, if you know what I mean."

I stared at the glass in my hand. Smashing it into his face would solve this problem. Unfortunately, with the amount of witnesses in the vicinity it would also lead to legal issues, messy news headlines, and general unpleasantness for me.

Dr. Frances' sage advice about putting myself in situations where losing control would be detrimental to my public image flitted through my mind.

He's going to get an earful from me on Monday.

"Stay away from her," I said as evenly as I could.

"Who?" Jordan's eyebrows arched up, contrasting with the smug smile twisting his mouth.

"Playing dumb is a bad look on you. Stay the fuck away from her."

"I'm the least of your worries. Victoria is an intelligent, gorgeous woman. And now that she's plastered all over the tabloid websites and gossip columns thanks to you, she'll get loads of attention."

A low growl rose in my throat. "Attention? Like the asshole you paid to harass her at that restaurant?"

Jordan's laugh chilled my blood. "Mate, I have no idea what you're talking about."

"The hell you don't." Keeping my tone civilized was challenging. "I hope you're not planning to ambush my girlfriend again."

The image of him cornering her on the sidewalk turned my blood to lava.

Distain colored Jordan's expression. "The only one being ambushed right now is me. I have little energy for your paranoia. I'm running a business. Speaking of," he reclined on his elbow, "I heard you secured Apex Jewelers. That's a big endorsement. Worldwide advertising campaign? Including in the States? You'll have endless admirers. I do hope Victoria can handle the spotlight."

"Leave her alone or I'll make your life miserable."

"Go back to charming your socialites. You never were very good at following through on any threats."

I stepped closer to him, resting my arm on the bar. His slight flinch didn't go unnoticed. "You're a coward, Jordan. You talk a lot of shit and then slink off to the shadows to let someone else do the dirty work. When I prove it was you behind Victoria's car being vandalized and that fucking guy putting his hands on her, I'll come for you when you least expect it." My voice remained calm, almost soothing.

Jordan picked invisible lint off his jacket. "I don't know anything about that."

"Christ," I taunted. "Lying is just like breathing for you, isn't it?"

"I'm tired of this conversation. Your life bores me. It always has. Don't know why you think I'd care so much about it." He pushed himself away from the bar. "I've told you numerous times before. You're nothing."

White hot rage tore through me, blacking out my current reality.

Why does Bennet keep inviting this asshole to these bonfires?

Jordan and I had been at each other's throats since he walked over spouting off his usual bitter taunts.

"Is the pretty boy goalkeeper using his sad mommy story to get more girls tonight?"

I threw him to the ground and straddled him with clenched fists.

"Yeah, go on," Jordan seethed. "Do your worst. Want a matching scar over your other eye?"

"Why don't you give it to me yourself this time instead of sending your mates to do it. Coward."

"I don't know what you're talking about. Those lads clearly had their reasons."

My blood boiled and simmered with enough anger to go total scorched earth on him. Cade ran over and pulled me off before I could throw a punch.

"Knock it off." Cade sounded exasperated. "Both of you."

"Listen to your boyfriend, Maddox. Spoiled prick." Jordan stood up. "I have better things to do than waste my time with your bullshit."

"Sounds like you haven't stopped crying over not being good enough for the development league again. What's the matter? Your fancy title still can't help you find the back of the net?"

He rounded on me with clenched fists. "I don't need football to make myself feel important. I am important. Unlike you. I can impress all the girls here tonight without any effort."

"Make sure you get their consent first, asshole."

Jordan's smug laughter stoked my anger. "Millie liked it and you know it. Did you know her friends are here? Twins. As I said, I have better things to do."

I shoved him hard when he turned to walk away. "Leave her alone."

He whipped around, standing nose-to-nose with me.

"The arrogance is strong with you tonight. You think you're so entitled to everything because you're a footballer. You're a fucking goalkeeper. And a shit one at that. You'll never get a contract. You're not as special as you think. You're nothing, you hear me. Noth—"

My fist crashed into his face and then his stomach. Hard. Hard enough for pain to shoot through my hand and wrist. He doubled over, gasping for air.

"Too bad your noble fucking bloodline can't hit back worth shit," I yelled. "You think I'm afraid of another scar? I'm not."

Sharp, wheezing laughter was all I heard. "Brave little twat, aren't you? Keep coming for me. You'll be locked up before your eighteenth birthday."

"My friends are just as powerful and influential as your family. You can't touch me."

"The Logans?" Jordan cackled. "You really think they care about your whiny ass? I'll say it again since you missed it the first time. You're nothing."

I launched myself at him, aiming to kick him right in the ribs. Air burned my lungs with each brutal inhale.

"Xavier." My shouted name echoed through the dark alley.

How the fuck did I get out here?

A slumped human form sat on the ground in front of me, their shirt bunched up in my hand.

Reality came rushing back, shattering the remnants of my unpleasant memory.

Cade forcibly grabbed my shoulders, turning me to face him. "Mate, you have to stop. Please. Just stop." The unnerving sound of his shaking voice finally snapped me awake.

"What…how did…?"

A firm squeeze preceded his response. "I saw you two talking at the bar. Didn't think much of it until he left. You seemed out of sorts. Then you ran after him. I tried to find you as fast as I could."

I glanced over my friend's shoulder. We were deep in the alley, far away from the street. Nobody could tell what was going on. At least, I hoped that was the case. This city was filled with CCTV cameras.

"Does Bennet—"

"I called him. He's sending some of his security team to handle this." Cade glanced down at what I assumed was Jordan's unconscious figure. "He also sent a car. It's waiting over there. We have to go."

"Is he…?"

"You knocked him out. He should be alright. We have to go. Now."

I don't remember coming out here. I don't remember attacking Jordan.

All I remembered was…*did you know her friends are here? Twins.*

Chapter
TWENTY-FIVE

Suppressing the urge to pace around the media room was harder than I wanted it to be. Besides, listening to the coach drone on and on about the final preseason loss wasn't exactly inspiring or relaxing.

We're seeing what works. Adjustments will be made. Blah, blah, blah.

I shifted on my feet. Only a couple more interviews to go and then I can head out. Thank goodness this was a home game.

Noah Tate was up next, then Jaxon Oliver. Both of them remained brief and on message. Jax threw in a couple of one-liners just to liven up the room but stuck to his talking points.

I barely said good night to Hannah and Glen before beelining it for my car. Well, not *my* car but I digress.

Marcus greeted me with a cordial nod and off we went. I'd hoped to talk to Xavier before the game started but he didn't answer when I tried calling him. He'd mentioned going out with Cade so maybe he got wrapped up in a spontaneous adventure. Still, it wasn't like him not to send a text if he saw a missed call from me.

Fortunately, there wasn't much traffic on the ride home. I thanked Marcus and wished him a good weekend. Since I didn't have any plans, I basically ordered him to take the next couple days off.

Calm silence greeted me when I walked into my condo. I went straight to the bathroom and filled the tub with warm water. A bubble bath sounded like heaven even though it was late.

Killian and Max were living it up at some swanky event. They'd been texting me most of the night, giving me updates on who's there, who they've met, and who looks dreadful. I'm hoping to get through this bath without being bombarded with more. Unless Killian met his favorite actor, who also happened to be at the same event. I was warned to expect not just texts, but photos and videos as well.

I'd just settled into the tub when my phone chimed.

Of course.

Unknown: Hi Victoria

I didn't recognize the number but the area code was local. A reporter maybe? What could they possibly want now? My jaw tensed in annoyance. They knew better than to text me on my personal phone after hours.

Unknown: Remember this?

A blurry photo accompanied the message. It looked like a still shot from a video. My brows pulled together as I tried to see what it could—

Panic curdled in my stomach.

I nearly dropped the phone in the bath water.

That was me. The photo was cropped to make it appear like I was the main target. My face wasn't visible but I'd recognize that sparkly red dress anywhere.

Bile rose in my throat.

My face wasn't visible because I was on my knees in front of someone. Someone who had their hands on my head while I—

Someone who was *not* Xavier.

Someone, judging by what little else I could see in the picture, I'd met at a party.

Remember this?

A party. Red sparkly dress.

I got out of the tub so fast water surged over the edge and soaked the floor. Grabbing a towel, I ran to my laptop and searched through my photos.

Draft parties. Championship parties. Ring presentations. Charity events.

Nothing.

So it wasn't a football or work related event. That means it could be from just about anything else. All I heard in the back of my head was Killian's voice.

I seem to remember one New Year's Eve when you and whoever the flavor of the month was at the time were going at it in the corner of my living room at the party. You have no shame.

I scrolled through more photos, pausing any time I saw flashes of red. I'd worn this red dress to a few parties but my hair was always pulled up. It was down in this random photo.

My phone chimed again. An eerie sensation crawled up the back of my neck.

Unknown: Looks like someone is enjoying themselves tonight

Another photo was attached. I gasped, staring at the image of a blonde woman sitting much too close to Xavier, and clearly flirting. I didn't like the seductive smile tilting her lips or the way she looked at him. I clenched my jaw, studying the picture.

I couldn't see his face, but I *could* see her hand resting on his leg. I looked closer. Actually, that was his upper thigh.

No you fucking don't.

Annoyance clouded my vision.

A surprised yelp passed my lips when my phone rang. It took me a second to calm the erratic beating of my heart before answering.

"Tori." Killian's voice was like a soothing balm. "Guess who you're talking to."

I indulged in several calming breaths before pretending everything was normal.

"NASA's selection for the first human on Mars?"

"Why are you like this? Better than that."

"Beyoncé's personal assistant?"

"Not quite as good as that. I'll give you one more guess."

Flicking my eyes over the dozens of photos still up on my screen, I clenched my hand into a fist.

"Host *and* musical guest for the season premiere of SNL?"

His exasperated sigh really did make all my button-pushing worth it. I could practically hear his violent eye roll.

"Your contract as my best friend is up for renegotiation this year," he grumbled.

"You wanted me to guess. And like an idiot, gave me three chances."

"Moving on. You are talking to the newly minted Chief Branding Officer for the Amber Sky Media Group."

My jaw dropped. Amber Sky was the biggest digital media corporation in Manhattan. "That's amazing. Tell me everything."

"I will. Tomorrow. I'm in a limo right now heading to the after party with Max and a bunch of others. I just wanted to tell you the good news before stuff got crazy."

If there's one thing Killian Monroe will always excel at, it's finding the biggest *see and be seen* social events in Manhattan. Normally I'd be right be his side with Maxim but once football season starts, my fun time diminishes dramatically.

"Don't do anything I wouldn't do."

"That's not a huge list to pull from." He paused. "Are you okay? You sound weird."

I absently scrolled through more photos, failing to find what I needed.

"Well, we lost tonight so I'm decompressing from that. Otherwise, I'm alright." *If* alright *means sitting in a towel fuming over a random photo of my boyfriend getting pawed by some blonde.*

"Isn't preseason like practice for you guys? The Legends lost." I heard muffled laughter in the background. "Max wants to say hi."

The low buzz of conversation and music vibrated through my ear when he passed the phone to Maxim.

"Hey gorgeous. We miss you. Dinner tomorrow?"

"Miss you more. Dinner sounds fantastic."

We made plans before hanging up. Asking them to meet for lunch was comical since they'd probably be out all night. Killian was as cuddly as a velociraptor if he didn't get enough sleep. Max wasn't as ornery but it's better to be safe than sorry.

Talking to the boys helped get my mind off the texts for a short time. And by short time, I meant thirty seconds.

For me, jealousy was a foreign emotion, especially when it came to relationships.

I stared at the photo. Knowing Xavier, he probably entertained her advances for a minute and then sent her on her way. From what I've seen of his interactions with women, he was always polite but set firm boundaries.

It wasn't my most romantic thought of Xavier but it triggered a longing so intense I gasped for air. Relationships were never really my thing. After my twin died, I figured nobody would want the mess that dwelled beneath my curated outer layer. Casual flings became routine. Dating was off limits. It had the potential to lead to sharing and being vulnerable; two things I refused to allow.

But now here I am, months into an actual relationship and missing him so much it fucking hurt.

Our communication had been so limited the last few weeks. Texting was fine but I wanted to see him, even if it was only on a video call, which we barely had time for.

An uneasy twinge fluttered through me. It really wasn't like him to go radio silent, especially if we'd planned to talk.

I glanced at the blurry photo of what I assumed was me in a red dress and scowled. Now that I'm splashed all over the gossip sites, it shouldn't surprise me that someone would stir up trouble. Just because I remained civilized about my encounters doesn't mean others will do the same.

The April version of me wouldn't be so bothered by messages like this. I'd have responded with a smart ass one-liner and gone on with my life.

Actually, the almost-September version of me would still do the same thing.

Seriously, screw this fucking person.

I grabbed my phone, typed *go touch grass*, and hit send.

Satisfied, I put on some pajamas and crawled into bed. Sleep was just about to welcome me with open arms when my phone chimed. I groaned into the pillow. It must be Killian so I chose to ignore it.

A few seconds passed before it beeped again. And again.

"This better be good," I muttered, grabbing the phone.

Mildly Hot: Are you still up?

Mildly Hot: Tori

Mildly Hot: Answer me

My hands went clammy. Xavier never texts me at this hour. It's the middle of the night in England. And middle of the night rapid-fire texts never led to anything good.

Me: What's wrong?

The phone rang in my hand when he started a video call.

"Hey." I answered, studying his face. It was pale and drawn. Dark circles shadowed his normally vibrant eyes. Christ, he looked awful.

"I'm sorry."

Tightness squeezed my chest. "For texting so late? Don't be."

"No. For what I did."

"I don't understand." Exhaustion spread across his features but his eyes dilated with the wildness of overwhelm. "Have you been awake all night?"

"Yeah. Mostly. I guess." The keyed up way he answered tore through me. "I was at dinner with Cade. I didn't know he'd be there. I relived it again. It hasn't happened in years. And *he* was there. Right fucking there and I went after him. I wanted to fucking kill him. I did it for—"

"Xavier, breathe."

"—you. Just like I had to after you showed me your sister's journal. I had to do something. I couldn't—"

"Xavier, please listen to—"

"—let him get away with it. I'm tired of—"

"*Xavier.*" I kept my tone calm and even. "Focus on me. Look at me."

Breathing fast, he stared at me but didn't quite *see* me. I've had enough anxiety attacks to recognize the beginnings of one.

"Listen to the sound of my voice, okay? I need you to take a deep breath. Slowly. In. Out. That's it, just like that. Can you do another one for me?" I inhaled and exhaled with him. "Perfect. Keep looking at me, Xavier. You know how much I love those pretty blue eyes."

I guided him through more breathing exercises, inhaling and exhaling with him. After a few minutes, he started to calm down. All I wanted to do was wrap him in my arms and never let go.

He ran a hand through his hair, looking a little lost.

"Does this happen to you often?" I asked, trying to disguise the shakiness in my voice.

"No. It only—" Our eyes locked through the screen, filling the air with electricity. "Thank you."

"For teaching you how to breathe? It's a hidden talent."

His lips curved into the crooked, dimpled smile I adore but he still looked off. Seeing him like this shredded my heart.

Several quiet minutes passed between us before he broke the silence with, "I fucking miss you."

"I miss you, too. Feeling a little better?"

He swallowed and nodded. "Yeah, I'm okay. Sorry for the…thing."

"No need to apologize. You'd do the same for me."

The intense stare he leveled at me stilled my heart.

"I would do anything for you, Tori. Anything. I'd risk it all for you."

His words seared through me, imprinting on the deepest parts of my soul. But it wasn't just *what* he said. It's *how* he said it.

Undaunted.

Almost as though he's daring someone to push him beyond his limits.

I did it for you.

I had to do something.

I relived it again.

"What happened tonight?" My question tumbled out soft and unforced. It hung in the air, suspended on twin pillars of curiosity and worry.

Xavier blew out a harsh breath. "Fucking McKennie. I got so goddam angry I lost it. I couldn't stop myself from…"

My head spun. "Stop yourself from what?"

"Fuck," he muttered. "Knocking him out again. I know. I shouldn't have done it but…"

I gripped the phone tighter. "Why did—"

"Because I relived a memory and took it out on him," he snapped. "It's too much to get into on a video call. I just…I need you. I needed to see you, hear you. It's the only way I can get myself right." His lips formed a tense line. "Thing is Victoria, I'd do it all again. I'll keep doing it. I won't let him hurt you any more than he has."

"This isn't about me." A dull pain spread in my chest. "And it's not about my sister. You have to let go of this grudge. Or at least try."

"No."

I bristled at his sharp tone.

"How is it helping to keep such a tight grip on it?"

No answer. Only a cool, disinterested stare.

"It's like what you said to me about the maybes and what ifs.

Holding onto this anger won't change what happened. You'll just keep reacting without considering the consequences every time you see him."

Don't get me wrong. I wanted Jordan McKennie to suffer for what he did to Charlotte and Xavier. I *didn't* want Xavier to put himself in situations where he'd either get hurt or do something he'd regret.

"There's more to it than you know, love."

"Then tell me. You started to once before. I really wish you trusted—" I stopped talking and squeezed my eyes shut. *Shit.* "I shouldn't have said that. I know you trust me. I'm sorry."

Processing all of this after the day I'd had and at this late hour gave me a splitting headache. Granted, I needed Xavier to answer so many more questions about a number of things but I don't want him to spiral out of control again. The timing, as usual, was the worst. He should be asleep.

"Don't you have a game in a few hours?" Maybe changing the subject will dissolve all this tension.

He dismissed my concern with a single shake of his head. "No. Not until Sunday. And even if we did, I've competed in matches on less sleep than this."

Okay. Not asking about *that* right now.

The lighting was so dim in the room it shadowed his tired expression. "Are you at least in bed?"

"No. I'm at Bennet's." He sounded less than thrilled about that.

"In the library?"

"Yeah." His piercing gaze burned through the screen. "I wish you were here with me. I really need you, Tori."

The flare of emotion encasing every word sliced through my chest, piercing an inner shield I didn't know existed. Maybe it was the late hour or the intense rush of concern I felt when he was so panicked. But this feeling? Utter fucking chaos.

Controlling my wild pulse was impossible.

"I'm with you as much as I can be." Not sure how I got those words out.

"Stay with me on the phone so we can keep talking until one of us falls asleep."

If I thought my feelings descended into chaos moments ago, I was so, so wrong. The noticeable tremble in his voice destroyed me.

I was *not* expecting his guard to collapse this way.

"Okay. Do you need to see me or is just hearing me enough?"

He smiled. "Put the phone down on something so you're comfortable. I'm not going make you hold it up."

"And you?"

"I'm putting you on the couch next to me."

I laid my phone on the pillow and snuggled under the blankets.

"All tucked in, city princess?"

Hearing his voice so close, yet knowing he was so far filled me with an intense longing. What I wouldn't give to have him right here.

"I am, country prince."

"You know that's not what I am."

"Right. You're a *gentleman*."

He remained quiet for so long I thought he'd fallen asleep. Good. The man needed rest. He'd never admit he was mortal.

"I'm not even that sometimes, love." Every ounce of air vibrated with an electric charge at the sound of his soothing, gentle tone. "The only thing I do know without question is I am undeniably in love with you. Nothing else matters."

Chapter
TWENTY-SIX

The only thing I do know without question is I am undeniably in love with you. Nothing else matters.

Xavier's words echoed in my head all day, including when I met the boys for dinner. Killian rambled on and on about his new job and meeting Jesse Rollins.

"He's so *nice*," Killian gushed. "And, like, a regular person. Not some *me, me, me* celebrity. So refreshing."

"I think we lost our audience," Maxim teased, nudging my foot under the table. "Are you okay, Victoria?"

I reached for a piece of bread and smiled. "I'm good. Hungry, tired, the usual."

"How's Xavier?" Max's dark eyes glinted in the candlelight.

Stressed, exhausted, ready to burn down the world for me. "He's good."

The boys shared a knowing glance. Both of them knew when I didn't reveal the entire truth. For some odd reason, they didn't gang up on me this time and let my non-answer slide.

"We have something exciting we want to tell you." Killian put his hand on Max's. "We're doing the thing."

"The thing?" I started to bite into the bread, paused, and pulled it out of my mouth. "Oh my God. The *thing*?" My heart leapt into my throat. "You're getting married? For real?"

"One hundred percent for real."

"Oh Killian." Tears filled my eyes. "When? Where?"

"New Year's Eve. Right here in Manhattan."

People seated at the tables near us stared at me when I squealed and jumped up to hug them. Happiness isn't a strong enough word to express how I felt. Killian and Max have been together nearly six years and always hinted at marriage but kept putting it off.

"What changed?" I asked, kissing each one of them on the cheek before returning to my seat.

"We wanted to get ours out of the way so *yours* could be front and center on all the society pages." Killian's smart ass grin glowed in the dim lighting.

"I'm not engaged." I calmly sipped some wine. "I don't plan to be any time soon."

Both of them snickered. I loved them to pieces but come on. Marriage was the furthest thing from my mind these days.

"Keep telling yourself that, baby girl. The public is obsessed with you two. How many followers do you have now?"

Two hundred thousand. "Good thing I don't equate my self-worth with the number of people who follow me on social media."

"That many, huh?" His gray eyes sparkled. "My branding services are available to you at the family and friends discount. Just saying."

Max elbowed him. "Leave her alone."

Dinner with the boys was just what I needed. I even tried to get Hannah to come out with us. Her polite refusal didn't surprise me. She'd been quieter than usual lately. Then again, I ran out of the stadium like my ass was on fire after the post-game presser last night without saying a word to her. I made a mental note to schedule a girls' night before the home opener. Or maybe a spa day.

"Oh!" I exclaimed. "Let me see the ring. Or rings."

I glanced at their hands. A silver ring glinted against Max's dark skin. Killian propped his hand up because if there's anyone who loves to be the center of attention as much as Xavier, it's Killian. He wiggled his fingers, showing off a ring with a thin row of glittering diamonds.

"Platinum?" I asked.

"Of course."

"Do you mind if I splash it all over social media?"

"Sweetie, I'd be pissed if you didn't." Killian slung his arm over Max's shoulders and smiled.

They are, without question, the most attractive couple I've ever seen.

Killian flagged down our server so I could be in a photo with them. By this time, several tables surrounding ours lifted a glass of wine or water or whatever they were drinking in celebration. I posted the photos with the caption *My loves are getting married*. No need to be pithy when the truth is way better. Within a few minutes, an incoming text chimed.

Mildly Hot: Tell the lads I said well done

Mildly Hot: And tell Killian my heart is broken beyond repair

"The fact that you still have him in your phone as *Mildly Hot* is hilarious and ridiculous." Killian's infectious laugh filled me with warmth. "Let Xavier know Max is willing to share."

"Uh, no he's not." Max arched an eyebrow.

"Neither am I." I flashed my best friend a smug smile. "Xavier's all mine, *sweetie*."

"Look at those claws. Get it girl."

Once we ordered and the food arrived we were knee deep in wedding talk. I haven't had much to look forward to this year outside of work. Ending it with my best friend's wedding could be the perfect remedy to the muddled chaos that's been following me around since, well, since forever it feels like.

"And then after the wedding, we'll be ready to go with Charlotte's foundation." Killian squeezed my hand. "Tracey and I just need to get Hannah's signature. Her family has been beyond generous."

The Caldwells offered to donate a sizable amount of money to help get the foundation off the ground. As grateful as I was to them, I insisted on providing most of the financial support.

We'd finalized which animal shelters and mental health clinics will receive the first grants. Our inaugural event next spring will be the big reveal for everyone.

"I have a couple of meetings lined up with potential donors," I said, clasping his hand in mine. "Thank you both for all the work you've done so far."

"Have you told your parents about it yet?"

"I'll tell my dad now that the name is official." I frowned. "I doubt my mother would care. She'll probably say it's an extravagant way for me to avoid taking responsibility for—"

"Enough." Killian's sharp tone startled me. The people at surrounding tables glanced in our direction. "Helena has her own shit to work through. *You* are not responsible for anything. Tell the voices in your head to shut the fuck up."

Heavy tension clouded our otherwise enjoyable dinner. Killian was right though. One of these days I'll silence the nagging, accusatory inner monologue that's plagued me since Charlotte took her own life.

"What name did you decide to use?" Max's tentative question sifted through the unpleasantness.

I sipped some water before answering. "The Seraphim Rising Foundation."

Max propped his chin on his hand, regarding me curiously. "What does seraphim mean?"

"It means..." I paused. "Well, I've seen several definitions for it but my favorite is *fiery ones*. Traditionally, Seraphim are red-winged angels. You know the tattoo I have? The twin phoenix feathers made from flames? A version of that will be the logo. I thought it would all tie in nicely." I caught Max's eye. "I guess you could say the meaning is really only significant to me. Always trying to rise from the ashes."

The boys remained quiet for a few seconds.

"I like it," Max finally said. "I know your sister would like it too. You're a smart one, Victoria. You never cease to amaze me."

Killian's eyes widened. I could tell he was ready to fire off a sarcastic remark. "Don't encourage her, Max. She loves to show off her Ivy League education to us regular university kids."

"Maybe if you cracked a book open once in a while, your vocabulary would expand beyond *like, follow, and share*."

Killian raised his middle finger and blew a kiss. I couldn't hold back my laughter when I mimicked his gesture.

"I'm marrying into this. Voluntarily." Max rubbed his eyes.

An incoming text disrupted us.

Unknown: No grass, but there was touching

An uncomfortable shiver passed through me. Ignoring it, I put the phone down and leaned back into our conversation.

"Someone just got a dirty message from their hot boyfriend." Killian folded his hands. "What did he say?"

Think, Victoria, think.

My day job is all about staying on message and talking points and controlling the conversation.

"Nothing."

"Liar." My best friend eyed me with suspicion. "Is something wrong? You've been acting strange since last night. Don't hide shit from me again."

I winced.

I'd been less than upfront with Killian about some things over the summer. Namely what I'd read in my twin's final diary entry. Not telling him what Charlotte had done all those years ago tore me up inside. Keeping it from him for as long as I did consumed me with guilt. When I finally sat him down for that conversation, we both had a good, long cry.

With that in mind, I resigned myself to coming clean. I told the boys about the text and the pictures and my unsuccessful search for any photographic evidence of me in a sparkly red dress.

The verbal diarrhea didn't stop there. Why would it?

I also unleashed what happened last night with Xavier's frantic call and the fight, plus being followed by a reporter in Paris and the encounter with that guy at the restaurant.

Once it was all out in the open, I leaned back into the chair and finished my glass of wine.

Two sets of eyes blinked at me in disbelief.

Killian started to say something and stopped. He gestured his hand at me, turned to Max, turned back to me, gestured again, and shook his head.

"I think what he's trying so eloquently to say is, are you alright." Max reached across the table and held my hand. "That's…a lot."

"I'm fine."

The most annoying phrase in the English language. *I'm fine.* Yet, so powerful. It could shut down a conversation, piss off any number of people, or provide a generic response to the equally annoying and slightly disingenuous *how are you* we throw around at each other on a daily basis.

"Maybe it's a good thing you still have a broad-shouldered shadow following you around." Killian scanned the restaurant. "Is he here?"

"No. He's off this weekend."

"Off? Like, not working?"

"Yeah. I told him to take the weekend off. I don't have any plans so—"

"No plans? Tori, we are literally out at dinner because we *planned* this."

"Since when did you become a huge fan of me having a bodyguard?"

"I'm not a huge fan of it but maybe it's a good idea."

"Why do you sound so concerned?"

Killian's eyes widened. "Did you not just hear yourself tell us all those things? He should be on the clock. Now."

"*Why* is everyone I know so overprotective?" I muttered. "I need to use the ladies' room. And no, I do not need an escort."

I balled up the napkin and dropped it on the table before walking toward the restrooms. Thankfully, I was the only person inside. Flattening my hands on the counter, I hung my head and exhaled slowly. As happy as I was for the boys, I needed a breather from them. Well, not so much Max. But anyway.

My exhausted reflection stared back at me in the mirror. Xavier's call left me so unsettled. I barely slept after ending the video chat. He'd fallen asleep first. I did linger for a while, listening to his even breathing. I wanted to make sure he got *some* rest.

Various scenarios of me getting on a plane and flying to London played out in my mind. I could confront Jordan on my own. He's a bully and an asshole, but not invincible. He must have a weakness. Everyone does.

My fingers wrapped around the ring hanging from my necklace. I can't sit back and watch Xavier continue down this path of destruction. I have to do something.

Chapter
TWENTY-SEVEN

XAVIER

The rundown farmhouse taunted me with its serene setting and frosty demeanor. Admittedly, I'd grown to like this painting after staring at it week after week.

Not today though. Today I wanted to set it on fire.

Dr. Frances shifted in his chair, pen in hand, notepad open. He'd grown on me too, mostly because he seemed to figure out my moods and learned not to push me to engage with him. I'd already said everything I needed to say about what happened at Constellations the other night. I even talked about yesterday's match, which we lost. All of that took a grand total of eight minutes, meaning I still had roughly forty more to suffer through.

Didn't matter to me if I sat here in silence. He's getting paid regardless.

My focus tightened on the painting, studying the layered details of the farmhouse. At first glance, nothing about this landscape had seemed extraordinary, but the intricacies jumped out at me now.

The fractured wooden facade.

A buckling snow-covered roof.

Several broken windows.

With every excruciating second that passed by, I noticed the flaws more and more.

"What is it about the painting that resonates with you so powerfully?" Dr. Frances' inquiry intruded on my thoughts.

"Everything," I answered without hesitation.

He jotted down a few notes before asking, "Can you give me a specific example?"

Closing my eyes, I leaned my head back. Normally, my resolve to give him just enough information to make these sessions bearable would kick in by now. But the more I thought about what happened the other night and the more I allowed my feelings for Victoria to consume me, the more I fell apart.

Just like that fucking painting. I glared at the imperfections. Their unveiling came faster and faster.

Chipped paint on the siding.

Uneven stairs.

Crooked door-frame.

"No."

"Do you…maybe…see yourself as the farmhouse?"

Fucking hell. "No."

An eyebrow arched over the rim of his glasses. Without saying another word, Dr. Frances wrote for a few seconds. He paused, looked at me, and wrote some more.

Not going to lie. It pissed me off.

"Is that what you're writing?" I nearly exploded. "That Xavier Maddox views himself as a broken structure, barely keeping himself together so the adoring public won't know how fucked up he is beneath it all?" I dug my fingers into the cushion, unable to stop myself from talking. "That my carefully curated life as a global superstar athlete is all for show? That I use attention and adoration as fucking bandages to hide my self-loathing and inadequacies?"

Stunned silence stretched between us.

Shit. I shouldn't have said all of that.

"Stay with this, Xavier. You're making a breakthrough that I think will help point you in the right direction."

"Fuck you."

I stood up and walked out.

An hour later I sprawled on the couch in the sitting room of Briarcliff Cottage, staring at the drum sander. My plan for the day was to do some work here after my session with Dr. Frances but that clearly went off the rails. Still, being in this house helped relieve some of the stress.

Cursing him out and leaving wasn't a good look. The man was just doing his job. And that's why I go to him, right? To stop denying all the shit I'd been burying for years.

If I can't handle it, that's on me.

Wow, look at me sounding all adult.

I sent Dr. Frances an email apologizing for my behavior and confirmed I'd be at the next appointment.

His response?

If and when something else throws you off, don't dismiss it. Don't ignore it. Really feel it.

He'd given me the exact same guidance a few months ago, word for word. At the time, it was in response to my reaction at a press conference. I'd ended up using it to sort out my feelings toward Victoria.

To say I'd initially fucked it up royally would be an understatement.

And now here I am again, faced with *really feeling it.*

I ignored the incoming text from Bennet and tossed my phone on the cushion. He wanted to talk about the fallout from my, as he'd so graciously put it, stupid fucking choices.

Jordan was livid. Not surprising. I don't know what Bennet said to him or how he managed to keep what happened under wraps, but he did. Lucky for me, Jordan wasn't seriously hurt. According to Bennet's private doctor, just a bump on the head. No black eye or broken nose or anything.

Pity.

At this point, I owed Bennet more than simple gratitude. The man already saved my career once. Not sure I'll get another chance if I screw up again.

I felt like I was being torn in two; the more I let down my guard with Victoria, the harder it became to deny the truth about my past. Trouble is, I only wanted to fall apart in front of *her.* Not a therapist or my friends. Just Victoria.

How would she even react if I told her I was at the bonfire the same night her sister encountered Jordan? That I'd fought with him and probably provoked him enough to carry through with what he did to Charlotte?

I didn't see her or Millie or anything else that happened but I couldn't help feel somewhat responsible.

More texts from Bennet flooded my phone. Then it started ringing. Swearing under my breath, I answered.

"What is it now?"

"We need you at the facility. Main offices." His words lacked any emotion. They hung frozen in the air.

"Why?"

"You know why. I already called your agent. Be here in an hour."

FUCK.

Benched for the next match.

"These unexpected bumps in the road need to be managed swiftly before things get out of hand." Bennet didn't mince words. "If anything like this happens again, we'll have no choice but to reevaluate the goalkeeper position."

I let the words simmer and fester in my mind.

The tips of my fingers glowed a purplish-red from how tight I clasped my hands together. Bennet and my agent, Gerard, talked around me. Eric, the Royal City manager, sat quietly, his face awash with disappointment.

"Christian will be in goal on Saturday." Bennet's stern amber glare focused on me. "You'll train as normal with the club until Wednesday."

My eye twitched. Christian was a decent keeper. He did well filling in during my suspension last season.

"What are we saying to the media? You know they'll ask." Gerard looked at his phone. He's represented me for the last fifteen years. I trusted he'd keep the real reason under wraps if it ever came to light.

"Illness," Bennet responded. "By midweek we'll make it known Xavier wasn't feeling well and left training early. We don't want supporters and the media to get carried away with speculation. If we just say he's not starting, it'll stir up quite the storm. This will keep it neat and tidy."

I bit down on my lip to keep silent. Fucking ridiculous.

They continued talking around me like I didn't exist while I stewed in anger. When Gerard and Eric finally left the office, I stood up and unleashed on Bennet.

"This is what you and that asshole agreed on? Pulling me from the pitch? Fuck you, Logan."

The force of Bennet's hand slamming against his desk ricocheted through the office. Within seconds, he was in front of me. "I am trying to prevent this from getting worse." Each word came out calm and measured. "There is CCTV footage of you going after him. Do you want that to go public? I know how much you love a fucking audience."

Reigning in my emotions sapped every bit of energy from me, but I managed to level a bored stare at my so-called best friend.

"And this footage just magically landed in your lap?"

"Don't be cute, Maddox. You know damn well I have connections in every corner of this city." He looked down his nose at me, his eyes glinting with steely knowledge.

"Yes, your grace." My shoulders stiffened. "This is all well above my pay grade."

Some of Bennet's measured control unraveled. "And it's a good fucking thing. I had all visual evidence of you chasing Jordan down that alley scrubbed from existence."

I suppressed a flinch at the mention of Jordan's name. "But he knows about it."

"Of course he does. This will keep him satisfied for the time being."

We stared at one another, silently communicating what's transpired over the years. Bennet looked exhausted. I sensed there was more going on than just my reckless decisions. Whatever it was, it's not my concern right now.

"Bench me," I snapped. "Tell the media whatever you want. Tell them I'm sick, I have a broken wrist, I need a fucking nap. Whatever. I'm going to New York."

"No, you're not." Bennet's slow, even delivery stopped me from walking out the door. "You will train with the club until midweek as directed. Then, you will stay inside your flat and out of the public eye until I tell you to return."

Keeping my mouth shut was an exercise in restraint. Bennet wasn't saying all this to me as a friend. He said it as my boss; the guy who controls my career and could sell me to another club if he wanted.

"I'm not only taking *your* best interests into consideration, I'm also protecting the team. Royal City is one of the founding members of this league and has been here for decades. Our name commands respect. This club will not be dragged into endless controversy because the fucking goalkeeper can't control himself."

Swallowing my pride was a bitter pill.

Balancing on the edge of this knife started to wear me down.

"Fine," I conceded. "We'll do it your way."

An exasperated sigh poured into the space between us. "I don't want to do this. My hands are tied. You know that."

Bennet's shoulders slumped but his whole body sagged under the weight of something.

"Yeah, I do." I studied him. "Can we speak as friends now?"

He eyed me warily. "Depends."

"What's going on with you? Nothing's been the same with all of us since Paris. Cade even noticed."

That garnered a smile. "If Gallagher noticed, then I must not be hiding it well."

Victoria's voice flitted through my head. *Be nice to Cade.*

"He thinks it's mostly work related. I think there's more to it."

Bennet smoothed down his tie, walked back to his chair, and sat. "You're both right. That's all I'm saying." The hardened edge to his statement signaled we were finished talking.

Later that night, after replaying the events of the day, I sipped on my third glass of whisky and called Victoria.

"The bossy chair makes another appearance." Her bright voice washed over me when she answered. "You look comfy."

"You look beautiful."

"Such a charmer." She leaned into the couch, tilted her head, and smiled. "Good day at practice?"

I winced, hoping she didn't notice. "It was alright. I stopped by your cottage this afternoon."

"Nice deflection."

I lifted a shoulder in a small shrug. "No deflections here."

"Whatever you say. Have you recovered from yesterday's loss?"

"For someone who doesn't actually play competitive sport for a living, you sure do know how to push an athlete's buttons."

"What happened to nothing about you being fragile? You're not going soft on me, are you?"

Normally I loved it when she teased me. Tonight? I couldn't bear it.

"Didn't really have the best day, Tori. Sorry." My voice tightened. "I don't like losing."

Concern lined her gloss-covered lips. "Did something else happen? Is it Jordan?"

Masking my reaction to that question wasn't easy. "No, love."

"The crazy thing about video calls is I can see your face. Talk to me, Xavier. I know something happened."

Swallowing the last of my drink didn't calm the growing storm festering inside me. Her emerald stare always pierced through to my deepest, hidden parts.

But this is what I wanted, right? To tell her all of it. Fall apart in front of her and no one else.

"There's CCTV footage of me chasing after Jordan." The words clawed their way out my throat. Victoria's eyes grew wide. "It's been dealt with but in order to keep everyone happy, I've been benched for this week's match."

"Benched? Is this something preemptive? Did the footage get leaked online or sent to a reporter? Is someone using it to blackmail you?"

I could see the no-nonsense, business side to her when she sat up straight and fired off questions without hesitation. I saw the poised Dartmouth graduate, the engaging woman engineered to command respect in the male-dominated sports industry.

"What's the story going out to the media?"

I wanted to kiss her. My girl is so clever. "Illness. The plan is for me to train until midweek, then go home because I'm not feeling well." I scowled. "I'll be locked in my flat until Bennet deems me worthy of seeing the light of day."

Victoria twisted a strand of hair. The subtle movement sparked intense yearning.

"That doesn't sound too horrible. Well, I mean, it's an unpleasant situation but the optics should be okay." The more she combed her fingers through her hair, the more I wanted to grab a fistful, pull her head back, and ravage her. "Is that the only thing bothering you?"

"Not even close."

We both startled at my raw honesty.

"I had a shit therapy session earlier. I stormed out."

"Why?"

The fucking thing in my chest raged. "I had a few…uncomfortable realizations. Dr. Frances wanted me to continue but—" *Fuck. I can't do this.*

"But what?" The gentle, reassuring way she asked almost gave me the courage to tell her. Almost.

"Sorry, love. I just…red."

Neither one of us has called *red* during a conversation in a long time. Even though Victoria was thousands of miles away, I could feel her overwhelming concern seep through the screen. But there was something else. Her mouth formed a determined line and her eyes darkened with steadfast anger. Noticeable tension lifted her shoulders as her jaw set with purpose.

I was used to the way her body reacted to me when she was aroused. But this? Seeing my sophisticated, intelligent, stunning girlfriend morph into something more feral, more protective? Sexy as fuck.

"Tori," I grit out. "What are you thinking?"

Fierce green eyes locked onto mine. "I'm starting to understand why you get so angry when it comes to Jordan. I can't stand what he's done to you."

The familiar surge of possessive pride flowed through me as I stroked my lip with my thumb.

"God, I fucking love you. But this isn't your fight. Let me handle him."

"Your fight *is* my fight, Xavier."

Chapter
TWENTY-EIGHT

This might be the worst decision I've ever made.

Or the best.

The jury was still out.

"Not much I can do to change it now," I muttered to myself while pacing around the hotel room. As soon as I'd ended the call with Xavier the other night, I set my plan into action.

After finessing a few things at work and straight up telling Marcus he wasn't coming with me, I chartered a private plane and flew to London.

This was the right thing to do, wasn't it? *Yes.* Then why does nothing about this feel comfortable? My gut kept telling me to go home.

A knock sounded at the door.

See? my gut taunted, as I opened it. *This is what you get for thinking you have autonomy when it comes to Jordan McKennie.*

Bennet stood expressionless with his hands tucked inside his pockets. "Victoria."

"Hi." I gestured toward the room. "Please come in."

Doesn't hurt to be polite, right? We haven't seen or spoken to one another since Paris.

His astute amber eyes surveyed me as he strode past. Bennet Logan doesn't simply enter a room, he announces his commanding presence with his entire body. I call him the god of thunder for a reason. Tall, broad-shouldered, and always impeccably dressed. The picture of modern British aristocracy with a nod to the old world elegance.

"You found me." I closed the door and faced him. "Should I ask how?"

Bennet flashed a grin that didn't quite meet his eyes. "I think you know, Ms. Chase. Next time you want to brush off your personal security, don't. Marcus has one job, and you just made it a million times more difficult."

The drama with this one.

"Spare me the lecture." I flicked my wrist. "I have to do this."

"Have you told Xavier?"

"You know I haven't. He'd do everything in his power to stop me."

A slow, resigned shake of his head made my heart wrench.

"As would I." The subtle lowering of his shoulders softened the pristine exterior of control. "That man is like a brother to me. I would do anything to prevent him from getting hurt." His tone sharpened. "You are the most important person in his life. I'm sure he tells you every chance he gets but it bears repeating. When we're finished here today, you'll go straight to him and tell him everything."

I'd prepared myself for one of Bennet's scoldings. I'd been around him enough to know he's surgical when being persuasive. This first cut was a doozy.

"How is he?"

"The best goalkeeper in England isn't playing this weekend for no good fucking reason other than his own inability to control his impulses. How do you *think* he's doing?"

"Point taken." I folded my arms. "So how is this going to play out? I'm assuming you know I scheduled a meeting with Jordan this afternoon."

"Is that your way of saying you'd like me to be there?"

"No. I need to take care of this on my own."

Something unnerving flashed behind Bennet's eyes. I couldn't figure out what it was exactly but I sensed he knew more than he was letting on.

"You're looking at me the same way your boyfriend does," he grumbled. "I can't tell you what to do or stop you from going. All I will say is this; be careful. You're an intelligent woman but Jordan is conniving and ruthless. If he can sense any weakness, he'll pounce."

Keeping my gaze locked on Bennet, I paced around the room. Dealing with asshole alpha males wasn't as difficult as people made it out to be. Sure, they're insufferable but not invincible. Besides, this guy ruined my sister's life.

"I can handle him."

"Now you *sound* like your boyfriend." The whisper of an amused grin pulled at Bennet's lips before disappearing like smoke in a breeze. "But I'm afraid you're being too impulsive, Victoria. Maybe you should go back to—"

"This isn't me being impulsive," I snapped. "This is me defending the people I love before the worst happens."

Twenty years of anguish surged from my fingertips to my toes in one giant, scalding wave. All the blame and guilt I've carried over Charlotte's actions at the bonfire and the subsequent fallout from her death ravaged me. I can't change the past. I know that. But I can prevent another life from descending into ruin.

A barely noticeable nod was Bennet's initial response. Then he dropped a bomb on me.

"He might not be the person behind your car getting vandalized earlier this summer."

I froze. "How do you know this?"

A slight tightening of his jaw was the only giveaway to any discomfort or apprehension. Bennet's exterior remained impenetrable.

"The details aren't important right now." Staunch whisky-colored eyes locked onto mine. "There was an issue with a former employee at your stadium. They've been dealt with."

My jaw almost hit the floor. "Who was it? What issue?"

"Nobody that concerns you."

"Did you tell Xavier? He's been out of his mind since—"

"No." Bennet's sharp response cut through the room. "I can't say anything more until the investigation is complete. Neither can you and that's all you need to know." Normally, he's unflappable. Seeing him come apart, even just a little, didn't sit right with me.

"Enough with the cagey shit. Give me a straight answer."

If I thought I'd seen Bennet at peak dominance, I was sorely mistaken. I've never spent any significant time around a true Dom, so I assumed they'd become tense or visibly agitated. Maybe some do, but Bennet simply morphed into a living, breathing statue of calm, calculated control.

"You aren't the only one defending the people you love the most." Velvet wrapped each word in a misleading cloak of serenity. "I'm choosing to trust you won't break my confidence, Ms. Chase. Don't step into an arena if you aren't prepared for the battle."

An air of finality settled around us.

The familiar screw that dwelled deep in my chest tightened. *I shouldn't have come here.*

But I am here. I'm here for Charlotte and Xavier. Nothing else matters, not even Bennet's concerning situation.

"One more thing," he said, straightening his cufflinks. "Jordan *is* targeting you. It's just not how you think."

The world must have spun off its axis. Thank goodness I stood so close to this couch. I sat before my legs gave out.

Bennet watched me with guarded concern.

The events of the last couple months flashed through my mind.

"How do you know?"

"Why did you come to London?"

"Answering my question with one of your own is annoying," I huffed.

Bennet smoothed down his tie while walking to the door. "The answer is obvious." He opened the door and leveled a fierce stare at me. "Cancel this meeting. Go to Xavier."

An hour later, I sank into the backseat of my taxi. Watching the familiar London landmarks pass by didn't do one damn thing to calm my nerves. I alternated between fidgeting with my necklace and checking my phone every two minutes in case Bennet tattled on me and told Xavier I was here.

Regardless of what he'd said, I didn't cancel the meeting. Call me stubborn or impulsive or whatever. I wasn't about to blow off a chance to do something I couldn't when I was sixteen.

When the taxi pulled to the curb, I stared at the nondescript glass office building. For someone so keen on flaunting his status, Jordan chose a rather mundane place to run his business. Even the name was boring: Sentinel Protection Services.

Probably by design, I thought as I entered the lobby.

The receptionist greeted me with a pleasant smile, pointed toward the elevator bank, and instructed me to go to the fifth floor.

My stupid heart wouldn't stop pounding. When the doors opened it took me a second to gather my wits and walk out. But then I saw Jordan standing in the hall talking with another man. I could feel his assholery saturate the air.

The night he'd approached me in Manhattan will forever be seared into my memory. Faking a southern accent, bombarding me with awful accusations about Xavier, and then gloating about what he'd done with Charlotte.

I raked my eyes over his tall, muscular build. The bastard still looked the same. Dark hair, dark eyes, expensive watch, and an expensive tailored suit.

He never looked in my direction but he knew I was there. His whole body reacted. He stood taller, adopting a more stern expression. Suppressing an eye roll, I strode toward him.

"These two will be our best bet." Jordan spoke in a tone edged with entitlement. "Make them fight for it. They're both in desperate need of our services."

The other man nodded once, looked me up and down, and went on his way.

"My most anticipated meeting of the day." A hint of amusement worked its way into Jordan's voice. "American football teams aren't really on my list of dream clients."

For a second, I fantasized about shoving my four-inch heel into his crotch and twisting it. Then again, he might like that.

"This meeting will be short and sweet since you're not on our dream list either." I flashed a smile that was both polite and menacing.

"Feisty. The legend of the fun twin continues to intrigue me." He opened his office door and gestured for me to enter.

My hand clenched into a fist. Standing with him in a hallway made my skin crawl. The thought of sitting in his office turned my stomach. Masking my discomfort would be a challenge.

I can do this. It can't be any worse than the league owners' meeting a few years ago.

Without acknowledging his remark, I took a seat in front of his desk. The bland theme continued in here. For a security firm, I expected cool, metal tones or maybe all-white furniture or something.

Nope.

Basic office. Basic asshole.

"I know what you're doing." I crossed my legs and leaned back in the chair when he sat down. "And you're going to tell me why."

"You'll have to be more specific." A wicked smile pulled at his too-wide mouth. "I'm juggling quite a few projects at the moment."

He splayed one of his big hands on the desk. Rotten images of those hands wrapped around my sister's neck fueled my courage.

"Cut the bullshit." I stood up, fighting off the urge to pace. "I'll dumb this down for you so there's no misunderstanding." He scoffed. He fucking *scoffed*. "Leave Xavier alone. I don't care if you see him at a restaurant, an event, on the sidewalk, on fucking television, wherever. Leave him the fuck alone or I will go to the authorities and have you formally charged with rape."

"Rape?" he sputtered. "Is this about your little tart of a sister? Jesus Christ. I didn't rape her."

Two decades worth of grief and rage gathered at the base of my neck, spreading until it enveloped my skull in a crushing grip. "*Stop lying*." I exploded. "We both know you did. I read all about it in her diary. She couldn't even talk to me. She never did tell me because she killed herself." Tears streamed down my cheeks. Somehow, I ended up on the other side of his office, pacing in my usual figure eight path. "Maybe I'll add murder charges to the list. I will bring you down if it's the last thing I do."

Jordan studied me briefly before responding, "I'd like to see you try."

With a swiftness that surprised even me, I stormed over to his desk, leaned forward and slammed my hands down. "England doesn't have a statute of limitations on sexual assault. Don't underestimate me. I'm not intimidated by your nobility. I have more power and influence than you think."

"Americans. Always so eager to show off their valor." Jordan rose from his chair like a demon coming out of hell. "How is your father these days? I hope my family's investments are still helping to support your lifestyle."

Shock paralyzed me.

"Well, this is an interesting development, isn't it? I see you're not as well versed on his business dealings as I thought. Did you also not know that my family invested heavily in his firm when you and your sister were in diapers? Must have been so lovely growing up in the wealthiest neighborhood, attending the fanciest schools," he paused, sliding his eyes over my body, "vacationing every summer in Briarcliff Village. Quite the little spoiled fucking brat, aren't you."

All the air disappeared. No matter how hard I tried, I couldn't breathe.

"I will say I'm impressed that you did your research regarding the statute of limitations. Technically, you *can* still bring charges against me for what allegedly happened with Charlotte." He moved closer. "But you won't."

The tiniest bit of oxygen reached my lungs. "I will."

"I was hoping you'd say that." Jordan stood inches away from me, blocking my path to the door. He lowered his head until our noses almost touched. "You won't. Want to know why?"

Heat from his breath brushed over my lips in a repulsive wave. He was too close.

Moving slow, I took a step back. Before I could take another, he grabbed my neck, putting me in a chokehold. On instinct, I clawed at his hand but he was too strong.

"I fucking own you, Victoria Ava Chase." Each squeeze of his fingers robbed me of precious air. "If you even think about going to the authorities, I will destroy not only you and your family, but Xavier as well." He yanked me closer, banding his other arm around me so my body pressed into him and his obvious arousal. "There is so much about him the public doesn't know."

The sound of his cold laugh whipped along my skin in brutal lashes.

"You are exquisite." He rubbed his erection against me. "Does that feel good? I imagine you like it fast and dirty."

"Fuck you," I growled through clenched teeth.

"I bet there was a time you would." His grip around my neck tightened. "You have quite the reputation yourself. And you have a specific type. Did you know I played football with Xavier and Cade in my younger days?"

Sucking in a breath was nearly impossible. The smug grin spreading across Jordan's mouth nauseated me.

"Getting quite the education today, aren't you? Tell me, how many professional athletes have you fucked? How many relationships have *you* ruined?"

Clamping my hands around his arm, I dug my nails into his skin. Jesus, he was so strong.

"Did you like the texts I sent you? That red dress is a stunner."

I went limp in his arms. My heart felt like it'd been dragged over hot coals. The text. The random photo of me kneeling in front of someone in a sparkly red dress.

"You?" I wheezed out the question. "How?"

"Having a little fun with a new project. Testing some new technology. It's amazing what can be generated to appear real these days." Malice laced his smile. "The one of your boyfriend and that sexy blonde is all too real. But I do have an entire arsenal of fabricated photos ready to go just in case. Ruining your professional and personal life will be so. Much. Fun."

Tears welled in my eyes. I refused to accept defeat but the overwhelming urge to run stretched my muscles taut. Jordan watched me with a sickening level of amusement.

"When Xavier met with me back in May he was so confident I'd fold. I will admit, watching him defend and protect his precious American girlfriend was entertaining. Want to know what I said to him?" His fingers sank into my skin. "I told him I knew what his weakness was and I'd find you." He affected a southern accent. "Did you enjoy meeting Wes in Manhattan? I still think about it." My stomach churned as I struggled in his grasp. "I'd hoped you'd come see me in London but I couldn't figure out how to get you here. Looks like I know your weakness, too. Thank you for making this so much easier."

The second he shoved me away and let go, I coughed and gulped for air. Each breath cut into my throat like razorblades.

I need to get out of here.

This was a mistake.

As much as I wanted to move, I was rooted to the ground. Jordan simply straightened his suit jacket and sat down.

"Was there anything else you'd like to discuss today, Victoria?" The question sounded so businesslike. Almost as though we'd reached an amicable agreement on some new partnership and he hadn't been choking me seconds ago. "I heard through various sources you're starting a foundation in your sister's memory. How righteous. Shall I make a donation?"

Glaring at him, I straightened my shoulders and regained some composure. "Stay away from my family."

Jordan's patronizing head tilt poured gasoline onto my expanding anger. "I don't think I will. Everything and everyone is fair game. Like I've told you before, you never know who's watching."

Enough. I have to leave.

Without saying another word, I grabbed my bag and headed to the door. Just as I was about to walk out I heard, "We should do this again in a more intimate setting. Ask Xavier if he still shares his girlfriends."

Chapter
TWENTY-NINE

VICTORIA

Why did you come to London?

Bennet's question rattled through my brain as I stood on the sidewalk in a downpour.

The answer is obvious.

Glancing up at Xavier's white stone townhouse, I finally allowed the tears to flow. I came here for him. Jordan knew I would and played on it and now…now I've ruined everything.

The rain fell harder, soaking me to the bone. I forced myself to approach the front door. As I attempted to ring the bell, the door swung open.

Xavier and I stared at one another in silence. Flickers of anger, concern, and regret cycled through his features.

Oh my God, he knows.

Arctic eyes swept over me in one steady, controlled movement. "Get out of the rain, Tori."

Reaching for my hand, he pulled me inside. He led me to his bedroom in silence, rummaged through his closet, and handed me dry clothes. I just stood there like an idiot, holding the clothes and fighting back tears.

After a few seconds Xavier took the clothes, put them on the bed, and started undressing me. Well, it wasn't so much undressing me as it was more *peeling* off my blouse, skirt, bra, and panties. Everything was drenched.

I've stood naked in front of him countless times but I've never felt as bare as I did now.

Xavier stared at my neck while he towel dried my hair. Rage twisted his mouth into a snarl when he brushed his fingers over my skin. I swallowed, looking down.

It didn't register with me that I'd been shivering until he pulled a sweatshirt over my head. When he knelt to help me step into his warmup pants, I grabbed onto his shoulders. He stopped, looking up at me briefly.

My heart did the thing it always does when I see him on his knees. It pounded with reckless abandon.

Slowly, and with great care, he pulled the pants up my legs and over my hips. Then he stroked a finger down my neck again before taking my hand.

The silence continued when he led me to the kitchen and I watched him prepare a kettle of water. He grabbed two mugs, two tea bags, and two spoons. I won't lie, all this quiet and the mundane tasks were getting to me.

"Xavier," I said, my voice barely above a whisper.

Scrubbing his face with his hands, he exhaled a harsh breath. "Jesus," he muttered, yanking me into a rough embrace. I clung to him while choking out a sob. "It's okay, love. You're okay."

"I'm sorry." I buried my face in his chest, embarrassed and furious with myself. "I thought I could handle him. I wanted—"

Xavier's kiss cut me off. "You," he whispered on my lips. Feather-light strokes along my jaw soothed my erratic pulse. "We have all night to talk about what happened. Right now, my only concern is getting you comfortable."

I nodded, melting into his hug.

The kettle clicked off once the water boiled. Xavier escorted me to the couch and finished preparing our tea. When he sat with me, I curled up next to him, resting my head in his lap. We stayed like this —me nestled against his thigh, him running a hand through my hair— listening to the rain.

Instead of enjoying the serenity, all the shitty things Jordan said polluted my mind.

"Xavier?"

"Yes, love."

"Did I make everything worse for us?"

His touch stilled, and he stiffened.

"Don't sugar coat it." I sat up. "I broke your trust. I did the one thing you asked me not to do."

Xavier closed his eyes, his expression oscillating between anguish and annoyance. "Nothing is broken." The heat behind his stare when he looked at me added emphasis to his words. A marked heaviness edged his tone. "Nothing will ever be broken between us."

"How did you know I went to see him?"

"Bennet texted me when your taxi pulled up here."

My mouth popped open. "He had me followed?"

"Apparently."

"You're not angry with me?"

He remained quiet long enough for me to regret asking.

"With you? No," he finally said. "I'm not happy you put yourself in that situation but I get it." Our eyes locked. "Although the possibility of losing you terrified me."

A lump burned in my throat. When I rubbed along the column of my neck, Xavier placed his hand over mine.

"He hurt you." His voice lowered to a dangerous decibel as the atmosphere turned ominous. "What happened?"

Telling him everything will trigger a series of events that cannot be undone. A long silence passed before I answered.

"I told him to leave you alone or I'll have him formally charged with rape for what he did to my sister." My lips thinned into a tense line. "He didn't like that so I ended up in a chokehold."

Slow, poisonous rage crept into Xavier's eyes. "I see. Is there anything else?"

I nodded, relaying what Jordan said about my dad and the investments, and his threats to destroy me and my family if I ever went to the authorities. "I don't know if he's lying about the investments. I need to talk to my father." I conveniently left out the part where he pressed his dick against my body.

"Is there more?"

"He threatened to go after you."

A small, joyless laugh shook his body for a moment. "Nothing new there." The feel of his hand on my thigh alleviated some stress. I almost relaxed into the cushions. Almost. Xavier's anger rolled in like a wave, slow and calculating as it devoured everything in sight but when he spoke, his tone was smooth and even-tempered.

"What aren't you telling me, Tori?"

"He, um," I swallowed, attempting to control the obvious shake in my voice. "He had a tight hold on me so we were standing close and—" I collected myself and continued with more confidence "—I could feel his erection. He said a few vulgar things to me. I guess intimidating women turns him on." Xavier's hand remained on my thigh, gently stroking it. I blurted out the rest in a rush. "He let go of me, mentioned he knew about the foundation, and then told me to ask you if you still share your girlfriends."

A rogue tear slid down my cheek. Not quite the image of composure I wanted to convey.

Xavier's chest rumbled from a low growl. He rubbed the tear away with his thumb, his touch calm and loving, but his eyes blazed with ruthless intentions.

"I see." I wasn't fooled by the measured softness in his tone. "Our tea must be cold by now. I'm going to put on the kettle. It'll only take a minute."

I sat in numb silence, watching him move through the townhouse with his trademark sleek fluidity. His body language betrayed nothing. On the surface, he appeared unbothered.

Slumping into the couch, I twisted the sweatshirt's hem in my fingers. It smelled like Xavier. Clean and outdoorsy and comforting. Grasping the neckline, I pulled it over my nose, breathing him in. Our encounters over the last few months played over and over in my mind.

His overconfident flirtatious advances.

My feeble attempts at resisting.

Our lives and pasts intersecting, becoming irrevocably entwined.

I will risk everything, Victoria. I will fucking destroy him if he comes near you again.

That day on the beach felt like a lifetime ago. Xavier's not-so-quiet promise of violence didn't concern me at the time. Even the best of us succumb to hyperbole when emotions run high.

Now?

Maybe I shouldn't like hearing he'd go to extreme lengths for me. But deep down, I did. I liked the way his dark, protective nature sizzled through me.

I liked knowing he would always be in my corner, no matter what.

But righting this wrong could shatter everything.

Xavier ambled back into the living room nearly ten minutes later, sans hot water or tea. He lowered himself, almost regally, onto the cushion. An eyebrow arched when he looked at me.

"Is there a reason your face is buried in my sweatshirt?"

I pulled it down. "It smells good."

"Thought so." Enough of a smile appeared to reveal his dimple. "Feeling okay?"

"I guess."

Xavier pushed a hand through his hair and nodded. "We should… there's quite a bit we should talk about."

My stomach tumbled into free fall. "What were you doing just now? You weren't making tea."

"Can't get anything past you, can I?"

I bristled at his flippant attitude. "I'm not in the mood for your nonsense."

"Sorry, love." He dipped his head and kissed my cheek. "I was taking care of a few things."

"What things?"

His lack of an immediate answer irked me. I folded my arms, leveling my best *I'm waiting* stare at him. Unease simmered beneath his eyes. It bubbled, growing impatient, the energy building like a restless spirit.

"I wanted to make sure Jordan wasn't planning to go to New York." His words poured out like hot steam. "The fucking coward chartered a flight somewhere. I'm not letting you out of my sight until I know where he is."

A dull ache throbbed behind my eyes. "I doubt he'll go to Manhattan. It's too obvious."

"Nothing is too obvious for him."

"Was that the only *thing* you were taking care of, or do you have more?"

"That's the only one that matters right now."

I sensed I was approaching the vault of secrets again so I steered the conversation another direction. "What is it you wanted to talk about?"

Xavier's whole body shuddered. "All of it."

I scooted closer to him, resting my head on his shoulder. That lasted a total of three seconds before he pulled me onto his lap.

"I was comfortable," I muttered.

"And now we're both comfortable."

When his fingers caressed my neck, I swallowed hard. "Is there a mark?"

"Yes."

"Is it super noticeable?"

Flames burned deep in his eyes. "It is to me."

I tipped his chin up until our gazes met. "Then keep those pretty blues here."

The strength of his stare made my cheeks flush, which then caused his breathing to stagger. Without missing a beat, he ran the pad of his thumb over my lips. A shiver skipped up and down my spine.

"You're doing the thing again." A wicked grin played on his mouth when he noticed my confusion. "Flipping the script on me. The push and pull."

"Oh, you mean our little game of cause and effect. You make me blush, I make you forget how to breathe. Stuff like that."

"Maybe." His deep, soft laugh stirred the embers smoldering deep inside me. "Whatever you want to call it, I like it."

Cupping a hand behind my neck, he pulled our foreheads together. I knew he was stalling. I knew he was avoiding the inevitable. Today has been explosive on so many levels. Taking this moment of solace seemed appropriate.

I pressed a hand to his chest. Xavier always felt strong and solid beneath my touch. The steady beat of his heart vibrated through my skin. Its rhythm invaded my senses, accelerating my longing to know every broken inch of him. Every shadow, every buried secret, every part of this beautiful, fractured, multilayered man.

Please don't ever take your light away.

Holding him tighter, I silently vowed to pour as much of my light into his soul as I could. I didn't have much, but what existed belonged to him.

"I was at the bonfire that night."

Pain clawed at my insides hearing his admission as the intersection of our pasts sharpened into vivid reality. "Did you see her?"

"No." A soft kiss brushed against my cheek. "I never saw her. But..." He released a shuddering breath. "Jordan and I got into a fight, as usual. Stupid shit. Football, girls. He mouthed off about Millie's friends being there." I stopped breathing. "Twins. He only said twins. I was hell bent on defending Millie, so I hit him again."

He covered my hand with his, anguish lining his mouth.

"If I'd known what he was about to do, I never would have provoked him like that. I feel...maybe..."

Resting my fingertips on his lips, I silenced him. "We didn't know one another back then. I'm not going to sit here and allow you to feel any responsibility for what happened. Charlotte made her own choices."

Echoes of her decisions continued to reverberate through so many people's lives. Tiny cracks of the aftermath spread along the fragile glass of time. Seeing the events of my teenage years through the lens of adulthood was something I'd struggled to achieve. My default was always to blame myself, drown in the ocean of guilt, and repeat the cycle.

This glimmer of clarity provided strength for me to say what I said next.

"Charlotte's death tore my family apart because we let it. We never healed. All we did was allow the grief to consume what remained."

"I know you now. I have a real fucking problem with him putting his hands on you and hurting you like this." Agony twisted Xavier's features while he gently stroked the bruised skin on my neck. "What he chooses to do to me is inconsequential. He will not touch you again. Ever."

"It's not inconsequential to me." Tears burned at the corners of my eyes. "He said...he said there's a lot the public doesn't know about you.

What did he mean by that?"

Shaking his head, Xavier slouched into the cushions. I'd never seen him look so distraught. Approaching this vault of secrets might not be the best idea right now.

"You don't have to—"

"I do." He rested his hands on my thighs. "I started to at your team's celebration and I've put it off long enough."

Anxiety settled in my stomach, bracing for what he'd say next.

"Millie and I dated when we were twenty-four. It only lasted about six months. I wasn't what anyone would consider boyfriend material. I preferred things to be less serious and I pretty much did as I pleased. But we'd been friends for a long time and she seemed to understand what my preferences were, so, I thought it would be okay."

"Did you—"

"No." His thumb caressed my jaw. "I know what you're going to ask, and the answer is no. She knew what I liked. We tried a few times but she wasn't comfortable with actually doing it." Another soft stroke of his thumb passed over my jaw. "I meant it when I said nobody has ever seen me the way you do."

Too many questions flooded my mind. I took a deep breath, attempting to pacify my ever increasing pulse rate.

"Do you want me to continue?"

For once I didn't fight against answering how he wanted. "Green."

Several seconds passed before he spoke. "I'm going to sound like an absolute cad when I say this. And I want you to know, at the time, I was."

I shifted on his lap to straddle him and laced my fingers behind his neck. A satisfied growl rumbled through his chest.

"You have no idea how much having you this close is helping," he whispered, dragging his hands up my thighs until they rested on my waist. "Cade wanted to show off his new house so he invited basically everyone he knew over one weekend. The party was massive. Drinking, drugs, girls everywhere."

"A lot of temptation for a group of young athletes."

He nodded. "Too much. And we were more than willing to take advantage of it."

I leaned back slightly, running my hands down his chest. "What happened?"

Anticipation filled the space between us.

"Millie and I weren't technically together anymore at this point but we hung out at the party. I got drunk. She got drunk. We started messing around on the couch in front of everyone. After a bit, she didn't feel comfortable and told me to stop, which I did. She excused herself to use the loo. I went to find Cade and ended up running into fucking McKennie."

"He was there?"

"Yeah." Bitterness coated his tone. "He made some vulgar remark about what I'd been doing with Millie on the couch. I almost punched him out but one of the lads from United walked over and Jordan left. I got wrapped up in a conversation. When I went back to the other room, she was gone."

"Gone? Like, she left?"

"That's the impression I got after asking around. A few people told me they saw her walk out. So, I stayed, hung out with Cade, had more drinks." He looked away. "I was young and reckless and impulsive. I didn't care about consequences. I let my selfish needs dictate my actions and— Cade and I flirted with these two girls. Things escalated and we all had sex."

My eyes widened. "All four of you?"

"Yes. Well, not Cade and I but we shared the girls. It's something we've done from time to time. In the middle of everything, Millie walked in. Turns out, she'd never left the party. She'd just gone outside with some friends."

"Xavier," I gasped. "Why did you do that?"

"Because I'm an arrogant asshole with the whole fucking world at my disposal." A scowl marred his mouth. "I thought I was untouchable, that I could do anything I wanted. You want to know the best part?" Acid dripped from his words. "Jordan was the one who told her to come back inside. He'd seen what Cade and I were doing, and made sure Millie did, too."

His grip on my waist tightened.

"After she ran out, he cornered me and said it was payback for shagging his fiancée."

I needed a minute to collect my thoughts. When Jordan found me in Manhattan, he'd mentioned something about Xavier stealing his fiancée.

When I'd pressed Xavier about it the night we reunited on the terrace, he'd told me he messed around with her. Although, he'd positioned it as she was cheating on Jordan with him and another soccer player.

My brain shifted into work mode, more for self-preservation than anything else.

"Going back to what Jordan said about the public not knowing a lot about you. Is this all he meant? Or is there more?"

"My reputation is well-known." Anger blazed behind his eyes. "I was sixteen when I entered this life. I worked hard. Nothing was handed to me. But after I signed my contract, something inside me became more," he struggled to find the word, "*aware*, I guess you could say. I burned the candle at both ends, never caring about any ramifications because there weren't any."

"Did it ever affect your ability to play the game?"

His dismissive laugh hung in the room. "No. I was good at keeping up appearances. But after what happened with Millie I sort of...I spiraled. I sought revenge on Jordan at every turn and became even more reckless. Bennet was always the one to clean up any messes in the media but things were slipping. I had more paparazzi on me. Not to mention anyone with a mobile phone who felt like recording a video or taking a picture. I couldn't control what was happening. Bennet finally reached his limit. He told me to get my shit together or he'd sell my contract to another club so I'd become someone else's problem."

My heart broke. "Why even—"

Something vibrated beneath me. Xavier shoved his hand in his pocket and grabbed his phone. He swore under his breath.

"What happened?"

"Nothing. Just...nothing."

"Xavier." I held his chin when he looked away. "Tell me."

He sighed. "Remember the woman on the sideline after the match in Paris?"

"Remember?" I huffed. "Yeah. She had her hands all over you. What does she want now?"

"There's a nonsense gossip article online about me. She wanted a comment."

"She's a *reporter*? After what you just told me you still fucked around with a—" Incredulity slackened my jaw. "What does the article say?"

He showed me the text. I opened the link and was floored by what I saw. The headline blared *Can't Keep Her Hands Off The Keeper: Has England's Number One Returned to His Old Ways*? A photo of Xavier laughing with a blonde woman accompanied the so-called article.

My heart skipped several beats. "I'll be right back."

Hopping off his lap, I trotted to the bedroom and grabbed my phone. When I returned, I repositioned myself on his lap and opened the texts I'd received the other night. Taking a deep breath, I showed him the screen. Shock washed across his face.

"Who sent this to you?"

"Jordan." I glanced at the photo of him and the same blonde. "Who is she?"

Xavier stiffened beneath me. "How did he get your number?"

"I don't know. He just said he sent the photos and—"

"Photos? There's more than one?"

Squeezing the phone, I braced myself for what was about to happen. "I got this one the same night." I showed him the screen. "At first, I thought it was someone from my past trying to stir up trouble but Jordan said he's experimenting with new technology. Creating fake photos that appear real."

"I see." The same measured softness colored his tone but indignation blazed in his eyes. "Change your number. Immediately."

"No. I already blocked—"

"Change it," he snapped. "That's final."

Frustration surged through me. I'm not one who takes too kindly to being ordered around. "Don't talk to me like that."

We stared at one another for a long stretch of uncomfortable beats. Stubbornness seemed to be a vice we both shared.

Xavier backed down first. "Sorry. I'm just trying to keep you out of his reach."

"I know. But if he found my phone number once, he'll find it again." I laced my fingers behind his neck. "Who is the blonde in the picture?"

"Nobody. She walked over to Cade and I at dinner with her friend. You know how Cade is. Never passes up an opportunity to flirt. They sat with us. She hit on me and invited me to her flat." Shivers rattled my body. Xavier pinned an intense stare on me. "I excused myself and ended up running into Jordan at the bar. You know what happened after that."

"You're not glossing over anything?" The question tumbled out with more animosity than I intended.

"I'm not. I would never—" he winced "—I'm not that guy anymore." Xavier frowned, keeping me locked in his cobalt gaze. "You believe me, right?"

I nodded, my head spinning. I didn't know what to focus on first. In my heart, I believed what he said about the blonde. His actions years ago didn't surprise me. I'd seen many young athletes get swept up in the fast lifestyle associated with going pro.

I would never judge him for any of it. I don't have the right. My track record with instant physical gratification was just as shocking.

The screw tightened in my chest. Exhaustion smothered every muscle in my body.

Part of me wanted to curl up with my boyfriend and fall asleep in his arms. The other part longed for a quiet space to make sense of everything.

"I should go back to the hotel," I said quietly.

Resignation swept through Xavier. He caressed my thighs for a brief moment before removing his hands. A hard swallow disrupted the strong column of his throat.

"Is there anything I can do to convince you to spend the night?"

Asking that question was more than enough to convince me. I wanted to. I wanted it so much I suffocated in the desire. Crushing sadness squeezed my chest.

"I fly out first thing in the morning. We have our home opener in two days." My shoulders sagged. "I just…I need time to process everything. If I stay with you, we'll fall into our usual pattern and," my voice hitched, "I really want to do this the right way."

Sapphire eyes pleaded for me to stay, their usual vibrance dulled by regret and fear.

In an effort to soothe any doubts, I leaned close and kissed the soft skin beneath his ear. "I'm not leaving forever. I'm just going home." I kissed his neck again, letting my lips linger.

Xavier held me in a vice-like grip. I felt every shudder, every ragged breath that tormented his body. Pieces of my fractured heart scraped through my veins. Leaving him in such a vulnerable state broke me.

Thick tears rolled down my cheeks. I wiped them away forcefully and stood up, somehow making my way to the bedroom to gather my belongings and call for a taxi.

When I returned to the living room, Xavier stood by the door. I couldn't stomach the utter look of defeat on his face. Without saying a word, I walked over to him, placed my hand on his chest, and stared into his eyes. They stared back, filled with dismay.

"I'll be back before you know it." I tried sounding cheerful but my voice betrayed me. "I promise."

Coming here wasn't a mistake. Learning more about his past wasn't a mistake.

Then why did I feel like nothing would ever be the same between us?

Chapter
THIRTY

Our next six matches were an absolute shit show.

Don't get me started on the one I watched from the couch or all the media fallout from it.

I had a chip on my shoulder the size of Greenland when I finally returned.

Too bad nothing has gone right since. Especially today's result.

I'd gladly press a reset button if it fell on the pitch in front of me. Our defenders played awful, including my step-brother, who remained in the starting eleven for some unknown reason. Cade bruised his knee on a cheap sliding challenge from the opponent's central midfielder. Our left winger got red-carded in the twentieth minute, leaving us down a man for the rest of the match.

And I couldn't stop a ball from hitting the back of the net if my life depended on it. I could hear fans taunting me from the section directly behind my goal.

Not what I'd call a banner fucking day.

Believe it or not, staying focused on football was the only way I survived the last few weeks. The aftermath of Victoria's visit weighed on me daily. We still texted as much as we could but it all felt different. More like two colleagues reaching out to see how the other was doing, rather than two people supposedly in love trying to stay connected.

Her season was now well underway. When I heard from her before today's game started, she was boarding a flight to Seattle.

I barely listened to the post-match lecture. I stared out into the changing room, observing my teammates. Our performance so far this season has been lackluster to say the least. Not living up to expectations started to affect the club's overall mood.

"We'll get back to the business of winning after the international break," Eric, our manager, told the room. "For those of you called up, good luck against the Dutch. See you all in a couple weeks."

After showering and changing, I walked out with Cade. His knee was wrapped but he seemed to be moving around just fine.

"Bloody cheap shot, that," he grumbled. "I saw him gunning for me. I'm lucky he didn't tear my ACL."

"Think you'll sit out for the qualifier?"

"Fuck no. I'll be dead before missing a chance to get England another trophy."

"Another?" I snickered. "You do realize the last time we won was before you and I were born."

He rolled his eyes. "I don't see your point."

We approached our cars in silence. The thought of returning to my flat to sit and wallow alone pressed down on me.

"Dinner at Black Rose?" Cade asked. "It's tradition."

Going to Briarcliff crossed my mind several times the last couple weeks but I never did.

"Sure."

"Last one there is buying." Cade punched my shoulder before trotting over to his car. I laughed, knowing full well he'd drive like a nutter to get there first.

Settling behind the steering wheel, I let the events of the day roll off me as best I could. I hated losing. Especially when I know I didn't do enough to help the club win.

Before I left, I debated on sending Victoria a quick text. I wasn't sure if she'd arrived yet but maybe she'd appreciate a little hello from me. Or maybe not.

Bloody hell.

Me: Hope the flight to Seattle was alright. Good luck tomorrow

Could I sound like more of a knobhead? And why the fuck was I so nervous to text my girlfriend?

Annoyed with myself, I turned the radio up and started driving.

The more of London I could see in my rearview mirror, the better I felt. By the time the roads became smaller and filled with curves, I relaxed. But as I approached the stretch of road where I first saw Victoria, my heart seized.

I could still picture her, clear as day, pacing in circles. After pulling off the road, I must have stayed in my car and watched her for longer than was socially acceptable. But I was just so damn captivated by her. I'd never felt anything like it. And then when I finally got out and she walked right into me? Jesus Christ, I wanted to take her in my arms right then and there. I didn't even know her name but all I wanted was her.

Blinking myself out of the memory, I focused on the road.

Ten minutes later I parked near Black Rose. Cade was already waiting for me by the door, surrounded by a few fans. We'd been coming here after matches for years so it's not surprising to see a small crowd.

We signed some autographs and posed for pictures before going inside.

The pub wasn't too crowded so we sat at the bar.

"My boys are here," Dawn exclaimed, flashing her megawatt smile when she walked over. "Just the two of you tonight?"

"You sound disappointed," Cade teased. "Don't tell me Bennet is your favorite."

"Stop." She swatted his arm playfully. "It's been ages since you've all been here together. I miss my three princes."

I smiled. "You say that to all the lads."

"You—" she reached out and ruffled my hair "—can't charm your way out of explaining why you haven't been here to say hello. I know for a fact you've been spending a lot of time at Victoria's cottage."

If there's one person who knows what goes on in Briarcliff Village, it's Dawn Halston. She and her husband, Ray, own this pub. Nothing gets past them.

My eyebrow winged up. "Spying on me?"

Dawn tilted her head and pursed her lips. "If I hear one more young lady talking about the dishy guy with tattoos walking around shirtless in front of that house I'll—"

"I can walk around shirtless in here," I cut in with a smirk. "Help drum up business."

"Mate, you'll scare everyone away," Cade jeered.

The pleasant smile on Dawn's face soothed my frayed nerves. One of the main reasons why I haven't been in here should be obvious. I knew Dawn would mention Victoria and I'm powerless to hide any type of reaction to hearing her name.

She clasped both our hands and told us she'd return with drinks.

A good thing about being out with Cade was his ability to sense when I refused to talk about certain topics. In this case, the banned topic was Victoria. After she left, I shut myself off to any conversation about her with him or Bennet. The only updates I wanted from Bennet involved Jordan. I still didn't know where he'd flown to. All I knew was he left England.

My hands clenched. When I do see him again, he'll regret touching her.

"Did I tell you what happened this week?" Cade slapped his hand down on the bar, jolting me from venomous thoughts of Jordan. "Most frustrating thing ever."

Dawn placed two beers in front of us, took our food orders, and went to assist other customers.

"You found a gray hair?" I asked, casually sipping my drink.

"Arse. No."

"Well I figured with all the dramatics it had to be something life changing."

"Like the sulky face you've put on the past few weeks? If you brood any harder, I'll have to create an emo playlist to turn on when you walk in a room."

"Just bloody tell me."

"I will. Then you're going to tell me what has your knickers in a twist." He took a long swallow of beer. "You know how I went to the children's hospital for a charity event?"

"Vaguely."

He frowned at me. "Thanks for paying attention, mate. Anyway, I ran into some of the lads from Holwood FC. We got to talking until their marketing representative sucked the fun out of everything. I can't remember her name but she was the biggest pain."

I could already feel myself losing interest in this conversation. "Did she turn you down when you asked her out?"

He ignored my question. "This girl had the largest stick wedged up her ass. She was a bloody ice queen. You know me. I like to finesse my way with the ladies, throw in a few one liners, have a laugh. Nothing worked with her. It drove me mad."

Now I was fully amused. My best friend wasn't used to getting snubbed. "It's called a challenge, Cade. Besides, not every woman has to fall for you. I like the sound of her."

"Of course you do. Did I mention she's American? Thought maybe you'd have some words of wisdom since you swept Victoria off her feet with your stupid dimple and all that so-called charm."

The genuine laugh that fell out of me felt good. I'd never admit it to him, but Cade was right about my lengthy brooding streak. A small weight lifted from my shoulders.

"She wasn't impressed by your jawline that could…what did that one girl say? Cut through steel like it was butter?"

Cade shrugged, taking another long pull of beer. "Dunno. Shit like this doesn't usually bother me. I went on a date that same night but couldn't stop thinking about this girl. And the other thing? She's older. Like, our age."

"Now I've heard everything." I smirked, reclining an elbow on the bar. "Cade Gallagher, World's Okayest Striker, fancies a woman his own age."

"I will let that half-assed remark slide on one condition."

"What?"

Cade's expression turned serious. "Tell me what's going on with you. And don't do the fucking Maddox thing you always do with deflecting and avoiding and scowling. You might be able to fool the rest of the lads but I know better. Spill it."

Any good will or lightened mood I'd felt deflated faster than I anticipated. Hiding this from Cade has been hard and not completely fair, but I also didn't want to drag him into something so multifaceted.

"I know Bennet knows," he griped. "And he's been less than forthcoming with what's going on in his gilded world of the posh and minted. The two of you keep shutting me out."

"You're right," I admitted. "It's just—" I paused, preparing myself for what's to come "—Victoria was here unexpectedly the week I was benched." I stared at the food one of the bar staff slid in front of us. "She'd gone to see Jordan."

I glanced at Cade. His full attention rested on me. Taking a deep breath, I told him what happened. A streak of anger flickered through his eyes when I relayed the part about Jordan putting her in a chokehold. His shoulders sagged a bit when I mentioned the party years ago.

I didn't leave out one detail.

More than a few minutes of silence elapsed between us.

"Our past selves weren't model citizens, were they?" A chagrined smile pulled at Cade's mouth. "We've both done a fair amount of maturing since then. Sounds like Victoria just needed some time to sort through it all. You still speak everyday though, yeah?"

"We do but nothing feels right."

"In all the years I've known you, I have never once seen you admit to your shortcomings or weaknesses so readily. At least not out loud. She sees you, mate. All of you. More than Bennet or I could ever fathom." He knocked back the rest of his beer. "I've said it a million times but I'll say it again. You've worked too fucking hard to get yourself right. Victoria is an amazing woman. Create a future with her. What's past is past. Let it stay there."

Confiding in him actually eased some of my discomfort. Our conversation turned away from past mistakes to the upcoming qualifier against the Netherlands. We both agreed it will be a tough match but not impossible to win.

"I'm telling you, we're taking the tournament next summer. Football's coming home." Cade's enthusiastic declaration was contagious, if not bordering on unrealistic.

"What if we do? Any idea what happens after we lift the trophy?"

"Make millions in endorsements. Retire a global phenomenon. Perfect ending to my career."

Hearing Cade mention retirement surprised me to a certain extent. We weren't getting any younger. Several commentators already planted seeds of doubt regarding our ability to play at a high level. We both turn thirty-seven later this year. Not that I ever let my age interfere with my desire to excel.

"Retirement, huh? I can't imagine having extra time on your hands is a good thing. Too much temptation out there." I took a bite of cottage pie.

"Nah. I'd go right into coaching. Start developing young talent for the next generation of—" he gestured at me and himself "—us. Reckon your kids will play better than you."

I choked on my food. "Kids? Fucking hell, Gallagher. You've actually gone mad."

"Deflect all you want. My predictions are never wrong."

Ridiculous comments aside, Cade is one of the best strikers to ever play the game. I never pictured him becoming a coach though. Maybe it's not such an outlandish idea.

By the time we finished dinner, I was in a significantly better mood than when the day started. Sitting alone in my house wasn't quite what I felt like doing, so I stuck around after Cade said his goodbyes. Dawn came over for a brief chat and mentioned someone wanted to meet me. A gentleman sitting at the other end of the bar lifted his glass when she gestured to him.

"Yeah, sure," I said. "Tell him it's fine."

The man made his way over slowly. He appeared to be around the same age as my dad. Tall, salt and pepper hair, well-dressed. There was something oddly familiar about him but I couldn't put my finger on it.

"Sorry for the interruption. Didn't think I'd be running into England's number one at this pub." He extended his hand. "I'm Trevor. Nice to meet you."

"Xavier," I responded, shaking his hand. "Pleasure's all mine. Can I refill your glass?"

Something warm and comforting reflected in his eyes. "I won't say no to that. Thank you."

Trevor and I chit-chatted about random things. I learned he grew up in Leeds and was definitely not a Royal City supporter.

"I am more than happy to cheer for you in England's jersey but other than that," he shook his head, "I'm afraid you'll get no support from me on the pitch."

I laughed. "You're not the first person to say that to me."

"Ready for the Dutch?"

"Think so. They're tough but I'm confident we'll get the points we need."

"Good." He looked down, turning the glass in his fingers. "So what brings you so far from London? I figured a popular young man like yourself would rather be out in the big city."

"It's a standing ritual for Cade and I. He was here with me just before. We always have dinner here after a home game."

"Cade Gallagher? The striker with the golden boot." Trevor smirked. "Same goes for him, you know. Love him in an England jersey. Will taunt him on the pitch every other time."

"Too bad you missed him. He loves a spirited debate."

Dawn came over to refill our glasses. "You gentlemen getting on alright?" Her genial tone matched her affectionate gaze.

"Always a pleasure coming here, Mrs. Halston. I'll be sure to stop in again when I'm back in town."

My phone vibrated while the two of them swapped travel stories.

Tori: Seattle is drizzly but good. Saw the final score for your game. Yikes.

Me: Yikes? We only lost by a goal

Tori: Only teasing. What are you up to?

Me: Dinner at Black Rose with Cade. Chatting with Dawn now

Tori: Tell her I said hello

Me: Will do

When she didn't respond straight away I figured this was the end of our polite discourse. Trepidation and misery strangled me from the inside out. I missed her with a vengeance. The skin she'd kissed beneath my ear tingled and burned. The sensation spread until every cell in my body threatened to detonate.

Tori: I miss you

Those three words stole the breath right out of my fucking lungs. The phone landed with a thud on the bar. I glanced up to see if Dawn or my new friend noticed. They were far too engrossed in conversation.

Me: I miss you too, love

Tori: I know you're in Birmingham next week for training but can we try to make time for a video call?

Me: Just tell me when and I'll be ready

Tori: Will do :P

"Look at that smile," Dawn exclaimed, grabbing my hand. "Did you just hear from your lovely girlfriend?"

"I did. She says to say hello."

"You better bring her here next time she visits." She turned to Trevor. "Have a good flight tomorrow. Don't be a stranger." Dawn excused herself to tend to other customers.

"I should be going," Trevor said, standing up. He regarded me with interest before saying, "Dawn is right about that smile. You haven't stopped since getting that text. I remember always having a silly grin on my face when I met my wife." He laughed at a memory only he could see. "Quite the spitfire, she was. My daughter takes after her."

"Sounds like you had your hands full."

Heartache passed briefly in his eyes. Again, I had the weird sensation of there being something oddly familiar about him.

"I did." Placing a hand on my shoulder, he squeezed it gently. "Your girlfriend is lucky to have you. Nice meeting you, Xavier. I'm sure we'll run into one another again."

Chapter
THIRTY-ONE

Late Wednesday afternoon, I sat in my office, exhausted in all ways possible.

Life has been hazy since returning from London. If sleepwalking through my existence was a professional sport, I'd be the best in the world at this point. I don't know how I made it through the home opener, let alone Seattle. My body operated on autopilot.

It had to.

Waking up each day missing Xavier poked fresh needles of pain in my chest. If I let it consume me, I'd never get anything done.

"Victoria." Hannah's stern tone sliced through my reverie. "Don't forget we have our weekly presser with Coach at nine tomorrow morning. And then Noah is scheduled to appear on Jake Kellerman's nationally televised radio program at ten-thirty."

"Got it." I glanced at my calendar. "Is that collaboration with the Knights still happening? The social media thing with the players?"

"Yeah. Tre and Jax are taking center stage on that with Tyler and Matt."

I laughed. "Kaylee will have her hands full."

Hannah's half-hearted smile gave me pause. She hasn't been herself in weeks. Not that I've been much of a shoulder for her to lean on. She looked as miserable as I felt.

"I have a meeting in ten minutes," I said, "but when I'm done, you and I need to plan a spa day."

Questioning brown eyes studied me. I leaned forward, resting my chin in my hand.

"Massages. Cucumber water. Fluffy robes. How can you resist?"

"Tempting."

"Think about it. I'll stop by your office before I leave."

Hannah rose to her feet like a queen and walked out not saying a word. I flopped back in my chair, exhaling until my lungs completely emptied. Thick silence saturated my office. I'd closed my eyes for not even a second when the phone rang.

"This is Victoria," I answered.

"Hello, sweetheart. Did I catch you at a bad time?"

My eyes flew open.

"Dad. No. I was just…no, it's not a bad time at all."

His soft chuckle and light British accent soothed some of my tense nerves.

"I'm in Manhattan this week. You sounded pretty adamant in your text that you wanted to know the next time I'd be here. So, here I am. I'd like to see you. Sooner, rather than later."

The last time my father was in town, he handed over the keys to Briarcliff Cottage. I could only imagine what this visit will bring.

"I'm free tomorrow, if that works for you." I typed his name into my calendar. "I actually have a few things to talk to you about."

"Sounds serious. Is it?"

My head spun recalling everything Jordan told me.

"I don't know," I answered honestly. "I'll find out when I see you."

After ending the call with my dad, I paced around my office just to shake off the nerves. The last thing I wanted was to appear out of sorts for my meeting. I'd only managed to do a few laps when my phone rang. I told the receptionist I'd be there in a minute.

Smoothing down my skirt, I inhaled slow, letting out a calming breath. This meeting was probably the least stressful part of my day. The closer I got to the main reception area, the better I felt.

A well-dressed brunette stood by one of the display cases, staring at the trophies.

"Shiny, aren't they?" I asked, approaching her.

She turned, her arms hugging her body just as tight as the black wrap dress she wore. Dark brown eyes examined my cheerful smile. At least, I hoped it was cheerful.

"They are. I'm sure my little brother appreciates seeing them every day." Noticeable sarcasm tinged her words.

My laughter was hard to stifle. "I'm Victoria," I said, extending my hand. "You must be Chelsea."

A genuine smile erupted across her face when she shook it. "Thank you so much for agreeing to see me. I know this was last minute."

We did the small talk thing on the way to my office. I offered her some water before sitting at my desk.

"So, what can I help you with?"

Chelsea glanced around at my display cases and shelves, her pretty face set in an expression of indifference. "I know Dante said I was looking for something in the sports world but to be honest, I don't want that."

"No problem. I have connections just about everywhere if—"

"Actually," she interrupted, "do you know anyone in the non-profit sector? The one thing I enjoy at the club is planning the charity appearances. I want to focus on work that has meaning. No offense to what you do."

"None taken."

I tapped my nails on the desk. Now that Killian started his new job, he hasn't been able to put much time into the foundation.

"I hope this doesn't sound too forward, but I just formed a non-profit and need a permanent foundation director."

Her eyes widened with hopeful optimism. "That's a big role to fill."

I smiled. "It sounds more intimidating than it is. I'm looking for someone to handle the marketing strategies and collaborative program development." I opened one of my desk drawers and pulled out an information packet. "Read through this. It explains pretty much everything."

"You don't need an answer right away, do you?" she asked, flipping through the packet. "I'm still under contract with Holwood FC and have to finish out the season."

"No. It's not officially launching until next spring. Take it home. Read it at your leisure."

Her expression softened while she read one of the sections. "This is all for your sister?" She sucked in a breath when she looked at me. "I'm sorry. I didn't mean to upset you."

"You didn't. This is my default reaction whenever I talk about her."

Glossy red lips curved into a warm smile. "I get a good vibe from you. You're not like the public relations guy at the club. He's so phony. I swear he's made of plastic."

I covered my mouth and tried not to giggle. "Some can be."

"That's probably why I need to get away from footballers. All those egos." She crossed her legs and leaned on an elbow. "Don't get me started on the guys in the Premier League. They're a special breed."

For the second time in as many minutes, I couldn't hold back my laughter. "I have a feeling we'd spend all night swapping stories about egomaniac athletes."

"Not Dante, though. He's a humble little angel." Her facetious grin and dramatic eye roll cemented my growing admiration.

We chatted for a few more minutes before ending the meeting. Since Chelsea lives in London, we agreed to get together again next month when the Legends play their international game. We exchanged numbers and planned to stay in touch until then.

My heart sped up thinking about returning to London. I glanced at the time. Xavier should be finished training for the day. We haven't texted much since the weekend. Apparently this game against the Netherlands was a pretty big one. According to all the online chatter, England should qualify for next summer's tournament with a win or draw.

Me: How's training?

Mildly Hot: Better than last time

Me: Are you busy?

Mildly Hot: Just relaxing. Still at work?

Me: Yeah. Just wrapped up my final meeting of the day

Mildly Hot: Have a few minutes to talk?

The phone vibrated in my hand before I could type a reply.

"Someone's impatient," I answered, staring at his handsome face. "Hi."

"Don't think I've actually ever seen you at work." Sapphire eyes scanned the shelves behind me. "Fancy office."

"Pfft. It's not."

An awkward cloud of silence settled over us. We stared at one another, wordless. Aside from social media posts, I haven't *looked* at him since I left London. All of our communication has been via text.

His brows furrowed. A hint of frustration passed through his features.

The longer we stayed quiet, the more my anxiety ramped up. I wish I had the right words to convey what I'd been feeling since he unlocked part of his past.

I *did* have the right words. The problem? I'd spent so many years convincing myself I didn't deserve the type of affection Xavier provided that I became used to shoving down what I truly felt. Leaving him hovering in a cloud of uncertainty didn't sit right with me.

I longed for things to be normal between him and I, whatever that is.

I know what it's not.

It's *not* sitting here agonizing over what to say to the man I love. It's not worrying if I broke him in some way when I left after he shared the most vulnerable parts of himself. It's not tossing and turning at night wondering if every word that came out of Jordan's mouth was true.

"Have you been able to go out and see Birmingham at all?" *What the hell kind of question is that?*

"I've been here quite a bit. Pretty much seen it."

I fidgeted with my necklace. This sucked. Especially since I was the one who suggested we find time for a video chat this week.

Good job, Chase. Way to make this even more uncomfortable than it's already been.

"So, um, what time is the game on Saturday?"

And the hits just keep on coming.

Uneasiness hissed through me, like a fire desperate to ignite. I couldn't drag enough oxygen into my lungs. All the cells in my body trembled. Why is this so *hard*?

"Seven," he responded, his tone flat. "Two your time."

The screw tightened deep in my chest. Invisible waves of needles rolled beneath my skin. I inhaled slow, annoyed with myself. We'd slipped into this unfeeling, disconnected way of speaking so easily it tore me up.

"Christ," Xavier muttered. "I can't do the small talk thing with you anymore. It— *fuck.*"

A lump of emotion clogged my throat, threatening to suffocate me.

"I can't either." The words fought their way out. "I miss how we were before."

"*Before*?" His strained repetition chilled me to the bone. "I see."

I squeezed my eyes shut. "That's not what I meant." When I looked at him, his sultry mouth twisted into a frown. "I know I've been a little distant lately. It's like a…I guess you could call it self preservation."

The frown deepened, draining the light from his eyes. "What aren't you saying, Tori?"

Struggling to say anything to him in this moment wrecked me. My entire professional career revolves around communication. Stay on message. Be direct. Shape public perception. But when it comes to Xavier, the more I surrender to my feelings for him, the more I falter.

Nothing will ever be broken between us.

"I just…" My lip trembled. A solitary tear rolled down my cheek. "I wish you were here."

Some of the tension in his shoulders melted. "Me too, love." He touched his neck, just below his left ear. A hard swallow expanded and contracted in his throat. "Cade says hello."

A small smile tugged at my mouth. "Tell my favorite striker I miss him."

"Do you have any big plans this week?"

"I'm having dinner with my dad tomorrow."

Much to my surprise, curiosity and warmth pushed through the apprehension.

"You must be excited to see him."

"I'm nervous. We haven't seen or spoken to each other this much in years. It's weird. And I have to bring up the whole…*thing*."

Our silent stare completed what I left unsaid.

"Want me to be there with you?"

My heart nearly stopped. "You have a game. You can't—"

"Tori." His low timbre vibrated through me. "I meant a video call. Although I'm more than willing to fly there right now if you asked."

I'm not a selfish person, but the temptation to have him abandon his responsibilities with England's national team and fly here for me was powerful.

"What is it you soccer players say? For club and country? Your team needs you. Besides, I saw the pictures you posted on social media. Playing for your childhood hero looks good on you."

A pleasant grin slanted his mouth. "You remembered."

"You still have to introduce him to me."

"Come to the match and I will."

"I'd be there in a heartbeat if I could."

"I know, love." Xavier cast his eyes down. "I mean it. I'll fly to you if you want. All this distance is killing me."

We both know he didn't mean only the physical distance. Our emotional connection was frayed.

"Me too. Let's make an effort to talk again. Like this. No more generic check ins."

When Xavier looked at me, my stomach fell. His guard was up. All the progress we've made in our relationship teetered on the edge of a cliff.

"Have you been doing okay after what happened with Jordan?"

Neither one of us has broached this topic head on since the night at his townhouse. A phantom hand burned around my neck.

"I've had a few restless nights. I try not to think about it. Have you been doing alright?"

Another round of poisonous rage crept into his eyes. "I still don't know where he is. As soon as I find out, I'm putting an end to this."

"Please don't do anything impulsive." The words felt hollow coming out of my mouth. I couldn't stop him any more than I could stop an out of control freight train.

"It won't be impulsive, trust me." Malice weaved through his tone. "He'll be sorry he ever put his hands on you."

"Premeditated isn't any better," I snapped. "I love you for wanting to defend me but I can't handle the thought of you getting hurt or losing your career over this."

Xavier's shoulders stiffened. He stroked his neck again and nodded. Part of me sensed he only backed down out of respect for my feelings but the look in his eyes said otherwise. Walls of tension pressed closer and closer around me.

A knot formed in my throat. My chest hurt, my lungs hurt, my heart hurt. Everything fucking hurt.

"I wish there was a way to stop him that didn't involve you beating the crap out of him at every turn. You can't keep doing that, Xavier. I will not lose someone else I love to that piece of shit."

The room went silent except for the low hum of my computer. Distant voices echoed in the hallway. This didn't feel like my office anymore.

It was an airtight prison.

One I needed to leave sooner rather than later.

The expression on Xavier's face oscillated between doubt and determination.

"Talk to me," I pleaded, my voice barely rising above a whisper. "Don't shut me out."

"I'm not shutting you out. I'm—" He exhaled, running a hand through his hair. "There's just so much to say."

"Then tell me something easy." My voice softened. "Tell me something about yourself. Something I wouldn't learn in news articles or player bios."

He remained quiet for a minute before he spoke.

"I didn't tell you all of it." His voice held an uncharacteristic tremble. "About what happened with my father."

The phone nearly slipped from my hand.

"I left out what I overheard him say to Rebecca one night. They thought I was up in my room but I'd gone downstairs for a drink. I heard voices in the living room. My dad sounded upset."

A quiet knock sounded on my office door. Hannah poked her head inside, saw my face, and abruptly left. Xavier was lost in his own memories and didn't notice the interruption.

"He was talking about me and Adam and how happy he was that I had someone to grow up with. Then he said…having me as a son was his greatest joy and the worst thing to ever happen to him." A bitter smile touched his lips. "Imagine saying that about your own child. Imagine *feeling* that way. I was only eleven when I heard him say it but I was old enough to understand what he meant."

"But he didn't—"

"I know. When I got older, I was able to fully comprehend the underlying pain he felt over my mother's death. But at the time, I was just a kid." He scowled. "It scarred me. I was *angry*. I felt inadequate. Like I told you, I channeled the unresolved hurt and took it out on Adam. I let it fuel me to succeed at football. All I wanted was to be noticed. I wanted to feel *wanted*. Football gave that to me. Cade and Bennet gave that to me. Indulging in all the temptations that came along with being a famous athlete gave that to me." His eyes flashed. "I vowed to never let anyone make me feel inadequate again. Not even Jordan."

Hearing that name punched a hole through my heart.

"When he finds out a person's weakness, he doesn't stop. Add jealousy to the mix, and he becomes a monster. He hated that I was better at football than he was. He despised that all the girls were drawn to me and not him. He would tell me I was nothing every chance he could. When I signed with the club and became one of the darlings of the league, it set off a new round of animosity. He was especially vicious when Millie and I started dating. I never understood it. I never will. The night he deliberately brought her into that room to see what Cade and I were doing…it…I hurt the person who, at the time, didn't make me feel like I wasn't enough."

He paused for a quick breath.

"And now he's hurt you. *You*." A myriad of emotions ravaged his face. "You are everything to me. You see me. You see my struggles and you still…you still love me. I've never loved anyone the way I love you. I will not let him ruin that. The only thing stopping me from killing him is the fact that I don't know where the fuck he is."

I sat in stunned silence. Too many questions littered my mind while unshed tears filled my eyes. I didn't have to ask him if he's ever told anyone this before. He hasn't. The man just broke apart into a million pieces in front of me, and I couldn't do anything other than stare at him through my stupid phone thousands of miles away.

"Xavier, I…"

"Not exactly something easy, was it?" His voice caught. "This wasn't how I wanted to tell you. This wasn't even *when* I wanted to tell you." Xavier's eyes flickered with emotion. "I balance on the edge of a sword every fucking day in order to keep up appearances. You shouldn't be dragged into this."

The quiet thickened with dread and confusion. I couldn't form a complete thought, let alone open my mouth to say something.

Xavier's expression stilled, almost as though he was preparing himself for the worst.

"Sorry I ended your work day on such a heavy topic. Get home safe. We'll speak later."

The screen went dark.

Chapter

THIRTY-TWO

It was funny how one moment could change a person's life.

My one moment started at birth and set off a chain reaction that continues to this day.

"Maddox." The goalkeeper coach yelled in frustration. "That's the fourth one you've missed. Run it again."

Training has been a disaster. My timing is off. I'm missing easy saves. My head is a mess.

This is the national team. I can't screw this up with a qualifier coming in two days. I've no doubt Ashton will replace me if I don't get my shit together.

I nodded, glancing at Cole, one of our backup keepers. He'd be more than willing to take my starting job for this match.

Determination lit a fire deep in my belly.

Losing control of my emotions was one thing. Losing control of my ability to focus and play at the highest level was another.

I refused to fail.

We started the drills again. Each time I punched the ball away or caught it, the velocity vibrated through my hands. I pushed harder with every dive and every lunge, stretching my body to its limit.

When the whistle blew to end the session, Zach walked over to me.

"You're practicing like you got something to prove," he remarked. "Want to run through some penalties with me?"

I grabbed my water bottle, pausing to drink. Cade and I practice penalty shoot outs all the time. Might be fun to work with Zach.

"Yeah. Let's see how good a striker you actually are."

Zach's knowing smile cemented my resolve. He placed the ball on the penalty marker and kicked it. No lead up, no theatrics, just a strong kick. A brisk whoosh of air streaked past me.

"Alright, mate. I see what you're doing." I smirked, picking up the ball. "You won't get it by me this time."

I tossed it back to him and stood on the line.

Zach kicked the ball hard. Jesus, what a leg. The sting from the ball hitting my hand burned halfway up my arm.

"Lucky stop," he commented. "Ready for more?"

We practiced for the next twenty minutes. I only play against West London twice a season but I've studied how Zach takes his penalties. I know which side of the net he prefers, if he kicks high or low, and how often he drills it down the middle. He doesn't give away much with his stance but he does feint in the run-up to his kicks.

I've seen this tactic many times. Unfortunately, I've been deceived by it more often than I care to admit.

His last attempt hit the crossbar, sending the ball over the net.

"Guess that means I won this round," I joked.

Zach laughed, placing his hands on his hips. "Fair enough, Maddox. Hope this little session got your mind back in the game."

Stunned by his observation, I followed him to the training facility. We'd almost made it to the changing room when he broke the silence.

"I realize we aren't proper friends or anything, but is everything alright? Off the pitch I mean. You've not been yourself."

I shrugged, not willing to pour my guts out to Zach Donovan. Tensions between us have certainly eased since the day I sucker-punched him during a match. Doesn't mean I'm sharing my life story with him.

"Can't complain," I answered in a brisk tone. "Just the usual stuff."

He stayed quiet for a few seconds.

"After I crashed my car into the store window, I thought my career was over. The media was hounding me. I was taken out of the starting eleven. All the distractions put me in a tailspin." He stopped walking and faced me. "One of the things that got me through it was my bond with my teammates. None of the other bullshit mattered. And do you know where I got that mentality from?" His hand rested on my shoulder. "You. You're a living legend, mate. And I don't say that lightly. All us lads are honored to represent England with you. We all have your back, on the pitch and off."

I remained frozen in place long after Zach disappeared into the changing room.

❦

VICTORIA

Having this conversation with my dad while sitting at home in pajamas wasn't quite how I pictured it.

I tossed our dinner plans out the window after yesterday's call with Xavier. I haven't been able to think straight since. All I saw was the tortured look in his eyes before the screen went black.

Bringing up the unpleasantness of Jordan's insinuations was the last thing I wanted to do. But I needed answers. I needed clarity. I needed to close this chapter of my life.

A soft knock sounded at my door. I shuffled over, numb to any emotion that tried to force its way into my reality. I've excelled at suppressing how I really felt for so long it was like second nature.

When I opened the door and saw my father, the dam broke.

All my pent-up emotion from the last twenty-four hours —hell, my entire *existence*— exploded. I didn't fight the tidal wave; I let it crash over me.

Gentle hands guided me to the couch. I sank into the cushions, drowning in anger, heartache, guilt, sadness, and hurt. My eyes burned with liquid fire. The tears I shed didn't play favorites. I cried for my sister, my family, and Xavier.

My dad stayed quiet, stroking my hair. I felt so small sitting with him, like I was still a little girl running to the unconditional comfort only a parent could provide. The fact that our relationship has been severed all these years made me feel even worse.

So much wasted time. And for what?

Focus. I have to focus.

Once the tears dried up and I could breathe without sniffling, my dad grabbed us some water from the kitchen. On his way back to the couch, he paused in front of the coffee table and picked up a small, framed photo.

"Where did you get this?" he asked quietly, turning the frame so I could see the picture of Charlotte and I.

"I found it when I was at the storage unit a few months ago."

A heartbreaking smile lifted my dad's mouth. "I remember this. Your sixteenth birthday. Charlotte wanted everything to be perfect. She was the consummate hostess, always making sure people had enough food and drink." He sat next to me. "You, on the other hand, kept flirting with the Anderson boy. Nobody else at the party existed."

"Oh my god." I smiled sheepishly. "I forgot about that. Thanks."

He chuckled, putting an arm around my shoulders. After staying quiet for a beat he asked, "What has you so upset, love? Is it your mother?"

I shook my head. "We haven't spoken since the cottage fiasco."

"Not even on your birthday?"

"Nope."

"Hmm." He squeezed my shoulder. "That surprises me."

"Yeah, well, it doesn't surprise me."

"Is it Xavier?"

A knot of emotion tangled in my throat. Such a loaded question. I decided on a brief, sanitized answer. "Yes and no. He's going through something right now and I feel helpless being so far away from him."

Astute hazel eyes studied me. "He's lucky to have you. I've no doubt he appreciates your support, no matter the distance."

I nodded, willing myself to get to the actual reason why I wanted to see my father.

"I need to ask you something." I clasped my hands together. "It's about one of your clients."

His brows furrowed in confusion.

"Someone from a long time ago, when Charlotte and I were babies or maybe even before we were born." I forged ahead, ignoring my erratic pulse. "The family name is McKennie. Are you familiar with them?"

A few moments of reflective silence passed.

"I knew a Samuel McKennie in my younger days. We went to the same school. Son of a lord if I remember correctly. He and his wife died in a boating accident about ten years ago."

My heart rate spiked.

"Did he ever invest with your firm?"

"I don't know. Maybe when I was just starting. What is all of this about, Victoria?"

Too many jumbled thoughts clouded my mind. Maybe I should have asked Xavier to be here for this conversation, even if it'd only been on a video call. His presence always calmed me.

Charming and affectionate, protective and fierce. My safety in the swirling storm.

Everything he told you is a half truth wrapped in a lie.

Xavier's words from our night on the terrace consumed me. Jordan preyed on weakness. I have to approach this from a position of strength.

Strategic, calm, steady.

"I need your help with something." I straightened, regaining my composure. "How feasible is it to locate investment records from when you started?"

An hour after my father went back to his hotel, I paced around the living room.

Bringing down Jordan will take finesse and the element of surprise. Not to mention balls of steel.

If Xavier was willing to blow up his career and reputation to put a stop to all of this, so was I.

I've never loved anyone the way I love you.

God, I missed him.

Purging all that emotion in front of my dad acted as a reset. The path to my happiness, to Xavier's happiness —*our* happiness— crystalized.

No more playing small. It's time to fight fire with fire.

I scrolled through my contacts list, dialed the number, and held my breath.

"I've been expecting your call." Bennet answered on the first ring. Does this man ever sleep? I could practically see his amber eyes light up with intrigue. "What can I do for you at this hour, Ms. Chase?"

I skipped over any pleasantries and got right to the point. Bennet Logan had more connections than the royal family. If I ended up in his debt for the rest of my life, it's a burden I'm willing to carry.

Chapter
THIRTY-THREE

VICTORIA

Asking for help wasn't something I did often.

Let me rephrase that.

I *never* asked for help. I preferred to hold my own in stressful situations and meet the challenges head on.

Reaching out to Bennet added more strength to my arsenal. He's like a brother to Xavier and would do anything for his friend.

Our phone call two days ago was short and to the point. I laid out what I needed, and Bennet confirmed he could get it. Now all I had to do was wait.

Ugh.

"Do we have enough food to watch the rest of this?" Killian walked through my living room carrying a tray covered in cheese, fruit, and nuts.

"I think you meant do *you* have enough food," Max chimed in.

The boys insisted on coming to my place to watch Xavier's game. Neither one of them has any interest in sports. I suspected they just wanted to keep me company.

The second half was well underway, with England and the Netherlands sitting at a scoreless tie.

"This is a good thing?" Killian lifted an eyebrow. "No points? How can they do whatever it is they have to do if nobody scores?"

I grabbed a slice of cheese off the tray. "Both teams can score as much as they want. England either has to win it or stay level with the Netherlands to qualify."

Killian snort-laughed. "Look at you using all the terminology."

"How much do these guys run? I'm exhausted just watching them," Max exclaimed, popping a grape into his mouth.

The two of them went off on a tangent about which athletes are the most athletic. They'd just entered the age old debate of golfers versus archers when a knock sounded at my door. My stomach swooped, not from nerves but from the unrealistic possibility it could be Xavier. A ridiculous thought seeing as he's currently on my television competing in a soccer game.

I opened the door.

"Victoria."

A completely different swoosh flooded my body.

"Bennet." I blinked at him, shocked. "What are you doing here?"

He glanced over my shoulder. "Hoping to catch the final few minutes of this qualifier, if that's alright with you."

I gestured for him to come in. His smile was unforced and warm. It reminded me of the night I met him in London. I peeked into the hallway to see if Hannah was also here but it was empty.

"Tori." Killian's loud voice made my ears ring. "Why didn't you tell me your hot, British friends were coming over?"

Bennet laughed as he sauntered through the room. Clad in jeans and a powder blue long-sleeved Henley, he looked like any other guy in his thirties hanging out with friends on the weekend. We shared a knowing glance when he sat on the couch next to Max.

Heat rushed to my face. He couldn't have done everything I'd requested this fast. Then again, I shouldn't underestimate the ultra-wealthy who have the world at their fingertips.

"It's called a surprise, Mr. Monroe." Amusement colored Bennet's tone. "I like keeping people on the edge."

Killian choked on a walnut. Max buried his face in his hands.

The announcer exclaimed something about a foul in the penalty box, drawing all our attention to the TV.

"Jesus Christ," Bennet muttered. "They bloody fouled Erik Vande Velde."

"Who's that?" I asked, sitting next to Killian.

"Only the best striker on the Netherlands side."

We watched the replay. I'm not sure who all the players were for England. I only knew Cade and Xavier. It appeared some guy stuck his foot out to stop the ball and tripped the Dutch player.

"VAR review confirms it," one of the announcers exclaimed. "Penalty for the Netherlands. Reckless decision by Zach Donovan to make that kind of move in the box. Oh boy, this couldn't have come at a worse time for England. Under two minutes left to play. If the Dutch score here, England have to win their next match to qualify."

"I literally don't know what he's talking about," Killian said. "But Xavier looks pissed."

Several emotions paralyzed me when Xavier popped up on the screen. He did look annoyed. But he also looked determined.

And fucking *hot*.

Blazing eyes, set jaw, larger-than-life stance.

It's been a minute since I've seen him in the heat of competition.

"This is a great duel for sure." Excitement dripped from the announcer's voice. "The best against the best. Xavier Maddox hasn't been tested much in goal tonight. Will the Royal City keeper be England's hero? Or will Vande Velde tame The Three Lions?"

Not one of us moved. All eyes remained glued to the TV. The Dutch player strolled to the penalty marker. When the camera switched to Xavier, I sucked in a breath. I've never seen him so focused. He stood on his line, rolled his shoulders, and waited.

Do all soccer players ooze such overt sexuality just doing their job? Seeing Xavier in his natural element hit all my hot buttons, and then some.

I swallowed, stealing a glance at Bennet. The corner of his mouth ticked up in a grin.

Nothing gets past this guy, I thought, turning my attention back to the game.

Both players stood motionless, staring the other down. The crowd noise hushed from a roar to scattered murmuring. My hands clasped so tight the knuckles turned white.

If I was this stressed out, I could only imagine how Xavier felt. Then again, ice water runs through his veins when he's competing.

The referee blew his whistle.

The Dutch striker trotted toward the ball, stopped short, then ran forward and kicked.

A resounding *smack* preceded pandemonium on the field. Xavier moved fast enough to block the kick, and slapped the ball away. He'd saved the penalty shot.

His actions resulted in a corner kick but that didn't seem to matter to England's players. When the final whistle blew, they piled on Xavier, celebrating a scoreless tie like they'd won a major tournament.

"That really didn't need to be so intense," Killian grumbled.

"Welcome to football," Bennet replied, glancing at his phone. "If you'll excuse me, I have a few calls to make."

The boys and I watched some of the post-game interviews. I recognized the brunette asking Xavier questions. Her professionalism was evident, but so were the demure glances and obvious attempts at charming England's hero.

Hiding my jealously from Killian was impossible.

"Ex-girlfriend?" he asked.

"Not quite."

He looked from me to the TV and back. "Xavier looks bored. You have nothing to worry about."

I laughed, giving my best friend a playful shove.

Max and Killian hung around for another hour while Bennet spent his time by the windows taking call after call. I declined the boys' dinner invitation, saying I had a few last minute details to iron out before tomorrow's game.

Nerves cascaded through my stomach. I could tell Killian knew I was hiding something and was bursting at the seams to ask why Bennet showed up unannounced. I didn't want to tell him or Max about my plan until all the pieces were in place. Besides, I hadn't told them what happened in London yet.

After the boys left, I turned to Bennet. "A heads up would have been helpful."

"And ruin the surprise?" he grinned.

"You sound like Xavier." I folded my arms. "I would have assumed you'd be at the game. Did you just arrive in New York?"

"I've been here since yesterday."

Interesting.

"Are you staying with Hannah?"

Apparently that question went over like a lead balloon. Bennet's expression iced slightly. "I leave tonight but wanted to see you first."

"Did you get what I need?"

"Mostly." He pulled a USB drive from his pocket. "Still working on a couple things but grab your laptop."

My heart skittered like a nervous bunny when I retrieved my computer. Either this information will put the Jordan situation to rest for good, or it'll open an entirely new, even more unpleasant situation.

"There's one item of notable interest," Bennet said, plugging in the USB. "I suggest starting with the McKennie family file."

Shooting him a skeptical look, I pulled up the finances folder. Their family history served no purpose at this time. I wanted financial records to prove once and for all that Jordan lied to me.

At first blush, the summary revealed nothing spectacular, aside from a couple of political scandals that had been covered up. Tempting, but not the knock-out punch I needed.

I opened a folder labeled *investments* and searched the files for mentions of my dad or his company.

"Jesus," I muttered, noticing their net worth of one billion pounds. Then I saw their titles. "He's a Duke?"

"The title is hereditary, much like mine." The corner of Bennet's mouth curved. "One might say we're a select elite within the elite."

Before I got swept up in the minutiae of British aristocracy, I refocused on searching the financial documents. Several revealed Jordan's interest in purchasing my family's cottage. My jaw clenched. He'd certainly done his research on Briarcliff Cottage, including its estimated worth.

Why he wanted it remained a mystery.

Shaking off the unpleasantness, I continued my search.

One record of interest popped up from thirty years ago. Samuel McKennie did invest with my dad's firm but the amount was less than one hundred thousand. Not exactly *investing heavily* for one of the wealthiest families in the United Kingdom.

I started another search, just in case I missed something. No additional records showed any financial connections.

Relieved, I clicked on the family file.

Again, nothing out of the ordinary, just a rundown of their lineage, including how long they've held a seat in Parliament's House of Lords. There was also information about the boating accident. Jordan's mom and dad were killed off the coast of Cyprus almost twelve years ago.

I scrolled through some photos of the couple. They appeared happy. Then again, pictures have the ability to convey a false narrative. I knew nothing about these people other than their son was a despicable human.

After pouring through as many files as possible, I couldn't find anything else of significance.

Just as I was about to close out of it, I noticed an addendum to the folder labeled *children* marked confidential.

I glanced up at Bennet. His small nod of encouragement sparked my curiosity.

I opened the file.

My jaw dropped.

No fucking way.

Chapter
THIRTY-FOUR

The great thing about being a national sports hero was people tend to forget any bad press or salacious rumors. In the days following the match, I had dozens of interviews scheduled to talk about our result against the Netherlands. Everyone wanted to hear about the penalty I'd saved.

My face was pretty much on every major sports broadcast across England. Not one reporter mentioned last season's suspension or the game I missed due to "illness."

And yet, with all this attention and adoration, my soul felt as empty as the glass in my hand. Never thought I'd see the day when public praise failed to satisfy my need to feel wanted.

Setting the glass on the table, I grabbed the bottle of whisky and downed it.

It's been over a week since I fell apart in front of Victoria. Not quite how I'd planned for the video call to go. I went into it just wanting to hear her voice and look into her mesmerizing eyes.

Telling her what I'd overheard as a child sort of just…came out. I was so emotionally shattered from confiding in Victoria that I refused to tell Dr. Frances what happened at my last session. I only told him I'd opened up to her about something painful.

He was less than pleased with all my deflections but did commend me for doing the whole *really feeling it* thing like he'd asked.

Every inch of me ached from missing her.

I'm not due back for training until next week. Part of me longed to get on a plane and spend the next five days in Manhattan with her. But I know she's traveling for work. The Legends have away games in Los Angeles and Houston before coming to London.

She can't get here fast enough. I might never let her leave when she does.

Competing in the qualifier was the only thing that kept me sane and focused.

Now?

I lifted the bottle to my lips and swallowed. The amber liquid didn't even fucking burn anymore.

What did burn, and never seemed to stop, was the skin beneath my ear where she'd kissed me. Victoria always liked kissing me there. The phantom flames from her lips lingered day and night.

She marked me.

Searing heat bloomed on my skin. I ran my fingers down the side of my neck, an idea taking shape. For the first time in weeks, I felt at peace.

Someone knocked at my door.

"Christ," I muttered, not moving. *So much for my peace.*

Another insistent knock, followed by a shouted, "Xavier."

My spine stiffened at the sound of Adam's voice.

Two seconds later, I opened the door in frustration. "Why the fuck are you here?"

"You smell like a distillery." My stepbrother scowled, waving a hand in front of his face. The guy standing behind him stared at me.

"Who the fuck is that?"

"This is how you greet your guests?" Adam's eyebrow arched. "Charming."

I flattened my hand on the doorframe. "Don't remember inviting anyone over. You have three seconds to tell me why you're here. Three."

"This is—"

"Two."

"We have somethi—"

"One." I slammed the door in their faces.

A heartbeat later, Adam barged into my living room with his friend in tow. I gritted my teeth, regretting not locking the door. Last thing I wanted was company.

"Not really how I pictured you spending your recovery days after all the heroics on the pitch. This is sad." Adam gestured around the room. "Drinking straight from the bottle and existing on take away?"

"What I do in my free time is none of your business," I snapped. "What do you want?"

Adam turned toward the other guy. "Give him the envelope."

Something that resembled a laugh passed through my lips. "I'm not taking anything from him. I don't even know who he is."

"You're going to take the bloody envelope and read what's in it." Adam's tone sharpened. Can't say I've ever heard him speak to me like this before. "This is Philip Edgewood. And before you start playing dumb again, he's the tech lead at Jordan's company."

Within seconds I had this guy backed up against a wall. "Where is he?"

Philip paled. "I don't know."

I grabbed his shirt collar. "The fuck you don't. Tell me where he is."

"I-I swear," he stammered, shrinking into the wall. "But I do think you should see what's in this envelope. Sooner rather than later."

My grasp on his shirt tightened. I didn't believe for a second that he had no idea where Jordan was hiding. Turning to Adam, I snarled,

"Do you know where he is? And don't even think about lying to me."

"I would have told you already if I knew." My stepbrother sounded offended. "Let Philip go and read what he brought."

I couldn't think straight. All I wanted to do was find Jordan and end this. After weeks of not knowing where he could be, I literally had someone in the palm of my hand who could point me in the right direction.

Eyeing Philip with distain, I loosened my hold on him. This stranger bearing gifts better provide the answers I needed.

"Show me," I bit out, releasing him and walking toward the couch. Stopping in front of Adam I muttered, "I hope you're not wasting my time."

"I'm not." He responded so quiet I almost missed it. "I just want to help you."

There it was again. That look he'd had when we first met as kids. Like he idolized me as the older brother he always wanted.

Confusion swirled through me. After all the years of animosity and fights, he still wanted to help. My chest seized with the oddest sensation.

Philip approached in silence, holding an envelope.

"What's in there?" I demanded.

"Information to keep you one step ahead." He paused. "Unless you want Jordan to get away with what he has planned for Victoria."

Barbed wire dug into my heart at the mention of her name associated with that prick. "Why should I trust you? You work for him."

Any signs of apprehension dissolved from Philip's expression. His mouth formed a hard line. "Let's just say I'm gearing up for a career change."

I glared at him. "I'm listening."

He laughed at my dark expression, and forged ahead. "Jordan tasked me with gathering as much information on the Chase family as possible last year. Mostly financial." Acid seeped into my veins. "He specifically asked me to target properties."

My head pounded. "Briarcliff Cottage."

"Yes. That's the only unused property still in the family's name. Everything else had been sold."

"Why does he want it?"

"No idea." Philip's response sounded nonchalant, but the tightness in his jaw told me otherwise. "We'd pretty much finalized the deal with Helena Chase. Then Victoria showed up and refused to sign the paperwork. I recognized her at some American football event in London. You were there, too. Jordan was less than thrilled when I told him. I went to the cottage to see if I could—"

"*That was you?*" My mind flashed to the day I'd seen Victoria arguing with the guy from the charity and the realtor. After they'd left, we went inside and someone had shown up unannounced.

"Imagine my surprise when you came running out," he said coolly. "I couldn't get back to my car fast enough."

I moved closer to him, clenching a fist. The little shit flinched. "I hope you weren't planning to hurt her that day."

"What?" His eyes grew large as saucers. "Don't be ridiculous. I'm not a psychopath."

"Oh no?" A dark smile tugged at my mouth. "You work for one."

Adam cleared his throat and stepped between us. "Let him finish explaining, Xavier. He's not the bad guy here."

Philip's confidence returned when Adam gently pulled me away. I stared at my stepbrother, surprised I'd allowed him put a hand on me, let alone remove me from a potential fight.

The volume of all this new information flowing in made it difficult to focus. Jordan has been going after Victoria's family since *last year*? I couldn't wrap my head around it.

Money can be so persuasive at times.

He'd sounded so fucking smug when he said that to me. At the time, I assumed he was pushing my buttons.

Familiar, wild energy simmered just below the surface of my skin, ready to erupt. I inhaled a deep breath, willing myself not to spiral.

"If this makes it any better," Philip said, "your girlfriend isn't the only person Jordan's targeting. Financially, her family is the most attractive, but he has several others in his sights."

"None of this makes an ounce of sense," I grumbled. "Show me what's in the envelope."

I tore it open the second he passed it over. A spreadsheet? Studying it closely, I noticed dates, times, phone numbers, and email addresses. All of the dates fell in October. The same dates Victoria will be here for the Legends game.

Two weeks from now.

"What is all this?"

Philip glanced from me to Adam, and back to me. "Blackmail. He's going to smear her reputation in the media until he gets what he wants."

Fury darkened the edges of my vision. *Breathe.* "How?"

A muscle in his jaw twitched. I stormed over to him, nearly losing my shit. Grabbing the collar of his shirt again, I growled, "Tell. Me. What. He. Is. Planning."

No answer.

"This won't end well for you if you don't start talking." I shoved him against the wall so hard the medals in my display case shook. "Tell me what he's doing, and then tell me where the fuck he is."

Philip's eyes flicked over to Adam. A low laugh rumbled in my chest. "He's not going to help you. He knows better than to get in my way a second time."

"Just tell him," Adam demanded. "Or I will."

All the color drained from Philip's face. "I don't know where he is."

I pressed my forearm into his throat. "We'll deal with the lies in a bit. What's he planning?"

The more this idiot squirmed in my grasp, the more annoyed I became. Rolling my eyes, I flattened a hand on his chest. Philip tensed.

"He has pictures and videos."

"Of?"

"Victoria with other men. Famous athletes and coaches, mostly."

Bile rose in my throat.

"How did he get them?"

Beads of sweat formed on his forehead. "S-some are fake. Others are real."

Pieces started clicking into place. "The tech start-up in Manhattan. Are they behind it?"

A shaky nod. "We hacked into the mainframe at the Legends facility to manipulate the wireless network. Every phone and computer connected was rendered vulnerable. Players, coaches, staff, visitors, basically anyone signed in to the network at the stadium. We gained access to phone numbers, texts, emails, the cloud, you name it. Our only target was Victoria but we messed around with other accounts and phones to deflect attention." He paused. "We, uh, we also hacked into her personal wireless network to access images on her laptop."

Clenching my jaw, I used every trick I've learned in training to keep my body still.

I had to.

If I didn't, I'd fucking throw him through the window and into the street.

After a few seconds, something else occurred to me. "Did you ever pay anyone to harass Victoria and Hannah?" I scowled. "Victoria was groped at dinner by some asshole."

Philip's neck bulged with a hard swallow. "Yes."

"And her car?" My voice dropped several decibels. "Are you behind that?"

"Technically."

"What the fuck does that mean?" I shouted. "You know what? Doesn't matter. I've heard enough." I slammed my fist into his face. "Where is he?"

Philip recoiled in pain and terror. "I don't—"

"Say *I don't know one* more time and you'll be hauled out of here in a pine box." Bunching his shirt in my grasp, I pressed his body into the wall.

A hand wrapped around my arm. "Xavier. Let him go." Adam's calming tone had zero effect on me.

Rage pumped through my veins like poison, corroding every cell until it pooled in my stomach.

"How much of this did you know?" I seethed, pinning a deadly stare on him. "Do not fucking lie to me."

Adam straightened his shoulders, looking affronted. "I only knew about the blackmail schedule. I'm just as surprised by the rest of it as you."

I studied him. Even though our relationship was frayed, I could tell when he was being truthful. Nodding, I released Philip, watching him slump to the floor.

Reality narrowed to a razor thin focus.

Dark thoughts. Spiral. Revenge. Redemption.

"Listen to me, you sniveling twat." I crouched down to make eye contact and flexed my hand into a fist. "I know you're lying. You know where Jordan is hiding, don't you?"

Fear enlarged his eyes.

"I'm going to get an answer out of you one way or another. Where. Is. He."

Philip touched his bruised cheekbone and winced. "He never left England. He just sent his plane to different locations to throw off Bennet because he knew you'd come after him."

A fresh wave of rage swept through me. "He's been here the whole time?"

The tiniest nod preceded his answer. "I don't know exactly where but my best guess is just south of Manchester at his house in Alderley Green."

Exasperation layered my sigh in spades. What a shithead. Hiding out in one of the wealthiest villages he could find.

When I pulled out my phone to text Bennet, Philip attempted to capitalize on my distraction and moved to stand up.

"Not so fast." I grabbed his shirt and shoved him back against the wall. "We're not done here."

"I told you everything I know."

"I'm sure you think you have."

Me: Alderley Green

"Are you texting Bennet Logan?" His voice spiked with panic. "Don't say it was me. I'll be—"

"Adam," I cut in. "What was it you told me about detecting and responding to cyberthreats as the tech lead for a security team?"

Philip's eyes darted to my stepbrother, pleading for help. Remaining nonchalant, I looked up at Adam and waited for his answer.

"He makes sure the clients' networks are safe. He could also *cause* cyberthreats."

I leveled a cool stare at Philip. "I imagine the punishment for committing that type of crime on foreign soil is severe."

Bennet: Sending a team now

Tucking my phone in my pocket, I turned my full attention back to Philip. "Answer this last question for me. What exactly does Jordan hope to get from blackmailing Victoria?"

He flinched when I let go of his shirt and smoothed it down. "Money."

"Bullshit. His family is worth almost a billion. He doesn't need money."

A bead of sweat trickled down the side of Philip's face. "His family is but he isn't."

Dismissing his cryptic remark, I leaned closer to him. "What else does he want?"

"He's baiting you into coming after him."

Prick. He knew that's exactly what I'd do.

Unless…

I looked up at my stepbrother.

"Do you still want to help me?"

Shock seized Adam's face. "Of course I do."

I smiled, not from joy but from resolve. "I have an idea."

Chapter

THIRTY-FIVE

Cade and Noah held up their respective jerseys and smiled for the camera. I looked down at mine, and then over at Tre Gideon.

As part of the international series being played here in London, the teams thought a jersey swap would be a fun little promotional stunt. Since Cade and Noah both wear the number nine, they were up first.

"You're officially invited to the number nines dinner," Cade proclaimed, slinging an arm around Noah's shoulders. "Only the best are allowed at the table."

The Legends quarterback laughed and glanced down at his newly acquired Royal City jersey, emblazoned with the name *Tate* on the back.

"Looks like we're next," Tre said, shaking out his Royal City jersey. "Do number ones have a dinner, too?"

"Not quite. Our egos haven't reached the same stratosphere as strikers."

"I heard that, Maddox," Cade shouted.

"Or quarterbacks," Tre joked.

"What was that, Gideon?" Noah lifted an eyebrow. "Did a wide receiver just claim to be less of a prima donna than the guy under center?"

The New York Legends arrived in London this morning and were already in the middle of a full day. After this photo session, they'll use our training facility for their normal practice. And then tonight, we're all getting together for a team dinner.

"Your place at five?" Cade asked on his way to the weight room.

"Sure."

He regarded me curiously. "Is Victoria meeting you at the venue?"

"That's the plan."

His brows furrowed. "Don't be nervous, mate. She probably can't wait to see you."

"I'm not nervous," I lied.

"Right. And I'm not better looking than you." A hard swat hit my arm. "See you after training."

I shook my head, shoving the Legends jersey in my bag.

Victoria and I had been texting all morning. She was setting up media availabilities for the players and coaches, and finalizing a few last minute interviews, so we haven't seen one another yet. To say I was growing impatient is an understatement.

I haven't told her what I'd learned about Jordan, or what I'd decided to do. Figured we should be somewhere quiet and private for that conversation.

The backlash from discovering his plan will be harsh. Knowing Jordan the way I do, he'll back Victoria into a corner and then come after me with everything he's got. Stopping him before it reached that point was my only goal. And in order to do that, I had to sacrifice everything I've worked so hard to achieve. It was the only way.

I made peace with my decision.

Victoria was worth it. Her happiness was worth it. *Our* happiness was worth it.

According to Bennet's daily updates, Jordan was still laying low in Alderley Green. Not driving out there myself was an exercise in self-control.

As the day dragged on and it became clear I wouldn't see Victoria until later tonight, I went about my usual schedule. Today's training consisted mostly of reaction timing.

I remained as focused as possible but kept one eye on the clock. *Tick, tick, tick.*

The seconds and minutes taunted me.

"Set!" The goalkeeping coach shouted.

I turned to face the goal, showing my back to him.

"Strike."

The ball was already sailing toward my left shoulder when I spun around. I somehow managed to catch it.

"Good reaction, Maddox. Let's go again. Set."

We ran this drill for the rest of our session. I never knew which direction the ball would come from when he shouted *strike*. Once we finished, I hit the showers and went home.

Prowling around my flat did nothing to calm me. Dinner wasn't for another two hours but Cade should be here any minute.

Not sure how much longer I could take all the waiting.

Just when I thought I'd crawl out of my fucking skin, a knock sounded at the door. My pulse ratcheted up several notches.

I flung it open and nearly had a heart attack.

Victoria.

She was right there in living color. Right in front of me.

Red hair fell in loose waves across her shoulders. Bright emerald eyes widened when she smiled. *My* smile. The one that brings me to my knees.

"Hi." Her greeting was breathy and sexy as hell. "I hope you don't mind me showing up unannounced. I had some extra time and thought maybe we could hang out for a little while and go to the event together."

My stomach clenched.

"I don't mind at all. Come inside."

Her musky, vanilla scent swirled around me when she walked by. The room vibrated with anticipation and unspoken words. Caressing her with my eyes, I dragged my gaze over her lush curves. The blue dress she wore fluttered around her thighs with every graceful step.

All the distance I'd felt the last few weeks evaporated. Victoria's presence consumed me, filling my soul and saturating the very air I breathe.

"I saw Cade outside just now." Victoria tucked a strand of hair behind her ear. I noticed a small tremble in her hand. "He looked totally surprised to see me and said he'd meet you at the restaurant instead. I didn't interfere with your plans, did I?"

"No, love." I reached for her. "Come to me."

A dusting of pink stained her cheeks at my low command. For a second, I feared she didn't want me to touch her.

How pretentious of me to assume we'd just fall back into our same pattern. So much has come to light since Paris. Who am I to think she'd even feel the same way?

But then she rushed toward me. The moment she melted into my embrace, any lingering doubts faded.

Neither of us spoke for the longest stretch of time. We simply stood wrapped in each other's arms. Burying my face in her neck, I whispered, "I'm never letting you go."

"Same," she murmured, her grasp tightening.

Skimming my palm down her back, I wanted nothing more than to pin her to the wall, and fuck her senseless. Feeling her body pressed to mine after weeks of separation fueled the pent-up fire burning through me. Reigning in my urges proved difficult.

Be a gentleman.

A noticeable chill settled between us when she pulled away.

"I have an ulterior motive for coming over." Victoria's melodic voice stilled my heart. "There's something I have to tell you. Several things, in fact."

Wariness edged out any overt lust at her serious tone. "Okay." My hand lingered on her back. "I have a few things to tell you, too."

She looked up at me through her lashes, a shrewd smile slanting her mouth. "You first."

"Me?" Incredulity strangled the laugh bubbling in my throat. "Don't you think I've said enough?"

"No." The tenderness in her eyes sank into my soul, filling cracks I didn't know existed. "I never want you to stop telling me things. The hard stuff, the easy stuff, all of it." She traced her thumb along my jaw, pausing when she reached my neck. Silence filled the room for a beat while she stared at the skin beneath my left ear. "You have a new tattoo?"

I nodded. "I got it two weeks ago."

"A rose on fire," she whispered, hovering her fingers over the ink. "Is that my name where the stem should be?"

"Yes, love." I reached for her hand and placed it over my heart. "It's for you. Every time you kiss me there, you leave a permanent mark. A beautiful, burning mark. I'm yours, Tori. And now everyone can see it."

A teasing sparkle illuminated her eyes. "Xavier Maddox, are you a secret romantic?"

I lifted a shoulder in a small shrug. "Maybe."

"I won't tell anyone."

Victoria's smile spread warmth through me. She grabbed my hand and pulled me toward the chair next to the fireplace. *The bossy chair*, as she calls it. After I sat, she positioned herself on my lap.

"Told you we'd fix this the next time I was here." Her lips brushed against my scar. "So what is it you have to tell me?"

Going over this conversation in my mind had been simple. But now that she's here, in my lap, wearing this dress, and looking so beautiful, I couldn't figure out how to say it.

She kissed my forehead again, letting her lips linger. I wrapped one arm around her, and rested the other on her legs.

"Remember when you told me these hands don't miss?" she asked, tangling her fingers through mine.

"I do." I searched her expression. "And they don't."

Victoria rolled her eyes, and I had to stifle a laugh at the familiar sight of her amused exasperation.

"Not that I want to inflate your ego any more than it already is—" she squealed when I squeezed her waist "—but I'd like to add something to your humble declaration."

"Please do."

Running a finger over my palm, she looked at me. "They don't miss. That is true. But they're also safe. I always feel safe in your hands." A thousand emotions passed over her face. "I hope you—"

I fisted her hair and pulled her close, my mouth pressing hot and insistent to hers. She kissed me back just as fierce, our breaths and heartbeats melding into one.

"You are my absolute fucking world," I said after breaking our mouths apart. "My safe haven when I feel alone. I never knew loving someone could be like this."

"Me either," Victoria whispered, her voice thick with emotion. "I wish I'd stayed with you that night."

I swept my thumb along her lower lip. "You're here now just like you said you'd be. That's all that matters."

A small shiver rippled through Victoria's body when she pulled me into a tight hug. Her fingers slid into my hair, tugging gently. I nuzzled into her neck, stroking her back slowly. Victoria's quiet, content moan was the most beautiful sound I'd ever heard.

Our time apart had been absolute hell. But now she's here, in my arms.

Safe hands.

The ferocious need to protect her consumed me. "Jordan is planning to blackmail you. He's been looking into your family's finances for over a year."

Victoria leaned back to look at me, but didn't appear overly surprised. "Have you been talking to Bennet?"

My brows pulled together in confusion. "Bennet? No. My stepbrother came over with some shit for brains friend and told me all about it."

"He wants Briarcliff Cottage. I knew that already."

"He wants more than that, love. He wants to publicly embarrass you and won't stop until you pay him."

A bitter laugh spilled from her. "Now it all makes sense."

"What does?"

"Finish telling me and then I'll fill in the blanks."

"Brace yourself," I grumbled before relaying what happened when Adam and Philip came over unannounced. I told her about the hacking, the guy at the restaurant, and her car. The hardest part was telling her about the photos and what Jordan planned to do with them.

A tremor of anger passed through her. "Does he know where Jordan is?"

"Yes. He never left England. Bennet's team has been tracking his every move since I found out."

I could see the gears spinning in Victoria's head as she processed the information. "How can you be sure this Philip guy won't turn tail and tell Jordan you know everything?"

I smirked. "The little shit orchestrated an international hack on a professional sports franchise in the United States. To top it off, he targeted a highly respected executive in some twisted revenge porn scheme to extort money. He doesn't have a leg to stand on. Silence is his only option."

This whole scenario was fucked up. The only game I wanted to play was football, not petty one-upmanship with a spoiled twat whose only leverage in life was his fucking noble bloodline.

Victoria's jaw set in determination. "Let Jordan go through with his plan. We'll draw him out easier that way."

"What do you mean *let him*?"

"Do you still have the spreadsheet with the list of media contacts?"

I nodded.

"Give it to me. This is my wheelhouse. I can finesse any narrative. Besides, I always have an ace up my sleeve." Her fiery stare burned through me. "I know this look, Maddox. Jordan's an egotistical asshole who likes to have the upper hand. If he thinks shaming me in public for my sexual history is going to make me run scared, he doesn't know who he's dealing with."

Despite her bravado, I picked up on a note of apprehension running beneath her words. The ever-present rage churned through my veins.

"I'm not letting him hurt you. Adam and I have already come up with a plan."

"And I'm not letting him hurt *you*. I refuse to watch you destroy everything you worked so hard for to take the bait and go after him. This is ultimately what he wants. We are each other's weakness. He's counting on that but he won't be expecting strength." A sly grin pulled at her mouth. "Someone once told me not to step into an arena if I wasn't prepared for the battle. Jordan won't know what hit him."

"Yes he will. Me."

Victoria pressed a soft kiss to my lips. "You're hot when get all growly and feral."

"And you're sexy as fuck when you're being this stubborn."

"Perfect match, don't you think?"

Another dark flame ignited between us.

"More than perfect. So, what are the blanks you're going to fill in?"

"I had Bennet do some digging for me so I could prove Jordan lied about investing with my dad's firm. Let's just say I learned more than I expected. Jordan is not as financially sound as he'd like everyone to believe."

"Philip mentioned the same thing," I murmured.

"What did he say?"

"Something about his family being worth almost a billion but not Jordan. Any idea what that means?"

Victoria examined me, an internal battle waging behind beautiful green eyes.

"Tori." I spoke low and deliberate. "What is it?"

"I told you. I always have an ace up my sleeve."

"Desperate people go to great lengths to get what they want, love." My fingers caressed down her neck. The red marks were gone but I won't ever forget seeing them. "If you know something, tell me. I don't want you putting yourself in harm's way alone."

"I'm not alone. I have you by my side." She slipped a hand under my shirt. "If I tell you, promise me you won't go scorched earth on him. This has to be strategic. Calm. Sort of like how you are in goal." She bit down on her lip and traced my body with a hungry stare. "Until you unleash your inner beast and get all ferocious."

I arched an eyebrow. "Is this your idea of flattery?"

"Maybe."

The dark flames intensified.

"It's working."

Rising from my lap with all the elegance of a queen, Victoria reached for me. "Come with me."

Curious, I took her hand and followed her outside to the patio. We haven't been out here in months. Actually, we were only here once. I can still picture her sitting naked on the table.

She hopped up on it now, fully clothed unfortunately. Pulling me close, she hooked her legs around my waist.

"Why are we out here?" I asked, sliding my hands over her hips.

"One of my favorite moments with you happened out here. I've had many more favorites since but..." She touched my scar and smiled. "This is where I started falling for you."

Flattening my hands on the table to brace myself was the only way I remained standing. This woman will in fact be the death of me.

"We are connected in ways I never dreamed possible," she continued. "The desire to find out what happened to Charlotte tortured me for years. And now I'm on the cusp of closing this chapter for good."

She tilted her head, gazing at the tattoo on my neck.

"You've told me numerous times that you'd risk it all for me." Heat bloomed on my skin at her touch. "I want you to know, I'd risk everything for you, too."

A strangled noise emerged from my throat. Grabbing her hips, I lowered my head until our mouths brushed together. "What do you know?"

Lacing her fingers behind my head, she parted her lips and kissed me. "Jordan McKennie is as common as you and me."

The heat and dampness of her mouth lingered near mine. I tasted her words as much as I heard them. When she slid her tongue between my lips, I allowed my instincts to take over. Pulling her flush against my chest, I kissed her hard, devouring her moans.

Fisting her hair, I yanked it until her head bent back.

"You're distracting me, dirty princess." I ran my tongue along the column of her neck. "Do I have to fuck this information out of you?"

A soft laugh preceded her answer. "You have to beg me, country prince."

All the air whooshed out of my lungs. Dark flames exploded in a raging inferno.

Fuck. Me.

I'd never been so turned on in my life.

Keeping her hair in a firm grasp, I used my other hand to lift her dress.

Bloody hell. No panties.

"That's not how this works, love." I slid my fingers inside her.

"I thought you liked when I flipped the script on you," she moaned, palming my erection through my clothes.

Feeling her hand on me was heaven. Any train of thought I had was now scrambled.

"I do. I love it."

"Good boy," she whispered, unzipping my pants. "Beg me."

My knees buckled the second she wrapped her hand around my cock and started stroking. Good thing I never wanted to join MI-6. I'd give up every national security secret if Victoria kidnapped me and used these coercive methods.

But I didn't beg her.

At least not yet.

I pulled on her hair, kissing her again. Harder, more possessive. When her stroking intensified, I roughly positioned her head so I could plunder the sweet softness of her mouth while I teased her clit.

Push and pull.

I will play this fucking game with her forever.

"Xavier," she gasped, shuddering from my touch.

The second her grip loosened around my cock, I spread her legs wider and sank into her, pushing deeper until I was buried to the hilt.

"Tell me what you know, love." I thrust in and out slowly, methodically.

"Harder, *please*." Victoria arched into me, digging her nails into my shoulders.

Lust surged from head to toe. "Good girl," I growled, turning her words back on her. "Beg me."

Shoving her hands in my hair and pulling, she stared into my soul. "I missed this. I missed you. Fuck. Xavier. *Please*. I need you untamed."

I stopped thrusting and framed her face gently with my hands. "I missed *us*." A dark smile tugged at my lips. "Careful what you wish for."

My blood flowed white hot when I slammed into her over and over. She was slick and tight and felt like heaven. I gave her what she wanted. What we both wanted. Hard and fast and uninhibited.

A groan ripped from my throat when she clenched and shattered around me, her cries echoing through the cool, evening air.

An orgasm raced through me, rendering me useless for longer than normal. Not that I mind. Staying wrapped in Victoria's arms while our bodies remained tangled together was the only place I wanted to be.

My heart stuttered when she kissed the tattoo on my neck.

"Again," she demanded, gazing up at me through her lashes.

I smoothed her hair out of her face and smiled. "Don't we have somewhere to be?"

"We do." A sexy glint illuminated her eyes. "Round two at the restaurant?"

"Naughty girl."

"You love it."

I curled my fingers under her chin. "I love *you*."

Victoria's face lit up with a smile that could topple kingdoms. "I love you, too."

I kissed her again, softer and more passionate. "I have to get you cleaned up before we go."

A tiny whine of displeasure escaped her. "On second thought, let's stay here."

"Yeah?" I kissed along her jaw. "Don't tempt me."

"I like tempting you." She banded her arms around me. "Have you ever used this table for, like, lunch or dinner?"

I thought for a second. "Uh, no. I've only had you on this table."

"Wow." Her laugh vibrated through me. "I don't know if this says something about me but I'm flattered."

For the first time in weeks, I felt lighter, more centered. Having Victoria close always settled the chaos that dwelled within. Knowing that she still loved me despite all my shortcomings filled me with an unrecognizable emotion.

Staring at her now and seeing how content and happy she looked boggled my mind.

I made her feel this way.

Unreal.

As much as I wanted to stay in our blissful post-sex bubble, there was still one thing we had to resolve.

"Tori." I held her tight. "Please tell me what you meant by Jordan is as common as you and me."

"I meant exactly that." She traced along my scar. "He's not noble born or whatever you call it. He has zero ties to the McKennie bloodline."

Well, this is a proper mind fuck. "What do you mean?"

"The man who raised him, Samuel McKennie, *isn't* his biological father. Someone named Daniel Southgate is."

I stared at her, slack-jawed. "How…how do you know this?"

"I saw his birth certificate." She leveled a determined stare at me. "The person who has bullied and tortured you since you were teenagers is a nobody. A fraud. Everything about his life is a lie. That's why he's trying to blackmail me. He has no claim to the McKennie fortune."

Chapter
THIRTY-SIX

Fifty direct messages in less than five minutes.

None of them were particularly kind.

Neither were the dozens and dozens of comments on any of the photos in my feed.

Maybe I'd been a little too overzealous when I insisted we let Jordan go through with his alleged smear campaign. The first so-called article exploded Friday afternoon, followed by two more on Saturday.

Photos of me and Tre Gideon from about a year ago saturated every gossip site imaginable. Most were harmless, but a few showed us getting more than cozy at a nightclub. One in particular caught us in the middle of a not-so chaste kiss.

That headline was eye roll inducing.

Tongues WAG Over Sultry Moments Between The Keeper's Girl and Past Lovers

Being called a WAG wasn't the worst thing I've experienced. The tabloids use it to refer to most wives and girlfriends of high-profile footballers. Can't get any more high-profile than England's number one.

Additional pictures featured me with other famous American football players. Only a handful of them were genuine. Those, again, were harmless.

Most of the artificially generated pictures were salacious.

The narrative was pretty clear. Some commenters labeled me as a "jersey chaser." That seemed to catch fire and showed up in multiple headlines.

"Shutting off your notifications will help," Hannah said, standing next to me on the sideline.

"I did."

"Then put your phone away. Torturing yourself won't make it any better."

Hannah didn't know what Xavier and I had planned. I had to play along like this was a burden, rather than exactly what I'd expected.

I tucked the phone in my pocket and watched some of the players do their pre-game warm-ups. The Legends were set to take the field for their highly anticipated international game later this afternoon. For his part, Tre remained professional and ignored the noise.

Granted, there wasn't much noise swirling around him. The British press found me much more interesting. Xavier morphed into protector mode the second the stories broke. He'd been traveling for his away game in Bournemouth but managed to text and call as much as he could.

He'll arrive here shortly, and then phase one of the plan will be set in motion.

When warm-ups finished, I escorted Noah, Jax, and Dante to the gaggle of reporters waiting in the end zone. Most of the questions for the guys were generic and simple. They could rattle off the answers in their sleep.

This was only a brief interview session, lasting about ten minutes.

Polite as always, the guys thanked the reporters and left. I hung back to finalize the post-game arrangements for locker room access.

Whispers fluttered through the reporters. Several glanced at their phones, their eyes widening.

At the same time, a few looked over at the sideline. I didn't have to look to know who they saw. I could feel Xavier's intense stare ripping through me.

One reporter held up his phone and asked, "Would you mind commenting on this latest photo?"

Expectant faces stared at me. My phone vibrated. According to the spreadsheet, another wave was due right about now.

"Excuse me for a minute," I told them, walking away.

When I looked at the phone, my heart thundered.

Panic blossomed in my stomach. Even though I knew *when* the pictures would be released, I didn't know *what* they'd show.

I stared at the image of me in a silver silk gown with my legs wrapped around Xavier's waist, and pure ecstasy etched on my face. He had me pressed against an ivy covered wall. Lights from the Manhattan cityscape glowed in the background. Even though the angle was high and most likely taken from a distance, whoever captured this photo used a powerful lens. It was easy to see what we were doing.

The terrace.

The night we reunited at the fundraiser.

Our intimate moment in a public setting was immortalized in Jordan's sick and twisted game.

Anger feasted on my panic, obliterating it. I straightened my shoulders. Now wasn't the time to shrivel up and call it quits. Now was the time to enter the arena.

Microphones and cameras pointed at me when I walked toward the reporters. Xavier remained on the sideline, watching my every move. An impassive expression dominated his features but his eyes flared with outrage.

I knew his instinct was to protect me and unleash his fury in front of the cameras. Convincing him to let me handle this part of our plan hadn't been easy. But even now, behind his anger and fear, I saw his trust and support.

"As you no doubt have seen, I've become somewhat of a minor celebrity on all the gossip sites this weekend." A smattering of nervous laughter rolled through the group. "I'll keep this short because today is about the New York Legends playing their first international game here in London. Our partnership with Royal City is exciting and we can't wait to watch it flourish in the coming years."

Despite my racing heart, I was strangely calm. Scanning the reporters, I locked eyes with the *actual* Justin Kirby from the London Independent News. He and I had a little meeting yesterday to discuss what I'd be saying here today, and what he'd ask. Fitting, since Jordan pretended to be him when he called the stadium last spring.

"It's come to my attention that I'm the target of an elaborate blackmail scheme. Many of the photos are fakes. My personal files were hacked and the photos were manipulated digitally." I took a deep breath. "Others are real. *All* of them are meant to intimidate me into paying out a large sum of money."

A wave of murmurs rumbled quietly through the reporters.

"Steps are being taken to shut this campaign down. That's all I have to say. Please enjoy the game."

Justin lifted his hand, recognizing his cue.

I gestured toward him. "I'm not taking questions, Justin."

"This seems personal," he pressed, ignoring my statement just like any good journalist would. "Calculated. You're being portrayed in a very specific light. Is there a jilted lover pulling the strings?"

I suppressed a pleased smile. He'd finessed our agreed-upon question, teeing up my answer perfectly.

"It is calculated. But it's not a jilted lover. Just someone desperate for attention." I stepped to the side. "Thanks again. See you all after the game."

The murmuring grew louder as I walked toward Xavier. His sapphire eyes burned in dynamic blue flames.

"You were brilliant." He reached for my hand.

"Years of training." I leaned closer and whispered, "Are they watching?"

His sinful, dark smile slid through me like rich, molten caramel. "Yes, love."

Xavier lowered his mouth to mine, softly brushing our lips together. Sliding his fingers through my hair, he pulled it gently to tilt my head back. Our mouths moved together in whispers of warmth and softness.

Then he captured my lower lip between his teeth and bit down hard.

Yanking me into his chest, he deepened the kiss. I surrendered to his touch and taste, losing myself in him. If my personal life was going to be splashed across the internet for everyone to see, it would be on my terms.

Xavier never left my side the rest of the day. Well, except for the game because he wasn't allowed on the sideline even with his all access credential.

"Can't really break this policy," I teased. "Go hang out with Cade and your teammates. We'll meet after the post-game interviews."

The Legends ended up winning a nail biter against Indianapolis. Our kicker scored the winning field goal as time expired. The atmosphere was unlike anything I'd experienced in all my years in the league. Fans sang songs, chanted, cheered, and just had a hell of a time. There were points in the game where it was hard to decipher which team they were rooting for.

I escorted the last of the reporters out of the locker room.

"We have to come back next season," Noah exclaimed, tossing his dirty uniform in the laundry bin. "That crowd was incredible."

"Even when they booed you?" Dante smirked.

"Pretty sure it was you, Milano. That pass was right on the numbers. Catch it next time." Noah turned to me. "You coming out with us, Victoria?"

"I sure am. You all better be on your best behavior."

The equipment crew made short work of gathering everything and packing crates for the flight home. Normally, we'd go straight to the airport after an away game, but we're officially on a bye week now so the plan was to meet at some swanky lounge in London.

After the last few days, a relaxing night out was needed.

Xavier waited for me in the hall outside the locker room. He handed me his credential with a smirk.

"Next time, I want the same access as you."

"I'm going to have to deny your request."

"A flat out denial? Again?" He pouted. *Why the hell was that so sexy?*

"You'll have to come work for the Legends if you want that kind of access," I teased, tucking the pass in my bag. "You know. Be the punter or something."

"Wow." He laughed. "And here I thought you liked me."

The taxi ride to Constellations was quick. When we pulled up, I noticed Xavier clench his jaw.

"Not your favorite place?"

"I like it just fine." He opened the door and stepped onto the sidewalk. "Haven't been here since I chased Jordan down that alley."

Shocked, I took his outstretched hand and followed him inside.

Dimly lit in shades of blue, cream, and lavender, the whole room gave off a relaxed, modern vibe. Some of my co-workers sat at the bar. Others crowded around tables, clinking glasses and enjoying appetizers.

"This place is incredible," I marveled, settling into a plush velvet couch.

Xavier draped an arm over my shoulders and dipped his head to my ear. "It has its moments." A light kiss warmed the skin on my cheek. "Still nothing new?"

"Nope. I'm guessing that means he got the message."

"His next move won't be subtle."

"I know." I rested a hand on his thigh. "I'm counting on it."

A low, sexy laugh rumbled in his chest. "You are fiery."

Turning toward him, I grinned. "You love it."

"I do. Makes me not want to be a gentleman in front of all these people."

His smooth, sultry tone hit all my hot buttons, and then some. When he licked his lower lip, I inched my hand up his thigh.

"You always look like you're savoring a secret that thrills you to no end when you do that."

"Do I?" He leaned close and stroked his tongue on my mouth. "What secret do you think it is?"

Laughter and conversations faded into the background until it was nothing more than a dull hum. Nobody else existed except for us. All I felt was Xavier.

Desire crashed through me. I haven't been with him since I arrived here three days ago. As spontaneous and hot as our moment on the patio had been, I craved more.

The muscles in his thigh tightened. I loved how his lethally athletic body reacted to me. It was perfectly honed for competition…and dirty, rough, unbridled sex.

Our breathing slowed, dovetailing into one connected breath.

Wordless promises passed between us.

"I don't know what your secret is," I whispered. "Want to know mine?"

Slipping a lock of hair behind my ear, Xavier slanted his head and lowered his mouth to mine. "Tell me all of them."

Lost in the heady fog of his scent and a fervent blue stare, I responded, "I love when you're not a gentleman with me."

He'd just locked me in a deep, passionate, very unsuitable-for-public-places kiss when I heard, "For fuck's sake you two. My virgin eyes can't handle this."

Xavier groaned in frustration at Cade's interruption. I glanced up at the striker.

"Virgin eyes?" Amusement colored my question as he flopped onto the couch next to us.

"Not buying it, huh?" Cade's little smile charmed me.

"Is there something you wanted, Gallagher?" Xavier's tone dripped razor blades.

"Don't let me stop you from shagging like minks." His normally playful demeanor faded. "Just needed to get away from the party for a few."

Xavier regarded his friend curiously. "Everything alright?"

Cade waved a dismissive hand. "Yeah. Maybe I'm getting too old for all this."

Releasing me from his embrace, Xavier leaned closer to his friend. I don't think I've ever seen Cade shy away from a crowd. He and Xavier were practically the same person when it came to attention.

I glanced towards the table where Jax, Dante, and Noah were sitting. Tracey was also there along with Hannah. Bennet was nowhere to be seen but Alex hovered in the shadows. A hulking figure appeared next to him. Marcus. *Of course.*

"I'll give you boys a few minutes to chat." I stood up, halted by Xavier's strong grasp. Shaking my head, I gestured to my friends. "I'll be right over there. You can stare at me the whole time."

"I will."

Laughing, I made my way toward the center of the lounge. Hannah caught my eye and rushed over.

"Are you okay?" Her breathless concern was touching. "Your

impromptu press conference is everywhere. Blackmail? I can have my secur—"

"I'm okay. I promise. Just controlling the narrative."

"Who's behind all of this?" Her brown eyes flared with anger.

"Hey," Noah shouted. "No secret meetings. This is mandatory fun. Besides, if you two are whispering about what I think you're whispering about, it looks like Victoria's *fuck around and find out* message is winning over the headlines."

"This is why we don't trust anyone else with our media handling," Dante declared, glancing over my shoulder. "Right, Chels?"

I spun around and came face to face with Dante's sister. The pretty brunette looked casual and cute in her brother's jersey. She tossed a sarcastic grin at Dante before greeting me. "Glad I could finally catch up with you. I've been dying to chat about the foundation."

Hannah's eyebrows shot up. "Are you the one interested in the director position?"

Chelsea clasped her hands together and nodded. "I think I might be. Can we meet for lunch this week? Unless you're busy with…" She gestured toward Xavier.

"He goes back to training on Tuesday. I'll have loads of time." I looked at Hannah. "Are you sticking around London for a bit? You should come with us."

"I'm here until Thursday." Her smile didn't touch her eyes. "I'd love to have a girls' lunch."

"It's settled," Chelsea exclaimed. "I'll make the arrangements. I know this great little cafe in Knightsbridge. And then if you're both up to it, we can hit Harrods."

"Food and shopping?" I laughed. "I'm in."

The three of us joined the guys. Every so often I'd glance over at Xavier and Cade. Their interactions always reminded me of siblings.

A balled up napkin flew into my lap. *Speaking of behaving like siblings…*

"Oh shit. Sorry, Victoria. That was meant for Jax." Noah's laugh drowned out his apologetic shrug.

"Noodle arm," Jax retaliated.

Shaking my head, I turned my attention back to Xavier and Cade.

They appeared deep in conversation. I figured Xavier was filling in his friend on what we put in motion this weekend.

Cade's eyes strayed to our table, lingering on something.

Someone?

Relaxing into the chair to make it look like I wasn't being nosy, I followed his gaze. The only people sitting in his line of sight were Dante and Chelsea.

Chelsea?!

Nah. From what I've seen of Cade's taste in women, Chelsea was not in the same universe as his type.

Before I fully turned my attention back to my friends, I noticed a dark-haired man leaning against the bar, sipping on a drink. Tall, broad shouldered, angry. My heart seized. *He wouldn't fucking dare.*

He would.

Jordan McKennie swept his eyes through the lounge, landing squarely on me.

Chapter
THIRTY-SEVEN

All the color drained from Victoria's face.

I jerked my head toward the bar. Atomic levels of rage tore me apart.

"Maddox, wait." Cade jumped up when I took off.

My long strides ate up the distance to where Jordan stood. He pursed his lips, discarding my presence with a glance.

"Leave. Now." I kept my voice low and threatening.

"It's a public venue. I can be here."

I saw Cade approaching out of the corner of my eye.

"The fuck you can. Leave while you still have the ability to walk."

Jordan's chastising laugh scraped at my insides. "Want to know the most annoying thing about you? Your threats are always hollow."

Grabbing his shirt collar, I yanked him toward the exit.

"This fucked up game of yours is over," I growled in his ear, releasing him when we got outside. The sidewalk wasn't empty. Several people stopped and stared.

Two footballers and an aristocrat storm out of a bar.

Reeling in a fraction of my aggression, I adopted a more civil level of speaking. "You should have left England when you had the chance."

He snorted. "Took you long enough to figure it out. The day I saw Logan's people tailing me, I knew I had you where I wanted you. Arrogant prick."

"What is this about?" Cade stepped between us.

"Gallagher," I spoke low. "Go back inside."

"How precious," Jordan taunted. "Protecting your boyfriend?"

I flexed my hand into a fist.

"Gentlemen," Bennet's authoritative voice carried on the night air as he approached. "Shall we take this discussion somewhere more discreet?"

I stared at my friend. "Where did you come from?"

No answer. Just a small smile.

The door burst open. Victoria rushed out, sweeping her eyes from me to Cade to Bennet to Jordan.

Not two seconds later, Alex and Marcus appeared.

"The media darling." Distain dripped from Jordan's words. "You think you're so clever. You won't win."

"I told you not to underestimate me." Confidence and determination radiated from Victoria. Her cheeks glowed red.

"I do think it's best if we go somewhere quiet to continue this." Bennet's regal stare pressed into Jordan. "The cars are this way."

Cars?

"I'm not going anywhere with any of you," Jordan snapped. "Logan, if you want a meeting, let's plan one for next—"

"Get in the car." I didn't recognize the sound of my own voice. "This ends tonight."

Half an hour later we gathered in the library at Logan Estate. Cade waited by the doors with Alex and Marcus.

Bennet took his place by the mantel. "This is a private matter between the three of you. We'll give you the room. Figure it out and end it. Stay in here as long as you need."

Without saying another word, he escorted Cade, Marcus, and Alex out. The doors clicked shut behind them.

An irritated-looking Jordan paced like a trapped animal before sitting on the couch. Satisfaction crept through me seeing him so out of sorts.

Regaining some bravado, he glared at us. "The keeper and his American tart. To what do I owe the pleasure of this gathering?"

A snarl rumbled in my throat. "Do not speak to her like that."

Victoria's hand curled around my arm. Her eyes said everything when I looked at her. *Calm. Strategic.*

Swallowing down my urge to beat the shit out of Jordan, I nodded. This was her moment.

Victoria sat on the couch across from him, emulating authority. Possessive pride rushed through me.

"For someone who's spent the better part of his life bullying and intimidating people, you sure do suck at blackmail." Rebuking him with a smile, she continued. "Is shaming me in public the best you can do?"

Silence.

They stared one another down before Jordan's laughter filled the library.

"You're just as arrogant as him," he said. "I didn't underestimate you. I assumed you'd have more bite." Shaking his head, his body vibrated with another laugh. "All those photos are nothing." He glared at me. "But the videos of *you* assaulting me at a club and chasing me down an alley will certainly make a bigger splash. I'll make sure your career ends in disgrace."

Victoria smiled, not rattled by Jordan's threat. I stepped toward him, ready to break every bone in his body.

"See? He can't wait to start a fight. It's too fucking easy." Jordan's chest puffed with overconfidence.

"More bite?" Victoria crossed her legs, her posture flawless and elegant.

We shared a glance.

Do you want to continue?

Green.

"You should really work on your methods of coercion," Victoria said. "Especially when you don't have that cushy title to shield you from any consequences. How's that for bite?"

Color leached from Jordan's face. The pompous self-satisfaction drained from his eyes. "My family and my title will—"

"Your family and your title are nonexistent. You are *not* of noble birth. You're just as common as we are." Her words detonated a silent explosion. Jordan recoiled from the impact, shrinking into the couch. This damage was much more satisfying to see than any bloody nose or broken jaw I could give him.

"Lies," he hissed.

"Does the name Daniel Southgate ring a bell?" I asked.

I didn't think a person's face could turn this shade of white or a body could cave in on itself in defeat. I swear if Jordan could have buried himself under the cushion, he would have.

"Looks like you know exactly who I'm talking about." I stood in front of him, relishing the obvious flinch when he moved away. "I told you, you can't hide behind your family name and your money forever."

Sitting next to Victoria, I watched him struggle with the realization that he had no move to make. No counterstrike.

A muscle flexed in his jaw. "Nobody will believe you."

"They will." Victoria's steady, calming tone accentuated her words. "Controlling the narrative is my job. I might be a jersey chaser but I know the media. I know what they salivate over. Imagine having all those reporters and all those cameras trained on you; the bitter, desperate man dragging a woman through the mud to save his ass and cover up the fact that he's nothing more than a rapist."

"Maybe *you* shouldn't underestimate *me*, Victoria."

My hands flexed into fists. "Threaten her again, McKennie. I fucking dare you."

The most dangerous people are the ones with nothing left to lose. Jordan scowled, shooting daggers at me. "Is the sex really that good?"

I flew off the couch, slamming my fist into his face before anyone could react. Blood poured from his nose. I was wrong. That *was* rather satisfying.

Grabbing him by the shirt, I snarled, "Say something about her again and what's left of you leaves here in a bag."

Shoving him into the couch, I returned to Victoria. Concern seeped from her but she remained poised and in control. Feeling her hand on my thigh helped quiet the urge to dismantle him. I exhaled a harsh breath, forcing myself to relax.

"Fuck," Jordan muttered, using his tie to wipe away the blood. "I had all the proof destroyed after my parents died. You have nothing."

Victoria felt the muscles in my thigh tighten. She slid her hand higher, her touch warm and reassuring.

"Xavier?"

"Yes, love."

"Did you bring it?"

I nodded, reaching into my pocket. Pulling out a folded copy of the birth certificate, I waved it in Jordan's face. "You mean this?" I smirked, tossing it on the coffee table.

Jordan's skin color morphed from translucent to bright red. His eyes ping-ponged from me to Victoria, and back. Snatching the certificate, he read it, his face turning chalk white again. "This was a secret file. How did you get it?"

Victoria shrugged. "Some secrets never stay buried. I know that better than anyone."

"Are you blackmailing me?"

"No. I'm not that vile."

"What do you want?" He choked on his words.

For the first time tonight, a slight tremble rattled Victoria's body. I laced my fingers through hers and squeezed.

"Admit what you did to my sister. Admit what you did to Xavier. I don't need to know why, I just need to hear you say it."

"And if I don't?"

Fierce determination swathed her beautiful face. "It would be a shame to wake up to news that you're not actually a high-ranking British aristocrat. It would be even more devastating to see excerpts from Charlotte's diary detailing the night you raped her."

I could tell he wanted to unleash his wrath. He wiped his nose with the tie instead.

"You *are* blackmailing me."

"I'm giving you the opportunity to come clean about what you did."

"You would do that to the memory of your sister? To your family? Put them through all that scrutiny just to get me to admit to something that never took place."

"We both know it happened."

The onyx pools in Jordan's eyes hardened. "If you do that, I'll expose Xavier. I'll release the CCTV footage. He'll have no choice but to retire from the league in shame."

"I'm retiring anyway," I blurted.

My words hung frozen in the air.

Victoria turned to me, shocked. So much for having this discussion with her in a more private setting.

I swept my thumb along her jaw.

"This will be my last season at Royal City. Next summer's tournament will be my final appearance with the national team." I glared at Jordan. "Admit what you did to her sister."

All the power rested with me and Victoria. Our united show of strength wiped out any leverage Jordan thought he had. She was willing to put her family's pain on display for the whole world to see.

I'm willing to walk away from my career.

We both risked everything.

And he fucking knew it.

If he refused, he'd be exposed as a fraud and a rapist.

If he caved, he'd walk away bruised and battered, with no hope of retaliation.

One step ahead. How he hated that.

The steady ticking of Bennet's grandfather clock was the only sound in the library. The passing seconds and minutes lasted an eternity. This might be more nerve-wracking than a penalty shoot out.

When Jordan's shoulders slumped, the thrill of victory darted through me. Nothing pleased me more than defeating a rival in competition.

"Fine," he acquiesced through clenched teeth. "I knew your sister didn't want to have sex, even though she pretended to be you and said otherwise. She cried the whole time. Happy now?"

Victoria's hand flew to her mouth, muffling a pained gasp.

Undeterred, Jordan leveled an angry stare at me. "You pissed me off acting all heroic like you didn't use and discard girls on a whim. Thought you needed a lesson."

The only reason I didn't get up and end his life was Victoria. She shook with rage beside me. I held her chin, turning her head to face me.

Jade-colored flames burned in the depths of her eyes.

"Strength," I whispered. "For Charlotte."

After a few seconds, Victoria stood and went toward Jordan. Her curvy, petite frame cast a large shadow over his seated form. "If you do anything to Xavier, *anything*, I will give the green light to not one, but *every* major news outlet in England run with the story." He scooted back an inch when she leaned closer. "That is not blackmail. That is a fucking promise."

She turned on a heel and strode toward the French doors.

I stared at Jordan. At his defeated posture, his sullen expression. After all the years of being at one another's throats, I finally saw him for what and who he really is.

Standing up, I shoved my hands in my pockets and approached him. An icy stare greeted me.

"Here to gloat?"

"No."

"Then what the fuck do you want?"

The overwhelming urge to slam a fist into his face dissipated. "Thought you should know one more thing before I leave."

A trickle of blood slid from a nostril and pooled on his lip.

"When Victoria told me what she'd learned, she said you were just as common us. I'll probably be in trouble for saying this, but she's wrong. You're not common." A slow, patronizing smile curled my lips. "You're nothing."

A muscle in his jaw jumped. The harshness of his new reality took hold.

Approaching Victoria, I pulled her into a tight embrace. "Well played, city princess."

"Couldn't have done it without you, country prince."

We walked out of the library, leaving Jordan behind for good.

"Everything alright?" Cade rushed over. "Bennet filled me in."

Victoria reached for Cade, and hugged him. Then she hugged Bennet. The sight of the three most important people in my life all in one place filled me with yet another unrecognizable emotion.

"Thought maybe one of you'd be coming out on a stretcher," Bennet said, nodding his head at the door. "Does he need medical attention?"

"No," I chuckled. "Maybe a new tie."

Holding Victoria's hand, I led her to the front door. We rode in silence back to my flat. The second we walked inside, I captured her mouth in a deep, tender kiss.

"What was that for?"

I lifted a shoulder in a small shrug. "Felt like it."

A thoughtful expression appeared. "Come here."

She led me to the bossy chair and sat. Tapping the ottoman with her foot, she grinned up at me. "Sit there, Mr. Maddox."

Intrigued, I did as she instructed and asked, "Feeling okay?"

"Yeah."

"You were absolutely brilliant, you know." I reached for her hand. Her soft palm nestled perfectly in mine. "Charlotte would be so proud of you."

"I know." A wistful smile touched her lips when she placed her hand over her heart. "I still feel her sometimes. It's like a peaceful warmth." Astute emerald eyes studied me. "Are you really retiring at the end of the season?"

A year ago, walking away from football was the furthest thought from my mind. Hell, six months ago it wasn't even a possibility. But that was before I pulled off the road to help what I'd thought was a stranded motorist.

"I am." I rested my fingers on her lips. "Let me explain." Inhaling slow, I spoke. "For the majority of my life, football filled a need. It still does to a certain extent. When Bennet threatened to take my livelihood away from me all those years ago, it opened my eyes. Nobody will dictate how I end my career. I love this sport. I love competing. There is nothing quite like the roar of a crowd and the adoration of millions."

I paused when Victoria knelt between my legs and reclined her forearm on my thigh. The movement was so graceful and natural and perfect. Finding my next breath, let alone my train of thought, was a struggle.

She'd done this only once before. *I will marry this woman.* The exact same thought I'd had at the time echoed through me.

I gazed into her eyes. "All of that pales in comparison to how I feel when I'm with you."

She sat up straight. "Don't tell me you're retiring because of me. That's ridiculous and I won't allow it."

I arched an eyebrow. "That's presumptuous."

"Really?" The fiery edge to her tone clued me in on what she was doing. "What about my policy? I only date British goalkeepers with dirty mouths and tattoos."

"I'm breaking it."

"I see." A sly grin pulled at her glossy lips. "Does that mean I have to go find another goalkeeper? How about a striker?"

Lowering my tone to the one that drives her mad, I leaned closer. "There are no other goalkeepers or strikers or anyone you classify as *the product*." I fisted her hair. "There's only me, and you're mine. Do I make myself clear?"

She cast her eyes down, parting her lips to suck in a breath. When she looked up at me again through her lashes, her pupils were so dilated I could barely see any green.

"Maybe."

Dark flames erupted into a ball of white hot desire in my chest.

"We can do this one of two ways." A raspy moan passed her lips when I pulled on her hair. "I can finish telling you what I have to say with my cock stuffed down your throat." The dusting of pink spreading across her cheeks was so fucking hot. "Or you can kneel at my feet like the dirty princess you are, listen to me talk while I stroke myself, and then clean the cum off me with your Ivy League mouth."

"And if I can't choose?"

I loosened my hold on her. "Then I'll choose for us." Standing up, I pulled her to her feet and tossed her over my shoulder.

"*Xavier*," she squealed with a giggle. "Put me down."

"Nope." My palm landed on her ass in a hard smack as I carried her to the bedroom. "I need to teach you a lesson about interrupting a heartfelt conversation to be cheeky with me."

A smile curved my mouth when she laughed and whacked my ass like a drum. "What kind of lesson?"

I placed her on the edge of the bed, admiring her flushed skin and sparkling eyes.

"Undress."

She complied, peeling off her clothes. Soft red waves of hair fell over her shoulders, framing the most beautiful curves known to man.

Fuck, she's gorgeous.

Rubbing my thumb on my lip, I grinned. "Don't move."

I went to my closet and dug out the Legends jersey from the photoshoot.

"Put this on," I commanded, tossing it to her.

She ran her hand over my name. "I bet you look hot in this."

"Put it on. If I have to say it again, the lesson will last all night."

"Promise?" Her mischievous grin delighted me. So did the sight of her wearing anything with my name on it.

"Get on the bed, on your hands and knees. Now."

"Want me to crawl to you again?" She got into position. "I really liked that."

Fuck yes.

"Not this time." I climbed on the mattress behind her and dragged a finger over her slick pussy. "I'll finish telling you why I'm retiring tomorrow." Her small growl went straight to my cock when I stroked her clit. "Maybe by then you'll learn some manners."

The crack of my hand slapping her ass echoed through the room.

A blush of red bloomed on her skin. Her groans intensified the more I teased her body.

"That doesn't feel like a lesson," she purred. "I thought you were going to reprimand me."

I stopped rubbing her clit to undo my jeans and release my cock.

"I am," I growled, filling her hard and fast. She buried her face in the pillows, muffling her screams. "I want to hear you, love." Thrusting as hard as I could, I fisted her hair again, pulling her head back. "Who do you belong to?"

"*You.*"

"That's right." I filled her until I had nothing left to give. "Who do I belong to?"

She looked over her shoulder, holding my stare. "Me."

"Forever." I clamped a hand around her neck. Panic surged through me and I released it. The last thing I wanted to do was hurt her.

Grabbing my thigh, she dug her nails into my skin. "Xavier. Put your hands on me. I *want* your hands on me. Be rough. Don't hold back."

Curling my fingers around her neck again, I asked, "Do you want to continue?"

"*Green*." She gasped when I tightened my grip. "Fuck me so hard all the tension and anxiety of these last few months disappear. For both of us. *Please*."

Without any further hesitation, I did.

Every thought, every bit of stress, every fucking worry melted away.

Victoria was all that mattered.

We were all that existed.

I surrendered to the feel of her, of heaven, of *us*.

Chapter
THIRTY-EIGHT

XAVIER

We spent the better part of Monday in my flat.

I didn't have training so we only came up for air to eat. I did sneak away for a couple minutes to reschedule my appointment with Dr. Frances. He wasn't pleased but I didn't give a shit. Being with Victoria was more important than rehashing everything we went through over the weekend. I'll tell him about it soon enough.

"Do you think we should get dressed and go out for dinner later?" Victoria snuggled into me, draping an arm across my stomach.

"No."

Her melodic laugh sent my heart racing. I buried my nose in her hair, inhaling her sensual scent. Staying like this forever seemed like a better option.

My phone vibrated on the nightstand. She reached over, grabbed it, and answered.

"Xavier's phone. How can I help you?"

I squeezed her waist, watching her cheerful expression.

"It is," she exclaimed. "Yep, I'm in London. Nice to talk to you too. Nope, we're not busy. We'd love to. Great. See you later."

"Who was that?"

Victoria smiled at me and tossed the phone on the mattress. "Your stepmother. She invited us over for dinner."

My stomach dropped into an endless free fall. "Tonight?"

An exaggerated eye roll preceded her sarcastic answer. "No. Next year." A pillow hit my face. "Yes, tonight. We've been in bed too long. Get up. You can take me to my cottage on the way."

Fine.

But before any of that would happen, I yanked her into the shower, claiming and ravaging her body until she shattered into a million pieces. And then I did it again.

The drive out to Briarcliff Village was enjoyable. Victoria messed around with my radio, playing DJ until she found something she liked, which always seemed to be pop music from the late nineties.

About ten minutes before we arrived at the cottage, she got a text.

"My dad's here." Her voice softened. "Can we stop at Black Rose first? He's there with Ray and Dawn."

Forget free fall. My stomach collapsed into oblivion. Introducing her to my family was a big enough challenge. Meeting her *father*?

Not ready for that at all.

"Of course we can."

I noticed a tiny smile when she saw my discomfort.

Black Rose Tavern was fairly empty at this time of day. The lunch crowd was already gone, so just a few people sat at the bar. Dawn saw us and beelined over, engulfing Victoria in a massive hug.

"I have missed this beautiful face," she exclaimed, cupping Victoria's cheeks. "You are glowing. Told you he was a charmer."

"You flatter me, Dawn." I grinned when she ruffled my hair.

"Is my dad still here? He texted me a few minutes ago."

"Yes." Dawn turned and waved someone over. "He's been waiting for you."

She hugged Victoria and looked at me. Something in her eyes gave me pause, like she was privy to specific information and I wasn't.

I almost fired off a snarky comment but was halted by the sight of an older gentleman walking our way.

Tall, well-dressed, salt and pepper hair.

A weird sensation swooped through my body.

I recognize this man.

"Hello sweetheart," he said, wrapping Victoria in a warn hug. "Congratulations on a successful game. Quite a stressful one at that."

"A win is a win. Even the ugly ones."

The man looked at me, a pleasant smile reflecting in his eyes. "Trevor *Chase.*" He offered his hand. "Not sure if you remember me. We met a few weeks ago in here."

Victoria's jaw dropped, meeting mine on the floor.

Trevor Chase. The random stranger Dawn said wanted to meet me when I was here with Cade.

I shook his hand. "I remember. You're not a Royal City supporter."

"Dad," Victoria hissed. "You told him that?"

When Trevor laughed a lightbulb went on in my brain. I'd thought there'd been something oddly familiar about him that night. And now I know.

His laugh.

It didn't sound like Victoria's but his smile and the way his eyes lit up were the same.

I should have known.

"Not going to lie to him, love." His smile grew bigger. "I'm Leeds 'til I die. But I'll always support England's number one."

Victoria folded her arms, glancing at both of us. "Unbelievable. What else did you two talk about?"

"Mostly football. Which reminds me. Hell of a save against the Dutch. Nearly had a heart attack when Donovan made that sliding block."

"You and me both." I relaxed into the conversation. "Good thing I spent extra time in training working on penalty shoot outs."

"Ready for the big tournament next summer? It's in Italy, right?" He addressed his daughter. "Will you be going?"

"Oh. Um, I don't…we haven't—"

"I'll convince her." I slipped an arm around Victoria's waist. "We've talked about going to Italy on holiday."

As we spent the next few minutes chatting, I felt Victoria soften in my embrace, leaning comfortably into my side. Her relationship with her dad hasn't been the greatest. Seeing them get along pleased me in a way I didn't expect.

"Before I go," Trevor said, reaching into his pocket. "I wanted to give you this."

He handed her a small box.

Victoria's breathing stuttered. "What is it?"

"A charm bracelet." A wisp of heartbreak passed through his eyes. "I know it's not something you'd wear but…I saw your mother a few weeks ago." Victoria's hands shook when she opened the box, revealing a delicate bracelet. "This belonged to her. The charms represent you and Charlotte. The silver crown is you. The gold crown is your sister. You're both named after royalty you know. Helena wanted you to have it. And she apologized for missing your birthday."

I held Victoria in a firm grip.

"I don't know…I don't know what to say." Her body trembled uncontrollably.

"You don't have to say anything, sweetheart." He looked at his daughter softly. "I told her about the foundation and how you created it to honor Charlotte."

Victoria slumped against me. "What did she say?"

"You know how your mother is. She's stubborn, like you. The words never came out of her mouth but I could see the pride in her eyes. Maybe someday the three of us can all sit down and work through this rift."

Trevor looked at me, holding my attention with a steady gaze.

"Take good care of my little girl."

Dawn caught my eye after Trevor said his goodbyes and left. A single tear rolled down her cheek.

"Do you still want to go to the cottage?" I asked, skimming my hand along Victoria's arm. "Or would you rather we go back to London?"

Regaining composure, she looked up at me through her lashes. "We have dinner plans."

"We don't—"

"We're going." Slipping the box in her bag, she turned to fully face me. "To the cottage *and* your family's house."

Discussion closed.

"Stunning work, Xavier." My stepmother gushed while looking at the photos Victoria took of her cottage. "I love the color on the walls. And the flooring is immaculate."

The two of them scrolled through picture after picture, smiling and chatting like old friends.

"I keep telling him this isn't a bad trait to have." Victoria slid a cool glance in my direction. "You should see the way he geeks out over architecture."

Squeezing the glass, I sipped my drink. My return glance said it all. *Another lesson later?*

"Sorry I'm late I—" Adam burst into the kitchen, stopping short next to Rebecca. He and Victoria stared at one another, shocked. Not as awkward as the day in the changing room, but not exactly comfortable.

"Right on time." Rebecca welcomed him with a hug. "I was just admiring your brother's work on Victoria's cottage." She glanced between the two of them. "Have you two met?"

"Kind of," Victoria answered.

"Not really," Adam responded.

"Right then. The three of you sort out the introductions and I'll grab your father." My stepmother left the kitchen but not before I noticed her self-satisfied grin. Agreeing to this dinner was not my best decision.

Victoria tucked her phone in her pocket, pinning an expectant stare on me. Adam looked at me warily.

Well, this will be fun.

"Adam, this is Victoria. Victoria, this is my stepbrother."

Adam narrowed his eyes. "You suck at this." Turning to Victoria, he smiled. "Lovely to meet you. Sorry about the whole Char— I mean, sorry I thought you were— *Christ*. Hi."

"And I'm the one who sucks?" I taunted.

"At least I don't sound like a robot. I thought you were supposed to be the charming one."

"I am."

"Right. And I'm the Prince of Wales."

A shrill whistle ended our bickering. We both looked at Victoria.

"Boys." She clasped her hands together and muttered, "Feels like I'm with Killian and Max."

Confusion spread across Adam's face. "Who are they?"

"Friends of mine that will obsess over your hair if you ever meet them."

Adam's confusion deepened as he touched his hair. "It is nice to meet you finally."

Victoria's soft smile melted my heart. "You, too. I hope this isn't weird or anything. I didn't know you'd be here."

"That's my mother. She probably sounded all apologetic and flustered when she called to ask if you were free for dinner, when in reality her plan was to get us all under one roof."

And just like that, Adam charmed my girlfriend and I was rendered invisible.

"No pouting, Maddox." Victoria laughed. "Come on. Show your brother all the great work you've done on my house."

We all squeezed on the couch together with Victoria seated between us. She kept a hand on my knee the whole time, knowing this was probably not what I'd expected.

Then again, neither did she.

The two of them danced around the elephant in the room until Victoria finally broke the impasse and asked, "So how did you meet my sister?"

It was an easy ice breaker seeing as she already knew and just wanted to hear his version.

Adam's stunned silence only lasted a few seconds before he launched into the story.

By the time we sat down for dinner, I'd unraveled my nerves and started to enjoy myself.

It's funny how one person could change the dynamic in a room. Victoria's light dazzled as she talked about American football and volunteering at the animal shelter, the latter being something she wished she had more time to do.

Even my dad engaged in the conversation.

"This might be the quietest Xavier's ever been," Adam chided. "Surprised you let someone else have center stage."

"A true gentleman knows when to be seen and not heard."

His burst of laughter ricocheted through the house. "The rubbish coming out of you."

"Try not to talk with your mouth full." I tilted my glass toward him in a fake toast before taking a sip.

I caught a glimpse of Rebecca trying, and failing, to suppress a smile.

When I turned back to Victoria, she was huddled in close with my dad, pointing at her phone screen. Dread flitted through me. As pleasant as this dinner has been, I wasn't prepared to start fixing all my relationships at once.

"Is this the original wood paneling?" he asked, turning the screen for me to see.

"Yeah. I used a medium-grit sandpaper on it. Wanted to keep the rustic, distressed look."

His little mouth shrug and head bob spoke volumes. For those fluent in the body language of James Maddox, that meant he was impressed.

Leaning back in my chair, I moved my eyes around the table, taking in every detail. A casserole dish with only a serving of cottage pie remaining, rumpled napkins, an empty soda can, and a basket of bread. Nothing about it seemed extraordinary. Just a normal Monday night at home.

But when I saw Victoria, Adam, my stepmother, and my father all gathered in one place, the same unrecognizable emotion I'd felt last night consumed me.

Only this time, it wasn't so unrecognizable.

Cade and Bennet have always been like brothers to me. Like family.

I'd closed myself off to my actual family years ago. Maybe this was the first step to allowing them back in.

Chapter

THIRTY-NINE

Killian and Max's wedding was a madhouse. Totally on brand for them but some of it was thanks to my date for the evening.

Press lined up in front of the venue, hoping to catch a glimpse of Xavier when he arrived. We'd offered for him to come in through the underground entrance. Never one to shy away from attention, he'd declined and spent a decent amount of time chatting with reporters and posing for pictures.

Killian wanted to let some of the media inside for exclusive coverage of the wedding. He was immediately shut down by Maxim.

The venue they'd chosen, Sky Raven, was breathtaking. Normally the boys pooh-pooh anything near Times Square. They don't like to be too close to touristy areas but this lounge won them over.

It fit their personalities. Floor-to-ceiling windows, magnificent panoramas of the city, including picture-perfect viewing for the ball drop, and a multi-level interior that boasted cozy, private areas along with glamorous open spaces.

Plus, it sat on top of a hotel where we all had rooms to spend the night.

I gazed down into the heart of Times Square from thirty stories high, watching the massive crowd of people waiting to celebrate the new year. Only forty-five minutes remaining.

"See anything you like?" Xavier slipped a hand around my waist.

"Are you referring to the obnoxiously huge billboard with your half naked body on it?"

Xavier's ad campaign for Apex Jewelers debuted after Halloween, and whipped up a frenzy. He's become much more recognizable here in the U.S.

He laughed, pulling me closer. "Not a fan of watches?"

"Stop. You know I love it. What's the next one going to be?" I faced him, lacing my fingers behind his neck. "You in a speedo leaning against a stack of firewood?"

"Only if you're in it with me wearing that so-called bikini." A light kiss brushed against my forehead. "On second thought, no. I'm the only one who gets to see you in that."

"Attention everyone, attention." The DJ's voice echoed through the room. "The ceremony will begin in fifteen minutes."

Guests started filing toward the rows of chairs set up in the center of the venue.

"That's my cue." I straightened Xavier's tie. Maybe I'll add *forcing the hot, British goalkeeper to wear a three-piece suit once a week* to my New Year's resolutions. I'd love nothing more than to take my time peeling it off him. "You clean up pretty good, Maddox."

The rasp in my voice gave me away. Xavier's friendly smile turned sultry. He fixed a heated stare on me that burned with sinful intentions.

"So do you. Can't wait to rip this dress off you later."

"Promise?"

I felt both his hands cup my backside. He squeezed hard, pulling me sharply into his rock hard body. "I'd tear it off you right now if you'd let me. Show everyone what a dirty princess you really are."

I swallowed hard. A wicked gleam brightened his eyes.

"You'd like that wouldn't you?"

"Yes."

The dimple appeared when he bit down on his lip and grinned. "Bad girl." Lowering his mouth to my neck, he left a searing trail of kisses along my skin. Unable to control myself, I slid my leg to hook around his.

Public sex will definitely be added to my list of resolutions.

"*Xavier.*" The closest people to us stood at a small table, their attention pinned on whatever was happening in Times Square. "Don't stop."

More open-mouthed kisses covered my neck.

Am I really going to do this at my best friend's wedding?

The change in the atmosphere was tangible when Xavier pulled away.

"Did I give you enough to reflect on during the ceremony, love?"

"Maybe."

He ran a finger beneath my lips. "Are you wet?"

"What do you think?" I huffed.

"Good girl."

Xavier sauntered away with a smirk, leaving me flustered and heated and wishing time moved faster so we could tear all of our clothes off. He'd arrived in Manhattan only a few hours ago after flying here following his game.

He'd done the same thing last week to come here for Christmas. In fact, every free moment he's had the last couple months was spent on a plane to be with me.

"*Tori.*" Killian's aggressive whisper pulled me back to the present. "Get your ass over here."

"What's the emergency now?" I half-trotted to him in five-inch heels. "Is there a piece of lint on your jacket?"

"Baby girl, I love you." He held my arms in a tight grip. "But I will replace you as my best man if the sarcasm continues."

"I thought I was your maid of honor."

"Victoria Ava."

"Killian Rhys."

His entire face scrunched up like I'd served him a plate of moldy cheese. "I banned you from using my middle name in seventh grade."

"Anyway." I wriggled out of his grip. "Where are the rings? You were supposed to give them to me twenty minutes ago."

"About that. Uh. Max lost his ring."

"That can't be possible. I put them both in the boxes myself when I got here and left them on the dresser."

"Well…yeah." Chagrin coated my best friend's face. "We sort of did a role play thing with them and—"

Grabbing his arm, I pulled him toward a quieter area. "Tell me you didn't have wild sex in the shower and—"

"Jacuzzi."

"The *jacuzzi*?" I pinched the bridge of my nose. "Did it get sucked down the drain?"

"We don't know. Can you look?"

I gestured at my dress. "I am not climbing into the jacuzzi wearing this to find your ring."

"All the water is gone. I just need you to look. Please."

Storm clouds filled his gray eyes. A calculated frown pulled at his mouth. When his bottom popped out it was game over. Killian knew I could never resist his sad, puppy dog face.

"Fine. Let's go."

A few minutes later, we walked into their suite. Max sat on the bed fidgeting with a pillow but looked rather handsome in his tuxedo.

"Without going into too much detail, were you wearing the ring the whole time?"

Max's shoulders slumped. "No. I put mine in the little soap dish on the edge of the counter."

Well that's surprising. Between the two of them, Max was always the more responsible one.

"Okay." I shot them both a look. "If I don't find it, I'll let you use this." I tugged at the ring hanging from my necklace.

Killian's eyes bugged out of his head. "Didn't Xavier give that to you last spring?"

"Yes. But if I can't find Max's, you'll need something to exchange during your vows. Xavier won't mind."

Killian opened his mouth to protest but Max clamped his hand over it. "Thanks, Victoria."

I went inside the bathroom. Towels were strewn all over the floor.

I scanned the area around the jacuzzi.

Candles. A box of chocolate. Nachos?

I laughed to myself, noticing the soap dish Max mentioned. Kicking aside some of the towels, a small object bounced and glittered on the tile.

Jackpot.

I picked up the platinum ring and put it on my finger.

"Found it," I proclaimed, holding up my hand. Two relieved faces broke into smiles. "But it stays with me. Where's the other box?"

"Here." Maxim handed it to me. "You're a lifesaver."

I smiled at the boys. They looked so excited and nervous. "Love you guys. If that was the pre-wedding sex romp, I can only imagine what you're planning for later."

"Bring Xavier up and we'll—"

I let the door shut behind me, ending Killian's proclamation. I did hear them laugh when I walked away.

Now that I had both rings in my possession, I went back to the event space, found Max's cousin and gave him the ring meant for Killian. Thanks to that unexpected little side adventure, the wedding was running late.

Max worked really hard to plan the timing to a tee. They'd have the ceremony at eleven-thirty, parade around the room to greet everyone, and then have roughly five minutes to spare before the clock struck midnight.

Conversation floated around us as we took our places near the civil officiant.

Guests quieted down when the opening notes of the entrance music played.

Max walked in the room first. Killian followed about thirty seconds later and stood next to Max. The way they stared at each other should be immortalized in sonnets.

They looked so happy. My heart swelled.

As they recited their vows, I scanned the crowd, finding Xavier with little effort. Then again, it's not hard to pinpoint a tall, athletic god with tousled dark hair, a tattoo on his neck, and his hands adorned with silver rings. He was seated at the end of the row, his face neutral but his eyes alight with emotion.

I couldn't help but smile. Not too big, just subtle enough so he knew it was only meant for him. Butterflies raced through my stomach when his mouth tipped up in a soft smile of his own.

A stolen moment just for us. Those were harder and harder to come by these days. Not that I minded. I knew being in a relationship with a superstar British soccer player could never be kept in the shadows.

Besides, it made stealing these moments fun.

I wanted to steal millions more.

The ceremony was short, concluding with about eight minutes remaining until midnight. I hugged the boys, congratulating them and kissing them both on the cheek. Before Killian waltzed off to celebrate, he pulled me into a tight hug.

"Love you, baby girl. I wouldn't want anyone else standing by my side to witness my wedding."

"Love you more." I looked up at him. "Of course, if you'd asked anyone else I would have disowned you."

"Pfft. You'd never." He reached in his pocket. "I have something for you. A belated Christmas present."

I took the small, black and gold marbled envelope. "Fancy. What is it?"

"Gee, maybe if you opened it."

"Oh hush." I lifted the flap and pulled out what looked like a business card. It, too, was black and gold marble. My eyes widened when I saw the scripted lettering. "The Guild."

"It's a trial pass to see if you'd like it there. Max and I secured it for you. You're allowed to bring one guest. And since you have company for a couple days…" his voice trailed off.

"Nothing says *I love you* like friends giving friends special access to an exclusive sex club," I teased.

"Oh my god, just bring him." Killian yanked me into another tight hug. "Also, if you don't leave here tonight engaged, I will riot."

Laughing, I squeezed him. "Manage your expectations."

He kissed my forehead, linked arms with his new husband, and disappeared in the crowd.

Five minutes until midnight.

"Hi." Xavier's low, rich voice invaded my senses.

"Hi." I felt the blush climbing my neck when he gestured toward the envelope.

"What's that?"

"A gift from Killian and Max."

"Aren't you supposed to be giving them a gift? It is their wedding night."

"It's actually for both of us."

Xavier's eyebrows shot up in surprise. "Us? May I see?"

I handed him the small card.

"What's The Guild?"

I thought back to the night we stood on the sidewalk in London, and he told me about Bennet's library parties. *How had he phrased it?*

"It's a place where people go to enjoy one another's company."

Curiosity morphed to something carnal. A hint of darkness glinted in his eyes. "Have you been before?" His voice lowered into a possessive growl.

God, I love this tone.

"No." I took the card and slipped it into my clutch. "It would be my first time. And I only want to go with you."

Three minutes until midnight.

"Good answer." He glanced to his left. "We should get a spot by the window. Come on."

Weaving our way through the crowd, we ended up at a window directly above the ball. The DJ announced all the lights in the room would dim thirty seconds before midnight, giving us a sharper view.

We stared down at the growing party on the street.

"Maybe next year we can ring in the New Year in London." Xavier stood behind me and wrapped his arms around my waist. "Just don't make me sing *Auld Lang Syne.*"

"I make no promises."

"About the singing or coming to London?"

Two minutes until midnight.

The nervous tremble in his voice surprised me. I turned to face him.

"The singing. I would spend the New Year with you in London, Barcelona, Rome, here, wherever."

"I like that answer, too."

Stepping closer, he pushed me back a step, then two, until I was pinned between him and the window. It wasn't lost on me that were we surrounded by wedding guests. Hot desire ripped through me.

"I'm curious," he whispered in my ear. "Would we enjoy one another's company like this at The Guild?" The light touch of his hand traced from my collarbone down to the swell of my breasts. "Would there be a crowd watching, like in your fantasy?"

My lips parted on a silent gasp.

One minute until midnight.

"Yes," I breathed.

A moan rumbled in his chest. The weight of his body cloaked me, leaving no space between us. "I want to bring that fantasy to life for you. Will you let me?"

I reached up, running my fingers through his hair. "Yes."

The damp warmth of his breath tickled my lips when he hovered his mouth over mine. "Dirty princess. How did I get so lucky to find you? You are my fantasy come true."

Was it wrong that I regretted wearing panties? They were soaked.

Thirty seconds until midnight.

The lights dimmed. The only awareness of us being in a room surrounded by people was the faint buzz of conversation. I was too locked in with Xavier, too consumed by his heat, his scent, his gorgeous blue stare.

"I want to bring all your fantasies to life for you. Will you let me?" His lips brushed against mine with every spoken word. The silky, smooth tone of his voice flowed through my veins.

I swallowed, barely able to control my racing pulse. "Yes."

We stood so close I felt every beat of his heart, every shallow breath, every small shudder.

"Victoria. I want to be the last person you kiss this year, the first person you kiss in the next, and the only person you kiss from now on. First. Last. Only. Will you let me?"

Ten seconds until midnight.

A myriad of emotions took hold of my heart. I couldn't breathe. I couldn't move. I couldn't think.

Five…four…three…

"Yes."

He kissed me on an exhale, soft and sweet. One of his hands cupped the back of my neck, his fingers gently scratching up into my hair.

Two…one.

Xavier sealed our mouths together, deepening our kiss. He possessed me, savored me, claimed me. Some kisses made a person feel a little disoriented. This kiss reached into my soul and reconfigured everything I thought I knew about love.

And yeah, it also made me dizzy.

"Tori," he whispered on my lips. "I want to spend the rest of my life with you. Will you let me?"

I melted into him, choking out a sob. Confetti and balloons fell silently around us. Time slowed to a near standstill.

Framing his face in my hands, I held his steady gaze. I spent so many years denying what I wanted. Denying myself happiness. Denying myself a chance.

Who knew this beautiful man would change my whole life when he pulled off the road in the English countryside to see if I needed help. In that one innocuous moment, he ignited a reality I never thought I deserved.

And then he showed me all the ways I did.

"Yes."

When Xavier kissed me again, portions of my life flashed before my eyes. The good parts, the terrible parts, the parts I never believed would be real.

Some might describe this as being similar to a near-death experience.

I don't think that's the case at all. For me, it's a rebirth. A transformation.

A vow to myself to never stop rising from the ashes.

EPILOGUE

"The couch stays."

Disbelief coated Victoria's face at my declaration. "You hate that couch."

"I don't hate it," I drawled. "It's unseemly."

She half coughed, half laughed. "Oh okay. That makes much more sense."

Snarky Victoria ranked quite high among my favorite Victorias. I chuckled, grabbing one of the last boxes sitting in the foyer.

"Where does this one go?"

"Upstairs. Charlotte's old room."

I trotted up the curved staircase to the first room on the right. Placing the box on a chair, I glanced around. We'd repainted the walls and donated most of the furniture. Victoria insisted on keeping the nightstand, which now displays a few photos of her and Charlotte from when they were teenagers. This room will mainly be just a quiet space for Victoria to use when she wants to feel closer to her twin.

"Hey." She poked her head in the doorway. "I was wrong. The other box goes in here. Would you mind bringing that one down to the living room and the other one up?"

"Do I look like your valet?"

"No. You look like my hot boyfriend who only has a few days to help me finish unpack and get our house set up before training takes you away from me."

Our house.

I fucking loved the way that sounded.

After I finished what little work needed to be done on this cottage, I sold my house and, well, we live here together now. At least while Victoria's in England, which will probably be during her off-season.

I also kept my flat in London at her request.

"You win, city princess." I picked up the box and stopped to kiss her on my way out. "But this is my last week of training. The season ends next Sunday. Then you can boss me around as much as you want."

"I'd have better luck taming a dragon."

"Maybe."

I heard her giggling when I went downstairs.

After we got all the boxes sorted and in the right rooms, we ordered take away from Black Rose and curled up on the couch to watch some TV.

"Does it feel weird knowing this is your last week with the team?" she asked, sopping up the rest of the mayonnaise with her chips.

"Sort of. Don't think it'll really hit me until the final whistle blows."

Announcing my retirement back in February set off a firestorm not just here in England, but around the football world. I was hounded by the media day and night. All of them wanted to know why I'd walk away from a storied twenty year career with the same club.

My responses of *it's time* and *I'm ready to start the next chapter of my life* didn't satisfy them at all.

Fans were a different story.

I've never received this much outpouring of support from every fan base. Players from all the clubs reached out, too. The countless messages and comments on social media from the lads around the league was humbling.

Not to mention the players from the German, Spanish, and Italian leagues, and the ones from as far away as Argentina and Brazil.

I was the most surprised to see the guys from the New York Legends send their congratulations. Noah, Tre, Jax, and Dante all posted photos from their time here in London with messages of support.

"Think you'll change your mind after the big tournament in Italy?" Victoria brushed crumbs off her leg. She'd thrown on jeans and one of my t-shirts this morning. No makeup or perfectly styled hair. It was tossed up in a messy ponytail. She was still the most stunning creature ever. "I've seen it happen. Athletes retire, then they have second thoughts and, poof. They're back."

"I won't change my mind." My heart rate spiked.

"Wanna make a bet?"

I shook my head with a grin. "No. But I do want dessert. You?"

"Actual dessert or…?" She struck a sexy pose.

"Actual." I pulled her close for a kiss. "I'll snack on you later."

"What did you order?"

"It's a surprise."

"I thought you didn't like surprises."

"I don't." I walked toward the kitchen trying like hell to calm my erratic pulse.

I expected to be nervous but not at this level. No, I wasn't nervous about dessert or her teasing me about changing my mind. Busying myself with getting plates, spoons, napkins, and more food kept the focus off the knots tangling in my stomach.

I was nervous about what I planned to give her.

Something had changed within me over the last year. The dark, heavy cloud of anger I'd allowed to hover over me for so many years was gone. There were days when it edged its way back but for the most part Victoria's light kept any darkness away.

At first, it felt weird. Holding onto all that anger was like a shield. Dr. Frances knew it the first time we met. He'd been rather pleased when I finally said it out loud at one of our sessions earlier this year. Letting it go allowed me to lower my defenses.

That shit was terrifying.

But I didn't need any barriers with Victoria. She saw through all of them anyway.

"Are you making the dessert yourself?" The sound of her voice startled me. "You've been in here forever." She hopped up on the stool and leaned forward onto the counter. "I see plates and utensils but no dessert. What are you up to, Maddox?"

I smirked, opening the refrigerator and pulling out a tin. "We still have to work on your patience, love."

Victoria's face lit up when she opened the container. "Eton Mess? I haven't had this in *years.*"

"No excuse for that anymore. You live ten minutes away from the best Eton Mess in England."

Spreading her arms, she squealed a little too enthusiastically over strawberries, meringue, and cream. "Get your sexy ass over here."

I did, wrapping her in my arms tight.

"If I'd known this was all it took, I would have bought you dessert the first night we met."

She dipped a finger in the cream and licked it off. "Too predictable. I wouldn't change a thing about how we got here."

The knots in my stomach tripled. I felt like the sixteen year old kid who walked onto the pitch at Royal City for the first time. Determined but scared about how the next chapter of my life would reveal itself.

It's now or never.

Reaching into my pocket, I pulled out a small velvet pouch. Victoria stilled, her emerald eyes growing wider and wider.

"I wouldn't change anything either." Turning the pouch upside down, a sparkling diamond ring landed softly in my palm. An official proposal was inevitable. Asking Victoria if she'd let me spend the rest of my life with her on New Year's Eve cemented that. But I wanted the proposal to be just for us. No crowds, no cameras, no friends, no outside attention. The rest of the world can wait.

This was one of the most important moments of my life.

I only wanted to share it with her.

"You once told me you didn't believe in fate. I didn't either. I didn't believe in anything that wasn't football, the adoration of millions, or winning." What the fuck is my voice doing? The shaking needs to stop. "But then one day I was driving home and saw this stunning redhead pacing frantically on the side of the road. I had to stop. Your smile captivated me immediately. Your sense of humor, intelligence, warmth, and compassion filled a part of my soul I'd neglected for years. All I wanted to do was heal your scars and make life beautiful for you. What I didn't anticipate was your ability to heal mine. And now, not only do I believe in fate, I also believe in love. I believe in forever."

A choked sob bled through the hand Victoria clasped over her mouth.

Clearing my throat, I held the ring up. "Victoria, will you spend forever with me?"

Her head bobbed up and down in a fierce nod.

Grinning, I pulled her hand away from her mouth. "I can't hear you, love."

"Yes." She kissed me. "Ask me again. Ask me every day for the rest of our lives so I can always remember how this feels."

"And how does it feel?" I slipped the ring on her finger. It fit perfectly.

"Like fire. Smoldering and warm and consuming." She traced the tattoo on my neck. "It feels beautiful."

Sweeping my thumb over her lips, I leaned my forehead to hers.

"I'll ask you every day."

"Promise?"

"Count on it."

When she kissed me again, a deep, euphoric ache spread through my chest, more intense than the *thing* I'd felt that first day we met. I don't know what I'd done to deserve her. I don't know how or why fate chose us.

What I did know was simple.

She was mine.

I was hers.

And I would never let her go.

"Let's go lads, *let's go*," Cade shouted, clapping his hands as he led us out of the tunnel and onto the pitch.

I looked down at Theo when he grabbed my hand and smiled. We always escort kids out with us before a game. I thought it was fitting to have my number one fan with me tonight.

Thousands of supporters roared and chanted and sang when we lined up on the pitch. The atmosphere hummed with anticipation. It was almost its own living, breathing beast.

The last match of the season was finally here.

My final match in a Royal City kit.

Of course it was against West London United. And yeah, it was for the league championship. Our third in a row if we walked away victorious.

The public service announcer asked everyone to turn their attention to the in-stadium monitor. Normally it featured the line-ups for each club.

Not this time.

My jaw dropped when a video started playing. I saw my sixteen year old self diving for the ball. Then I saw my sixteen year old self stumble his way through an interview.

Bloody hell.

I knew the club planned something but I was not expecting this.

Cade elbowed me. "Look at that handsome little face. What happened?"

"Piss off."

"A bit heavy on the pomp and circumstance, don't you think?"

"Wait until it's your turn."

He laughed. "Take it all in, Maddox. You're a massive hero. An arse, but a well-loved one. You deserve it."

"Just get the ball in the back of the net, mate."

If I let myself get caught up in the tribute video it'll throw me off. I needed to be focused. Especially with Zach Donovan ready to make my final appearance an unpleasant one.

We'd texted a handful of spirited jabs back and forth in the lead up to this game. Although I do think he tried to take the piss out of me a few times. The last thing I wanted was to end my Royal City career with someone scoring on me.

Thank goodness the video only lasted a minute. We had football to get to.

We all gathered in a huddle near midfield before the whistle.

As the captain, Cade usually espoused some words of wisdom. Tonight was no different.

"Listen up, gents. We know what we have to do. That trophy is ours. Let's win it for the fans and for each other. And let's give Maddox a final match to fucking remember."

When we broke the huddle and I walked toward my goal, the fans started chanting my name. Always the crowd pleaser, I lifted an arm and waved.

I took my place on my line and looked up into the crowd.

Victoria was there, along with Bennet. I couldn't see them from where I stood but I could feel her presence. Nobody knew we were officially engaged yet. We decided to keep it just between us for a little bit longer.

This last week with her has been absolute heaven.

I glanced up into the crowd again. I knew approximately where she'd be sitting.

My heart stilled.

A familiar red ponytail bounced as she trotted down the stairs to her seat. It helped that she wore my jersey. Not a store bought one. Mine. She'd kept it from when I spent last summer with her in Manhattan.

I loved seeing my name on her.

I loved knowing someday soon she'll be my wife.

I loved that every struggle, every setback, and every triumph led to this very moment.

The whistle sounded to start the match.

The next chapter of my life has begun.

Not all masks hide the truth…

She's the sole heiress to a fortune and the most successful American football team in history.

But she doesn't want that life.

He's the aristocrat who owns the Premier League's marquee club, and has the world at his beck and call.

But he can't have her.

Bennet and Hannah's forbidden relationship is put to the test in the decadent world of money, power, and dark secrets in *The Legacy*.

Still to come in the Royals and Legends series...
The Elite
The Striker
The Trophy

Thank you so much for reading *The Penalty*. If you enjoyed this book, please consider leaving a review on the platform(s) of your choice. I would be so grateful. Reviews help spread the word. Every single one is appreciated.

xo,

Lynn

ACKNOWLEDGMENTS

Thank you to everyone for reading Xavier and Victoria's story. This couple will live in my head rent free forever. They've literally consumed my life for the past year. Now that their story is complete and out in the world, I hope you love them as much as I do.

There are so many people to thank but I want to shine a light on some important ones (yes, you're all important).

To Deana, for being the most patient, understanding human on the planet. My writing cave swallowed me whole but you were (and always are) there every day with a text or one hundred reels to keep me going. My DMs are a never-ending basket of laughter. I owe you, like, a year's worth of girls' nights. Love you.

To my beta readers, for devouring this book in pieces (sorry about that) while I continued to tweak and finesse their story. I'm forever grateful.

To my proofreader, Emma Malito, for taking a chance on an unknown author and being my second set of eyes. I can't wait to work with you on the rest of this series.

To my cover designer, Lori Jackson, for creating beautiful, eye-popping covers that literally stop people in their tracks when I'm at book signings.

To the team at E.M. Tippets Book Designs for creating such pretty interiors for these books and formatting them (so I don't have to).

And I wanted to give a little shoutout to the narrators who brought Xavier and Victoria to life. To Elliot and Branden, thank you for lending your gorgeous voices to these characters. You are both perfection.

Finally, a massive thank you to everyone on BookTok, Bookstagram, and all the bookish platforms for showing *The Keeper* and *The Penalty* so much love and excitement. Getting your DMs and being tagged in your posts really does make my day. Your support truly keeps me going.

On a personal note, writing a soccer (sorry, *football*) romance has been the most fun I've had as an author. It also doesn't hurt that I've been a fan of the sport forever and will always use the excuse "but it's *research*" when I hop on a plane to England for the next Premier League match. See you soon, Newcastle.

I'm excited to share the rest of this series with you. Bennet, Hannah, Cade, and Chelsea can't wait to melt your hearts (after they break them).

xo,
Lynn

ABOUT THE AUTHOR

Lynn Montagano is a contemporary romance author, cat mom, and unapologetic football fan. Her books feature delicious British alpha heroes and the feisty American women who steal their hearts. They're filled with darker themes, humor, a cast of relatable characters, and plenty of steam mixed in.

When Lynn isn't writing, you can find her cheering loudly for her beloved New England Patriots, traveling (probably to London), or binge-watching 90 Day Fiancé.

She lives in the suburbs outside of Boston with her husband and three rescue cats, Loki, Bentley, and Negan. (Bentley, the pantry door isn't a toy)

Want to know more?
www.lynnmontagano.com